Russia revisited—

The world of 19th century Russian literature is as fascinating today to the Western world as it was half a century or more ago. It is a world both exotic and familiar, and it is a world now gone. Yet its characters live—those people with impossibly long names, who talk and love and weep and laugh with equal ease. And they live because the great writers of that age—Tolstoy, Dostoevsky, Turgenev, Chekhov—wrote with fidelity to human nature, with love and pity for all human beings, and with consummate art.

If you already know some of these superb stories, they are worth rereading; if you are discovering them for the first time, so much the better; and if you think Russians are always sad, you have a surprise in store for you.

About the Editor

Although Norris Houghton, being a man of the theatre, is more closely associated with Russian drama than with fiction, he brings to this collection a keen eye for literary excellence, combined with a sure feeling for what is entertaining, a long acquaintance with the works of Russian writers, and first-hand knowledge of Russian life gained on a Guggenheim Fellowship and other visits to Russia. Mr. Houghton, formerly co-managing director of the Phoenix Theatre in New York, is most recently Professor of Drama at Vassar College. He is also the author of several books about the theatre, including *Moscow Rehearsals,* and edited *The Seeds of Modern Drama, The Golden Age,* and *The Romantic Influence* in the Laurel Masterpieces of Continental Drama series.

Great Russian Short Stories

Edited and introduced by
NORRIS HOUGHTON

Published by
DELL PUBLISHING CO., INC.
750 Third Avenue
New York 17, N. Y.

Designed and produced by
Western Printing and Lithographing Company

Printed in U.S.A.

ACKNOWLEDGMENTS The following translations in this collection are
reprinted by permission of the translators, their publishers or their agents:

"The Queen of Spades," by Alexander Pushkin, translated by T. Keane.
Reprinted by permission of G. Bell & Sons, Ltd.

"Taman," from *A Hero of Our Time*, by Mikhail Lermontov, translated
by J. H. Wisdom & Marr Murray. Reprinted by permission of Alfred
A. Knopf, Inc.

"Bezhin Meadows," from *A Sportsman's Sketches*, by Ivan Turgenev, translated by Constance Garnett. Reprinted by permission of The Macmillan Co. and William Heinemann Ltd.

"How a Muzhik Fed Two Officials," by Mikhail Saltykov, translated by
Vera Volkhovsky. Published by Chatto & Windus Ltd. Reprinted by
permission of the translator.

"A Gentle Spirit," from *The Eternal Husband and Other Stories*, by Fyodor Dostoevsky, translated by Constance Garnett. Reprinted by permission of the Macmillan Co. and William Heinemann Ltd.

"The Crocodile," from *An Honest Thief and Other Stories*, by Fyodor
Dostoevsky, translated by Constance Garnett. Reprinted by permission
of The Macmillan Co. and William Heinemann Ltd.

"The Lady with the Dog," from *The Lady with the Dog, and Other Stories*,
by Anton Chekhov, translated by Constance Garnett. Copyright, 1917,
by The Macmillan Co.; 1945, by Constance Garnett. Reprinted by
permission of The Macmillan Co. and Chatto & Windus Ltd.

"Anna on the Neck," from *Party, and Other Stories*, by Anton Chekhov,
translated by Constance Garnett. Copyright, 1917, by The Macmillan
Co.; 1945, by Constance Garnett. Reprinted by permission of The
Macmillan Co. and Chatto & Windus Ltd.

"The Outrage," by Alexander Kuprin, translated by S. Koteliansky and J.
M. Murry, from *Best Russian Short Stories*, edited by Thomas Seltzer.
Reprinted by permission of Random House, Inc.

"In the Steppes," by Maxim Gorky, from the book *Short Stories by Russian
Authors*, translated by R. S. Townsend. Published by E. P. Dutton &
Co., Inc. and J. M. Dent & Sons Ltd. in Everyman's Library edition.
Reprinted by permission of the publishers.

"The Seven Who Were Hanged," by Leonid Andreyev, translated by Eu-
genia Schimanskaya & M. Elizabeth Gow. Published 1947 by Lindsay
Drummond Ltd. Reprinted by permission of Ernest Benn Ltd.

First printing—August, 1958   Seventh printing—March, 1965
Second printing—July, 1960   Eighth printing—September, 1966
Third printing—December, 1960   Ninth printing—April, 1969
Fourth printing—February, 1963   Tenth printing—May, 1970
Fifth printing—April, 1964   Eleventh printing—August, 1971
Sixth printing—March, 1965   Twelfth printing—August, 1972

CONTENTS

EDITOR'S NOTE: *It will be readily observed that there has been no attempt to achieve uniformity in the transliteration of Russian proper names, which varies greatly among the translators of these stories.*

INTRODUCTION

Each year the old Russia becomes a fainter image; but twenty-four years ago when I first went to Moscow, remnants of the tsarist age were still in evidence. I recall, for instance, at the Moscow Art Theatre on a Chekhov gala night, the elderly couple beside me, figures of thirty years before: she in a faded, yellow-white starched blouse with a high net collar supported by whalebone, he with his high, pale forehead, his pince-nez and his carefully clipped, white, pointed beard; and again I recall, as I looked from a train at the snow-covered platform of a provincial railroad station, the men in their fur hats and greatcoats stamping up and down in thick boots, the people from the train darting into the shed to refill their teapots with boiling water from the station's samovar, the horse-drawn sleighs lined up on the far side of the platform. All this had not changed in thirty years and more.

The Russians still eat dinner at four o'clock in the afternoon, still drink tea and talk until the wee small hours; still laugh uproariously and weep unshamedly. The men still kiss one another without self-consciousness, still get drunk on innumerable tiny glasses of vodka, still dream of a great tomorrow, and the steppes still stretch empty to the horizon.

So the world of these short stories is both utterly remote —never to be recalled—and at the same time unexpectedly immediate. The actual life that they depict is encompassed within one hundred years—even less, for Russian literature didn't really begin until the nineteenth century, and this volume ends at the Revolution (although its last three authors did live beyond that momentous 1917). When Chaucer was writing his great *Canterbury Tales* that were really short stories in verse, Russia scarcely had an alphabet; when La Fontaine and Boccaccio in later centuries were delighting the western world with their fables and short romances and satires, there were not yet any Russian story-writers.

Not until the time of Lord Byron—two centuries after Shakespeare—did Russia finally produce her first great literary figure, Alexander Pushkin. Born in the last year of the eighteenth century and living only thirty-eight years (he was killed in a duel in 1837), Pushkin was a handsome, romantic figure, inheriting a strain of African Negro blood, "inspired and frivolous," reminiscent a little of that same Byron, whose work, incidentally, influenced him considerably.

At parties in communist Moscow today young people stand up, a glass of Caucasian red wine in hand, and recite long excerpts of Pushkin's poetry, which every literate youngster knows by heart, for he is Russia's national poet. "No Russian writer," said Dostoevsky once in a famous speech, "was ever so intimately at one with the Russian people as Pushkin." And at the red and gold and white Bolshoi Opera House in Moscow there is always a sell-out whenever his great works-turned-into-operas are performed: *Boris Godunov, Eugene Onegin, Russlan and Ludmilla, The Queen of Spades.*

It is with this last, in its original short story form, that I have chosen to introduce the Russians. Actually, it makes the introduction easy, for while the story itself is fantastic, the world in which it transpires is reassuringly western in appearance. Save for those odd Russian names (which I predict will grow cozily familiar by the end of this collection), the atmosphere is almost Parisian, end-of-the-eighteenth-century. It is, furthermore, the only story in this volume that is played out in court circles, which accounts too for its western feeling, for St. Petersburg society was strongly oriented—or should I say occidented—toward the West at the beginning of the nineteenth century.

At those parties in Russia today at which I described

guests reciting Pushkin over the samovar, much as I imagine our grandfathers and grandmothers recited Longfellow and Tennyson to one another, the other author most in demand is Lermontov, Pushkin's "successor to the throne of Russian letters," as one critic dubs him. The modern Russians' delight in Mikhail Lermontov is not surprising for he was a lyric poet of great beauty and a true romantic. *A Hero of Our Time,* from which my selection "Taman" is taken, transports us to the wild and craggy Caucasus, to a world that reminds one a little of Robert Louis Stevenson's, crossed perhaps by Chateaubriand's.

Lermontov was only twenty-seven (the year was 1841) when, like Pushkin, he was killed in a duel. With them Russia's Byronic world collapsed and after a little while a new world emerged, a world alien to duels and periwigs alike.

It has been widely observed that the history of Russian literature has been profoundly affected by public events. Perhaps this is always true in an autocracy, where artistic expression is directly controlled. At any rate, censorship, which we abhor in the Soviet world today, is an old story to Russian writers. It existed in the reigns of tyrannical tsars, also, and as a result the literary output dwindled in significance; under more liberal-minded tsars literature flourished.

The explanation for this liability to censorship (and this cannot be underlined too strongly), is that almost from its inception Russian literature has been outspokenly devoted to humanitarian ideals. The nineteenth-century current of liberalism flowed deeply in the writers of Europe's least liberal land. Their sentiment and their compassion drew them strongly to the side of the little man, the underdog; their antipathy was for bureaucracy, for tyranny in any form.

The first man to express this fully was Nikolai Gogol. He was a realist, a satirist, a humanitarian—the combination which we shall find recurring throughout the nineteenth century to form the hallmark of Russian letters. *Dead Souls* is his great novel, *The Inspector General* his great play, "The Overcoat" his great piece of short fiction.

"We were all brought up under Gogol's 'Overcoat,' " asserted Dostoevsky. (Had it not been included in Dell's *Six Great Modern Short Novels*, "The Overcoat" would, of course, appear in this volume.) In it you find the same simplicity, close observation of life and warm sympathy for the unfortunate as Gogol's successors will all exhibit.

Gogol did not live to see the emancipation of the serfs. This took place during the reign of Alexander II, who ascended the throne in 1855, three years after the great writer's death. This Alexander was something of a liberal and there is probably a connection between the political and intellectual climate he created, or at least permitted, and Russia's golden age of literature. For in the quarter century of his reign the great triumvirate of Russian letters— Turgenev, Dostoevsky, Tolstoy—came to their magnificent fruition. Indeed, Dostoevsky died in the same year that Alexander was assassinated (1881), Turgenev died two years later, and although Tolstoy lived on until 1910, the spiritual transformation that altered the direction and area of his writing took place also about 1880.

Since Russian literature has achieved a reputation for unrelieved melancholy, I suspect that some of my readers, like the countess in "The Queen of Spades," will have picked up this volume half afraid it will be full of stranglings and drownings. While they will not be altogether disappointed, I want them to be pleasantly surprised to find that Russian writing is also full of laughter. Some of it will be happy laughter, some bitter. Nowhere is this laughter more evident than in the writing of Mikhail Saltykov.

Saltykov (born in 1826, two years before Tolstoy and five years after Dostoevsky), who wrote under the pen-name of Shchedrin, was one of the world's great satirists; his eye was as keen as Gogol's, his pen as sharp as Swift's. In the short story, "How a Muzhik Fed Two Officials," the laughter is, of course, ironic and a Swiftean *saeva indignatio* makes itself felt. But this situation is so broad, so preposterous that the modern reader can scarcely be moved to

Father of the golden age

Alexander Pushkin
1799 – 1837

THE QUEEN OF SPADES

There was a card party at the rooms of Narumov of the Horse Guards. The long winter night passed away imperceptibly, and it was five o'clock in the morning before the company sat down to supper. Those who had won, ate with a good appetite; the others sat staring absently at their empty plates. When the champagne appeared, however, the conversation became more animated, and all took a part in it.

"And how did you fare, Surin?" asked the host.

"Oh, I lost, as usual. I must confess that I am unlucky: I play mirandole, I always keep cool, I never allow anything to put me out, and yet I always lose!"

"And you did not once allow yourself to be tempted to back the red? . . . Your firmness astonishes me."

"But what do you think of Hermann?" said one of the guests, pointing to a young Engineer. "He has never had a card in his hand in his life, he has never in his life laid a wager, and yet he sits here till five o'clock in the morning watching our play."

"Play interests me very much," said Hermann, "but I am not in the position to sacrifice the necessary in the hope of winning the superfluous."

"Hermann is a German: he is economical—that is all!" observed Tomsky. "But if there is one person that I cannot understand, it is my grandmother, the Countess Anna Fedotovna."

"How so?" inquired the guests.

"I cannot understand," continued Tomsky, "how it is that my grandmother does not play."

"What is there remarkable about an old lady of eighty not playing?" said Narumov.

"Then you do not know the reason why?"

"No, really; haven't the faintest idea."

"Oh! then listen. About sixty years ago, my grandmother went to Paris, where she created quite a sensation. People used to run after her to catch a glimpse of the 'Muscovite Venus.' Richelieu made love to her, and my grandmother maintains that he almost blew out his brains in consequence of her cruelty. At that time ladies used to play at faro. On one occasion at the Court, she lost a very considerable sum to the Duke of Orleans. On returning home, my grandmother removed the patches from her face, took off her hoops, informed my grandfather of her loss at the gaming-table, and ordered him to pay the money. My deceased grandfather, as far as I remember, was a sort of house-steward to my grandmother. He dreaded her like fire; but, on hearing of such a heavy loss, he almost went out of his mind; he calculated the various sums she had lost, and pointed out to her that in six months she had spent half a million francs, that neither their Moscow nor Saratov estates were in Paris, and finally refused point blank to pay the debt. My grandmother gave him a box on the ear and slept by herself as a sign of her displeasure. The next day she sent for her husband, hoping that this domestic punishment had produced an effect upon him, but she found him inflexible. For the first time in her life, she entered into reasonings and explanations with him, thinking to be able to convince him by pointing out to him that there are debts and debts, and that there is a great difference between a Prince and a coachmaker. But it was all in vain, my grandfather still remained obdurate. But the matter did not rest there. My grandmother did not know what to do. She had shortly before become acquainted with a very remarkable man. You have heard of Count St. Germain, about whom so many marvellous stories are told. You know that he represented himself as the Wandering Jew, as the discoverer of the elixir of life, of the philosopher's stone, and so forth. Some laughed at him as a charlatan; but Casanova, in his memoirs, says that he was a spy. But be that as it may, St. Germain, in spite of the mystery surrounding him, was a very fascinating person, and was much sought after in the best circles of society. Even to this day my grandmother retains an affectionate recollection of him, and becomes quite angry if any one speaks disrespectfully of him. My grandmother knew that St. Germain had large sums of money at his disposal. She resolved to have recourse to him, and she wrote a letter to him asking him to come to her without delay. The queer old man immediately waited upon her and found her overwhelmed with grief. She described to him in the blackest colours the barbarity of her husband, and ended by declaring that her whole hope depended upon his friendship and amiability.

"St. Germain reflected.

"'I could advance you the sum you want,' said he; 'but I know that you would not rest easy until you had paid me back, and I should not like to bring fresh troubles upon you. But there is another way of getting out of your difficulty: you can win back your money.'

"'But, my dear Count,' replied my grandmother, 'I tell you that I haven't any money left.'

"'Money is not necessary,' replied St. Germain. 'Be pleased to listen to me.'

"Then he revealed to her a secret, for which each of us would give a good deal . . .''

The young officers listened with increased attention. Tomsky lit his pipe, puffed away for a moment and then continued:

"That same evening my grandmother went to Versailles to the *jeu de la reine*. The Duke of Orleans kept the bank; my grandmother excused herself in an off-hand manner for not having yet paid her debt, by inventing some little story, and then began to play against him. She chose three cards and played them one after the other: all three won *sonika*,[1] and my grandmother recovered every farthing that she had lost."

"Mere chance!" said one of the guests.

"A tale!" observed Hermann.

"Perhaps they were marked cards!" said a third.

"I do not think so," replied Tomsky gravely.

"What!" said Narumov, "you have a grandmother who knows how to hit upon three lucky cards in succession, and you have never yet succeeded in getting the secret of it out of her?"

"That's the deuce of it!" replied Tomsky. "She had four sons, one of whom was my father; all four were determined gamblers, and yet not to one of them did she ever reveal her secret, although it would not have been a bad thing either for them or for me. But this is what I heard from my uncle, Count Ivan Ilyich, and he assured me, on his honour, that it was true. The late Chaplitzky—the same who died in poverty after having squandered millions—once lost, in his youth, about three hundred thousand rubles—to Zorich, if I remember rightly. He was in despair. My grandmother, who was always very severe upon the extravagance of young men, took pity, however, upon Chaplitzky. She gave him three cards, telling him to play them one after the other, at the same time exacting from him a solemn promise that he would never play at cards again as long as he lived. Chaplitzky then went to his victorious opponent, and they began a fresh game. On the first card he staked fifty thousand rubles and won *sonika;* he doubled the stake and won again, till at last, by pursuing the same tactics, he won back more than he had lost . . .

"But it is time to go to bed: it is a quarter to six already."

And indeed it was already beginning to dawn: the young men emptied their glasses and then took leave of each other.

[1] Said of a card when it wins or loses in the quickest possible time.

II

The old Countess A—— was seated in her dressing-room in front of her looking-glass. Three waiting maids stood around her. One held a small pot of rouge, another a box of hair-pins, and the third a tall cap with bright red ribbons. The Countess had no longer the slightest pretensions to beauty, but she still preserved the habits of her youth, dressed in strict accordance with the fashion of seventy years before, and made as long and as careful a toilette as she would have done sixty years previously. Near the window, at an embroidery frame, sat a young lady, her ward.

"Good morning, grandmamma," said a young officer, entering the room. *"Bonjour, Mademoiselle Lise.* Grandmamma, I want to ask you something."

"What is it, Paul?"

"I want you to let me introduce one of my friends to you, and to allow me to bring him to the ball on Friday."

"Bring him direct to the ball and introduce him to me there. Were you at B——'s yesterday?"

"Yes; everything went off very pleasantly, and dancing was kept up until five o'clock. How charming Yeletzkaya was!"

"But, my dear, what is there charming about her? Isn't she like her grandmother, the Princess Daria Petrovna? By the way, she must be very old, the Princess Daria Petrovna."

"How do you mean, old?" cried Tomsky thoughtlessly; "she died seven years ago."

The young lady raised her head and made a sign to the young officer. He then remembered that the old Countess was never to be informed of the death of any of her contemporaries, and he bit his lips. But the old Countess heard the news with the greatest indifference.

"Dead!" said she; "and I did not know it. We were appointed maids of honour at the same time, and when we were presented to the Empress. . . ."

And the Countess for the hundredth time related to her grandson one of her anecdotes.

"Come, Paul," said she, when she had finished her story, "help me to get up. Lizanka, where is my snuff-box?"

And the Countess with her three maids went behind a screen to finish her toilette. Tomsky was left alone with the young lady.

"Who is the gentleman you wish to introduce to the Countess?" asked Lizaveta Ivanovna in a whisper.

"Narumov. Do you know him?"

"No. Is he a soldier or a civilian?"

"A soldier."

"Is he in the Engineers?"

"No, in the Cavalry. What made you think he was in the Engineers?"

The young lady smiled, but made no reply.

"Paul," cried the Countess from behind the screen, "send me some new novel, only pray don't let it be one of the present day style."

"What do you mean, grandmother?"

"That is, a novel, in which the hero strangles neither his father nor his mother, and in which there are no drowned bodies. I have a great horror of drowned persons."

"There are no such novels nowadays. Would you like a Russian one?"

"Are there any Russian novels? Send me one, my dear, pray send me one!"

"Good-bye, grandmother: I am in a hurry. . . . Good-bye, Lizaveta Ivanovna. What made you think that Narumov was in the Engineers?"

And Tomsky left the boudoir.

Lizaveta Ivanovna was left alone: she laid aside her work and began to look out of the window. A few moments afterwards, at a corner house on the other side of the street, a young officer appeared. A deep blush covered her cheeks; she took up her work again and bent her head down over the frame. At the same moment the Countess returned completely dressed.

"Order the carriage, Lizaveta," said she; "we will go out for a drive."

Lizaveta arose from the frame and began to arrange her work.

"What is the matter with you, my child, are you deaf?" cried the Countess. "Order the carriage to be got ready at once."

"I will do so this moment," replied the young lady, hastening into the ante-room.

A servant entered and gave the Countess some books from Prince Paul Aleksandrovich.

"Tell him that I am obliged to him," said the Countess. "Lizaveta! Lizaveta! where are you running to?"

"I am going to dress."

"There is plenty of time, my dear. Sit down here. Open the first volume and read to me aloud."

Her companion took the book and read a few lines.

"Louder," said the Countess. "What is the matter with you, my child? Have you lost your voice? Wait—give me that footstool—a little nearer—that will do."

Lizaveta read two more pages. The Countess yawned.

"Put the book down," said she. "What a lot of nonsense! Send it back to Prince Paul with my thanks. . . . But where is the carriage?"

"The carriage is ready," said Lizaveta, looking out into the street.

"How is it that you are not dressed?" said the Countess. "I must always wait for you. It is intolerable, my dear!"

Liza hastened to her room. She had not been there two minutes, before the Countess began to ring with all her might. The three waiting-maids came running in at one door and the valet at another.

"How is it that you cannot hear me when I ring for you?" said the Countess. "Tell Lizaveta Ivanovna that I am waiting for her."

Lizaveta returned with her hat and cloak on.

"At last you are here!" said the Countess. "But why such an elaborate toilette? Whom do you intend to captivate? What sort of weather is it? It seems rather windy."

"No, your Ladyship, it is very calm," replied the valet.

"You never think of what you are talking about. Open the window. So it is: windy and bitterly cold. Unharness the horses. Lizaveta, we won't go out—there was no need for you to deck yourself like that."

"What a life is mine!" thought Lizaveta Ivanovna.

And, in truth, Lizaveta Ivanovna was a very unfortunate creature. "The bread of the stranger is bitter," says Dante, "and his staircase hard to climb." But who can know what the bitterness of dependence is so well as the poor companion of an old lady of quality? The Countess A—— had by no means a bad heart, but she was capricious, like a woman who had been spoilt by the world, as well as being avaricious and egotistical, like all old people who have seen their best days, and whose thoughts are with the past and not the present. She participated in all the vanities of the great world, went to balls, where she sat in a corner, painted and dressed in old-fashioned style, like a deformed but indispensable ornament of the ball-room; all the guests on entering approached her and made a profound bow, as if in accordance with a set ceremony, but after that nobody took any further notice of her. She received the whole town at her house, and observed the strictest etiquette, although she could no longer recognise the faces of people. Her numerous domestics, growing fat and old in her ante-chamber and servants' hall, did just as they liked, and vied with each other in robbing the aged Countess in the most barefaced manner. Lizaveta Ivanovna was the martyr of the household. She made tea, and was reproached with using too much sugar; she read novels aloud to the Countess, and the faults of the author were visited upon her head; she accompanied the Countess in her walks, and was held answerable for the weather or the state of the pavement. A salary was attached to the post, but she very rarely received it, although she was expected to dress like everybody else, that is to say, like very few indeed. In society she played the most pitiable rôle. Everybody knew her, and nobody paid her any attention. At balls she danced only when a partner was wanted, and ladies would only take hold of her arm when it was necessary to lead her out of the room to attend to their dresses. She was very self-conscious, and felt her position keenly, and she looked about her with impatience for a deliverer to come to her rescue; but the young men, calculating in their giddiness, honoured her with but very little attention, although

Lizaveta Ivanovna was a hundred times prettier than the bare-faced and cold-hearted marriageable girls around whom they hovered. Many a time did she quietly slink away from the glittering but wearisome drawing-room, to go and cry in her own poor little room, in which stood a screen, a chest of drawers, a looking-glass and a painted bedstead, and where a tallow candle burnt feebly in a copper candle-stick.

One morning—this was about two days after the evening party described at the beginning of this story, and a week previous to the scene at which we have just assisted—Lizaveta Ivanovna was seated near the window at her embroidery frame, when, happening to look out into the street, she caught sight of a young Engineer officer, standing motionless with his eyes fixed upon her window. She lowered her head and went on again with her work. About five minutes afterwards she looked out again—the young officer was still standing in the same place. Not being in the habit of coquetting with passing officers, she did not continue to gaze out into the street, but went on sewing for a couple of hours, without raising her head. Dinner was announced. She rose up and began to put her embroidery away, but glancing casually out of the window, she perceived the officer again. This seemed to her very strange. After dinner she went to the window with a certain feeling of uneasiness, but the officer was no longer there—and she thought no more about him.

A couple of days afterwards, just as she was stepping into the carriage with the Countess, she saw him again. He was standing close behind the door, with his face half-concealed by his fur collar, but his dark eyes sparkled beneath his cap. Lizaveta felt alarmed, though she knew not why, and she trembled as she seated herself in the carriage.

On returning home, she hastened to the window—the officer was standing in his accustomed place, with his eyes fixed upon her. She drew back, a prey to curiosity and agitated by a feeling which was quite new to her.

From that time forward not a day passed without the young officer making his appearance under the window at the customary hour, and between him and her there was established a sort of mute acquaintance. Sitting in her place at work, she used to feel his approach; and raising her head, she would look at him longer and longer each day. The young man seemed to be very grateful to her: she saw with the sharp eye of youth, how a sudden flush covered his pale cheeks each time that their glances met. After about a week she commenced to smile at him. . . .

When Tomsky asked permission of his grandmother the Countess to present one of his friends to her, the young girl's heart beat violently. But hearing that Narumov was not an Engineer, she regretted that by her thoughtless question, she had betrayed her secret to the volatile Tomsky.

Hermann was the son of a German who had become a naturalised Russian, and from whom he had inherited a small capital. Being firmly convinced of the necessity of preserving his independence, Hermann did not touch his private income, but lived on his pay, without allowing himself the slightest luxury. Moreover, he was reserved and ambitious, and his companions rarely had an opportunity of making merry at the expense of his extreme parsimony. He had strong passions and an ardent imagination, but his firmness of disposition preserved him from the ordinary errors of young men. Thus, though a gamester at heart, he never touched a card, for he considered his position did not allow him—as he said—"to risk the necessary in the hope of winning the superfluous," yet he would sit for nights together at the card table and follow with feverish anxiety the different turns of the game.

The story of the three cards had produced a powerful impression upon his imagination, and all night long he could think of nothing else. "If," he thought to himself the following evening, as he walked along the streets of St. Petersburg, "if the old Countess would but reveal her secret to me! if she would only tell me the names of the three winning cards. Why should I not try my fortune? I must get introduced to her and win her favour—become her lover. . . . But all that will take time, and she is eighty-seven years old: she might be dead in a week, in a couple of days even! . . . But the story itself: can it really be true? . . . No! Economy, temperance and industry: those are my three winning cards; by means of them I shall be able to double my capital—increase it sevenfold, and procure for myself ease and independence."

Musing in this manner, he walked on until he found himself in one of the principal streets of St. Petersburg, in front of a house of antiquated architecture. The street was blocked with equipages; carriages one after the other drew up in front of the brilliantly illuminated doorway. At one moment there stepped out on to the pavement the well-shaped little foot of some young beauty, at another the heavy boot of a cavalry officer, and then the silk stockings and shoes of a member of the diplomatic world. Furs and cloaks passed in rapid succession before the gigantic porter at the entrance.

Hermann stopped. "Whose house is this?" he asked of the watchman at the corner.

"The Countess A——'s," replied the watchman.

Hermann started. The strange story of the three cards again presented itself to his imagination. He began walking up and down before the house, thinking of its owner and her strange secret. Returning late to his modest lodging, he could not go to sleep for a long time, and when at last he did doze off, he could dream of nothing but cards, green tables, piles of banknotes and heaps of ducats. He played one card after the other, winning uninterruptedly, and then he gathered up the gold and filled his pockets with the notes. When he woke up late the next morning, he sighed over the loss of his imaginary wealth, and then sallying out into the town, he found himself once more in front of the Countess's residence. Some unknown power seemed to have attracted him thither. He stopped and looked up at the windows. At one of these he saw a head with luxuriant black hair, which was bent down probably over some book or an embroidery frame. The head was raised. Hermann saw a fresh complexion and a pair of dark eyes. That moment decided his fate.

Lizaveta Ivanovna had scarcely taken off her hat and cloak, when the Countess sent for her and again ordered her to get the carriage ready. The vehicle drew up before the door, and they prepared to take their seats. Just at the moment when two footmen were assisting the old lady to enter the carriage, Lizaveta saw her Engineer standing close beside the wheel; he grasped her hand; alarm caused her to lose her presence of mind, and the young man disappeared—but not before he had left a letter between her fingers. She concealed it in her glove, and during the whole of the drive she neither saw nor heard anything. It was the custom of the Countess, when out for an airing in her carriage, to be constantly asking such questions as: "Who was that person that met us just now? What is the name of this bridge? What is written on that signboard?" On this occasion, however, Lizaveta returned such vague and absurd answers, that the Countess became angry with her.

"What is the matter with you, my dear?" she exclaimed. "Have you taken leave of your senses, or what is it? Do you not hear me or understand what I say? . . . Heaven be thanked, I am still in my right mind and speak plainly enough!"

Lizaveta Ivanovna did not hear her. On returning home she ran to her room, and drew the letter out of her glove: it was not sealed. Lizaveta read it. The letter contained a declaration of love; it was tender, respectful, and copied word for word from a German novel. But Lizaveta did not know anything of the German language, and she was quite delighted.

For all that, the letter caused her to feel exceedingly uneasy. For the first time in her life she was entering into secret and confidential relations with a young man. His boldness alarmed her. She reproached herself for her imprudent behaviour, and knew not what to do. Should she cease to sit at the window and, by assuming an appearance of indifference towards him, put a check upon the young officer's desire for further acquaintance with her? Should she send his letter back to him, or should she answer him in a cold and decided manner? There was nobody to whom she could turn in her perplexity, for she had neither female friend nor adviser. . . . At length she resolved to reply to him.

She sat down at her little writing-table, took pen and paper, and began to think. Several times she began her letter, and then tore it up: the way she had expressed herself seemed to her either too inviting or too cold and decisive. At last she succeeded in writing a few lines with which she felt satisfied.

"I am convinced," she wrote, "that your intentions are honourable, and that you do not wish to offend me by any imprudent behaviour, but our acquaintance must not begin in such a manner. I return you your letter, and I hope that I shall never have any cause to complain of this undeserved slight."

The next day, as soon as Hermann made his appearance, Lizaveta rose from her embroidery, went into the drawing-room, opened the ventilator and threw the letter into the street, trusting that the young officer would have the perception to pick it up.

Hermann hastened forward, picked it up and then repaired to a confectioner's shop. Breaking the seal of the envelope, he found inside it his own letter and Lizaveta's reply. He had expected this, and he returned home, his mind deeply occupied with his intrigue.

Three days afterwards, a bright-eyed young girl from a milliner's establishment brought Lizaveta a letter. Lizaveta opened it with great uneasiness, fearing that it was a demand for money, when suddenly she recognised Hermann's hand-writing.

"You have made a mistake, my dear," said she. "This letter is not for me."

"Oh, yes, it is for you," replied the girl, smiling very knowingly. "Have the goodness to read it."

Lizaveta glanced at the letter. Hermann requested an interview.

"It cannot be," she cried, alarmed at the audacious request, and the manner in which it was made. "This letter is certainly not for me."

And she tore it into fragments.

"If the letter was not for you, why have you torn it up?" said the girl. "I should have given it back to the person who sent it."

"Be good enough, my dear," said Lizaveta, disconcerted by this remark, "not to bring me any more letters in the future, and tell the person who sent you that he ought to be ashamed. . . ."

But Hermann was not the man to be thus put off. Every day Lizaveta received from him a letter, sent now in this way, now in that. They were no longer translated from the German. Hermann wrote them under the inspiration of passion, and spoke in his own language, and they bore full testimony to the inflexibility of his desire and the disordered condition of his uncontrollable imagination. Lizaveta no longer thought of sending them back to him: she became intoxicated with them and began to reply to them, and little by little her answers became longer and more affectionate. At last she threw out of the window to him the following letter:

"This evening there is going to be a ball at the Embassy. The Countess will be there. We shall remain until two o'clock. You have now an opportunity of seeing me alone. As soon as the Countess is gone, the servants will very probably go out, and there will be nobody left but the Swiss, but he usually goes to sleep in his lodge. Come about half-past eleven. Walk straight upstairs. If you meet anybody in the ante-room, ask if the Countess is at home. You will be told 'No,' in which case there will be nothing left for you to do but to go away again. But it is most probable that you will meet nobody. The maidservants will all be together in one room. On leaving the ante-room, turn to the left, and walk straight on until you reach the Countess's bedroom. In the bedroom, behind a screen, you will find two doors: the one on the right leads to a cabinet, which the Countess never enters; the one on the left leads to a corridor, at the end of which is a little winding staircase; this leads to my room."

Hermann trembled like a tiger, as he waited for the appointed time to arrive. At ten o'clock in the evening he was already in front of the Countess's house. The weather was terrible; the wind blew with great violence; the sleety snow fell in large flakes; the lamps emitted a feeble light, the streets were deserted; from time to time a sledge, drawn by a sorry-looking hack, passed by, on the look-out for a belated passenger. Hermann was enveloped in a thick overcoat, and felt neither wind nor snow.

At last the Countess's carriage drew up. Hermann saw two footmen carry out in their arms the bent form of the old lady, wrapped in sable fur, and immediately behind her, clad in a warm mantle, and with her head ornamented with a wreath of fresh flowers, followed Lizaveta. The door was closed. The carriage rolled away heavily through the yielding snow. The porter shut the street-door; the windows became dark.

Hermann began walking up and down near the deserted house; at length he stopped under a lamp, and glanced at his watch: it was twenty minutes past eleven. He remained standing under the lamp, his eyes fixed upon the watch, impatiently waiting for the remaining minutes to pass. At half-past eleven precisely, Hermann ascended the steps of the house, and made his way into the brightly-illuminated vestibule. The porter was not there. Hermann hastily ascended the staircase, opened the door of the ante-room and saw a footman sitting asleep in an antique chair by the side of a lamp. With a light firm step Hermann passed by him. The drawing-room and dining-room were in darkness, but a feeble reflection penetrated thither from the lamp in the ante-room.

Hermann reached the Countess's bedroom. Before a shrine, which was full of old images, a golden lamp was burning. Faded stuffed chairs and divans with soft cushions stood in melancholy symmetry around the room, the walls of which were hung with China silk. On one side of the room hung two portraits painted in Paris by Madame Lebrun. One of these represented a stout, red-faced man of about forty years of age in a bright-green uniform and with a star upon his breast; the other—a beautiful young woman, with an aquiline nose, forehead curls and a rose in her powdered hair. In the corners stood porcelain shepherds and shepherdesses, dining-room clocks from the workshop of the celebrated Lefroy, bandboxes, roulettes, fans and the various playthings for the amusement of ladies that were in vogue at the end of the last century, when Montgolfier's balloons and Mesmer's magnetism were the rage. Hermann stepped behind the screen. At the back of it stood a little iron bedstead; on the right was the door which led to the cabinet; on the left—the other which led to the corridor. He opened the latter, and saw the little winding staircase which led to the room of the poor companion. . . . But he retraced his steps and entered the dark cabinet.

The time passed slowly. All was still. The clock in the drawing-room struck twelve; the strokes echoed through the room one after the other, and everything was quiet again. Hermann stood leaning against the cold stove. He was calm; his heart beat regularly, like that of a man resolved upon a dangerous but inevitable undertaking. One o'clock in the morning struck; then two; and he heard the distant noise of carriage-wheels. An involuntary agitation took possession of him. The carriage drew near and stopped. He heard the sound of the carriage-steps being let down. All was bustle within the house. The servants were running hither and thither, there was a confusion of voices, and the rooms were lit up. Three antiquated chambermaids entered the bedroom, and they were shortly afterwards followed by the Countess who, more dead than alive, sank into a Voltaire armchair. Hermann peeped through a chink. Lizaveta Ivanovna passed close by him, and he heard her hurried steps as she hastened up the little spiral staircase. For a moment his heart was assailed by something like a pricking of conscience, but the emotion was only transitory, and his heart became petrified as before.

The Countess began to undress before her looking-glass. Her rose-bedecked cap was taken off, and then her powdered wig was removed from off her white and closely-cut hair. Hairpins fell in showers around her. Her yellow satin dress, brocaded with silver, fell down at her swollen feet.

Hermann was a witness of the repugnant mysteries of her toilette; at last the Countess was in her night-cap and dressing-gown, and in this costume, more suitable to her age, she appeared less hideous and deformed.

Like all old people in general, the Countess suffered from sleeplessness. Having undressed, she seated herself at the window in a Voltaire armchair and dismissed her maids. The candles were taken away, and once more the room was left with only one lamp burning in it. The Countess sat there looking quite yellow, mumbling with her flaccid lips and swaying to and fro. Her dull eyes expressed complete vacancy of mind, and, looking at her, one would have thought that the rocking of her body was not a voluntary action of her own, but was produced by the action of some concealed galvanic mechanism.

Suddenly the death-like face assumed an inexplicable expression. The lips ceased to tremble, the eyes became animated: before the Countess stood an unknown man.

"Do not be alarmed, for Heaven's sake, do not be alarmed!" said he in a low but distinct voice. "I have no intention of doing you any harm, I have only come to ask a favour of you."

The old woman looked at him in silence, as if she had not heard what he had said. Hermann thought that she was deaf, and, bending down towards her ear, he repeated what he had said. The aged Countess remained silent as before.

"You can insure the happiness of my life," continued Hermann, "and it will cost you nothing. I know that you can name three cards in order—"

Hermann stopped. The Countess appeared now to understand what he wanted; she seemed as if seeking for words to reply.

"It was a joke," she replied at last. "I assure you it was only a joke."

"There is no joking about the matter," replied Hermann angrily. "Remember Chaplitzky, whom you helped to win."

The Countess became visibly uneasy. Her features expressed strong emotion, but they quickly resumed their former immobility.

"Can you not name me these three winning cards?" continued Hermann.

The Countess remained silent; Hermann continued:

"For whom are you preserving your secret? For your grandsons? They are rich enough without it; they do not know the worth of money. Your cards would be of no use to a spendthrift. He who cannot preserve his paternal inheritance will die in want, even though he had a demon at his service. I am not a man of that sort; I know the value of money. Your three cards will not be thrown away upon me. Come!" . . .

He paused and tremblingly awaited her reply. The Countess remained silent; Hermann fell upon his knees.

"If your heart has ever known the feeling of love," said he, "if you remember its rapture, if you have ever smiled at the cry of your new-born child, if any human feeling has ever entered into your breast, I entreat you by the feelings of a wife, a lover, a mother, by all that is most sacred in life, not to reject my prayer. Reveal to me your secret. Of what use is it to you? . . . Maybe it is connected with some terrible sin, with the loss of eternal salvation, with some bargain with the devil. . . . Reflect,—you are old; you have not long to live—I am ready to take your sins upon my soul. Only reveal to me your secret. Remember that the happiness of a man is in your hands, that not only I, but my children, and grandchildren will bless your memory and reverence you as a saint. . . ."

The old Countess answered not a word.

Hermann rose to his feet.

"You old hag!" he exclaimed, grinding his teeth, "then I will make you answer!"

With these words he drew a pistol from his pocket.

At the sight of the pistol, the Countess for the second time exhibited strong emotion. She shook her head and raised her hands as if to protect herself from the shot. . . . then she fell backwards and remained motionless.

"Come, an end to this childish nonsense!" said Hermann, taking hold of her hand. "I ask you for the last time: will you tell me the names of your three cards, or will you not?"

The Countess made no reply. Hermann perceived that she was dead.

IV

Lizaveta Ivanovna was sitting in her room, still in her ball dress, lost in deep thought. On returning home, she had hastily dismissed the chambermaid who very reluctantly came forward to assist her, saying that she would undress herself, and with a trembling heart had gone up to her own room, expecting to find Hermann there, but yet hoping not to find him. At the first glance she convinced herself that he was not there, and she thanked her fate for having prevented him keeping the appointment. She sat down without undressing, and began to recall to mind all the circumstances which in so short a time had carried her so far. It was not three weeks since the time when she first saw the young officer from the window—and yet she was already in correspondence with him, and he had succeeded in inducing her to grant him a nocturnal interview! She knew his name only through his having written it at the bottom of some of his letters; she had never spoken to him, had never heard his voice, and had never heard him spoken of until that evening. But, strange to say, that very evening at the ball, Tomsky, being piqued with the young Princess Pauline N——, who, contrary to her usual custom, did not flirt with him, wished to revenge himself by assuming an air of indifference: he therefore engaged Lizaveta Ivanovna and danced an endless mazurka with her. During the whole of the time he kept teasing her about her partiality for Engineer officers; he assured her that he knew far more than she imagined, and some of his jests were so happily aimed, that Lizaveta thought several times that her secret was known to him.

"From whom have you learnt all this?" she asked, smiling.

"From a friend of a person very well known to you," replied Tomsky, "from a very distinguished man."

"And who is this distinguished man?"

"His name is Hermann."

Lizaveta made no reply; but her hands and feet lost all sense of feeling.

"This Hermann," continued Tomsky, "is a man of romantic personality. He has the profile of a Napoleon, and the soul of a Mephistopheles. I believe that he has at least three crimes upon his conscience. . . . How pale you have become!"

"I have a headache . . . But what did this Hermann— or whatever his name is—tell you?"

"Hermann is very much dissatisfied with his friend: he says that in his place he would act very differently . . . I even think that Hermann himself has designs upon you; at least, he listens very attentively to all that his friend has to say about you."

"And where has he seen me?"

"In church, perhaps; or on the parade—God alone knows where. It may have been in your room, while you were asleep, for there is nothing that he—"

Three ladies approaching him with the question: *"oubli ou regret?"* interrupted the conversation, which had become so tantalisingly interesting to Lizaveta.

The lady chosen by Tomsky was the Princess Pauline herself. She succeeded in effecting a reconciliation with him during the numerous turns of the dance, after which he conducted her to her chair. On returning to his place, Tomsky thought no more either of Hermann or Lizaveta. She longed to renew the interrupted conversation, but the mazurka came to an end, and shortly afterwards the old Countess took her departure.

Tomsky's words were nothing more than the customary small talk of the dance, but they sank deep into the soul of the young dreamer. The portrait, sketched by Tomsky, coincided with the picture she had formed within her own mind, and thanks to the latest romances, the ordinary countenance of her admirer became invested with attributes capable of alarming her and fascinating her imagination at the same time. She was now sitting with her bare arms crossed and with her head, still adorned with flowers, sunk upon her uncovered bosom. Suddenly the door opened and Hermann entered. She shuddered.

"Where were you?" she asked in a terrified whisper.

"In the old Countess's bedroom," replied Hermann. "I have just left her. The Countess is dead."

"My God! What do you say?"

"And I am afraid," added Hermann, "that I am the cause of her death."

Lizaveta looked at him, and Tomsky's words found an echo in her soul: "This man has at least three crimes upon his conscience!" Hermann sat down by the window near her, and related all that had happened.

Lizaveta listened to him in terror. So all those passionate letters, those ardent desires, this bold obstinate pursuit— all this was not love! Money—that was what his soul yearned for! She could not satisfy his desire and make him happy! The poor girl had been nothing but the blind tool of a robber, of the murderer of her aged benefactress! . . . She wept bitter tears of agonised repentance. Hermann gazed at her in silence: his heart, too, was a prey to violent emotion, but neither the tears of the poor girl, nor the wonderful charm of her beauty, enhanced by her grief, could produce any impression upon his hardened soul. He felt no pricking of conscience at the thought of the dead old woman. One thing only grieved him: the irreparable loss of the secret from which he had expected to obtain great wealth.

"You are a monster!" said Lizaveta at last.

"I did not wish for her death," replied Hermann. "My pistol was not loaded."

Both remained silent.

The day began to dawn. Lizaveta extinguished her candle: a pale light illumined her room. She wiped her tear-stained eyes and raised them towards Hermann: he was sitting near the window, with his arms crossed and with a fierce frown upon his forehead. In this attitude he bore a striking resemblance to the portrait of Napoleon. This resemblance struck Lizaveta even.

"How shall I get you out of the house?" said she at last. "I thought of conducting you down the secret staircase, but in that case it would be necessary to go through the Countess's bedroom, and I am afraid."

"Tell me how to find this secret staircase—I will go alone."

Lizaveta arose, took from her drawer a key, handed it to Hermann and gave him the necessary instructions. Hermann pressed her cold, limp hand, kissed her bowed head, and left the room.

He descended the winding staircase, and once more entered the Countess's bedroom. The dead old lady sat as if petrified; her face expressed profound tranquillity. Hermann stopped before her, and gazed long and earnestly at her, as if he wished to convince himself of the terrible reality; at last he entered the cabinet, felt behind the tapestry for the door, and then began to descend the dark staircase, filled with strange emotions. "Down this very staircase," thought he, "perhaps coming from the very same room, and at this very same hour sixty years ago, there may have glided, in an embroidered coat, with his hair dressed *à l'oiseau royal* and pressing to his heart his three-cornered hat, some young gallant, who has long been mouldering in the grave, but the heart of his aged mistress has only today ceased to beat. . . ."

At the bottom of the staircase Hermann found a door, which he opened with a key, and then traversed a corridor which conducted him into the street.

V

Three days after the fatal night, at nine o'clock in the morning, Hermann repaired to the Convent of——, where the last honours were to be paid to the mortal remains of the old Countess. Although feeling no remorse, he could not altogether stifle the voice of conscience, which said to him: "You are the murderer of the old woman!" In spite of his entertaining very little religious belief, he was exceedingly superstitious; and believing that the dead Countess might exercise an evil influence on his life, he resolved to be present at her obsequies in order to implore her pardon.

The church was full. It was with difficulty that Hermann made his way through the crowd of people. The coffin was placed upon a rich catafalque beneath a velvet baldachin. The deceased Countess lay within it, with her hands crossed upon her breast, with a lace cap upon her head and dressed in a white satin robe. Around the catafalque stood the members of her household: the servants in black *caftans*, with armorial ribbons upon their shoulders, and candles in their hands; the relatives—children, grandchildren, and great-grandchildren—in deep mourning.

Nobody wept; tears would have been *une affectation*. The Countess was so old, that her death could have surprised nobody, and her relatives had long looked upon her as being out of the world. A famous preacher pronounced the funeral sermon. In simple and touching words he described the peaceful passing away of the righteous, who had passed long years in calm preparation for a Christian end. "The angel of death found her," said the orator, "engaged in pious meditation and waiting for the midnight bridegroom."

The service concluded amidst profound silence. The relatives went forward first to take farewell of the corpse. Then followed the numerous guests, who had come to render the last homage to her who for so many years had been a participator in their frivolous amusements. After these followed the members of the Countess's household. The last of these was an old woman of the same age as the deceased. Two young women led her forward by the hand. She had not strength enough to bow down to the ground—she merely shed a few tears and kissed the cold hand of her mistress.

Hermann now resolved to approach the coffin. He knelt down upon the cold stones and remained in that position for some minutes; at last he arose, as pale as the deceased

Countess herself; he ascended the steps of the catafalque and bent over the corpse. . . . At that moment it seemed to him that the dead woman darted a mocking look at him and winked with one eye. Hermann started back, took a false step and fell to the ground. Several persons hurried forward and raised him up. At the same moment Lizaveta Ivanovna was borne fainting into the porch of the church. This episode disturbed for some minutes the solemnity of the gloomy ceremony. Among the congregation arose a deep murmur, and a tall thin chamberlain, a near relative of the deceased, whispered in the ear of an Englishman who was standing near him, that the young officer was a natural son of the Countess, to which the Englishman coldly replied: "Oh!"

During the whole of that day, Hermann was strangely excited. Repairing to an out-of-the-way restaurant to dine, he drank a great deal of wine, contrary to his usual custom, in the hope of deadening his inward agitation. But the wine only served to excite his imagination still more. On returning home, he threw himself upon his bed without undressing, and fell into a deep sleep.

When he woke up it was already night, and the moon was shining into the room. He looked at his watch: it was a quarter to three. Sleep had left him; he sat down upon his bed and thought of the funeral of the old Countess.

At that moment somebody in the street looked in at his window, and immediately passed on again. Hermann paid no attention to this incident. A few moments afterwards he heard the door of his ante-room open. Hermann thought that it was his orderly, drunk as usual, returning from some nocturnal expedition, but presently he heard footsteps that were unknown to him: somebody was walking softly over the floor in slippers. The door opened, and a woman dressed in white, entered the room. Hermann mistook her for his old nurse, and wondered what could bring her there at that hour of the night. But the white woman glided rapidly across the room and stood before him—and Hermann recognised the Countess!

"I have come to you against my wish," she said in a firm voice, "but I have been ordered to grant your request. Three, seven, ace, will win for you if played in succession, but only on these conditions: that you do not play more than one card in twenty-four hours, and that you never play again during the rest of your life. I forgive you my death, on condition that you marry my companion, Lizaveta Ivanovna."

With these words she turned round very quietly, walked with a shuffling gait towards the door and disappeared. Hermann heard the street-door open and shut, and again he saw some one look in at him through the window.

For a long time Hermann could not recover himself. He then rose up and entered the next room. His orderly was lying asleep upon the floor, and he had much difficulty in waking him. The orderly was drunk as usual, and no information could be obtained from him. The street-door was locked. Hermann returned to his room, lit his candle, and wrote down all the details of his vision.

VI

Two fixed ideas can no more exist together in the moral world than two bodies can occupy one and the same place in the physical world. "Three, seven, ace," soon drove out of Hermann's mind the thought of the dead Countess. "Three, seven, ace," were perpetually running through his head and continually being repeated by his lips. If he saw a young girl, he would say: "How slender she is! quite like the three of hearts." If anybody asked: "What is the time?" he would reply: "Five minutes to seven." Every stout man that he saw reminded him of the ace. "Three, seven, ace" haunted him in his sleep, and assumed all possible shapes. The threes bloomed before him in the forms of magnificent flowers, the sevens were represented by Gothic portals, and the aces became transformed into gigantic spiders. One thought alone occupied his whole mind—to make a profitable use of the secret which he had purchased so dearly. He thought of applying for a furlough so as to travel abroad. He wanted to go to Paris and tempt fortune in some of the public gambling-houses that abounded there. Chance spared him all this trouble.

There was in Moscow a society of rich gamesters, presided over by the celebrated Chekalinsky, who had passed all his life at the card-table and had amassed millions, accepting bills of exchange for his winnings and paying his losses in ready money. His long experience secured for him the confidence of his companions, and his open house, his famous cook, and his agreeable and fascinating manners gained for him the respect of the public. He came to St. Petersburg. The young men of the capital flocked to his rooms, forgetting balls for cards, and preferring the emotions of faro to the seductions of flirting. Narumov conducted Hermann to Chekalinsky's residence.

They passed through a suite of magnificent rooms, filled with attentive domestics. The place was crowded. Generals and Privy Counsellors were playing at whist; young men were lolling carelessly upon the velvet-covered sofas, eating ices and smoking pipes. In the drawing-room, at the head of a long table, around which were assembled about a score of players, sat the master of the house keeping the bank. He was a man of about sixty years of age, of a very dignified appearance; his head was covered with silvery-white hair; his full, florid countenance expressed good-nature, and his eyes twinkled with a perpetual smile. Narumov introduced Hermann to him. Chekalinsky shook him by the hand in a friendly manner, requested him not to stand on ceremony, and then went on dealing.

The game occupied some time. On the table lay more than thirty cards. Chekalinsky paused after each throw, in order to give the players time to arrange their cards and note down their losses, listened politely to their requests, and more politely still, put straight the corners of cards that some player's hand had chanced to bend. At last the game was finished. Chekalinsky shuffled the cards and prepared to deal again.

"Will you allow me to take a card?" said Hermann, stretching out his hand from behind a stout gentleman who was playing.

Chekalinsky smiled and bowed silently, as a sign of acquiescence. Narumov laughingly congratulated Hermann on his abjuration of that abstention from cards which he had practised for so long a period, and wished him a lucky beginning.

"Stake!" said Hermann, writing some figures with chalk on the back of his card.

"How much?" asked the banker, contracting the muscles of his eyes; "excuse me, I cannot see quite clearly."

"Forty-seven thousand rubles," replied Hermann.

At these words every head in the room turned suddenly round, and all eyes were fixed upon Hermann.

"He has taken leave of his senses!" thought Narumov.

"Allow me to inform you," said Chekalinsky, with his eternal smile, "that you are playing very high; nobody here has ever staked more than two hundred and seventy-five rubles at once."

"Very well," replied Hermann; "but do you accept my card or not?"

Chekalinsky bowed in token of consent.

"I only wish to observe," said he, "that although I have the greatest confidence in my friends, I can only play against ready money. For my own part, I am quite convinced that your word is sufficient, but for the sake of the order of the game, and to facilitate the reckoning up, I must ask you to put the money on your card."

Hermann drew from his pocket a bank-note and handed it to Chekalinsky, who, after examining it in a cursory manner, placed it on Hermann's card.

He began to deal. On the right a nine turned up, and on the left a three.

"I have won!" said Hermann, showing his card.

A murmur of astonishment arose among the players. Chekalinsky frowned, but the smile quickly returned to his face.

"Do you wish me to settle with you?" he said to Hermann.

"If you please," replied the latter.

Chekalinsky drew from his pocket a number of bank-notes and paid at once. Hermann took up his money and left the table. Narumov could not recover from his astonishment. Hermann drank a glass of lemonade and returned home.

The next evening, he again repaired to Chekalinsky's. The host was dealing. Hermann walked up to the table; the punters immediately made room for him. Chekalinsky greeted him with a gracious bow.

Hermann waited for the next deal, took a card and placed upon it his forty-seven thousand rubles, together with his winnings of the previous evening.

Chekalinsky began to deal. A knave turned up on the right, a seven on the left.

Hermann showed his seven.

There was a general exclamation. Chekalinsky was evidently ill at ease, but he counted out the ninety-four thousand rubles and handed them over to Hermann, who pocketed them in the coolest manner possible and immediately left the house.

The next evening Hermann appeared again at the table. Every one was expecting him. Ten generals and Privy Counsellors left their whist in order to watch such extraordinary play. The young officers quitted their sofas, and even the servants crowded into the room. All pressed round Hermann. The other players left off the game, impatient to see how it would end. Hermann stood at the table and prepared to play alone against the pale, but still smiling Chekalinsky. Each opened a pack of cards. Chekalinsky shuffled. Hermann took a card and covered it with a pile of bank-notes. It was like a duel. Deep silence reigned around.

Chekalinsky began to deal; his hands trembled. On the right a queen turned up, and on the left an ace.

"Ace has won!" cried Hermann, showing his card.

"Your queen has lost," said Chekalinsky, politely.

Hermann started; instead of an ace, there lay before him the queen of spades! He could not believe his eyes, nor could he understand how he had made such a mistake.

At that moment it seemed to him that the queen of spades smiled ironically and winked her eye at him. He was struck by her remarkable resemblance. . . .

"The old Countess!" he exclaimed, seized with terror.

Chekalinsky gathered up his winnings. For some time, Hermann remained perfectly motionless. When at last he left the table, there was a general commotion in the room.

"Splendidly done!" said the players. Chekalinsky shuffled the cards afresh, and the game went on as usual.

Hermann went out of his mind, and is now confined in room Number 17 of the Obukhov Hospital. He never answers any questions, but he constantly mutters with unusual rapidity: "Three, seven, ace!" "Three, seven, queen!"

Lizaveta Ivanovna has married a very amiable young man, a son of the former steward of the old Countess. He is in the service of the State somewhere, and is in receipt of a good income. Lizaveta is also supporting a poor relative.

Tomsky has been promoted to the rank of captain, and has become the husband of the Princess Pauline.

Mikhail Lermontov
1814 – 1841

TAMAN

Taman is the nastiest little hole of all the seaports of Russia. I was all but starved there, to say nothing of having a
narrow escape from being drowned.

I arrived late at night by the post-car. The driver stopped
the tired troika at the gate of the only stone-built house
that stood at the entrance to the town. The sentry, a Cossack from the Black Sea, hearing the jingle of the bell,
cried out sleepily in his barbarous voice, "Who goes
there?" An under-officer of Cossacks and a headborough
came out. I explained that I was an officer bound for
the active-service detachment on government business, and
I proceeded to demand official quarters. The headborough
conducted us round the town. Whatever hut we drove up
to we found to be occupied. The weather was cold; I had
not slept for three nights; I was tired out, and I began to
lose my temper.

"Take me somewhere or other, you scoundrel!" I cried;
"to the devil himself, as long as there's a place to put up
at!"

"There *is* one other lodging," answered the headborough,
scratching his head. "Only you won't like it, sir. It is uncanny!"

Failing to grasp the exact signification of the last phrase,
I ordered him to go on, and, after a lengthy peregrination
through muddy byways, at the sides of which I could see

nothing but old fences, we drove up to a small cabin, right on the shore of the sea.

The full moon was shining on the little reed-thatched roof and the white walls of my new dwelling. In the court-yard, which was surrounded by a wall of rubble-stone, there stood another miserable hovel, smaller and older than the first and all askew. The shore descended precipi-tously to the sea, almost from its very walls, and down below, with incessant murmur, plashed the dark-blue waves. The moon gazed softly upon the watery element, restless but obedient to it, and I was able by its light to distinguish two ships lying at some distance from the shore, their black rigging motionless and standing out, like cobwebs, against the pale line of the horizon.

"There are vessels in the harbor," I said to myself. "To-morrow I will set out for Gelenjik."

I had with me, in the capacity of soldier-servant, a Cos-sack of the frontier army. Ordering him to take down the portmanteau and dismiss the driver, I began to call the master of the house. No answer! I knocked—all was si-lent within! . . . What could it mean? At length a boy of about fourteen crept out from the hall.

"Where is the master?"

"There isn't one."

"What! No master?"

"None!"

"And the mistress?"

"She has gone off to the village."

"Who will open the door for me, then?" I said, giving it a kick.

The door opened of its own accord, and a breath of moisture-laden air was wafted from the hut. I struck a lucifer match and held it to the boy's face. It lit up two white eyes. He was totally blind, obviously so from birth. He stood stock-still before me, and I began to examine his features.

I confess that I have a violent prejudice against all blind, one-eyed, deaf, dumb, legless, armless, hunchbacked, and such-like people. I have observed that there is always a cer-tain strange connection between a man's exterior and his soul; as if when the body loses a limb, the soul also loses some power of feeling.

And so I began to examine the blind boy's face. But what could be read upon a face from which the eyes were missing? . . . For a long time I gazed at him with involuntary compassion, when suddenly a scarcely perceptible smile flitted over his thin lips, producing, I know not why, a most unpleasant impression upon me. I began to feel a suspicion that the blind boy was not so blind as he appeared to be. In vain I endeavored to convince myself that it was impossible to counterfeit cataracts; and besides, what reason could there be for doing such a thing? But I could not help my suspicions. I am easily swayed by prejudice. . . .

"You are the master's son?" I asked at length.

"No."

"Who are you, then?"

"An orphan—a poor boy."

"Has the mistress any children?"

"No, her daughter ran away and crossed the sea with a Tartar."

"What sort of a Tartar?"

"The devil only knows! A Crimean Tartar, a boatman from Kerch."

I entered the hut. Its whole furniture consisted of two benches and a table, together with an enormous chest beside the stove. There was not a single ikon to be seen on the wall—a bad sign! The sea-wind burst in through the broken windowpane. I drew a wax candle-end from my portmanteau, lit it, and began to put my things out. My saber and gun I placed in a corner, my pistols I laid on the table. I spread my felt cloak out on one bench, and the Cossack his on the other. In ten minutes the latter was snoring, but I could not go to sleep—the image of the boy with the white eyes kept hovering before me in the dark.

About an hour passed thus. The moon shone in at the window and its rays played along the earthen floor of the hut. Suddenly a shadow flitted across the bright strip of moonshine which intersected the floor. I raised myself up a little and glanced out of the window. Again somebody ran by it and disappeared—goodness knows where! It seemed impossible for anyone to descend the steep cliff overhanging the shore, but that was the only thing that could have happened. I rose, threw on my tunic, girded on a dagger, and with the utmost quietness went out of the hut. The blind boy was coming toward me. I hid by the fence, and he passed by me with a sure but cautious step. He was carrying a parcel under his arm. He turned toward the harbor and began to descend a steep and narrow path.

"On that day the dumb will cry out and the blind will see," I said to myself, following him just close enough to keep him in sight.

Meanwhile the moon was becoming overcast by clouds and a mist had risen upon the sea. The lantern alight in the stern of a ship close at hand was scarcely visible through the mist, and by the shore there glimmered the foam of the waves, which every moment threatened to submerge it. Descending with difficulty, I stole along the steep declivity, and all at once I saw the blind boy come to a standstill and then turn down to the right. He walked so close to the water's edge that it seemed as if the waves would straightway seize him and carry him off. But, judging by the confidence with which he stepped from rock to rock and avoided the water-channels, this was evidently not the first time that he had made that journey. Finally he stopped, as though listening for something, squatted down upon the ground, and laid the parcel beside him. Concealing myself behind a projecting rock on the shore, I kept watch on his movements. After a few minutes a white figure made its appearance from the opposite direction. It came up to the blind boy and sat down beside him. At times the wind wafted their conversation to me.

"Well?" said a woman's voice. "The storm is violent; Yanko will not be here."

"Yanko is not afraid of the storm!" the other replied.

"The mist is thickening," rejoined the woman's voice, sadness in its tone.

"In the mist it is all the easier to slip past the guard-ships," was the answer.

"And if he is drowned?"

"Well, what then? On Sunday you won't have a new ribbon to go to church in."

An interval of silence followed. One thing, however, struck me—in talking to me the blind boy spoke in the Little Russian dialect, but now he was expressing himself in pure Russian.

"You see, I am right!" the blind boy went on, clapping his hands. "Yanko is not afraid of sea, nor winds, nor mist, nor coast guards! Just listen! That is not the water plashing, you can't deceive me—it is his long oars."

The woman sprang up and began anxiously to gaze into the distance. "You are raving!" she said. "I cannot see anything."

I confess that, much as I tried to make out in the distance something resembling a boat, my efforts were unsuccessful. About ten minutes passed thus, when a black speck appeared between the mountains of the waves! At one time it grew larger, at another smaller. Slowly rising upon the crests of the waves and swiftly descending from them, the boat drew near to the shore.

"He must be a brave sailor," I thought, "to have determined to cross the twenty versts of strait on a night like this, and he must have had a weighty reason for doing so."

Reflecting thus, I gazed with an involuntary beating of the heart at the poor boat. It dived like a duck, and then, with rapidly swinging oars—like wings—it sprang forth from the abyss amid the splashes of the foam. "Ah!" I thought, "it will be dashed against the shore with all its force and broken to pieces!" But it turned aside adroitly and leaped unharmed into a little creek. Out of it stepped a man of medium height, wearing a Tartar sheepskin cap. He waved his hand, and all three set to work to drag something out of the boat. The cargo was so large that, to this day, I cannot understand how it was that the boat did not sink.

Each of them shouldered a bundle, and they set off along the shore, and I soon lost sight of them. I had to return home; but I confess I was rendered uneasy by all these strange happenings, and I found it hard to await the morning.

My Cossack was very much astonished when, on waking up, he saw me fully dressed. I did not, however, tell him the reason. For some time I stood at the window, gazing admiringly at the blue sky all studded with wisps of cloud, and at the distant shore of the Crimea, stretching out in a lilac-colored streak and ending in a cliff, on the summit of which the white tower of the lighthouse was gleaming. Then I betook myself to the fortress, Phanagoriya, in order to ascertain from the Commandant at what hour I should depart for Gelenjik.

But the Commandant, alas! could not give me any definite information. The vessels lying in the harbor were all either guard-ships or merchant vessels which had not yet even begun to take in lading.

"Maybe in about three or four days' time a mailboat will come in," said the Commandant, "and then we shall see."

I returned home sulky and wrathful. My Cossack met me at the door with a frightened countenance.

"Things are looking bad, sir!" he said.

"Yes, my friend; goodness only knows when we shall get away!"

Hereupon he became still more uneasy, and, bending toward me, he said in a whisper:

"It is uncanny here! I met an under-officer from the Black Sea today—he's an acquaintance of mine—he was in my detachment last year. When I told him where we were staying, he said, 'That place is uncanny, old fellow, they're wicked people there!' . . . And, indeed, what sort of a blind boy is that? He goes everywhere alone, to fetch water and to buy bread at the bazaar. It is evident they have become accustomed to that sort of thing here."

"Well, what then? Tell me, though, has the mistress of the place put in an appearance?"

"During your absence today, an old woman and her daughter arrived."

"What daughter? She has no daughter!"

"Goodness knows who it can be if it isn't her daughter; but the old woman is sitting over there in the hut now."

I entered the hovel. A blazing fire was burning in the stove, and they were cooking a dinner which struck me as being a rather luxurious one for poor people. To all my questions the old woman replied that she was deaf and could not hear me. There was nothing to be got out of her. I turned to the blind boy who was sitting in front of the stove, putting twigs into the fire.

"Now, then, you little blind devil," I said, taking him by the ear. "Tell me, where were you roaming with the bundle last night, eh?"

The blind boy suddenly burst out weeping, shrieking and wailing.

"Where did I go? I did not go anywhere. . . . With the bundle? . . . What bundle?"

This time the old woman heard, and she began to mutter:

"Hark at them plotting, and against a poor boy too! What are you touching him for? What has he done to you?"

I had enough of it, and went out, firmly resolved to find the key to the riddle.

I wrapped myself up in my felt cloak and, sitting down on a rock by the fence, gazed into the distance. Before me stretched the sea, agitated by the storm of the previous night, and its monotonous roar, like the murmur of a town over which slumber is beginning to creep, recalled bygone years to my mind, and transported my thoughts northward to our cold capital. Agitated by my recollections, I became oblivious to my surroundings.

About an hour passed thus, perhaps even longer. Suddenly something resembling a song struck upon my ear. It *was* a song, and the voice was a woman's, young and fresh—but where was it coming from? . . . I listened; it was a harmonious melody—now long-drawn-out and plaintive, now swift and lively. I looked around me—there was nobody to be seen. I listened again—the sounds seemed to be falling from the sky. I raised my eyes. On the roof of my cabin was standing a young girl in a striped dress and with her hair hanging loose—a regular water-nymph. Shading her eyes from the sun's rays with the palm of her hand, she was gazing intently into the distance. At one time, she would laugh and talk to herself, at another, she would strike up her song anew.

I have retained that song in my memory, word for word:

> At their own free will
> They seem to wander
> O'er the green sea yonder,
> Those ships, as still
> They are onward going,
> With white sails flowing.
>
> And among those ships
> My eye can mark
> My own dear barque:
> By two oars guided
> (All unprovided
> With sails) it slips.
>
> The storm-wind raves:
> And the old ships—see!
> With wings spread free,
> Over the waves
> They scatter and flee!
>
> The sea I will hail
> With obeisance deep:
> "Thou base one, hark:
> Thou must not fail
> My little barque
> From harm to keep!"
>
> For lo! 'tis bearing
> Most precious gear,
> And brave and daring
> The arms that steer
> Within the dark
> My little barque.

Involuntarily the thought occurred to me that I had heard the same voice the night before. I reflected for a moment, and when I looked up at the roof again there was no girl to be seen. Suddenly she darted past me, with another song on her lips, and, snapping her fingers, she ran up to the old woman. Thereupon a quarrel arose between them. The old woman grew angry, and the girl laughed loudly. And then I saw my Undine running and gamboling again. She came up to where I was, stopped, and gazed fixedly into my face as if surprised at my presence. Then she turned carelessly away and went quietly toward the harbor. But this was not all. The whole day she kept hovering around my lodging, singing and gamboling without a moment's interruption. Strange creature! There was not the slightest sign of insanity in her face; on the contrary, her eyes, which were continually resting upon me, were bright and piercing. Moreover, they seemed to be endowed with a certain magnetic power, and each time they looked at me they appeared to be expecting a question. But I had only to open my lips to speak, and away she would run, with a sly smile.

Certainly never before had I seen a woman like her. She was by no means beautiful; but, as in other matters, I have my own prepossessions on the subject of beauty. There was a good deal of breeding in her. . . . Breeding in women, as in horses, is a great thing: a discovery, the credit of which belongs to young France. It—that is to say, breeding, not young France—is chiefly to be detected in the gait, in the hands and feet; the nose, in particular, is of the greatest significance. In Russia a straight nose is rarer than a small foot.

My songstress appeared to be not more than eighteen years of age. The unusual suppleness of her figure, the characteristic and original way she had of inclining her head, her long, light-brown hair, the golden sheen of her slightly sunburned neck and shoulders, and especially her straight nose—all these held me fascinated. Although in her sidelong glances I could read a certain wildness and disdain, although in her smile there was a certain vagueness, yet—such is the force of predilections—that straight nose of hers drove me crazy. I fancied that I had found Goethe's Mignon—that queer creature of his German imagination. And, indeed, there was a good deal of similarity between them: the same rapid transitions from the utmost restlessness to complete immobility, the same enigmatical speeches, the same gambols, the same strange songs.

Toward evening I stopped her at the door and entered into the following conversation with her.

"Tell me, my beauty," I asked, "what were you doing on the roof today?"

"I was looking to see from what direction the wind was blowing."

"What did you want to know for?"

"Whence the wind blows comes happiness."

"Well? Were you invoking happiness with your song?"

"Where there is singing there is also happiness."

"But what if your song were to bring you sorrow?"

"Well, what then? Where things won't be better, they will be worse; and from bad to good again is not far."

"And who taught you that song?"

"Nobody taught me; it comes into my head and I sing; whoever is to hear it, he will hear it, and whoever ought not to hear it, he will not understand it."

"What is your name, my songstress?"

"He who baptized me knows."

"And who baptized you?"

"How should I know?"

"What a secretive girl you are! But look here, I have learned something about you"—she neither changed countenance nor moved her lips, as though my discovery was of no concern to her—"I have learned that you went to the shore last night."

And, thereupon, I very gravely retailed to her all that I had seen, thinking that I should embarrass her. Not a bit of it! She burst out laughing heartily.

"You have seen much, but know little; and what you do know, see that you keep it under lock and key."

"But supposing, now, I was to take it into my head to inform the Commandant?" and here I assumed a very serious, not to say stern, demeanor.

She gave a sudden spring, began to sing, and hid herself like a bird frightened out of a thicket. My last words were altogether out of place. I had no suspicion then how momentous they were, but afterwards I had occasion to rue them.

As soon as the dusk of the evening fell, I ordered the Cossack to heat the teapot, campaign fashion. I lighted a candle and sat down by the table, smoking my traveling-pipe. I was just about to finish my second tumbler of tea when suddenly the door creaked and I heard behind me the sound of footsteps and the light rustle of a dress. I started and turned around.

It was she—my Undine. Softly and without saying a word she sat down opposite to me and fixed her eyes upon me. Her glance seemed wondrously tender, I know not why; it reminded me of one of those glances which, in years gone by, so despotically played with my life. She seemed to be waiting for a question, but I kept silence, filled with an inexplicable sense of embarrassment. Mental agitation was evinced by the dull pallor which overspread her countenance; her hand, which I noticed was trembling slightly, moved aimlessly about the table. At one time her breast heaved, and at another she seemed to be holding her breath. This little comedy was beginning to pall upon me, and I was about to break the silence in a most prosaic manner, that is, by offering her a glass of tea; when suddenly, springing up, she threw her arms around my neck, and I felt her moist, fiery lips pressed upon mine. Darkness came before my eyes, my head began to swim. I embraced her with the whole strength of youthful passion. But, like a snake, she glided from between my arms, whispering in my ear as she did so:

"Tonight, when everyone is asleep, go out to the shore."

Like an arrow she sprang from the room.

In the hall she upset the teapot and a candle which was standing on the floor.

"Little devil!" cried the Cossack, who had taken up his position on the straw and had contemplated warming himself with the remains of the tea.

It was only then that I recovered my senses.

In about two hours' time, when all had grown silent in the harbor, I awakened my Cossack.

"If I fire a pistol," I said, "run to the shore."

He stared open-eyed and answered mechanically:

"Very well, sir."

I stuffed a pistol in my belt and went out. She was waiting for me at the edge of the cliff. Her attire was more than light, and a small kerchief girded her supple waist.

"Follow me!" she said, taking me by the hand, and we began to descend.

I cannot understand how it was that I did not break my neck. Down below we turned to the right and proceeded to take the path along which I had followed the blind boy the evening before. The moon had not yet risen, and only two little stars, like two guardian lighthouses, were twinkling in the dark-blue vault of heaven. The heavy waves, with measured and even motion, rolled one after the other, scarcely lifting the solitary boat which was moored to the shore.

"Let us get into the boat," said my companion.

I hesitated. I am no lover of sentimental trips on the sea; but this was not the time to draw back. She leaped into the boat, and I after her; and I had not time to recover my wits before I observed that we were adrift.

"What is the meaning of this?" I said angrily.

"It means," she answered, seating me on the bench and throwing her arms around my waist, "it means that I love you!" . . .

Her cheek was pressed close to mine, and I felt her burning breath upon my face. Suddenly something fell noisily into the water. I clutched at my belt—my pistol was gone! Ah, now a terrible suspicion crept into my soul, and the blood rushed to my head! I looked round. We were about fifty fathoms from the shore, and I could not swim a stroke! I tried to thrust her away from me, but she clung like a cat to my clothes, and suddenly a violent wrench all but threw me into the sea. The boat rocked, but I righted myself, and a desperate struggle began.

Fury lent me strength, but I soon found that I was no match for my opponent in point of agility. . . .

"What do you want?" I cried, firmly squeezing her little hands.

Her fingers crunched, but her serpentlike nature bore up against the torture, and she did not utter a cry.

"You saw us," she answered. "You will tell on us."

And with a supernatural effort, she flung me onto the side of the boat; we both hung half-overboard; her hair touched the water. The decisive moment had come. I planted my knee against the bottom of the boat, caught her by the tresses with one hand and by the throat with the other; she let go my clothes, and, in an instant I had thrown her into the waves.

It was now rather dark; once or twice her head appeared for an instant amidst the sea foam, and I saw no more of her.

I found the half of an old oar at the bottom of the boat, and somehow or other, after lengthy efforts, I made fast to the harbor. Making my way along the shore toward my hut, I involuntarily gazed in the direction of the spot where, on the previous night, the blind boy had awaited the nocturnal mariner. The moon was already rolling through the sky, and it seemed to me that somebody in white was sitting on the shore. Spurred by curiosity, I crept up and crouched down in the grass on the top of the cliff. By thrusting my head out a little way I was able to get a good view of everything that was happening down below, and I was not very much astonished, but almost rejoiced, when I recognized my water-nymph. She was wringing the seafoam from her long hair. Her wet garment outlined her supple figure and her high bosom.

Soon a boat appeared in the distance; it drew near rapidly; and, as on the night before, a man in a Tartar cap stepped out of it, but he now had his hair cropped round in the Cossack fashion, and a large knife was sticking out behind his leather belt.

"Yanko," the girl said, "all is lost!"

Then their conversation continued, but so softly that I could not catch a word of it.

"But where is the blind boy?" said Yanko at last, raising his voice.

"I have told him to come," was the reply.

After a few minutes the blind boy appeared, dragging on his back a sack, which they placed in the boat.

"Listen!" said Yanko to the blind boy. "Guard that place! You know where I mean? There are valuable goods there. Tell"—I could not catch the name—"that I am no longer his servant. Things have gone badly. He will see me no more. It is dangerous now. I will go seek work in another place, and he will never be able to find another daredevil like me. Tell him also that if he had paid me a little better for my labors, I would not have forsaken him. For me there is a way anywhere, if only the wind blows and the sea roars."

After a short silence Yanko continued:

"She is coming with me. It is impossible for her to remain here. Tell the old woman that it is time for her to die; she has been here a long time, and the line must be drawn somewhere. As for us, she will never see us any more."

"And I?" said the blind boy in a plaintive voice.

"What use have I for you?" was the answer.

In the meantime my Undine had sprung into the boat. She beckoned to her companion with her hand. He placed something in the blind boy's hand and added:

"There, buy yourself some gingerbreads."

"Is this all?" said the blind boy.

"Well, here is some more."

The money fell and jingled as it struck the rock.

The blind boy did not pick it up. Yanko took his seat in the boat; the wind was blowing from the shore; they hoisted the little sail and sped rapidly away. For a long time the white sail gleamed in the moonlight amid the dark waves. Still the blind boy remained seated upon the shore, and then I heard something which sounded like sobbing. The blind boy was, in fact, weeping, and for a long, long time his tears flowed. . . . I grew heavy-hearted. For what reason should fate have thrown me into the peaceful circle of *honorable smugglers?* Like a stone cast into a smooth well, I had disturbed their quietude, and I barely escaped going to the bottom like a stone.

I returned home. In the hall the burned-out candle was spluttering on a wooden platter, and my Cossack, contrary to orders, was fast asleep, with his gun held in both hands. I left him at rest, took the candle, and entered the hut. Alas! my cashbox, my saber with the silver chasing, my Daghestan dagger—the gift of a friend—all had vanished! It was then that I guessed what articles the cursed blind boy had been dragging along. Roughly shaking the Cossack, I woke him up, rated him, and lost my temper. But what was the good of that? And would it not have been ridiculous to complain to the authorities that I had been robbed by a blind boy and all but drowned by an eighteen-year-old girl?

Thank heaven an opportunity of getting away presented itself in the morning, and I left Taman.

What became of the old woman and the poor blind boy I know not. And, besides, what are the joys and sorrows of mankind to me—me, a traveling officer, and one, moreover, with an order for post-horses on government business?

Ivan Turgenev
1818 – 1883

BEZHIN MEADOWS

It was a glorious July day, one of those days which only
come after many days of fine weather. From earliest morning the sky is clear; the sunrise does not glow with fire; it
is suffused with a soft roseate flush. The sun, not fiery, not
red-hot as in time of stifling drought, not dull purple as
before a storm, but with a bright and genial radiance,
rises peacefully behind a long and narrow cloud, shines out
freshly, and plunges again into its lilac mist. The delicate
upper edge of the strip of cloud flashes in little gleaming
snakes; their brilliance is like polished silver. But, lo! the
dancing rays flash forth again, and in solemn joy, as though
flying upward, rises the mighty orb. About mid-day there
is wont to be, high up in the sky, a multitude of rounded
clouds, golden-grey, with soft white edges. Like islands
scattered over an overflowing river, that bathes them in its
unbroken reaches of deep transparent blue, they scarcely
stir; farther down the heavens they are in movement,
packing closer; now there is no blue to be seen between
them, but they are themselves almost as blue as the sky,
filled full with light and heat. The colour of the horizon, a
faint pale lilac, does not change all day, and is the same
all round; nowhere is there storm gathering and darkening;
only somewhere rays of bluish colour stretch down from
the sky; it is a sprinkling of scarce-perceptible rain. In the
evening these clouds disappear; the last of them, blackish

and undefined as smoke, lie streaked with pink, facing the setting sun; in the place where it has gone down, as calmly as it rose, a crimson glow lingers long over the darkening earth, and, softly flashing like a candle carried carelessly, the evening star flickers in the sky. On such days all the colours are softened, bright but not glaring; everything is suffused with a kind of touching tenderness. On such days the heat is sometimes very great; often it is even "steaming" on the slopes of the fields, but a wind dispels this growing sultriness, and whirling eddies of dust—sure sign of settled, fine weather—move along the roads and across the fields in high white columns. In the pure dry air there is a scent of wormwood, rye in blossom, and buckwheat; even an hour before nightfall there is no moisture in the air. It is for such weather that the farmer longs, for harvesting his wheat. . . .

On just such a day I was once out grouse-shooting in the Tchern district of the province of Tula. I started and shot a fair amount of game; my full game-bag cut my shoulder mercilessly; but already the evening glow had faded, and the cool shades of twilight were beginning to grow thicker, and to spread across the sky, which was still bright, though no longer lighted up by the rays of the setting sun, when I at last decided to turn back homewards. With swift steps I passed through the long "square" of underwoods, clambered up a hill, and instead of the familiar plain I expected to see, with the oakwood on the right and the little white church in the distance, I saw before me a scene completely different, and quite new to me. A narrow valley lay at my feet, and directly facing me a dense wood of aspen-trees rose up like a thick wall. I stood still in perplexity, looked round me. . . . "Aha!" I thought, "I have somehow come wrong; I kept too much to the right," and surprised at my own mistake, I rapidly descended the hill. I was at once plunged into a disagreeable clinging mist, exactly as though I had gone down into a cellar; the thick high grass at the bottom of the valley, all drenched with dew, was white like a smooth tablecloth; one felt afraid somehow to walk on it. I made haste to get on the other side, and walked along beside the aspenwood, bearing to the left. Bats were already hovering over its slumbering tree-tops, mysteriously flitting and quivering across the clear obscure of the sky; a young belated hawk flew in swift, straight course upwards, hastening to its nest. "Here, directly I get to this corner," I thought to myself, "I shall find the road at once; but I have come a mile out of my way!"

I did at last reach the end of the wood, but there was no road of any sort there; some kind of low bushes overgrown with long grass extended far and wide before me; behind them in the far, far distance could be discerned a tract of waste land. I stopped again. "Well? Where am I?" I began ransacking my brain to recall how and where I had been walking during the day. . . . "Ah! but these are the bushes at Parahin," I cried at last; "of course! then this must be Sindyev wood. But how did I get here? So far? . . . Strange! Now I must bear to the right again."

I went to the right through the bushes. Meantime the night had crept close and grown up like a storm-cloud; it seemed as though, with the mists of evening, darkness was rising up on all sides and flowing down from overhead. I had come upon some sort of little, untrodden, overgrown path; I walked along it, gazing intently before me. Soon all was blackness and silence around—only the quail's cry was heard from time to time. Some small night-bird, flitting noiselessly near the ground on its soft wings, almost flapped against me and scurried away in alarm. I came out on the further side of the bushes, and made my way along a field by the hedge. By now I could hardly make out distant objects; the field showed dimly white around; beyond it rose up a sullen darkness, which seemed moving up closer in huge masses every instant. My steps gave a muffled sound in the air, that grew colder and colder. The pale sky began again to grow blue—but it was the blue of night. The tiny stars glimmered and twinkled in it.

What I had been taking for a wood turned out to be a dark round hillock. "But where am I, then?" I repeated again aloud, standing still for the third time and looking inquiringly at my spot and tan English dog, Dianka by name, certainly the most intelligent of four-footed creatures.

But the most intelligent of four-footed creatures only wagged her tail, blinked her weary eyes dejectedly, and gave me no sensible advice. I felt myself disgraced in her eyes and pushed desperately forward, as though I had suddenly guessed which way I ought to go; I scaled the hill, and found myself in a hollow of no great depth, ploughed round.

A strange sensation came over me at once. This hollow had the form of an almost perfect cauldron, with sloping sides; at the bottom of it were some great white stones standing upright—it seemed as though they had crept there for some secret council—and it was so still and dark in it, so dreary and weird seemed the sky, overhanging it, that my heart sank. Some little animal was whining feebly and piteously among the stones. I made haste to get out again on to the hillock. Till then I had not quite given up all hope of finding the way home; but at this point I finally decided that I was utterly lost, and without any further attempt to make out the surrounding objects, which were almost completely plunged in darkness, I walked straight forward, by the aid of the stars, at random. . . . For about half an hour I walked on in this way, though I could hardly move one leg before the other. It seemed as if I had never been in such a deserted country in my life; nowhere was there the glimmer of a fire, nowhere a sound to be heard. One sloping hillside followed another; fields stretched endlessly upon fields; bushes seemed to spring up out of the earth under my very nose. I kept walking and was just making up my mind to lie down somewhere till morning, when suddenly I found myself on the edge of a horrible precipice.

I quickly drew back my lifted foot, and through the almost opaque darkness I saw far below me a vast plain. A long river skirted it in a semi-circle, turned away from me; its course was marked by the steely reflection of the water still faintly glimmering here and there. The hill on which I found myself terminated abruptly in an almost overhanging precipice, whose gigantic profile stood out black against the dark-blue waste of sky, and directly below me, in the corner formed by this precipice and the plain near the river, which was there a dark, motionless mirror, under the lee of the hill, two fires side by side were smoking and throwing up red flames. People were stirring round them, shadows hovered, and sometimes the front of a little curly head was lighted up by the glow.

I found out at last where I had got to. This plain was well known in our parts under the name of Bezhin Meadows. . . . But there was no possibility of returning home, especially at night; my legs were sinking under me from weariness. I decided to get down to the fires and to wait for the dawn in the company of these men, whom I took for drovers. I got down successfully, but I had hardly let go of the last branch I had grasped, when suddenly two large shaggy white dogs rushed angrily barking upon me. The sound of ringing boyish voices came from round the fires; two or three boys quickly got up from the ground. I called back in response to their shouts of inquiry. They ran up to me, and at once called off the dogs, who were specially struck by the appearance of my Dianka. I came down to them.

I had been mistaken in taking the figures sitting round the fires for drovers. They were simply peasant boys from a neighbouring village, who were in charge of a drove of horses. In hot summer weather with us they drive the horses out at night to graze in the open country: the flies and gnats would give them no peace in the daytime; they drive out the drove towards evening, and drive them back in the early morning: it's a great treat for the peasant boys. Bareheaded, in old fur capes, they bestride the most spirited nags, and scurry along with merry cries and hooting and ringing laughter, swinging their arms and legs, and leaping into the air. The fine dust is stirred up in yellow clouds and moves along the road; the tramp of hoofs in unison resounds afar; the horses race along, pricking up their ears; in front of all, with his tail in the air and thistles in his tangled mane, prances some shaggy chestnut, constantly shifting his paces as he goes.

I told the boys I had lost my way, and sat down with them. They asked me where I came from, and then were silent for a little and turned away. Then we talked a little

again. I lay down under a bush, whose shoots had been
nibbled off, and began to look round. It was a marvellous
picture; about the fire a red ring of light quivered and
seemed to swoon away in the embrace of a background of
darkness; the flame flaring up from time to time cast swift
flashes of light beyond the boundary of this circle; a fine
tongue of light licked the dry twigs and died away at once;
long thin shadows, in their turn breaking in for an instant,
danced right up to the very fires; darkness was struggling
with light. Sometimes, when the fire burnt low and the
circle of light shrank together, suddenly out of the en-
croaching darkness a horse's head was thrust in, bay, with
striped markings or all white, stared with intent blank eyes
upon us, nipped hastily the long grass, and drawing back
again, vanished instantly. One could only hear it still
munching and snorting. From the circle of light it was
hard to make out what was going on in the darkness; everything close at hand seemed shut off by an almost black
curtain; but farther away hills and forests were dimly visible in long blurs upon the horizon.

The dark unclouded sky stood, inconceivably immense,
triumphant, above us in all its mysterious majesty. One felt
a sweet oppression at one's heart, breathing in that peculiar,
overpowering, yet fresh fragrance—the fragrance of a
summer night in Russia. Scarcely a sound was to be heard
around. . . . Only at times, in the river near, the sudden
splash of a big fish leaping, and the faint rustle of a reed
on the bank, swaying lightly as the ripples reached it . . .
the fires alone kept up a subdued crackling.

The boys sat round them: there too sat the two dogs,
who had been so eager to devour me. They could not for
long after reconcile themselves to my presence, and,
drowsily blinking and staring into the fire, they growled
now and then with an unwonted sense of their own dignity;
first they growled, and then whined a little, as though de-
ploring the impossibility of carrying out their desires.
There were altogether five boys: Fedya, Pavlusha, Ilyusha, Kostya and Vanya. (From their talk I learnt their
names, and I intend now to introduce them to the reader.)

The first and eldest of all, Fedya, one would take to be

about fourteen. He was a well-made boy, with good-looking, delicate, rather small features, curly fair hair, bright eyes, and a perpetual half-merry, half-careless smile. He belonged, by all appearances, to a well-to-do family, and had ridden out to the meadows, not through necessity, but for amusement. He wore a gay print shirt, with a yellow border; a short new overcoat slung round his neck was almost slipping off his narrow shoulders; a comb hung from his blue belt. His boots, coming a little way up the leg, were certainly his own—not his father's. The second boy, Pavlusha, had tangled black hair, grey eyes, broad cheek-bones, a pale face pitted with smallpox, a large but well-cut mouth; his head altogether was large—"a beer-barrel head," as they say—and his figure was square and clumsy. He was not a good-looking boy—there's no denying it!—and yet I liked him; he looked very sensible and straightforward, and there was a vigorous ring in his voice. He had nothing to boast of in his attire; it consisted simply of a homespun shirt and patched trousers. The face of the third, Ilyusha, was rather uninteresting; it was a long face, with short-sighted eyes and a hook nose; it expressed a kind of dull, fretful uneasiness; his tightly-drawn lips seemed rigid; his contracted brow never relaxed; he seemed continually blinking from the firelight. His flaxen—almost white—hair hung out in thin wisps under his low felt hat, which he kept pulling down with both hands over his ears. He had on new bast-shoes and leggings; a thick string, wound three times round his figure, carefully held together his neat black smock. Neither he nor Pavlusha looked more than twelve years old. The fourth, Kostya, a boy of ten, aroused my curiosity by his thoughtful and sorrowful look. His whole face was small, thin, freckled, pointed at the chin like a squirrel's; his lips were barely perceptible; but his great black eyes, that shone with liquid brilliance, produced a strange impression; they seemed trying to express something for which the tongue—his tongue, at least—had no words. He was undersized and weakly, and dressed rather poorly. The remaining boy, Vanya, I had not noticed at first; he was lying on the ground, peacefully curled up under a square rug, and only occasionally thrust his curly brown head out from under it: this boy was seven years old at the most.

So I lay under the bush at one side and looked at the boys. A small pot was hanging over one of the fires; in it potatoes were cooking. Pavlusha was looking after them, and on his knees he was trying them by poking a splinter of wood into the boiling water. Fedya was lying leaning on his elbow, and smoothing out the skirts of his coat. Ilyusha was sitting beside Kostya, and still kept blinking constrainedly. Kostya's head drooped despondently, and he looked away into the distance. Vanya did not stir under his rug. I pretended to be asleep. Little by little, the boys began talking again.

At first they gossiped of one thing and another, the work of tomorrow, the horses; but suddenly Fedya turned to Ilyusha, and, as though taking up again an interrupted conversation, asked him:

"Come then, so you've seen the domovoy?"

"No, I didn't see him, and no one ever can see him," answered Ilyusha, in a weak hoarse voice, the sound of which was wonderfully in keeping with the expression of his face; "I heard him. . . . Yes, and not I alone."

"Where does he live—in your place?" asked Pavlusha.

"In the old paper-mill."

"Why, do you go to the factory?"

"Of course we do. My brother Avdushka and I, we are paper-glazers."

"I say—factory-hands!"

"Well, how did you hear it, then?" asked Fedya.

"It was like this. It happened that I and my brother Avdushka, with Fyodor of Mihyevska, and Ivashka the Squint-eyed, and the other Ivashka who comes from the Red Hills, and Ivashka of Suhorukov too—and there were some other boys there as well—there were ten of us boys there altogether—the whole shift, that is—it happened that we spent the night at the paper-mill; that's to say, it didn't happen, but Nazarov, the overseer, kept us. 'Why,' said he, 'should you waste time going home, boys; there's a lot of work tomorrow, so don't go home, boys.' So we stopped, and were all lying down together, and Avdushka had just begun to say, 'I say, boys, suppose the domovoy were to come?' And before he'd finished saying so, some one suddenly began walking over our heads; we were lying down below, and he began walking upstairs overhead, where the wheel is. We listened: he walked; the boards seemed to be bending under him, they creaked so; then he crossed over, above our heads; all of a sudden the water began to drip and drip over the wheel; the wheel rattled and rattled and again began to turn, though the sluices of the conduit above had been let down. We wondered who could have lifted them up so that the water could run; any way, the wheel turned and turned a little, and then stopped. Then he went to the door overhead and began coming downstairs, and came down like this, not hurrying himself; the stairs seemed to groan under him too. . . . Well, he came right down to our door, and waited and waited . . . and all of a sudden the door simply flew open. We were in a fright; we looked—there was nothing. . . . Suddenly what if the net on one of the vats didn't begin moving; it got up, and went rising and ducking and moving in the air as though some one were stirring with it, and then it was in its place again. Then, at another vat, a hook came off its nail, and then was on its nail again; and then it seemed as if some one came to the door, and suddenly coughed and choked like a sheep, but so loudly! . . . We all fell down in a heap and huddled against one another. . . . Just weren't we in a fright that night!"

"I say!" murmured Pavel, "what did he cough for?"

"I don't know; perhaps it was the damp."

All were silent for a little.

"Well," inquired Fedya, "are the potatoes done?"

Pavlusha tried them.

"No, they are raw. . . . My, what a splash!" he added, turning his face in the direction of the river; "that must be a pike. . . . And there's a star falling."

"I say, I can tell you something, brothers," began Kostya, in a shrill little voice; "listen what my dad told me the other day."

"Well, we are listening," said Fedya with a patronising air.

"You know Gavrila, I suppose, the carpenter up in the big village?"

"Yes, we know him."

"And do you know why he is so sorrowful always, never speaks? do you know? I'll tell you why he's so sorrowful; he went one day, daddy said, he went, brothers, into the forest nutting. So he went nutting into the forest and lost his way; he went on—God only can tell where he got to. So he went on and on, brothers—but 'twas no good!—he could not find the way; and so night came on out of doors. So he sat down under a tree. 'I'll wait till morning,' thought he. He sat down and began to drop asleep. So as he was falling asleep, suddenly he heard some one call him. He looked up; there was no one. He fell asleep again; again he was called. He looked and looked again; and in front of him there sat a russalka on a branch, swinging herself and calling him to her, and simply dying with laughing; she laughed so. . . . And the moon was shining bright, so bright, the moon shone so clear—everything could be seen plain, brothers. So she called him, and she herself was as bright and as white sitting on the branch as some dace or a roach, or like some little carp so white and silvery. . . . Gavrila the carpenter almost fainted, brothers, but she laughed without stopping, and kept beckoning him to her like this. Then Gavrila was just getting up; he was just going to yield to the russalka, brothers, but—the Lord put it into his heart, doubtless—he crossed himself like this. . . . And it was so hard for him to make that cross, brothers; he said, 'My hand was simply like a stone; it would not move.' . . . Ugh! the horrid witch. . . . So when he made the cross, brothers, the russalka, she left off laughing, and all at once how she did cry. . . . She cried, brothers, and wiped her eyes with her hair, and her hair was green as any hemp. So Gavrila looked and looked at her, and at last he fell to questioning her. 'Why are you weeping, wild thing of the woods?' And the russalka began to speak to him like this: 'If you had not crossed yourself, man,' she says, 'you should have lived with me in gladness of heart to the end of your days; and I weep, I am grieved at heart because you crossed yourself; but I will not grieve alone; you too shall grieve at heart to the end of your days.' Then she vanished, brothers, and at once it was plain to Gavrila how to get out of the forest. . . . Only since then he goes always sorrowful, as you see."

"Ugh!" said Fedya after a brief silence; "but how can such an evil thing of the woods ruin a Christian soul—he did not listen to her?"

"And I say!" said Kostya. "Gavrila said that her voice was as shrill and plaintive as a toad's."

"Did your father tell you that himself?" Fedya went on.

"Yes. I was lying in the loft; I heard it all."

"It's a strange thing. Why should he be sorrowful? . . . But I suppose she liked him, since she called him."

"Ay, she liked him!" put in Ilyusha. "Yes, indeed! she wanted to tickle him to death, that's what she wanted. That's what they do, those russalkas."

"There ought to be russalkas here too, I suppose," observed Fedya.

"No," answered Kostya, "this is a holy open place. There's one thing, though: the river's near."

All were silent. Suddenly from out of the distance came a prolonged, resonant, almost wailing sound, one of those inexplicable sounds of the night, which break upon a profound stillness, rise upon the air, linger, and slowly die away at last. You listen: it is as though there were nothing, yet it echoes still. It is as though some one had uttered a long, long cry upon the very horizon, as though some other had answered him with shrill harsh laughter in the forest, and a faint, hoarse hissing hovers over the river. The boys looked round about shivering. . . .

"Christ's aid be with us!" whispered Ilyusha.

"Ah, you craven crows!" cried Pavel, "what are you frightened of? Look, the potatoes are done." (They all came up to the pot and began to eat the smoking potatoes; only Vanya did not stir.) "Well, aren't you coming?" said Pavel.

But he did not creep out from under his rug. The pot was soon completely emptied.

"Have you heard, boys," began Ilyusha, "what happened with us at Varnavitsi?"

"Near the dam?" asked Fedya.

"Yes, yes, near the dam, the broken-down dam. That is a haunted place, such a haunted place, and so lonely. All round there are pits and quarries, and there are always snakes in pits."

"Well, what did happen? Tell us."

"Well, this is what happened. You don't know, perhaps, Fedya, but there a drowned man was buried; he was drowned long, long ago, when the water was still deep; only his grave can still be seen, though it can only just be seen . . . like this—a little mound. . . . So one day the bailiff called the huntsman Yermil, and says to him, 'Go to the post, Yermil.' Yermil always goes to the post for us; he has let all his dogs die; they never will live with him, for some reason, and they have never lived with him, though he's a good huntsman, and everyone liked him. So Yermil went to the post, and he stayed a bit in the town, and when he rode back, he was a little tipsy. It was night, a fine night; the moon was shining. . . . So Yermil rode across the dam; his way lay there. So, as he rode along, he saw, on the drowned man's grave, a little lamb, so white and curly and pretty, running about. So Yermil thought, 'I will take him,' and he got down and took him in his arms. But the little lamb didn't take any notice. So Yermil goes back to his horse, and the horse stares at him, and snorts and shakes his head; however, he said 'wo' to him and sat on him with the lamb, and rode on again; he held the lamb in front of him. He looks at him, and the lamb looks him straight in the face, like this. Yermil the huntsman felt upset. 'I don't remember,' he said, 'that lambs ever look at any one like that'; however, he began to stroke it like this on its wool, and to say, 'Chucky! chucky!' And the lamb suddenly showed its teeth and said too, 'Chucky! chucky!' "

The boy who was telling the story had hardly uttered this last word, when suddenly both dogs got up at once, and, barking convulsively, rushed away from the fire and disappeared in the darkness. All the boys were alarmed.

Vanya jumped up from under his rug. Pavlusha ran shouting after the dogs. Their barking quickly grew fainter in the distance. . . . There was the noise of the uneasy tramp of the frightened drove of horses. Pavlusha shouted aloud: "Hey Grey! Beetle!" . . . In a few minutes the barking ceased; Pavel's voice sounded still in the distance. . . . A little time more passed; the boys kept looking about in perplexity, as though expecting something to happen. . . . Suddenly the tramp of a galloping horse was heard; it stopped short at the pile of wood, and, hanging on to the mane, Pavel sprang nimbly off it. Both the dogs also leaped into the circle of light and at once sat down, their red tongues hanging out.

"What was it? what was it?" asked the boys.

"Nothing," answered Pavel, waving his hand to his horse; "I suppose the dogs scented something. I thought it was a wolf," he added, calmly drawing deep breaths into his chest.

I could not help admiring Pavel. He was very fine at that moment. His ugly face, animated by his swift ride, glowed with hardihood and determination. Without even a switch in his hand, he had, without the slightest hesitation, rushed out into the night alone to face a wolf. . . . "What a splendid fellow!" I thought, looking at him.

"Have you seen any wolves, then?" asked the trembling Kostya.

"There are always a good many of them here," answered Pavel; "but they are only troublesome in the winter."

He crouched down again before the fire. As he sat down on the ground, he laid his hand on the shaggy head of one of the dogs. For a long while the flattered brute did not turn his head, gazing sidewise with grateful pride at Pavlusha. Vanya lay down under his rug again.

"What dreadful things you were telling us, Ilyusha!" began Fedya, whose part it was, as the son of a well-to-do peasant, to lead the conversation. (He spoke little himself, apparently afraid of lowering his dignity.) "And then some evil spirit set the dogs barking. . : . Certainly I have heard that place was haunted."

"Varnavitsi? . . . I should think it was haunted! More

than once, they say, they have seen the old master there—
the late master. He wears, they say, a long skirted coat,
and keeps groaning like this, and looking for something on
the ground. Once grandfather Trofimitch met him. 'What,'
says he, 'your honour, Ivan Ivanitch, are you pleased to
look for on the ground?' "

"He asked him?" put in Fedya in amazement.

"Yes, he asked him."

"Well, I call Trofimitch a brave fellow after that. . . .
Well, what did he say?"

" 'I am looking for the herb that cleaves all things,' says
he. But he speaks so thickly, so thickly. 'And what, your
honour, Ivan Ivanitch, do you want with the herb that
cleaves all things?' 'The tomb weighs on me; it weighs on
me, Trofimitch: I want to get away—away.' "

"My word!" observed Fedya, "he didn't enjoy his life
enough, I suppose."

"What a marvel!" said Kostya. "I thought one could only
see the departed on All Hallows' day."

"One can see the departed any time," Ilyusha interposed
with conviction. From what I could observe, I judged he
knew the village superstitions better than the others. . . .
"But on All Hallows' day you can see the living too; those,
that is, whose turn it is to die that year. You need only sit
in the church porch, and keep looking at the road. They
will come by you along the road; those, that is, who will
die that year. Last year old Ulyana went to the porch."

"Well, did she see anyone?" asked Kostya inquisitively.

"To be sure she did. At first she sat a long, long while,
and saw no one and heard nothing . . . only it seemed as
if some dog kept whining and whining like this somewhere. . . . Suddenly she looks up: a boy comes along the
road with only a shirt on. She looked at him. It was
Ivashka Fedosyev."

"He who died in the spring?" put in Fedya.

"Yes, he. He came along and never lifted up his head.
But Ulyana knew him. And then she looks again: a woman
came along. She stared and stared at her. . . . Ah, God
Almighty! . . . it was herself coming along the road;
Ulyana herself."

"Could it be herself?" asked Fedya.

"Yes, by God, herself."

"Well, but she is not dead yet, you know?"

"But the year is not over yet. And only look at her; her life hangs on a thread."

All were still again. Pavel threw a handful of dry twigs on to the fire. They were soon charred by the suddenly leaping flame; they cracked and smoked, and began to contract, curling up their burning ends. Gleams of light in broken flashes glanced in all directions, especially upwards. Suddenly a white dove flew straight into the bright light, fluttered round and round in terror, bathed in the red glow, and disappeared with a whirr of its wings.

"It's lost its home, I suppose," remarked Pavel. "Now it will fly till it gets somewhere, where it can rest till dawn."

"Why, Pavlusha," said Kostya, "might it not be a just soul flying to heaven?"

Pavel threw another handful of twigs on to the fire.

"Perhaps," he said at last.

"But tell us, please, Pavlusha," began Fedya, "what was seen in your parts at Shalamovy at the heavenly portent?" [1]

"When the sun could not be seen? Yes, indeed."

"Were you frightened then?"

"Yes; and we weren't the only ones. Our master, though he talked to us beforehand, and said there would be a heavenly portent, yet when it got dark, they say he himself was frightened out of his wits. And in the house-serfs' cottage the old woman, directly it grew dark, broke all the dishes in the oven with the poker. 'Who will eat now?' she said; 'the last day has come.' So the soup was all running about the place. And in the village there were such tales about among us: that white wolves would run over the earth, and would eat men, that a bird of prey would pounce down on us, and that they would even see Trishka." [2]

[1] This is what the peasants call an eclipse.—*Author's Note.*

[2] The popular belief in Trishka is probably derived from some tradition of Antichrist.—*Author's Note.*

"What is Trishka?" asked Kostya.

"Why, don't you know?" interrupted Ilyusha warmly. "Why, brother, where have you been brought up, not to know Trishka? You're a stay-at-home, one-eyed lot in your village, really! Trishka will be a marvellous man, who will come one day, and he will be such a marvellous man that they will never be able to catch him, and never be able to do anything with him; he will be such a marvellous man. The people will try to take him; for example, they will come after him with sticks, they will surround him, but he will blind their eyes so that they fall upon one another. They will put him in prison, for example; he will ask for a little water to drink in a bowl; they will bring him the bowl, and he will plunge into it and vanish from their sight. They will put chains on him, but he will only clap his hands—they will fall off him. So this Trishka will go through villages and towns; and this Trishka will be a wily man; he will lead astray Christ's people. . . . and they will be able to do nothing to him. . . . He will be such a marvellous, wily man."

"Well, then," continued Pavel, in his deliberate voice, "that's what he's like. And so they expected him in our parts. The old men declared that directly the heavenly portent began, Trishka would come. So the heavenly portent began. All the people were scattered over the street, in the fields, waiting to see what would happen. Our place, you know, is open country. They look; and suddenly down the mountain-side from the big village comes a man of some sort; such a strange man, with such a wonderful head . . . that all scream: 'Oy, Trishka is coming! Oy, Trishka is coming!' and all run in all directions! Our elder crawled into a ditch; his wife stumbled on the door-board and screamed with all her might; she terrified her yard-dog, so that he broke away from his chain and over the hedge and into the forest; and Kuzka's father, Dorofyitch, ran into the oats, lay down there, and began to cry like a quail. 'Perhaps' says he, 'the Enemy, the Destroyer of Souls, will spare the birds, at least.' So they were all in such a scare! But he that was coming was our cooper Vavila; he had bought himself a new pitcher, and had put the empty pitcher over his head."

All the boys laughed; and again there was a silence for a while, as often happens when people are talking in the open air. I looked out into the solemn, majestic stillness of the night; the dewy freshness of late evening had been succeeded by the dry heat of midnight; the darkness still had long to lie in a soft curtain over the slumbering fields; there was still a long while left before the first whisperings, the first dewdrops of dawn. There was no moon in the heavens; it rose late at that time. Countless golden stars, twinkling in rivalry, seemed all running softly towards the Milky Way, and truly, looking at them, you were almost conscious of the whirling, never-resting motion of the earth. . . . A strange, harsh, painful cry, sounded twice together over the river, and a few moments later, was repeated farther down. . . .

Kostya shuddered. "What was that?"

"That was a heron's cry," replied Pavel tranquilly.

"A heron," repeated Kostya. . . . "And what was it, Pavlusha, I heard yesterday evening," he added, after a short pause; "you perhaps will know."

"What did you hear?"

"I will tell you what I heard. I was going from Stony Ridge to Shashkino; I went first through our walnut wood, and then passed by a little pool—you know where there's a sharp turn down to the ravine—there is a water-pit there, you know; it is quite overgrown with reeds; so I went near this pit, brothers, and suddenly from this came a sound of some one groaning, and piteously, so piteously; oo-oo, oo-oo! I was in such a fright, my brothers; it was late, and the voice was so miserable. I felt as if I should cry myself. . . . What could that have been, eh?"

"It was in that pit the thieves drowned Akim the forester, last summer," observed Pavel; "so perhaps it was his soul lamenting."

"Oh, dear, really, brothers," replied Kostya, opening wide his eyes, which were round enough before, "I did not know they had drowned Akim in that pit. Shouldn't I have been frightened if I'd known!"

"But they say there are little, tiny frogs," continued Pavel, "who cry piteously like that."

"Frogs? Oh, no, it was not frogs, certainly not. (A heron again uttered a cry above the river.) Ugh, there it is!" Kostya cried involuntarily; "it is just like a wood-spirit shrieking."

"The wood-spirit does not shriek; it is dumb," put in Ilyusha; "it only claps its hands and rattles."

"And have you seen it then, the wood-spirit?" Fedya asked him ironically.

"No, I have not seen it, and God preserve me from seeing it; but others have seen it. Why, one day it misled a peasant in our parts, and led him through the woods and all in a circle in one field. . . . He scarcely got home till daylight."

"Well, and did he see it?"

"Yes. He says it was a big, big creature, dark, wrapped up, just like a tree; you could not make it out well; it seemed to hide away from the moon, and kept staring and staring with its great eyes, and winking and winking with them. . . ."

"Ugh!" exclaimed Fedya with a slight shiver, and a shrug of the shoulders; "pfoo."

"And how does such an unclean brood come to exist in the world?" said Pavel; "it's a wonder."

"Don't speak ill of it; take care, it will hear you," said Ilyusha.

Again there was a silence.

"Look, look, brothers," suddenly came Vanya's childish voice; "look at God's little stars; they are swarming like bees!"

He put his fresh little face out from under his rug, leaned on his little fist, and slowly lifted up his large soft eyes. The eyes of all the boys were raised to the sky, and they were not lowered quickly.

"Well, Vanya," began Fedya caressingly, "is your sister Anyutka well?"

"Yes, she is very well," replied Vanya with a slight lisp.

"You ask her, why doesn't she come to see us?"

"I don't know."

"You tell her to come."

"Very well."

"Tell her I have a present for her."

"And a present for me too?"

"Yes, you too."

Vanya sighed.

"No; I don't want one. Better give it to her; she is so kind to us at home."

And Vanya laid his head down again on the ground. Pavel got up and took the empty pot in his hand.

"Where are you going?" Fedya asked him.

"To the river, to get water; I want some water to drink." The dogs got up and followed him.

"Take care you don't fall into the river!" Ilyusha cried after him.

"Why should he fall in?" said Fedya. "He will be careful."

"Yes, he will be careful. But all kinds of things happen; he will stoop over, perhaps, to draw the water, and the water-spirit will clutch him by the hand, and drag him to him. Then they will say, 'The boy fell into the water.' . . . Fell in, indeed! . . . There, he has crept in among the reeds," he added, listening.

The reeds certainly "shished," as they call it among us, as they were parted.

"But is it true," asked Kostya, "that crazy Akulina has been mad ever since she fell into the water?"

"Yes, ever since. . . . How dreadful she is now! But they say she was a beauty before then. The water-spirit bewitched her. I suppose he did not expect they would get her out so soon. So down there at the bottom he bewitched her."

(I had met this Akulina more than once. Covered with rags, fearfully thin, with face as black as a coal, bleareyed and for ever grinning, she would stay whole hours in one place in the road, stamping with her feet, pressing her fleshless hands to her breast, and slowly shifting from one leg to the other, like a wild beast in a cage. She understood nothing that was said to her, and only chuckled spasmodically from time to time.)

"But they say," continued Kostya, "that Akulina threw herself into the river because her lover had deceived her."

"Yes, that was it."

"And do you remember Vasya?" added Kostya, mournfully.

"What Vasya?" asked Fedya.

"Why, the one who was drowned," replied Kostya, "in this very river. Ah, what a boy he was! What a boy he was! His mother, Feklista, how she loved him, her Vasya! And she seemed to have a foreboding, Feklista did, that harm would come to him from the water. Sometimes, when Vasya went with us boys in the summer to bathe in the river, she used to be trembling all over. The other women did not mind; they passed by with the pails, and went on, but Feklista put her pail down on the ground, and set to calling him, 'Come back, come back, my little joy; come back, my darling!' And no one knows how he was drowned. He was playing on the bank, and his mother was there haymaking; suddenly she hears, as though some one was blowing bubbles through the water, and behold! there was only Vasya's little cap to be seen swimming on the water. You know since then Feklista has not been right in her mind: she goes and lies down at the place where he was drowned; she lies down, brothers, and sings a song—you remember Vasya was always singing a song like that—so she sings it too, and weeps and weeps, and bitterly rails against God."

"Here is Pavlusha coming," said Fedya.

Pavel came up to the fire with a full pot in his hand.

"Boys," he began, after a short silence, "something bad happened."

"Oh, what?" asked Kostya hurriedly.

"I heard Vasya's voice."

They all seemed to shudder.

"What do you mean? what do you mean?" stammered Kostya.

"I don't know. Only I went to stoop down to the water; suddenly I hear my name called in Vasya's voice, as though it came from below water: 'Pavlusha, Pavlusha, come here.' I came away. But I fetched the water, though."

"Ah, God, have mercy upon us!" said the boys, crossing themselves.

"It was the water-spirit calling you, Pavel," said Fedya; "we were just talking of Vasya."

"Ah, it's a bad omen," said Ilyusha, deliberately.

"Well, never mind, don't bother about it," Pavel declared stoutly, and he sat down again; "no one can escape his fate."

The boys were still. It was clear that Pavel's words had produced a strong impression on them. They began to lie down before the fire as though preparing to go to sleep.

"What is that?" asked Kostya, suddenly lifting his head. Pavel listened.

"It's the curlews flying and whistling."

"Where are they flying to?"

"To a land where, they say, there is no winter."

"But is there such a land?"

"Yes."

"Is it far away?"

"Far, far away, beyond the warm seas."

Kostya sighed and shut his eyes.

More than three hours had passed since I first came across the boys. The moon at last had risen; I did not notice it at first; it was such a tiny crescent. This moonless night was as solemn and hushed as it had been at first. . . . But already many stars, that not long before had been high up in the heavens, were setting over the earth's dark rim; everything around was perfectly still, as it is only still towards morning; all was sleeping the deep unbroken sleep that comes before daybreak. Already the fragrance in the air was fainter; once more a dew seemed falling. . . . How short are nights in summer! . . . The boys' talk died down when the fires did. The dogs even were dozing; the horses, so far as I could make out, in the hardly-perceptible, faintly shining light of the stars, were asleep with downcast heads. . . . I fell into a state of weary unconsciousness, which passed into sleep.

A fresh breeze passed over my face. I opened my eyes; the morning was beginning. The dawn had not yet flushed the sky, but already it was growing light in the east. Every-

thing had become visible, though dimly visible, around.
The pale grey sky was growing light and cold and bluish;
the stars twinkled with a dimmer light, or disappeared; the
earth was wet, the leaves covered with dew, and from the
distance came sounds of life and voices, and a light morning breeze went fluttering over the earth. My body responded to it with a faint shudder of delight. I got up
quickly and went to the boys. They were all sleeping as
though they were tired out round the smouldering fire;
only Pavel half rose and gazed intently at me.

I nodded to him, and walked homewards beside the
misty river. Before I had walked two miles, already all
around me, over the wide dew-drenched meadows, and in
front from forest to forest, where the hills were growing
green again, and behind, over the long dusty road and the
sparkling bushes, flushed with the red glow, and the river
faintly blue now under the lifting mist, flowed fresh streams
of burning light, first pink, then red and golden. . . . All
things began to stir, to awaken, to sing, to flutter, to speak.
On all sides thick drops of dew sparkled in glittering diamonds; to welcome me, pure and clear as though bathed in
the freshness of morning, came the notes of a bell, and
suddenly there rushed by me, driven by the boys I had
parted from, the drove of horses, refreshed and rested. . . .

Sad to say, I must add that in that year Pavel met his
end. He was not drowned; he was killed by a fall from his
horse. Pity! he was a splendid fellow!

Mikhail Saltykov
1826 – 1889

HOW A MUZHIK FED
TWO OFFICIALS

Once upon a time there were two Officials. They were both empty-headed, and so they found themselves one day suddenly transported to an uninhabited isle, as if on a magic carpet.

They had passed their whole life in a Government Department, where records were kept; had been born there, bred there, grown old there, and consequently hadn't the least understanding for anything outside of the Department, and the only words they knew were: "With assurances of the highest esteem, I am your humble servant."

But the Department was abolished, and as the services of the two Officials were no longer needed, they were given their freedom. So the retired Officials migrated to Podyacheskaya Street in St. Petersburg. Each had his own home, his own cook, and his pension.

Waking up on the uninhabited isle, they found themselves lying under the same cover. At first, of course, they couldn't understand what had happened to them, and they spoke as if nothing extraordinary had taken place.

"What a peculiar dream I had last night, Your Excellency," said the one Official. "It seemed to me as if I were on an uninhabited isle."

Scarcely had he uttered the words, when he jumped to his feet. The other Official also jumped up.

"Good Lord, what does this mean? Where are we?" they cried out in astonishment.

They felt each other to make sure that they were no longer dreaming, and finally convinced themselves of the sad reality.

Before them stretched the ocean, and behind them was a little spot of earth, beyond which the ocean stretched again. They began to cry—the first time since their Department had been shut down.

They looked at each other, and each noticed that the other was clad in nothing but his nightshirt with his order hanging about his neck.

"We really should be having our coffee now," observed the one Official. Then he bethought himself again of the strange situation he was in and a second time fell to weeping.

"What are we going to do now?" he sobbed. "Even supposing we were to draw up a report, what good would that do?"

"You know what, Your Excellency," replied the other Official, "you go to the east and I will go to the west. Toward evening we will come back here again, and, perhaps, we shall have found something."

They started to ascertain which was the east and which was the west. They recalled that the head of their Department had once said to them, "If you want to know where the east is, then turn your face to the north, and the east will be on your right." But when they tried to find out which was the north, they turned to the right and to the left and looked around on all sides. Having spent their whole life in the Department of Records, their efforts were all in vain.

"To my mind, Your Excellency, the best thing to do would be for you to go to the right and me to go to the left," said one Official, who had served not only in the Department of Records, but had also been teacher of handwriting in the School for Reserves, and so was a little bit cleverer.

So said, so done. The one Official went to the right. He came upon trees bearing all sorts of fruits. Gladly would he have plucked an apple, but they all hung so high that he would have been obliged to climb up. He tried to climb up in vain. All he succeeded in doing was tearing his night-shirt. Then he struck upon a brook. It was swarming with fish.

"Wouldn't it be wonderful if we had all this fish in Podya-cheskaya Street!" he thought, and his mouth watered. Then he entered woods and found partridges, grouse, and hares.

"Good Lord, what an abundance of food!" he cried. His hunger was going up tremendously.

But he had to return to the appointed spot with empty hands. He found the other Official waiting for him.

"Well, Your Excellency, how went it? Did you find anything?"

"Nothing but an old number of the *Moscow Gazette*, not another thing."

The Officials lay down to sleep again, but their empty stomachs gave them no rest. They were partly robbed of their sleep by the thought of who was now enjoying their pension, and partly by the recollection of the fruit, fishes, partridges, grouse, and hares that they had seen during the day.

"The human pabulum in its original form flies, swims, and grows on trees. Who would have thought it, Your Excellency?" said the one Official.

"To be sure," rejoined the other Official. "I, too, must admit that I had imagined that our breakfast rolls came into the world just as they appear on the table."

"From which it is to be deduced that if we want to eat a pheasant, we must catch it first, kill it, pull its feathers, and roast it. But how's that to be done?"

"Yes, how's that to be done?" repeated the other Official.

They turned silent and tried again to fall asleep, but their hunger scared sleep away. Before their eyes swarmed flocks of pheasants and ducks, herds of porklings; and they were all so juicy, done so tenderly and garnished so deliciously with olives, capers, and pickles.

"I believe I could devour my own boots now," said the one Official.

"Gloves are not bad either, especially if they have been born quite mellow," said the other Official.

The two Officials stared at each other fixedly. In their

glances gleamed an evil-boding fire, their teeth chattered, and a dull groaning issued from their breasts. Slowly they crept upon each other and suddenly they burst into a fearful frenzy. There was a yelling and groaning, the rags flew about, and the Official who had been teacher of handwriting bit off his colleague's order and swallowed it. However, the sight of blood brought them both back to their senses.

"God help us!" they cried at the same time. "We certainly don't mean to eat each other up. How could we have come to such a pass as this? What evil genius is making sport of us?"

"We must, by all means, entertain each other to pass the time away, otherwise there will be murder and death," said the one Official.

"You begin," said the other.

"Can you explain why it is that the sun first rises and then sets? Why isn't it the reverse?"

"Aren't you a funny man, Your Excellency? You get up first, then you go to your office and work there, and at night you lie down to sleep."

"But why can't one assume the opposite, that is, that one goes to bed, sees all sorts of dream figures, and then gets up?"

"Well, yes, certainly. But when I was still an Official, I always thought this way: 'Now it is dawn, then it will be day, then will come supper, and finally will come the time to go to bed.' "

The word "supper" recalled that incident in the day's doings, and the thought of it made both Officials melancholy, so that the conversation came to a halt.

"A doctor once told me that human beings can sustain themselves for a long time on their own juices," the one Official began again.

"What does that mean?"

"It is quite simple. You see, one's own juices generate other juices, and these in their turn still other juices, and so it goes on until finally all the juices are consumed."

"And then what happens?"

"Then food has to be taken into the system again."

"The devil!"

No matter what topic the Officials chose, the conversation invariably reverted to the subject of eating; which only increased their appetite more and more. So they decided to give up talking altogether, and, recollecting the *Moscow Gazette* that the one of them had found, they picked it up and began to read it eagerly.

BANQUET GIVEN BY THE MAYOR

The table was set for one hundred persons. The magnificence of it exceeded all expectations. The remotest provinces were represented at this feast of the gods by the costliest gifts. The golden sturgeon from Sheksna and the silver pheasant from the Caucasian woods held a rendezvous with strawberries so seldom to be had in our latitude in winter. . . .

"The devil! For God's sake, stop reading, Your Excellency. Couldn't you find something else to read about?" cried the other Official in sheer desperation. He snatched the paper from his colleague's hands, and started to read something else.

Our correspondent in Tula informs us that yesterday a sturgeon was found in the Upa (an event which even the oldest inhabitants cannot recall, and all the more remarkable since they recognized the former police captain in this sturgeon). This was made the occasion for giving a banquet in the club. The prime cause of the banquet was served in a large wooden platter garnished with vinegar pickles. A bunch of parsley stuck out of its mouth. Doctor P——, who acted as toastmaster, saw to it that everybody present got a piece of the sturgeon. The sauces to go with it were unusually varied and delicate—

"Permit me, Your Excellency, it seems to me you are not so careful either in the selection of reading matter," interrupted the first Official, who secured the *Gazette* again and started to read:

One of the oldest inhabitants of Viatka has discovered a new and highly original recipe for fish soup. A live codfish (*lota vulgaris*) is taken and beaten with a rod until its liver swells up with anger. . . .

The Officials' heads drooped. Whatever their eyes fell upon had something to do with eating. Even their own thoughts were fatal. No matter how much they tried to keep their minds off beefsteak and the like, it was all in vain; their fancy returned invariably, with irresistible force, back to that for which they were so painfully yearning.

Suddenly an inspiration came to the Official who had once taught handwriting.

"I have it!" he cried delightedly. "What do you say to this, Your Excellency? What do you say to our finding a muzhik?"

"A muzhik, Your Excellency? What sort of a muzhik?"

"Why a plain ordinary muzhik. A muzhik like all other muzhiks. He would get the breakfast rolls for us right away, and he could also catch partridges and fish for us."

"Hm, a muzhik. But where are we to fetch one from, if there is no muzhik here?"

"Why shouldn't there be a muzhik here? There are muzhiks everywhere. All one has to do is hunt for them. There certainly must be a muzhik hiding here somewhere so as to get out of working."

This thought so cheered the Officials that they instantly jumped up to go in search of a muzhik.

For a long while they wandered about on the island without the desired result, until finally a concentrated smell of black bread and old sheepskin assailed their nostrils and guided them in the right direction. There under a tree was a colossal muzhik lying fast asleep with his hands under his head. It was clear that to escape his duty to work he had impudently withdrawn to this island. The indignation of the Officials knew no bounds.

"What, lying asleep here, you lazy-bones you!" they raged at him. "It is nothing to you that there are two Officials here who are fairly perishing of hunger. Up, forward march, work."

The Muzhik rose and looked at the two severe gentlemen standing in front of him. His first thought was to make his escape, but the Officials held him fast.

He had to submit to his fate. He had to work.

First he climbed up on a tree and plucked several dozen of the finest apples for the Officials. He kept a rotten one for himself. Then he turned up the earth and dug out some potatoes. Next he started a fire with two bits of wood that he rubbed against each other. Out of his own hair he made a snare and caught partridges. Over the fire, by this time burning brightly, he cooked so many kinds of food that the question arose in the Officials' minds whether they shouldn't give some to this idler.

Beholding the efforts of the Muzhik, they rejoiced in their hearts. They had already forgotten how the day before they had nearly been perishing of hunger, and all they thought of now was: "What a good thing it is to be an Official. Nothing bad can ever happen to an Official."

"Are you satisfied, gentlemen?" the lazy Muzhik asked.

"Yes, we appreciate your industry," replied the Officials.

"Then you will permit me to rest a little?"

"Go take a little rest, but first make a good strong cord."

The Muzhik gathered wild hemp stalks, laid them in water, beat them and broke them, and toward evening a good stout cord was ready. The Officials took the cord and bound the Muzhik to a tree, so that he should not run away. Then they laid themselves to sleep.

Thus day after day passed, and the Muzhik became so skillful that he could actually cook soup for the Officials in his bare hands. The Officials had become round and well-fed and happy. It rejoiced them that here they needn't spend any money and that in the meanwhile their pensions were accumulating in St. Petersburg.

"What is your opinion, Your Excellency," one said to the other after breakfast one day, "is the story of the Tower of Babel true? Don't you think it is simply an allegory?"

"By no means, Your Excellency, I think it was something that really happened. What other explanation is there for the existence of so many different languages on earth?"

"Then the Flood must really have taken place, too?"

"Certainly, else how would you explain the existence of antediluvian animals? Besides, the *Moscow Gazette* says—"

They made search for the old number of the *Moscow Gazette,* seated themselves in the shade, and read the whole sheet from beginning to end. They read of festivities in Moscow, Tula, Penza, and Riazan, and strangely enough felt no discomfort at the description of the delicacies served.

There is no saying how long this life might have lasted. Finally, however, it began to bore the Officials. They often thought of their cooks in St. Petersburg, and even shed a few tears in secret.

"I wonder how it looks in Podyacheskaya Street now, Your Excellency," one of them said to the other.

"Oh, don't remind me of it, Your Excellency. I am pining away with homesickness."

"It is very nice here. There is really no fault to be found with this place, but the lamb longs for its mother sheep. And it is a pity, too, for the beautiful uniforms."

"Yes, indeed, a uniform of the fourth class is no joke. The gold embroidery alone is enough to make one dizzy."

Now they began to importune the Muzhik to find some way of getting them back to Podyacheskaya Street, and strange to say, the Muzhik even knew where Podyacheskaya Street was. He had once drunk beer and mead there, and as the saying goes, everything had run down his beard, alas, but nothing into his mouth. The Officials rejoiced and said: "We are Officials from Podyacheskaya Street."

"And I am one of those men—do you remember—who sit on a scaffolding hung by ropes from the roofs and paint the outside walls. I am one of those who crawl about on the roofs like flies. That is what I am," replied the Muzhik.

The Muzhik now pondered long and heavily on how to give great pleasure to his Officials, who had been so gracious to him, the lazy-bones, and had not scorned his work. And he actually succeeded in constructing a ship. It was not really a ship, but still it was a vessel that would carry them across the ocean close to Podyacheskaya Street.

"Now, take care, you dog, that you don't drown us," said the Officials, when they saw the raft rising and falling on the waves.

"Don't be afraid. We muzhiks are used to this," said the Muzhik, making all the preparations for the journey. He gathered swan's-down and made a couch for his two Officials, then he crossed himself and rowed off from shore.

How frightened the Officials were on the way, how seasick they were during the storms, how they scolded the coarse Muzhik for his idleness, can neither be told nor described. The Muzhik, however, just kept rowing on and fed his Officials on herring. At last, they caught sight of dear old Mother Neva. Soon they were in the glorious Catherine Canal, and then, oh joy! they struck the grand Podyacheskaya Street. When the cooks saw their Officials so well-fed, round, and so happy, they rejoiced immensely. The Officials drank coffee and ate rolls, then put on their uniforms and drove to the Pension Bureau. How much money they collected there is another thing that can neither be told nor described. Nor was the Muzhik forgotten. The Officials sent a glass of whisky out to him and five kopeks.

Now, Muzhik, rejoice.

Fyodor Dostoevsky
1821 – 1881

A GENTLE SPIRIT

PART ONE

I WHO I WAS AND WHO SHE WAS

Oh, while she is still here, it is still all right; I go up and look at her every minute; but tomorrow they will take her away—and how shall I be left alone? Now she is on the table in the drawing-room, they put two card tables together, the coffin will be here tomorrow—white, pure white "gros de Naples"—but that's not it . . .

I keep walking about, trying to explain it to myself. I have been trying for the last six hours to get it clear, but still I can't think of it all as a whole.

The fact is, I walk to and fro, and to and fro.

This is how it was. I will simply tell it in order. (Order!)

Gentlemen, I am far from being a literary man and you will see that; but no matter, I'll tell it as I understand it myself. The horror of it for me is that I understand it all!

It was, if you care to know, that is to take it from the beginning, that she used to come to me simply to pawn things, to pay for advertising in the *Voice* to the effect that a governess was quite willing to travel, to give lessons at home, and so on, and so on. That was at the very beginning, and I, of course, made no difference between her and the others: "She comes," I thought, "like any one else," and so on.

But afterwards I began to see a difference. She was such a slender, fair little thing, rather tall, always a little awkward with me, as though embarrassed (I fancy she was the same with all strangers, and in her eyes, of course, I was exactly like anybody else—that is, not as a pawnbroker but as a man).

As soon as she received the money she would turn round at once and go away. And always in silence. Other women argue so, entreat, haggle for me to give them more; this one did not ask for more. . . .

I believe I am muddling it up.

Yes; I was struck first of all by the things she brought: poor little silver gilt earrings, a trashy little locket, things not worth sixpence. She knew herself that they were worth next to nothing, but I could see from her face that they were treasures to her, and I found out afterwards as a fact that they were all that was left her belonging to her father and mother.

Only once I allowed myself to scoff at her things. You see I never allow myself to behave like that. I keep up a gentlemanly tone with my clients: few words, politeness and severity. "Severity, severity!"

But once she ventured to bring her last rag, that is, literally the remains of an old hareskin jacket, and I could not resist saying something by way of a joke. My goodness! how she flared up! Her eyes were large, blue and dreamy but—how they blazed. But she did not drop one word; picking up her "rags" she walked out.

It was then for the first time I noticed her *particularly*, and thought something of the kind about her—that is, something of a particular kind. Yes, I remember another impression—that is, if you will have it, perhaps the chief impression, that summed up everything. It was that she was terribly young, so young that she looked just fourteen. And yet she was within three months of sixteen. I didn't mean that, though, that wasn't what summed it all up. Next day she came again. I found out later that she had been to Dobronravov's and to Mozer's with that jacket, but they take nothing but gold and would have nothing to say to it. I once took some stones from her (rubbishy little ones) and, thinking it over afterwards, I wondered: I, too, only lend on gold and silver, yet from her I accepted stones. That was my second thought about her then; that I remember. That time, that is when she came from Mozer's, she brought an amber cigar-holder. It was a connoisseur's article, not bad, but, again, of no value to us, because we only deal in gold. As it was the day after her "mutiny," I received her sternly. Sternness with me takes the form of dryness. As I gave her two roubles, however, I could not resist saying, with a certain irritation, "I only do it for *you*, of course; Mozer wouldn't take such a thing."

The words "for *you*" I emphasized particularly, and with a particular implication.

I was spiteful. She flushed up again when she heard that "for you," but she did not say a word, she did not throw down the money, she took it—that is poverty! But how hotly she flushed! I saw I had stung her. And when she had gone out, I suddenly asked myself whether my triumph over her was worth two roubles. He! He!! He!!! I remember I put that question to myself twice over, "Was it worth it? was it worth it?"

And, laughing, I inwardly answered it in the affirmative. And I felt very much elated. But that was not an evil feeling; I said it with design, with a motive; I wanted to test her, because certain ideas with regard to her had suddenly come into my mind. That was the third thing I thought particularly about her. . . . Well, it was from that time it all began. Of course, I tried at once to find out all her circumstances indirectly, and awaited her coming with a special impatience. I had a presentiment that she would come soon. When she came, I entered into affable conversation with her, speaking with unusual politeness. I have not been badly brought up and have manners. H'm. It was then I guessed that she was soft-hearted and gentle.

The gentle and soft-hearted do not resist long, and though they are by no means very ready to reveal themselves, they do not know how to escape from a conversation; they are niggardly in their answers, but they do answer, and the more readily the longer you go on. Only, on your side you must not flag, if you want them to talk. I need hardly say that she did not explain anything to me then. About the *Voice* and all that I found out afterwards. She was at that time spending her last farthing on advertising, haughtily at first, of course. "A governess prepared to travel and will send terms on application," but, later on: "willing to do anything, to teach, to be a companion, to be a housekeeper, to wait on an invalid, plain sewing, and so on, and so on," the usual thing! Of course, all this was added to the advertisement a bit at a time, and finally, when she was reduced to despair, it came to: "without salary in return for board." No, she could not find a situation. I made up my mind then to test her for the last time. I suddenly took up the *Voice* of the day and showed her an advertisement. "A young person, without friends and relations, seeks a situation as a governess to young children, preferably in the family of middle-aged widower. Might be a comfort in the home."

"Look here how this lady has advertised this morning, and by the evening she will certainly have found a situation. That's the way to advertise."

Again she flushed crimson and her eyes blazed, she turned round and went straight out. I was very much pleased, though by that time I felt sure of everything and had no apprehensions; nobody will take her cigar-holders, I thought. Besides, she has got rid of them all. And so it was, two days later, she came in again, such a pale little creature, all agitation—I saw that something had happened to her at home, and something really had. I will explain directly what had happened, but now I only want to recall how I did something *chic,* and rose in her opinion. I suddenly decided to do it. The fact is she was pawning the ikon (she had brought herself to pawn it!) . . . Ah, listen! listen! This is the beginning now, I've been in a muddle. You see I want to recall all this, every detail, every little point. I want to bring them all together and look at them as a whole and—I cannot. . . . It's these little things, these little things. . . . It was an ikon of the Madonna. A Madonna with the Babe, an old-fashioned, homely one, and the setting was silver gilt, worth—well, six roubles, perhaps. I could see the ikon was precious to her; she was pawning it whole, not taking it out of the setting. I said to her—

"You had better take it out of the setting, and take the ikon home; for it's not the thing to pawn."

"Why, are you forbidden to take them?"

"No, it's not that we are forbidden, but you might, perhaps, yourself . . ."

"Well, take it out."

"I tell you what. I will not take it out, but I'll set it here in the shrine with the other ikons," I said, on reflection. "Under the little lamp" (I always had the lamp burning as soon as the shop was opened), "and you simply take ten roubles."

"Don't give me ten roubles. I only want five; I shall certainly redeem it."

"You don't want ten? The ikon's worth it," I added, noticing that her eyes flashed again.

She was silent. I brought out five roubles.

"Don't despise any one; I've been in such straits myself; and worse too, and that you see me here in this business . . . is owing to what I've been through in the past. . . ."

"You're revenging yourself on the world? Yes?" she interrupted suddenly with rather sarcastic mockery, which, however, was to a great extent innocent (that is, it was general, because certainly at that time she did not distinguish me from others, so that she said it almost without malice).

"Aha," thought I; "so that's what you're like. You've got character; you belong to the new movement."

"You see!" I remarked at once, half-jestingly, half mysteriously, "I am part of that part of the Whole that seeks to do ill, but does good. . . ."

Quickly and with great curiosity, in which, however, there was something very childlike, she looked at me.

"Stay . . . what's that idea? Where does it come from? I've heard it somewhere . . ."

"Don't rack your brains. In those words Mephistopheles introduces himself to Faust. Have you read *Faust?*"

"Not . . . not attentively."

"That is, you have not read it at all. You must read it. But I see an ironical look in your face again. Please don't imagine that I've so little taste as to try to use Mephistopheles to commend myself to you and grace the rôle of pawnbroker. A pawnbroker will still be a pawnbroker. We know."

"You're so strange . . . I didn't mean to say anything of that sort."

She meant to say: "I didn't expect to find you were an educated man"; but she didn't say it; I knew, though, that she thought that. I had pleased her very much.

"You see," I observed, "one may do good in any calling —I'm not speaking of myself, of course. Let us grant that I'm doing nothing but harm, yet. . . ."

"Of course, one can do good in every position," she said, glancing at me with a rapid, profound look. "Yes, in any position," she added suddenly.

Oh, I remember, I remember all those moments! And I want to add, too, that when such young creatures, such sweet young creatures want to say something so clever and profound, they show at once so truthfully and naïvely in their faces, "Here I am saying something clever and profound now"—and that is not from vanity, as it is with any one like me, but one sees that she appreciates it awfully herself, and believes in it, and thinks a lot of it, and imagines that you think a lot of all that, just as she does. Oh, truthfulness! it's by that they conquer us. How exquisite it was in her!

I remember it, I have forgotten nothing! As soon as she had gone, I made up my mind. That same day I made my last investigations and found out every detail of her position at the moment; every detail of her past I had learned already from Lukerya, at that time a servant in the family, whom I had bribed a few days before. This position was so awful that I can't understand how she could laugh as she had done that day and feel interest in the words of Mephistopheles, when she was in such horrible straits. But—that's youth! That is just what I thought about her at the time with pride and joy; for, you know, there's a greatness of soul in it—to be able to say, "Though I am on the edge of the abyss, yet Goethe's grand words are radiant with light." Youth always has some greatness of soul, if it's only a spark and that distorted. Though it's of her I am speaking, of her alone. And, above all, I looked upon her then as *mine* and did not doubt of my power. You know that's a voluptuous idea when you feel no doubt of it.

But what is the matter with me? If I go on like this, when shall I put it all together and look at it as a whole. I must make haste, make haste—that is not what matters, oh, my God!

II   THE OFFER OF MARRIAGE

The "details" I learned about her I will tell in one word: her father and mother were dead, they had died three years before, and she had been left with two disreputable aunts: though it is saying too little to call them disreputable. One aunt was a widow with a large family (six children, one smaller than another), the other a horrid old maid. Both were horrid. Her father was in the service, but only as a copying clerk, and was only a gentleman by courtesy; in fact, everything was in my favour. I came as though from a higher world; I was anyway a retired lieutenant of a brilliant regiment, a gentleman by birth, independent and all the rest of it, and as for my pawnbroker's shop, her aunts could only have looked on that with respect. She had been living in slavery at her aunts' for those three years: yet she had managed to pass an examination somewhere—she managed to pass it, she wrung the time for it, weighed down as she was by the pitiless burden of daily drudgery, and that proved something in the way of striving for what was higher and better on her part! Why, what made me want to marry her? Never mind me, though; of that later on . . . As though that mattered!—She taught her aunt's children; she made their clothes; and towards the end not only washed the clothes, but with her weak chest even scrubbed the floors. To put it plainly, they used to beat her, and taunt her with eating their bread. It ended by their scheming to sell her. Tfoo! I omit the filthy details. She told me all about it afterwards.

All this had been watched for a whole year by a neighbour, a fat shopkeeper, and not a humble one but the owner of two grocer's shops. He had ill-treated two wives and now he was looking for a third, and so he cast his eye on her. "She's a quiet one," he thought; "she's grown up in poverty, and I am marrying for the sake of my motherless children."

He really had children. He began trying to make the match and negotiating with the aunts. He was fifty years old, besides. She was aghast with horror. It was then she began coming so often to me to advertise in the *Voice*. At last she began begging the aunts to give her just a little time to think it over. They granted her that little time, but would not let her have more; they were always at her: "We don't know where to turn to find food for ourselves, without an extra mouth to feed."

I had found all this out already, and the same day, after what had happened in the morning, I made up my mind. That evening the shopkeeper came, bringing with him a pound of sweets from the shop; she was sitting with him, and I called Lukerya out of the kitchen and told her to go and whisper to her that I was at the gate and wanted to say something to her without delay. I felt pleased with myself. And altogether I felt awfully pleased all that day.

On the spot, at the gate, in the presence of Lukerya, before she had recovered from her amazement at my sending for her, I informed her that I should look upon it as an honour and happiness . . . telling her, in the next place, not to be surprised at the manner of my declaration and at my speaking at the gate, saying that I was a straightforward man and had learned the position of affairs. And I was not lying when I said I was straightforward. Well, hang it all. I did not only speak with propriety—that is, showing I was a man of decent breeding, but I spoke with originality and that was the chief thing. After all, is there any harm in admitting it? I want to judge myself and am judging myself. I must speak *pro* and *contra*, and I do. I remembered afterwards with enjoyment, though it was stupid, that I frankly declared, without the least embarrassment, that, in the first place, I was not particularly talented, not particularly intelligent, perhaps not particularly good-natured, rather a cheap egoist (I remember that expression, I thought of it on the way and was pleased with it) and that very probably there was a great deal that was disagreeable in me in other respects. All this was said with a special sort of pride—we all know how that sort of thing is said. Of course, I had good taste enough not to proceed to enlarge on my virtues after honourably enumerating my defects, not to say "to make up for that I have this and that and the other." I saw that she was still horribly frightened, but I softened nothing; on the contrary, seeing she was frightened I purposely exaggerated. I told her straight out that she would have enough to eat, but that fine clothes, theatres, balls—she would have none of, at any rate not till later on, when I had attained my object. This severe tone was a positive delight to me. I added as cursorily as possible, that in adopting such a calling— that is, in keeping a pawnbroker's shop, I had only one object, hinting there was a special circumstance . . . But I really had a right to say so: I really had such an aim and there really was such a circumstance. Wait a minute, gentlemen; I have always been the first to hate this pawnbroking business, but in reality, though it is absurd to talk about oneself in such mysterious phrases, yet, you know, I was "revenging myself on society," I really was, I was, I was! So that her gibe that morning at the idea of my revenging myself was unjust. That is, do you see, if I had said to her straight out in words: "Yes, I am revenging myself on society," she would have laughed as she did that morning, and it would, in fact, have been absurd. But by indirect hints, by dropping mysterious phrases, it appeared that it was possible to work upon her imagination. Besides, I had no fears then: I knew that the fat shopkeeper was anyway more repulsive to her than I was, and that I, standing at the gate, had appeared as a deliverer. I understood that, of course. Oh, what is base a man understands particularly well! But was it base? How can a man judge? Didn't I love her even then?

Wait a bit: of course, I didn't breathe a word to her of doing her a benefit; the opposite, oh, quite the opposite; I made out that it was *I* that would be under an obligation to her, not *she* to me. Indeed, I said as much—I couldn't resist saying it—and it sounded stupid, perhaps, for I noticed a shade flit across her face. But altogether I won the day completely. Wait a bit, if I am to recall all that vileness, then I will tell of that worst beastliness. As I stood there what was stirring in my mind was, "You are tall, a good

figure, educated and—speaking without conceit—good looking." That is what was at work in my mind. I need hardly
say that, on the spot, out there at the gate she said *"yes."*
But . . . but I ought to add: that out there by the gate she
thought a long time before she said *"yes."* She pondered for
so long that I said to her, "Well?"—and could not even
refrain from asking it with a certain swagger.

"Wait a little. I'm thinking."

And her little face was so serious, so serious that even
then I might have read it! And I was mortified: "Can she
be choosing between me and the grocer!" I thought. Oh, I
did not understand then! I did not understand anything, anything, then! I did not understand till today! I remember
Lukerya ran after me as I was going away, stopped me on
the road and said, breathlessly: "God will reward you, sir,
for taking our dear young lady; only don't speak of that to
her—she's proud."

Proud, is she! "I like proud people," I thought. Proud
people are particularly nice when . . . well, when one has
no doubt of one's power over them, eh? Oh, base, tactless
man! Oh, how pleased I was! You know, when she was
standing there at the gate, hesitating whether to say "yes" to
me, and I was wondering at it, you know, she may have had
some such thought as this: "If it is to be misery either way,
isn't it best to choose the very worst"—that is, let the fat
grocer beat her to death when he was drunk! Eh! what do
you think, could there have been a thought like that?

And, indeed, I don't understand it now, I don't understand it at all, even now. I have only just said that she may
have had that thought: of two evils choose the worst—that
is, the grocer. But which was the worst for her then—the
grocer or I? The grocer or the pawnbroker who quoted
Goethe? That's another question! What a question! And
even that you don't understand: the answer is lying on the
table and you call it a question! Never mind me, though. It's
not a question of me at all . . . and, by the way, what is there
left for me now—whether it's a question of me or whether
it is not? That's what I am utterly unable to answer. I had
better go to bed. My head aches. . . .

I could not sleep. And how should I? There is a pulse throb-bing in my head. One longs to master it all, all that degrada-tion. Oh, the degradation! Oh, what degradation I dragged her out of then! Of course, she must have realized that, she must have appreciated my action! I was pleased, too, by various thoughts—for instance, the reflection that I was forty-one and she was only sixteen. That fascinated me, that feeling of inequality was very sweet, was very sweet.

I wanted, for instance, to have a wedding *à l'anglaise,* that is only the two of us, with just the two necessary witnesses, one of them Lukerya, and from the wedding straight to the train to Moscow (I happened to have business there, by the way), and then a fortnight at the hotel. She opposed it, she would not have it, and I had to visit her aunts and treat them with respect as though they were relations from whom I was taking her. I gave way, and all befitting respect was paid the aunts. I even made the creatures a present of a hundred roubles each and promised them more—not telling her anything about it, of course, that I might not make her feel humiliated by the lowness of her surroundings. The aunts were as soft as silk at once. There was a wrangle about the trousseau too; she had nothing, almost literally, but she did not want to have anything. I succeeded in proving to her, though, that she must have something, and I made up the trousseau, for who would have given her anything? But there, enough of me. I did, however, succeed in communicat-ing some of my ideas to her then, so that she knew them any-way. I was in too great a hurry, perhaps. The best of it was that, from the very beginning, she rushed to meet me with love, greeted me with rapture, when I went to see her in the evening, told me in her chatter (the enchanting chatter of innocence) all about her childhood and girlhood, her old home, her father and mother. But I poured cold water upon all that at once. That was my idea. I met her enthusiasm with silence, friendly silence, of course . . . but, all the same, she could quickly see that we were different and that

I was—an enigma. And being an enigma was what I made a point of most of all! Why, it was just for the sake of being an enigma, perhaps—that I have been guilty of all stupidity. The first thing was sternness—it was with an air of sternness that I took her into my house. In fact, as I went about then feeling satisfied, I framed a complete system. Oh, it came of itself without any effort. And it could not have been otherwise. I was bound to create that system owing to one inevitable fact—why should I libel myself, indeed! The system was a genuine one. Yes, listen; if you must judge a man, better judge him knowing all about it . . . listen.

How am I to begin this, for it is very difficult. When you begin to justify yourself—then it is difficult. You see, for instance, young people despise money—I made money of importance at once; I laid special stress on money. And laid such stress on it that she became more and more silent. She opened her eyes wide, listened, gazed and said nothing. You see, the young are heroic, that is the good among them are heroic and impulsive, but they have little tolerance; if the least thing is not quite right they are full of contempt. And I wanted breadth, I wanted to instill breadth into her very heart, to make it part of her inmost feeling, did I not? I'll take a trivial example: how should I explain my pawn-broker's shop to a character like that? Of course, I did not speak of it directly, or it would have appeared that I was apologizing, and I, so to speak, worked it through pride, I almost spoke without words, and I am masterly at speaking without words. All my life I have spoken without words, and I have passed through whole tragedies on my own account without words. Why, I, too, have been unhappy! I was abandoned by every one, abandoned and forgotten, and no one, no one knew it! And all at once this sixteen-year-old girl picked up details about me from vulgar people and thought she knew all about me, and, meanwhile, what was precious remained hidden in this heart! I went on being silent, with her especially I was silent, with her especially, right up to yesterday—why was I silent? Because I was proud. I wanted her to find out for herself, without my help, and not from the tales of low people; I wanted her to *divine of herself* what manner of man I was and to understand me!

Taking her into my house I wanted all her respect, I wanted her to be standing before me in homage for the sake of my sufferings—and I deserved it. Oh, I have always been proud, I always wanted all or nothing! You see it was just because I am not one who will accept half a happiness, but always wanted all, that I was forced to act like that then: it was as much as to say, "See into me for yourself and appreciate me!" For you must see that if I had begun explaining myself to her and prompting her, ingratiating myself and asking for her respect—it would have been as good as asking for charity . . . But . . . but why am I talking of that!

Stupid, stupid, stupid, stupid! I explained to her then, in two words, directly, ruthlessly (and I emphasize the fact that it was ruthlessly) that the heroism of youth was charming, but—not worth a farthing. Why not? Because it costs them so little, because it is not gained through life; it is, so to say, merely "first impressions of existence," but just let us see you at work! Cheap heroism is always easy, and even to sacrifice life is easy too; because it is only a case of hot blood and an overflow of energy, and there is such a longing for what is beautiful! No, take the deed of heroism that is laborious, obscure, without noise or flourish, slandered, in which there is a great deal of sacrifice and not one grain of glory—in which you, a splendid man, are made to look like a scoundrel before every one, though you might be the most honest man in the world—you try that sort of heroism and you'll soon give it up! While I—have been bearing the burden of that all my life. At first she argued—ough, how she argued—but afterwards she began to be silent, completely silent, in fact, only opened her eyes wide as she listened, such big, big eyes, so attentive. And . . . and what is more, I suddenly saw a smile, mistrustful, silent, an evil smile. Well, it was with that smile on her face I brought her into my house. It is true that she had nowhere else to go.

IV   PLANS AND PLANS

Which of us began it first?

Neither. It began of itself from the very first. I have said that with sternness I brought her into the house. From the first step, however, I softened it. Before she was married it was explained to her that she would have to take pledges and pay out money, and she said nothing at the time (note that). What is more, she set to work with positive zeal. Well, of course, my lodging, my furniture all remained as before. My lodging consisted of two rooms, a large room from which the shop was partitioned off, and a second one, also large, our living room and bedroom. My furniture is scanty: even her aunts had better things. My shrine of ikons with the lamp was in the outer room where the shop is; in the inner room my bookcase with a few books in and a trunk of which I keep the key; of course, there is a bed, tables and chairs. Before she was married I told her that one rouble a day and not more, was to be spent on our board— that is, on food for me, her and Lukerya whom I had enticed to come to us. "I must have thirty thousand in three years," said I, "and we can't save the money if we spend more." She fell in with this, but I raised the sum by thirty kopecks a day. It was the same with the theatre. I told her before marriage that she would not go to the theatre, and yet I decided once a month to go to the theatre, and in a decent way, to the stalls. We went together. We went three times and saw *The Hunt after Happiness*, and *Singing Birds*, I believe. (Oh, what does it matter!) We went in silence and in silence we returned. Why, why, from the very beginning, did we take to being silent? From the very first, you know, we had no quarrels, but always the same silence. She was always, I remember, watching me stealthily in those days; as soon as I noticed it I became more silent than before. It is true that it was I insisted on the silence, not she. On her part there were one or two outbursts, she rushed to embrace me; but as these outbursts were hysterical, painful, and I wanted secure happiness, with respect from her, I received them coldly. And indeed, I was right; each time the outburst was followed next day by a quarrel.

Though, again, there were no quarrels, but there was silence and—and on her side a more and more defiant air. "Rebellion and independence," that's what it was, only she didn't know how to show it. Yes, that gentle creature was becoming more and more defiant. Would you believe it, I was becoming revolting to her? I learned that. And there could be no doubt that she was moved to frenzy at times. Think, for instance, of her beginning to sniff at our poverty, after her coming from such sordidness and destitution—from scrubbing the floors! You see, there was no poverty; there was frugality, but there was abundance of what was necessary, of linen, for instance, and the greatest cleanliness. I always used to dream that cleanliness in a husband attracts a wife. It was not our poverty she was scornful of, but my supposed miserliness in the housekeeping: "He has his objects," she seemed to say, "he is showing his strength of will." She suddenly refused to go to the theatre. And more and more often an ironical look. . . . And I was more silent, more and more silent.

I could not begin justifying myself, could I? What was at the bottom of all this was the pawnbroking business. Allow me, I knew that a woman, above all at sixteen, must be in complete subordination to a man. Women have no originality. That—that is an axiom; even now, even now, for me it is an axiom! What does it prove that she is lying there in the outer room? Truth is truth, and even Mill is no use against it! And a woman who loves, oh, a woman who loves idealizes even the vices, even the villainies of the man she loves. He would not himself even succeed in finding such justification for his villainies as she will find for him. That is generous but not original. It is the lack of originality alone that has been the ruin of women. And, I repeat, what is the use of your pointing to that table? Why, what is there original in her being on that table? O—O—Oh!

Listen. I was convinced of her love at that time. Why, she used to throw herself on my neck in those days. She loved me; that is, more accurately, she wanted to love. Yes, that's just what it was, she wanted to love; she was trying to love. And the point was that in this case there were no villainies for which she had to find justification. You will say, I'm a pawnbroker; and every one says the same. But what if I am a pawnbroker? It follows that there must be reasons since the most generous of men had become a pawnbroker. You see, gentlemen, there are ideas . . . that is, if one expresses some ideas, utters them in words, the effect is very stupid. The effect is to make one ashamed. For what reason? For no reason. Because we are all wretched creatures and cannot hear the truth, or I do not know why. I said just now, "the most generous of men"—that is absurd, and yet that is how it was. It's the truth, that is, the absolute, the absolute truth! Yes, I *had the right* to want to make myself secure and open that pawnbroker's shop: "You have rejected me, you—people, I mean—you have cast me out with contemptuous silence. My passionate yearning towards you you have met with insult all my life. Now I have the right to put up a wall against you, to save up that thirty thousand roubles and end my life somewhere in the Crimea, on the south coast, among the mountains and vineyards, on my own estate bought with that thirty thousand, and above everything, far away from you all, living without malice against you, with an ideal in my soul, with a beloved woman at my heart, and a family, if God sends one, and—helping the inhabitants all around."

Of course, it is quite right that I say this to myself now, but what could have been more stupid than describing all that aloud to her? That was the cause of my proud silence, that's why we sat in silence. For what could she have understood? Sixteen years old, the earliest youth—yes, what could she have understood of my justification, of my sufferings? Undeviating straightness, ignorance of life, the cheap convictions of youth, the hen-like blindness of those "noble hearts," and what stood for most was—the pawnbroker's shop and—enough! (And was I a villain in the pawnbroker's shop? Did not she see how I acted? Did I extort too much?)

Oh, how awful is truth on earth! That exquisite creature, that gentle spirit, that heaven—she was a tyrant, she was the insufferable tyrant and torture of my soul! I should be unfair to myself if I didn't say so! You imagine I didn't love her? Who can say that I did not love her! Do you see, it was a case of irony, the malignant irony of fate and nature! We were under a curse, the life of men in general is under a curse! (mine in particular). Of course, I understand now that I made some mistake! Something went wrong. Everything was clear, my plan was clear as daylight: "Austere and proud, asking for no moral comfort, but suffering in silence." And that was how it was. I was not lying, I was not lying! "She will see for herself, later on, that it was heroic, only that she had not known how to see it, and when, some day, she divines it she will prize me ten times more and will abase herself in the dust and fold her hands in homage"—that was my plan. But I forgot something or lost sight of it. There was something I failed to manage. But, enough, enough! And whose forgiveness am I to ask now? What is done is done. Be bolder, man, and have some pride! It is not your fault! . . .

Well, I will tell the truth, I am not afraid to face the truth; it was *her fault, her fault!* . . .

V A GENTLE SPIRIT IN REVOLT

Quarrels began from her suddenly beginning to pay out loans on her own account, to price things above their worth, and even, on two occasions, she deigned to enter into a dispute about it with me. I did not agree. But then the captain's widow turned up.

This old widow brought a medallion—a present from her dead husband, a souvenir, of course. I lent her thirty roubles on it. She fell to complaining, begged me to keep the thing for her—of course, we do keep things. Well, in short, she came again to exchange it for a bracelet that was not worth eight roubles; I, of course, refused. She must have guessed something from my wife's eyes, anyway she came again when I was not there and my wife changed it for the medallion.

Discovering it the same day, I spoke mildly but firmly and reasonably. She was sitting on the bed, looking at the ground and tapping with her right foot on the carpet (her characteristic movement); there was an ugly smile on her lips. Then, without raising my voice in the least, I explained calmly that the money was *mine,* that I had a right to look at life with *my own* eyes and—and that when I had offered to take her into my house, I had hidden nothing from her.

She suddenly leapt up, suddenly began shaking all over and—what do you think—she suddenly stamped her foot at me; it was a wild animal, it was a frenzy, it was the frenzy of a wild animal. I was petrified with astonishment; I had never expected such an outburst. But I did not lose my head. I made no movement even, and again, in the same calm voice, I announced plainly that from that time forth I should deprive her of the part she took in my work. She laughed in my face, and walked out of the house.

The fact is, she had not the right to walk out of the house. Nowhere without me, such was the agreement before she was married. In the evening she returned; I did not utter a word.

The next day, too, she went out in the morning, and the day after again. I shut the shop and went off to her aunts. I had cut off all relations with them from the time of the wedding—I would not have them to see me, and I would not go to see them. But it turned out that she had not been with them. They listened to me with curiosity and laughed in my face: "It serves you right," they said. But I expected their laughter. At that point, then, I bought over the younger aunt, the unmarried one, for a hundred roubles, giving her twenty-five in advance. Two days later she came to me: "There's an officer called Efimovitch mixed up in this," she said; "a lieutenant who was a comrade of yours in the regiment."

I was greatly amazed. That Efimovitch had done me more harm than any one in the regiment, and about a month ago, being a shameless fellow, he once or twice came into the shop with a pretence of pawning something, and I remember, began laughing with my wife. I went up at the time and told him not to dare to come to me, recalling our relations; but there was no thought of anything in my head, I simply thought that he was insolent. Now the aunt suddenly informed me that she had already appointed to see him and that the whole business had been arranged by a former friend of the aunt's, the widow of a colonel, called Yulia Samsonovna. "It's to her," she said, "your wife goes now."

I will cut the story short. The business cost me three hundred roubles, but in a couple of days it had been arranged that I should stand in an adjoining room, behind closed doors, and listen to the first *rendezvous* between my wife and Efimovitch, *tête-à-tête*. Meanwhile, the evening before, a scene, brief but very memorable for me, took place between us.

She returned towards evening, sat down on the bed, looked at me sarcastically, and tapped on the carpet with her foot. Looking at her, the idea suddenly came into my mind that for the whole of the last month, or rather, the last fortnight, her character had not been her own; one might even say that it had been the opposite of her own; she had suddenly shown herself a mutinous, aggressive creature; I cannot say shameless, but regardless of decorum and eager for trouble. She went out of her way to stir up trouble. Her gentleness hindered her, though. When a girl like that rebels, however outrageously she may behave, one can always see that she is forcing herself to do it, that she is driving herself to do it, and that it is impossible for her to master and overcome her own modesty and shamefacedness. That is why such people go such lengths at times, so that one can hardly believe one's eyes. One who is accustomed to depravity, on the contrary, always softens things, acts more disgustingly, but with a show of decorum and seemliness by which she claims to be superior to you.

"It is true that you were turned out of the regiment because you were afraid to fight a duel?" she asked suddenly, apropos of nothing—and her eyes flashed.

"It is true that by the sentence of the officers I was asked to give up my commission, though, as a fact, I had sent in my papers before that."

"You were turned out as a coward?"

"Yes, they sentenced me as a coward. But I refused to fight a duel, not from cowardice, but because I would not submit to their tyrannical decision and send a challenge when I did not consider myself insulted. You know," I could not refrain from adding, "that to resist such tyranny and to accept the consequences meant showing far more manliness than fighting any kind of duel."

I could not resist it. I dropped this phrase, as it were, in self-defence, and that was all she wanted, this fresh humiliation for me.

She laughed maliciously.

"And is it true that for three years afterwards you wandered about the streets of Petersburg like a tramp, begging for coppers and spending your nights in billiard-rooms?"

"I even spent the night in Vyazemsky's House in the Haymarket. Yes, it is true; there was much disgrace and degradation in my life after I left the regiment, but not moral degradation, because even at the time I hated what I did more than any one. It was only the degradation of my will and my mind, and it was only caused by the desperateness of my position. But that is over. . . ."

"Oh, now you are a personage—a financier!"

A hint at the pawnbroker's shop. But by then I had succeeded in recovering my mastery of myself. I saw that she was thirsting for explanations that would be humiliating to me and—I did not give them. A customer rang the bell very opportunely, and I went out into the shop. An hour later, when she was dressed to go out, she stood still, facing me, and said—

"You didn't tell me anything about that, though, before our marriage?"

I made no answer and she went away.

And so next day I was standing in that room, the other side of the door, listening to hear how my fate was being decided, and in my pocket I had a revolver. She was dressed better than usual and sitting at the table, and Efimovitch was showing off before her. And, after all, it turned out exactly (I say it to my credit) as I had foreseen and had assumed it would, though I was not conscious of having foreseen and assumed it. I do not know whether I express myself intelligibly.

This is what happened.

I listened for a whole hour. For a whole hour I was present at a duel between a noble, lofty woman and a worldly, corrupt, dense man with a crawling soul. And how, I wondered in amazement, how could that naïve, gentle, silent girl have come to know all that? The wittiest author of a society comedy could not have created such a scene of mockery, of naïve laughter, and of the holy contempt of virtue for vice. And how brilliant her sayings, her little phrases were: what wit there was in her rapid answers, what truths in her condemnation. And, at the same time, what almost girlish simplicity. She laughed in his face at his declarations of love, at his gestures, at his proposals. Coming coarsely to the point at once, and not expecting to meet with opposition, he was utterly nonplussed. At first I might have imagined that it was simply coquetry on her part—"the coquetry of a witty, though depraved creature to enhance her own value." But no, the truth shone out like the sun, and to doubt was impossible. It was only an exaggerated and impulsive hatred for me that had led her, in her inexperience, to arrange this interview, but, when it came off—her eyes were opened at once. She was simply in desperate haste to mortify me, came what might, but though she had brought herself to do something so low she could not endure unseemliness. And could she, so pure and sinless, with an ideal in her heart, have been seduced by Efimovitch or any worthless snob? On the contrary, she was only moved to laughter by him. All her goodness rose up from her soul and her indignation roused her to sarcasm. I repeat, the buffoon was completely nonplussed at last and sat frowning, scarcely answering, so much so that I began to be afraid that he might dare to insult her, from a mean desire for revenge. And I repeat again: to my credit, I listened to that scene almost without surprise. I met, as it were, nothing but what I knew well. I had gone, as it were, on purpose to meet it, believing not a word of it, not a word said against her, though I did take the revolver in my pocket—that is the truth. And could I have imagined her different? For what did I love her, for what did I prize her, for what had I married her? Oh, of course, I was quite convinced of her hate for me, but at the same time I was quite convinced of her sinlessness. I suddenly cut short the scene by opening the door. Efimovitch leapt up. I took her by the hand and suggested she should go home with me. Efimovitch recovered himself and suddenly burst into loud peals of laughter.

"Oh, to sacred conjugal rights I offer no opposition; take her away, take her away! And you know," he shouted after me, "though no decent man could fight you, yet from respect to your lady I am at your service . . . If you are ready to risk yourself."

"Do you hear?" I said, stopping her for a second in the doorway.

After which not a word was said all the way home. I led her by the arm and she did not resist. On the contrary, she was greatly impressed, and this lasted after she got home. On reaching home she sat down in a chair and fixed her eyes upon me. She was extremely pale; though her lips were compressed ironically yet she looked at me with solemn and austere defiance and seemed convinced in earnest, for the first minute, that I should kill her with the revolver. But I took the revolver from my pocket without a word and laid it on the table! She looked at me and at the revolver. (Note that the revolver was already an object familiar to her. I had kept one loaded ever since I opened the shop. I made up my mind when I set up the shop that I would not keep a huge dog or a strong manservant, as Mozer does, for instance. My cook opens the doors to my visitors. But in our trade it is impossible to be without means of self-defence in case of emergency, and I kept a loaded revolver. In early days, when first she was living in my house, she took great interest in that revolver, and asked questions about it, and I even explained its construction and working; I even persuaded her once to fire at a target. Note all that.) Taking no notice of her frightened eyes, I lay down on the bed, half-undressed. I felt very much exhausted; it was by then about eleven o'clock. She went on sitting in the same place, not stirring, for another hour. Then she put out the candle and she, too, without undressing, lay down on the sofa near the wall. For the first time she did not sleep with me—note that too. . . .

VI   A TERRIBLE REMINISCENCE

Now for a terrible reminiscence. . . .

I woke up, I believe, before eight o'clock, and it was very nearly broad daylight. I woke up completely to full consciousness and opened my eyes. She was standing at the table holding the revolver in her hand. She did not see that I had woken up and was looking at her. And suddenly I saw that she had begun moving towards me with the revolver in her hand. I quickly closed my eyes and pretended to be still asleep.

She came up to the bed and stood over me. I heard everything; though a dead silence had fallen I heard that silence. All at once there was a convulsive movement and, irresistibly, against my will, I suddenly opened my eyes. She was looking straight at me, straight into my eyes, and the revolver was at my temple. Our eyes met. But we looked at each other for no more than a moment. With an effort I shut my eyes again, and at the same instant I resolved that I would not stir and would not open my eyes, whatever might be awaiting me.

It does sometimes happen that people who are sound asleep suddenly open their eyes, even raise their heads for a second and look about the room, then, a moment later, they lay their heads again on the pillow unconscious, and fall asleep without understanding anything. When meeting her eyes and feeling the revolver on my forehead, I closed my eyes and remained motionless, as though in a deep sleep—she certainly might have supposed that I really was asleep, and that I had seen nothing, especially as it was utterly improbable that, after seeing what I had seen, I should shut my eyes again at *such* a moment.

Yes, it was improbable. But she might guess the truth all the same—that thought flashed upon my mind at once, all at the same instant. Oh, what a whirl of thoughts and sensations rushed into my mind in less than a minute. Hurrah for the electric speed of thought! In that case (so I felt), if she guessed the truth and knew that I was awake, I should crush her by my readiness to accept death, and her hand might tremble. Her determination might be shaken by a new, overwhelming impression. They say that people standing on a height have an impulse to throw themselves down. I imagine that many suicides and murders have been committed simply because the revolver has been taken in the hand. It is like a precipice, with an incline of an angle of forty-five degrees, down which you cannot help sliding, and something impels you irresistibly to pull the trigger. But the knowledge that I had seen, that I knew it all, and was waiting for death at her hands without a word —might hold her back on the incline.

The stillness was prolonged, and all at once I felt on my temple, on my hair, the cold contact of the iron. You will ask: did I confidently expect to escape? I will answer you as God is my judge: I had no hope of it, except one chance in a hundred. Why did I accept death? But I will ask, what use was life to me after that revolver had been raised against me by the being I adored? Besides, I knew with the whole strength of my being that there was a struggle going on between us, a fearful duel for life and death, the duel fought by the coward of yesterday, rejected by his comrades for cowardice. I knew that and she knew it, if only she guessed the truth that I was not asleep.

Perhaps that was not so, perhaps I did not think that then, but yet it must have been so, even without conscious thought, because I've done nothing but think of it every hour of my life since.

But you will ask me again: why did you not save her from such wickedness? Oh! I've asked myself that question a thousand times since—every time that, with a shiver down my back, I recall that second. But at that moment my soul was plunged in dark despair! I was lost, I myself was lost—how could I save any one? And how do you know whether I wanted to save any one then? How can one tell what I could be feeling then?

My mind was in a ferment, though; the seconds passed; she still stood over me—and suddenly I shuddered with hope! I quickly opened my eyes. She was no longer in the room: I got out of bed: I had conquered—and she was conquered for ever!

I went to the samovar. We always had the samovar brought into the outer room and she always poured out the tea. I sat down at the table without a word and took a glass of tea from her. Five minutes later I looked at her. She was fearfully pale, even paler than the day before, and she looked at me. And suddenly . . . and suddenly, seeing that I was looking at her, she gave a pale smile with her pale lips, with a timid question in her eyes. "So she still doubts and is asking herself: does he know or doesn't he know; did he see, or didn't he?" I turned my eyes away indifferently. After tea I closed the shop, went to the market and bought an iron bedstead and a screen. Returning home, I directed that the bed should be put in the front room and shut off with a screen. It was a bed for her, but I did not say a word to her. She understood without words, through that bedstead, that I "had seen and knew all," and that all doubt was over. At night I left the revolver on the table, as I always did. At night she got into her new bed without a word: our marriage bond was broken, "she was conquered but not forgiven." At night she began to be delirious, and in the morning she had brain-fever. She was in bed for six weeks.

PART TWO

I THE DREAM OF PRIDE

Lukerya had just announced that she couldn't go on living here and that she is going away as soon as her lady is buried. I knelt down and prayed for five minutes. I wanted to pray for an hour, but I keep thinking and thinking, and always sick thoughts, and my head aches—what is the use of praying?—it's only a sin! It is strange, too, that I am not sleepy: in great, too great sorrow, after the first outbursts one is always sleepy. Men condemned to death, they say, sleep very soundly on the last night. And so it must be, it is the law of nature, otherwise their strength would not hold out. . . . I lay down on the sofa but I did not sleep. . . .

. . . For the six weeks of her illness we were looking after her day and night—Lukerya and I together with a trained nurse whom I had engaged from the hospital. I spared no expense—in fact, I was eager to spend money for her. I called in Dr. Shreder and paid him ten roubles a visit. When she began to get better I did not show myself so much. But why am I describing it? When she got up again, she sat quietly and silently in my room at a special table, which I had bought for her, too, about that time. . . . Yes, that's the truth, we were absolutely silent; that is, we began talking afterwards, but only of the daily routine. I purposely avoided expressing myself, but I noticed that she, too, was glad not to have to say a word more than was necessary. It seemed to me that this was perfectly natural on her part: "She is too much shattered, too completely conquered," I thought, "and I must let her forget and grow used to it." In this way we were silent, but every minute I was preparing myself for the future. I thought that she was too, and it was fearfully interesting to me to guess what she was thinking about to herself then.

I will say more: oh! of course, no one knows what I went through, moaning over her in her illness. But I stifled my moans in my own heart, even from Lukerya. I could not imagine, could not even conceive of her dying without knowing the whole truth. When she was out of danger and began to regain her health, I very quickly and completely, I remember, recovered my tranquillity. What is more, I made up my mind to *defer our future* as long as possible, and meanwhile to leave things just as they were. Yes, something strange and peculiar happened to me then, I cannot call it anything else: I had triumphed, and the mere consciousness of that was enough for me. So the whole winter passed. Oh! I was satisfied as I had never been before, and it lasted the whole winter.

You see, there had been a terrible external circumstance in my life which, up till then—that is, up to the catastrophe with my wife—had weighed upon me every day and every hour. I mean the loss of my reputation and my leaving the regiment. In two words, I was treated with tyrannical injustice. It is true my comrades did not love me because of my difficult character, and perhaps because of my absurd character, though it often happens that what is exalted, precious and of value to one, for some reason amuses the herd of one's companions. Oh, I was never liked, not even at school! I was always and everywhere disliked. Even Lukerya cannot like me. What happened in the regiment, though it was the result of their dislike of me, was in a sense accidental. I mention this because nothing is more mortifying and insufferable than to be ruined by an accident, which might have happened or not have happened, from an unfortunate accumulation of circumstances which might have passed over like a cloud. For an intelligent being it is humiliating. This was what happened.

In an interval, at a theatre, I went out to the refreshment bar. A hussar called A—— came in and began, before all the officers present and the public, loudly talking to two other hussars, telling them that Captain Bezumtsev, of our regiment, was making a disgraceful scene in the passage and was, "he believed, drunk." The conversation did not go further and, indeed, it was a mistake, for Captain Bezumtsev was not drunk and the "disgraceful scene" was not really disgraceful. The hussars began talking of something else, and the matter ended there, but next day the story reached our regiment, and then they began saying at once that I was the only officer of our regiment in the refreshment bar at the time, and that when A—— the hussar, had spoken insolently of Captain Bezumtsev, I had not gone up to A—— and stopped him by remonstrating. But on what grounds could I have done so? If he had a grudge against Bezumtsev, it was their personal affair and why should I interfere? Meanwhile, the officers began to declare that it was not a personal affair, but that it concerned the regiment, and as I was the only officer of the regiment present I had thereby shown all the officers and other people in the refreshment bar that there could be officers in our regiment who were not over-sensitive on the score of their own honour and the honour of their regiment. I could not agree with this view. They let me know that I could set everything right if I were willing, even now, late as it was, to demand a formal explanation from A——. I was not willing to do this, and as I was irritated I refused with pride. And thereupon I forthwith resigned my commission—that is the whole story. I left the regiment, proud but crushed in spirit. I was depressed in will and mind. Just then it was that my sister's husband in Moscow squandered all our little property and my portion of it, which was tiny enough, but the loss of it left me homeless, without a farthing. I might have taken a job in a private business, but I did not. After wearing a distinguished uniform I could not take work in a railway office. And so—if it must be shame, let it be shame; if it must be disgrace, let it be disgrace; if it must be degradation, let it be degradation—(the worse it is, the better) that was my choice. Then followed three years of gloomy memories, and even Vyazemsky's House. A year and a half ago my godmother, a wealthy old lady, died in Moscow, and to my surprise left me three thousand in her will. I thought a little and immediately decided on my course of action. I determined on setting up as a pawnbroker, without apologizing to any one: money, then a home, as far as possible from memories of the past, that was my plan. Nevertheless, the gloomy past and my ruined reputation fretted me every day, every hour. But then I married. Whether it was by chance or not I don't know. But when I brought her into my home I thought I was bringing a friend, and I needed a friend so much. But I saw clearly that the friend must be trained, schooled, even conquered. Could I have explained myself straight off to a girl of sixteen with her prejudices? How, for instance, could I, without the chance help of the horrible incident with the revolver, have made her believe I was not a coward, and that I had been unjustly accused of cowardice in the regiment? But that terrible incident came just in the nick of time. Standing the test of the revolver, I scored off all my gloomy past. And though no one knew about it, *she* knew, and for me that was everything, because she was everything for me, all the hope of the future that I cherished in my dreams! She was the one person I had prepared for myself, and I needed no one else—and here she knew everything; she knew, at any rate, that she had been in haste to join my enemies against me unjustly. That thought enchanted me. In her eyes I could not be a scoundrel now, but at most a strange person, and that thought after all that had happened was by no means displeasing to me; strangeness is not a vice—on the contrary, it sometimes attracts the feminine heart. In fact, I purposely deferred the climax: what had happened was, meanwhile, enough for my peace of mind and provided a great number of pictures and materials for my dreams. That is what is wrong, that I am a dreamer: I had enough material for my dreams, and about her, I thought she could *wait*.

So the whole winter passed in a sort of expectation. I liked looking at her on the sly, when she was sitting at her little table. She was busy at her needlework, and sometimes in the evening she read books taken from my bookcase. The choice of books in the bookcase must have had an influence in my favour too. She hardly ever went out. Just before dusk, after dinner, I used to take her out every day for a walk. We took a constitutional, but we were not absolutely silent, as we used to be. I tried, in fact, to make a show of our not being silent, but talking harmoniously, but as I have said already, we both avoided letting ourselves go. I did it purposely, I thought it was essential to "give her time." Of course, it was strange that almost till the end of the winter it did not once strike me that, though I loved to watch her stealthily, I had never once, all the winter, caught her glancing at me! I thought it was timidity in her. Besides, she had an air of such timid gentleness, such weakness after her illness. Yes, better to wait and—"she will come to you all at once of herself. . . ."

That thought fascinated me beyond all words. I will add one thing; sometimes, as it were purposely, I worked myself up and brought my mind and spirit to the point of believing she had injured me. And so it went on for some time. But my anger could never be very real or violent. And I felt myself as though it were only acting. And though I had broken off our marriage by buying that bedstead and screen, I could never, never look upon her as a criminal. And not that I took a frivolous view of her crime, but because I had the sense to forgive her completely, from the very first day, even before I bought the bedstead. In fact, it is strange on my part, for I am strict in moral questions. On the contrary, in my eyes, she was so conquered, so humiliated, so crushed, that sometimes I felt agonies of pity for her, though sometimes the thought of her humiliation was actually pleasing to me. The thought of our inequality pleased me. . . .

I intentionally performed several acts of kindness that winter. I excused two debts, I gave one poor woman money without any pledge. And I said nothing to my wife about it, and I didn't do it in order that she should know; but the woman came herself to thank me, almost on her knees. And in that way it became public property; it seemed to me that she heard about the woman with pleasure.

But spring was coming, it was mid-April, we took out the double windows and the sun began lighting up our silent room with its bright beams. But there was, as it were, a veil before my eyes and a blindness over my mind. A fatal, terrible veil! How did it happen that the scales suddenly fell from my eyes, and I suddenly saw and understood? Was it a chance, or had the hour come, or did the ray of sunshine kindle a thought, a conjecture, in my dull mind? No, it was not a thought, not a conjecture. But a chord suddenly vibrated, a feeling that had long been dead was stirred and came to life, flooding all my darkened soul and devilish pride with light. It was as though I had suddenly leaped up from my place. And, indeed, it happened suddenly and abruptly. It happened towards evening, at five o'clock, after dinner. . . .

II   THE VEIL SUDDENLY FALLS

Two words first. A month ago I noticed a strange melancholy in her, not simply silence, but melancholy. That, too, I noticed suddenly. She was sitting at her work, her head bent over her sewing, and she did not see that I was looking at her. And it suddenly struck me that she had grown so delicate-looking, so thin, that her face was pale, her lips were white. All this, together with her melancholy, struck me all at once. I had already heard a little dry cough, especially at night. I got up at once and went off to ask Shreder to come, saying nothing to her.

Shreder came next day. She was very much surprised and looked first at Shreder and then at me.

"But I am well," she said, with an uncertain smile.

Shreder did not examine her very carefully (these doctors are sometimes superciliously careless), he only said to me in the other room, that it was just the result of her illness, and that it wouldn't be amiss to go for a trip to the sea in the spring, or, if that were impossible, to take a cottage out of town for the summer. In fact, he said nothing except that there was weakness, or something of that sort. When Shreder had gone, she said again, looking at me very earnestly—

"I am quite well, quite well."

But as she said this she suddenly flushed, apparently from shame. Apparently it was shame. Oh! now I understand: she was ashamed that I was still *her husband*, that I was looking after her still as though I were a real husband. But at the time I did not understand and put down her blush to humility (the veil!).

And so, a month later, in April, at five o'clock on a bright sunny day, I was sitting in the shop making up my accounts. Suddenly I heard her, sitting in our room, at work at her table, begin softly, softly . . . singing. This novelty made an overwhelming impression upon me, and to this day I don't understand it. Till then I had hardly ever heard her sing, unless, perhaps, in those first days, when we were still able to be playful and practise shooting at a target. Then her voice was rather strong, resonant; though not quite true it was very sweet and healthy. Now her little song was so faint —it was not that it was melancholy (it was some sort of ballad), but in her voice there was something jangled, broken, as though her voice were not equal to it, as though the song itself were sick. She sang in an undertone, and suddenly, as her voice rose, it broke—such a poor little voice, it broke so pitifully; she cleared her throat and again began softly, softly singing. . . .

My emotions will be ridiculed, but no one will understand why I was so moved! No, I was still not sorry for her, it was still something quite different. At the beginning, for the first minute, at any rate, I was filled with sudden perplexity and terrible amazement—a terrible and strange, painful and almost vindictive amazement: "She is singing, and before me; *has she forgotten about me?*"

Completely overwhelmed, I remained where I was, then I suddenly got up, took my hat and went out, as it were, without thinking. At least I don't know why or where I was going. Lukerya began giving me my overcoat.

"She is singing?" I said to Lukerya involuntarily. She did not understand, and looked at me still without understanding; and, indeed, I was really unintelligible.

"Is it the first time she is singing?"

"No, she sometimes does sing when you are out," answered Lukerya.

I remember everything. I went downstairs, went out into the street and walked along at random. I walked to the corner and began looking into the distance. People were passing by, they pushed against me. I did not feel it. I called a cab and told the man, I don't know why, to drive to Politseysky Bridge. Then suddenly changed my mind and gave him twenty kopecks.

"That's for my having troubled you," I said, with a meaningless laugh, but a sort of ecstasy was suddenly shining within me.

I returned home, quickening my steps. The poor little jangled, broken note was ringing in my heart again. My breath failed me. The veil was falling, was falling from my eyes! Since she sang before me, she had forgotten me—that is what was clear and terrible. My heart felt it. But rapture was glowing in my soul and it overcame my terror.

Oh! the irony of fate! Why, there had been nothing else, and could have been nothing else but that rapture in my soul all the winter, but where had I been myself all that winter? Had I been there together with my soul? I ran up the stairs in great haste, I don't know whether I went in timidly. I only remember that the whole floor seemed to be rocking and I felt as though I were floating on a river. I went into the room. She was sitting in the same place as before, with her head bent over her sewing, but she wasn't singing now. She looked cursorily and without interest at me; it was hardly a look but just an habitual and indifferent movement upon somebody's coming into the room.

I went straight up and sat down beside her in a chair abruptly, as though I were mad. She looked at me quickly, seeming frightened; I took her hand and I don't remember what I said to her—that is, tried to say, for I could not even speak properly. My voice broke and would not obey me and I did not know what to say. I could only gasp for breath.

"Let us talk . . . you know . . . tell me something!" I muttered something stupid. Oh! how could I help being stupid? She started again and drew back in great alarm, looking at my face, but suddenly there was an expression of *stern surprise* in her eyes. Yes, surprise and *stern*. She looked at me with wide-open eyes. That sternness, that stern surprise shattered me at once: "So you still expect love? Love?" that surprise seemed to be asking, though she said nothing. But I read it all, I read it all. Everything within me seemed quivering, and I simply fell down at her feet. Yes, I grovelled at her feet. She jumped up quickly, but I held her forcibly by both hands.

And I fully understood my despair—I understood it! But, would you believe it? ecstasy was surging up in my head so violently that I thought I should die. I kissed her feet in delirium and rapture. Yes, in immense, infinite rapture, and that, in spite of understanding all the hopelessness of my despair. I wept, said something, but could not speak. Her alarm and amazement were followed by some uneasy misgiving, some grave question, and she looked at me strangely, wildly even; she wanted to understand something quickly and she smiled. She was horribly ashamed at my kissing her feet and she drew them back. But I kissed the place on the floor where her foot had rested. She saw it and suddenly began laughing with shame (you know how it is when people laugh with shame). She became hysterical, I saw that her hands trembled—I did not think about that but went on muttering that I loved her, that I would not get up. "Let me kiss your dress . . . and worship you like this all my life." . . . I don't know, I don't remember—but suddenly she broke into sobs and trembled all over. A terrible fit of hysterics followed. I had frightened her.

I carried her to the bed. When the attack had passed off, sitting on the edge of the bed, with a terribly exhausted look, she took my two hands and begged me to calm myself: "Come, come, don't distress yourself, be calm!" and she began crying again. All that evening I did not leave her side.

I kept telling her I should take her to Boulogne to bathe in the sea now, at once, in a fortnight, that she had such a broken voice, I had heard it that afternoon, that I would shut up the shop, that I would sell it to Dobronravov, that everything should begin afresh and, above all, Boulogne, Boulogne! She listened and was still afraid. She grew more and more afraid. But that was not what mattered most for me: what mattered most to me was the more and more irresistible longing to fall at her feet again, and again to kiss and kiss the spot where her foot had rested, and to worship her; and—"I ask nothing, nothing more of you," I kept repeating, "do not answer me, take no notice of me, only let me watch you from my corner, treat me as your dog, your thing. . . ." She was crying.

"I thought you would let me go on like that," suddenly broke from her unconsciously, so unconsciously that, perhaps, she did not notice what she had said, and yet—oh, that was the most significant, momentous phrase she uttered that evening, the easiest for me to understand, and it stabbed my heart as though with a knife! It explained everything to me, everything, but while she was beside me, before my eyes, I could not help hoping and was fearfully happy. Oh, I exhausted her fearfully that evening. I understood that, but I kept thinking that I should alter everything directly. At last, towards night, she was utterly exhausted. I persuaded her to go to sleep and she fell sound asleep at once. I expected her to be delirious, she was a little delirious, but very slightly. I kept getting up every minute in the night and going softly in my slippers to look at her. I wrung my hands over her, looking at that frail creature in that wretched little iron bedstead which I had bought her for three roubles. I knelt down, but did not dare to kiss her feet in her sleep (without her consent). I began praying but leapt up again. Lukerya kept watch over me and came in and out from the kitchen. I went in to her, and told her to go to bed, and that tomorrow "things would be quite different."

And I believed in this, blindly, madly.

Oh, I was brimming over with rapture, rapture! I was eager for the next day. Above all, I did not believe that anything could go wrong, in spite of the symptoms. Reason had

not altogether come back to me, though the veil had fallen
from my eyes, and for a long, long time it did not come back
—not till today, not till this very day! Yes, and how could
it have come back then: why she was still alive then; why,
she was here before my eyes, and I was before her eyes:
"Tomorrow she will wake up and I will tell her all this, and
she will see it all." That was how I reasoned then, simply
and clearly, because I was in an ecstasy! My great idea was
the trip to Boulogne. I kept thinking for some reason that
Boulogne would be everything, that there was something
final and decisive about Boulogne. "To Boulogne, to Boulogne!" . . . I waited frantically for the morning.

III   I UNDERSTAND TOO WELL

But you know that was only a few days ago, five days, only
five days ago, last Tuesday! Yes, yes, if there had only been
a little longer, if she had only waited a little—and I would
have dissipated the darkness!—It was not as though she had
not recovered her calmness. The very next day she listened
to me with a smile, in spite of her confusion. . . . All this
time, all these five days, she was either confused or ashamed.
She was afraid, too, very much afraid. I don't dispute it, I
am not so mad as to deny it. It was terror, but how could she
help being frightened? We had so long been strangers to
one another, had grown so alienated from one another, and
suddenly all this. . . . But I did not look at her terror. I
was dazzled by the new life beginning! . . . It is true, it is
undoubtedly true that I made a mistake. There were even,
perhaps, many mistakes. When I woke up next day, the first
thing in the morning (that was on Wednesday), I made a
mistake: I suddenly made her my friend. I was in too great
a hurry, too great a hurry, but a confession was necessary,
inevitable—more than a confession! I did not even hide
what I had hidden from myself all my life. I told her straight
out that the whole winter I had been doing nothing but
brood over the certainty of her love. I made clear to her that
my money-lending had been simply the degradation of my
will and my mind, my personal idea of self-castigation and
self-exaltation. I explained to her that I really had been

cowardly that time in the refreshment bar, that it was owing to my temperament, to my self-consciousness. I was impressed by the surroundings, by the theatre: I was doubtful how I should succeed and whether it would be stupid. I was not afraid of a duel, but of its being stupid . . . and afterwards I would not own it and tormented every one and had tormented her for it, and had married her so as to torment her for it. In fact, for the most part I talked as though in delirium. She herself took my hands and made me leave off. "You are exaggerating . . . you are distressing yourself," and again there were tears, again almost hysterics! She kept begging me not to say all this, not to recall it.

I took no notice of her entreaties, or hardly noticed them: "Spring, Boulogne! There there would be sunshine, there our new sunshine," I kept saying that! I shut up the shop and transferred it to Dobronravov. I suddenly suggested to her giving all our money to the poor except the three thousand left me by my godmother, which we would spend on going to Boulogne, and then we would come back and begin a new life of real work. So we decided, for she said nothing. . . . She only smiled. And I believe she smiled chiefly from delicacy, for fear of disappointing me. I saw, of course, that I was burdensome to her, don't imagine I was so stupid or egoistic as not to see it. I saw it all, all, to the smallest detail, I saw better than any one; all the hopelessness of my position stood revealed.

I told her everything about myself and about her. And about Lukerya. I told her that I had wept. . . . Oh, of course, I changed the conversation. I tried, too, not to say a word more about certain things. And, indeed, she did revive once or twice—I remember it, I remember it! Why do you say I looked at her and saw nothing? And if only *this* had not happened, everything would have come to life again. Why, only the day before yesterday, when we were talking of reading and what she had been reading that winter, she told me something herself, and laughed as she told me, recalling the scene of Gil Blas and the Archbishop of Granada. And with what sweet, childish laughter, just as in old days when we were engaged (one instant! one instant!); how glad I was! I was awfully struck, though, by the story of the Archbishop; so she had found peace of mind and happiness enough to laugh at that literary masterpiece while she was sitting there in the winter. So then she had begun to be fully at rest, had begun to believe confidently that I should leave her *like that*. "I thought you would leave me like that," those were the words she uttered then on Tuesday! Oh! the thought of a child of ten! And you know she believed it, she believed that really everything would remain *like that*: she at her table and I at mine, and we both should go on like that till we were sixty. And all at once—I come forward, her husband, and the husband wants love! Oh, the delusion! Oh, my blindness!

It was a mistake, too, that I looked at her with rapture; I ought to have controlled myself, as it was my rapture frightened her. But, indeed, I did not control myself, I did not kiss her feet again. I never made a sign of . . . well, that I was her husband—oh, there was no thought of that in my mind, I only worshipped her! But, you know, I couldn't be quite silent, I could not refrain from speaking altogether! I suddenly said to her frankly, that I enjoyed her conversation and that I thought her incomparably more cultured and developed than I. She flushed crimson and said in confusion that I exaggerated. Then, like a fool, I could not resist telling her how delighted I had been when I had stood behind the door listening to her duel, the duel of innocence with that low cad, and how I had enjoyed her cleverness, the brilliance of her wit, and, at the same time, her childlike simplicity. She seemed to shudder all over, was murmuring again that I exaggerated, but suddenly her whole face darkened, she hid it in her hands and broke into sobs. . . . Then I could not restrain myself: again I fell at her feet, again I began kissing her feet, and again it ended in a fit of hysterics, just as on Tuesday. That was yesterday evening—and—in the morning. . . .

In the morning! Madman! why, that morning was today, just now, only just now!

Listen and try to understand: why, when we met by the samovar (it was after yesterday's hysterics), I was actually struck by her calmness, that is the actual fact! And all night I had been trembling with terror over what happened yesterday. But suddenly she came up to me and, clasping her hands (this morning, this morning!) began telling me that she was a criminal, that she knew it, that her crime had been torturing her all the winter, was torturing her now. . . . That she appreciated my generosity. . . . "I will be your faithful wife, I will respect you . . ."

Then I leapt up and embraced her like a madman. I kissed her, kissed her face, kissed her lips like a husband for the first time after a long separation. And why did I go out this morning, only for two hours . . . our passports for abroad. . . . Oh, God! if only I had come back five minutes, only five minutes earlier! . . . That crowd at our gates, those eyes all fixed upon me. Oh, God!

Lukerya says (oh! I will not let Lukerya go now for anything. She knows all about it, she has been here all the winter, she will tell me everything!), she says that when I had gone out of the house and only about twenty minutes before I came back—she suddenly went into our room to her mistress to ask her something, I don't remember what, and saw that her ikon (that same ikon of the Mother of God) had been taken down and was standing before her on the table, and her mistress seemed to have only just been praying before it. "What are you doing, mistress?" "Nothing, Lukerya, run along." "Wait a minute, Lukerya." "She came up and kissed me. 'Are you happy, mistress?' I said. 'Yes, Lukerya.' 'Master ought to have come to beg your pardon long ago, mistress. . . . Thank God that you are reconciled.' " "Very good, Lukerya," she said. "Go away, Lukerya," and she smiled, but so strangely. So strangely that Lukerya went back ten minutes later to have a look at her.

"She was standing by the wall, close to the window, she had laid her arm against the wall, and her head was pressed on her arm, she was standing like that thinking. And she was standing so deep in thought that she did not hear me come and look at her from the other room. She seemed to be smiling—standing, thinking and smiling. I looked at her, turned softly and went out wondering to myself, and suddenly I heard the window opened. I went in at once to say: 'It's fresh, mistress; mind you don't catch cold,' and suddenly I saw she had got on the window and was standing there, her full height, in the open window, with her back to me, holding the ikon in her hand. My heart sank on the spot. I cried, 'Mistress, mistress.' She heard, made a movement to turn back to me, but, instead of turning back, took a step forward, pressed the ikon to her bosom, and flung herself out of window."

I only remember that when I went in at the gate she was still warm. The worst of it was they were all looking at me. At first they shouted and then suddenly they were silent, and then all of them moved away from me . . . and she was lying there with the ikon. I remember, as it were, in a darkness, that I went up to her in silence and looked at her a long while. But all came round me and said something to me. Lukerya was there too, but I did not see her. She says she said something to me. I only remember that workman. He kept shouting to me that, "Only a handful of blood came from her mouth, a handful, a handful!" and he pointed to the blood on a stone. I believe I touched the blood with my finger, I smeared my finger, I looked at my finger (that I remember), and he kept repeating: "a handful, a handful!"

"What do you mean by a handful?" I yelled with all my might, I am told, and I lifted up my hands and rushed at him.

Oh, wild! wild! Delusion! Monstrous! Impossible!

IV   I WAS ONLY FIVE MINUTES TOO LATE

Is it not so? Is it likely? Can one really say it was possible? What for, why did this woman die?

Oh, believe me, I understand, but why she died is still a question. She was frightened of my love, asked herself seriously whether to accept it or not, could not bear the question and preferred to die. I know, I know, no need to rack my brains: she had made too many promises, she was afraid she could not keep them—it is clear. There are circumstances about it quite awful.

For why did she die? That is still a question, after all.

The question hammers, hammers at my brain. I would have left her *like that* if she had wanted to remain *like that*. She did not believe it, that's what it was! No—no. I am talking nonsense, it was not that at all. It was simply because with me she had to be honest—if she loved me, she would have had to love me altogether, and not as she would have loved the grocer. And as she was too chaste, too pure, to consent to such love as the grocer wanted she did not want to deceive me. Did not want to deceive me with half love, counterfeiting love, or a quarter love. They are honest, too honest, that is what it is! I wanted to instil breadth of heart in her, in those days, do you remember? A strange idea.

It is awfully interesting to know: did she respect me or not? I don't know whether she despised me or not. I don't believe she did despise me. It is awfully strange: why did it never once enter my head all the winter that she despised me? I was absolutely convinced of the contrary up to that moment when she looked at me with *stern surprise*. *Stern* it was. I understood on the spot that she despised me. I understood once for all, for ever! Ah, let her, let her despise me all her life even, only let her be living. Only yesterday she was walking about, talking. I simply can't understand how she threw herself out of the window! And how could I have imagined it five minutes before? I have called Lukerya. I won't let Lukerya go now for anything!

Oh, we might still have understood each other! We had simply become terribly estranged from one another during the winter, but couldn't we have grown used to each other again? Why, why, couldn't we have come together again and begun a new life again? I am generous, she was too— that was a point in common! Only a few more words, another two days—no more, and she would have understood everything.

What is most mortifying of all is that it is chance—simply a barbarous, lagging chance. That is what is mortifying! Five minutes, only five minutes too late! Had I come five minutes earlier, the moment would have passed away like a cloud, and it would never have entered her head again. And it would have ended by her understanding it all. But now again empty rooms, and me alone. Here the pendulum is ticking; it does not care, it has no pity. . . . There is no one—that's the misery of it!

I keep walking about, I keep walking about. I know, I know, you need not tell me; it amuses you, you think it absurd that I complain of chance and those five minutes. But it is evident. Consider one thing: she did not even leave a note, to say, "Blame no one for my death," as people always do. Might she not have thought that Lukerya might get into trouble. "She was alone with her," might have been said, "and pushed her out." In any case she would have been taken up by the police if it had not happened that four people, from the windows, from the lodge, and from the yard, had seen her stand with the ikon in her hands and jump out of herself. But that, too, was a chance, that the people were standing there and saw her. No, it was all a moment, only an irresponsible moment. A sudden impulse, a fantasy! What if she did pray before the ikon? It does not follow that she was facing death. The whole impulse lasted, perhaps, only some ten minutes; it was all decided, perhaps, while she stood against the wall with her head on her arm, smiling. The idea darted into her brain, she turned giddy and—and could not resist it.

Say what you will, it was clearly misunderstanding. It would have been possible to live with me. And what if it were anæmia? Was it simply from poorness of blood, from the flagging of vital energy? She had grown tired during the winter, that was what it was. . . .

I was too late! ! !

How thin she is in her coffin, how sharp her nose has grown! Her eyelashes lie straight as arrows. And, you know, when she fell, nothing was crushed, nothing was broken! Nothing but that "handful of blood." A dessertspoonful, that is. From internal injury. A strange thought: if only it were possible not to bury her? For if they take her away, then . . . oh, no, it is almost incredible that they should take her away! I am not mad and I am not raving—on the contrary, my mind was never so lucid—but what shall I do when again there is no one, only the two rooms, and me alone with the pledges? Madness, madness, madness! I worried her to death, that is what it is!

What are your laws to me now? What do I care for your customs, your morals, your life, your state, your faith! Let your judge judge me, let me be brought before your court, let me tried by jury, and I shall say that I admit nothing. The judge will shout, "Be silent, officer." And I will shout to him, "What power have you now that I will obey? Why did blind, inert force destroy that which was dearest of all? What are your laws to me now? They are nothing to me." Oh, I don't care!

She was blind, blind! She is dead, she does not hear! You do not know with what a paradise I would have surrounded you. There was paradise in my soul, I would have made it blossom around you! Well, you wouldn't have loved me—so be it, what of it? Things should still have been *like that*, everything should have remained *like that*. You should only have talked to me as a friend—we should have rejoiced and laughed with joy looking at one another. And so we should have lived. And if you had loved another—well, so be it, so be it! You should have walked with him laughing, and I should have watched you from the other side of the street. . . . Oh, anything, anything, if only she would open her eyes just once! For one instant, only one! If she would look at me as she did this morning, when she stood before me and made a vow to be a faithful wife! Oh, in one look she would have understood it all!

Oh, blind force! Oh, nature! Men are alone on earth—that is what is dreadful! "Is there a living man in the country?" cried the Russian hero. I cry the same, though I am not a hero, and no one answers my cry. They say the sun gives life to the universe. The sun is rising and—look at it, is it not dead? Everything is dead and everywhere there are dead. Men are alone—around them is silence—that is the earth! "Men, love one another"—who said that? Whose commandment is that? The pendulum ticks callously, heartlessly. Two o'clock at night. Her little shoes are standing by the little bed, as though waiting for her. . . . No, seriously, when they take her away tomorrow, what will become of me?

Fyodor Dostoevsky

THE CROCODILE

A true story of how a gentleman of a certain age and of respectable appearance was swallowed alive by the crocodile in the Arcade, and of the consequences that followed.

Ohé Lambert! Où est Lambert?
As tu vu Lambert?

On the thirteenth of January of this present year, 1865, at half-past twelve in the day, Elena Ivanovna, the wife of my cultured friend Ivan Matveitch, who is a colleague in the same department, and may be said to be a distant relation of mine, too, expressed the desire to see the crocodile now on view at a fixed charge in the Arcade. As Ivan Matveitch had already in his pocket his ticket for a tour abroad (not so much for the sake of his health as for the improvement of his mind), and was consequently free from his official duties and had nothing whatever to do that morning, he offered no objection to his wife's irresistible fancy, but was positively aflame with curiosity himself.

"A capital idea!" he said, with the utmost satisfaction. "We'll have a look at the crocodile! On the eve of visiting Europe it is as well to acquaint ourselves on the spot with its indigenous inhabitants." And with these words, taking his wife's arm, he set off with her at once for the Arcade. I joined them, as I usually do, being an intimate friend of the family. I have never seen Ivan Matveitch in a more agreeable frame of mind than he was on that memorable morning—how true it is that we know not beforehand the fate that awaits us! On entering the Arcade he was at once full of admiration for the splendours of the building, and when we reached the shop in which the monster lately arrived in Petersburg was being exhibited, he volunteered to pay the quarter-rouble for me to the crocodile owner—a thing which had never happened before. Walking into a little room, we observed that besides the crocodile there were in it parrots of the species known as cockatoo, and also a group of monkeys in a special case in a recess. Near the entrance, along the left wall stood a big tin tank that looked like a bathtub covered with a thin iron grating, filled with water to the depth of two inches. In this shallow pool was kept a huge crocodile, which lay like a log absolutely motionless and apparently deprived of all its faculties by our damp climate, so inhospitable to foreign visitors. This monster at first aroused no special interest in any one of us.

"So this is the crocodile!" said Elena Ivanovna, with a pathetic cadence of regret. "Why, I thought it was . . . something different."

Most probably she thought it was made of diamonds. The owner of the crocodile, a German, came out and looked at us with an air of extraordinary pride.

"He has a right to be," Ivan Matveitch whispered to me, "he knows he is the only man in Russia exhibiting a crocodile."

This quite nonsensical observation I ascribe also to the extremely good-humoured mood which had overtaken Ivan Matveitch, who was on other occasions of rather envious disposition.

"I fancy your crocodile is not alive," said Elena Ivanovna, piqued by the irresponsive stolidity of the proprietor, and addressing him with a charming smile in order to soften his churlishness—a manœuvre so typically feminine.

"Oh, no, madam," the latter replied in broken Russian; and instantly moving the grating half off the tank, he poked the monster's head with a stick.

Then the treacherous monster, to show that it was alive, faintly stirred its paws and tail, raised its snout and emitted something like a prolonged snuffle.

"Come, don't be cross, Karlchen," said the German caressingly, gratified in his vanity.

"How horrid that crocodile is! I am really frightened," Elena Ivanovna twittered, still more coquettishly. "I know I shall dream of him now."

"But he won't bite you if you do dream of him," the German retorted gallantly, and was the first to laugh at his own jest, but none of us responded.

"Come, Semyon Semyonitch," said Elena Ivanovna, addressing me exclusively, "let us go and look at the monkeys. I am awfully fond of monkeys; they are such darlings . . . and the crocodile is horrid."

"Oh, don't be afraid, my dear!" Ivan Matveitch called after us, gallantly displaying his manly courage to his wife. "This drowsy denison of the realms of the Pharaohs will do us no harm." And he remained by the tank. What is more, he took his glove and began tickling the crocodile's nose with it, wishing, as he said afterwards, to induce him to snort. The proprietor showed his politeness to a lady by following Elena Ivanovna to the case of monkeys.

So everything was going well, and nothing could have been foreseen. Elena Ivanovna was quite skittish in her raptures over the monkeys, and seemed completely taken up with them. With shrieks of delight she was continually turning to me, as though determined not to notice the proprietor, and kept gushing with laughter at the resemblance she detected between these monkeys and her intimate friends and acquaintances. I, too, was amused, for the resemblance was unmistakable. The German did not know whether to laugh or not, and so at last was reduced to frowning. And it was at that moment that a terrible, I may say unnatural, scream set the room vibrating. Not knowing what to think, for the first moment I stood still, numb with horror, but noticing that Elena Ivanovna was screaming too, I quickly turned round —and what did I behold! I saw—oh heavens!—I saw the luckless Ivan Matveitch in the terrible jaws of the crocodile, held by them round the waist, lifted horizontally in the air and desperately kicking. Then—one moment, and no trace remained of him. But I must describe it in detail, for I stood all the while motionless, and had time to watch the whole process taking place before me with an attention and interest such as I never remember to have felt before.

"What," I thought at that critical moment, "what if all that had happened to me instead of to Ivan Matveitch—how unpleasant it would have been for me!"

But to return to my story. The crocodile began by turning the unhappy Ivan Matveitch in his terrible jaws so that he could swallow his legs first; then bringing up Ivan Matveitch, who kept trying to jump out and clutching at the sides of the tank, sucked him down again as far as his waist. Then bringing him up again, gulped him down, and so again and again. In this way Ivan Matveitch was visibly disappearing before our eyes. At last, with a final gulp, the crocodile swallowed my cultured friend entirely, this time leaving no trace of him. From the outside of the crocodile we could see the protuberances of Ivan Matveitch's figure as he passed down the inside of the monster. I was on the point of screaming again when destiny played another treacherous trick upon us. The crocodile made a tremendous effort, probably oppressed by the magnitude of the object he had swallowed, once more opened his terrible jaws, and with a final hiccup he suddenly let the head of Ivan Matveitch pop out for a second, with an expression of despair on his face. In that brief instant the spectacles dropped off his nose to the bottom of the tank. It seemed as though that despairing countenance had only popped out to cast one last look on the objects around it, to take its last farewell of all earthly pleasures. But it had not time to carry out its intention; the crocodile made another effort, gave a gulp and instantly it vanished again—this time for ever. This appearance and disappearance of a still living human head was so horrible, but at the same—either from its rapidity and unexpectedness or from the dropping of the spectacles—there was something so comic about it that I suddenly quite unexpectedly exploded with laughter. But pulling myself together and realising that to laugh at such a moment was not the thing for an old family friend, I turned at once to Elena Ivanovna and said with a sympathetic air:

"Now it's all over with our friend Ivan Matveitch!"

I cannot even attempt to describe how violent was the agitation of Elena Ivanovna during the whole process. After the first scream she seemed rooted to the spot, and stared at the catastrophe with apparent indifference, though her eyes looked as though they were starting out of her head; then she suddenly went off into a heart-rending wail, but I seized her hands. At this instant the proprietor, too, who had at first been also petrified by horror, suddenly clasped his hands and cried, gazing upwards:

"Oh my crocodile! *Oh mein allerliebster Karlchen! Mutter, Mutter, Mutter!*"

A door at the rear of the room opened at this cry, and the *Mutter,* a rosy-cheeked, elderly but dishevelled woman in a cap made her appearance, and rushed with a shriek to her German.

A perfect Bedlam followed. Elena Ivanovna kept shrieking out the same phrase, as though in a frenzy, "Flay him! flay him!" apparently entreating them—probably in a moment of oblivion—to flay somebody for something. The proprietor and *Mutter* took no notice whatever of either of us; they were both bellowing like calves over the crocodile.

"He did for himself! He will burst himself at once, for he did swallow a *ganz* official!" cried the proprietor.

"Unser Karlchen, unser allerliebster Karlchen wird sterben," howled his wife.

"We are bereaved and without bread!" chimed in the proprietor.

"Flay him! flay him! flay him!" clamoured Elena Ivanovna, clutching at the German's coat.

"He did tease the crocodile. For what did your man tease the crocodile?" cried the German, pulling away from her. "You will if *Karlchen wird* burst, therefore pay, *das war mein Sohn, das war mein einziger Sohn.*"

I must own I was intently indignant at the sight of such egoism in the German and the cold-heartedness of his dishevelled *Mutter;* at the same time Elena Ivanovna's reiterated shriek of "Flay him! flay him!" troubled me even more and absorbed at last my whole attention, positively alarming me. I may as well say straight off that I entirely misunderstood this strange exclamation: it seemed to me that Elena Ivanovna had for the moment taken leave of her senses, but nevertheless wishing to avenge the loss of her beloved Ivan Matveitch, was demanding by way of compensation that the crocodile should be severely thrashed, while she was meaning something quite different. Looking round at the door, not without embarrassment, I began to entreat Elena Ivanovna to calm herself, and above all not to use the shocking word "flay." For such a reactionary desire here, in the midst of the Arcade and of the most cultured society, not two paces from the hall where at this very minute Mr. Lavrov was perhaps delivering a public lecture, was not only impossible but unthinkable, and might at any moment bring upon us the hisses of culture and the caricatures of Mr. Stepanov. To my horror I was immediately proved to be correct in my alarmed suspicions: the curtain that divided the crocodile room from the little entry where the quarter-roubles were taken suddenly parted, and in the opening there appeared a figure with moustaches and beard, carrying a cap, with the upper part of its body bent a long way forward, though the feet were scrupulously held beyond the threshold of the crocodile room in order to avoid the necessity of paying the entrance money.

"Such a reactionary desire, madam," said the stranger, trying to avoid falling over in our direction and to remain standing outside the room, "does no credit to your development, and is conditioned by lack of phosphorous in your brain. You will be promptly held up to shame in the *Chronicle of Progress* and in our satirical prints . . ."

But he could not complete his remarks; the proprietor coming to himself, and seeing with horror that a man was talking in the crocodile room without having paid entrance money, rushed furiously at the progressive stranger and turned him out with a punch from each fist. For a moment both vanished from our sight behind a curtain, and only then I grasped that the whole uproar was about nothing. Elena Ivanovna turned out quite innocent; she had, as I have mentioned already, no idea whatever of subjecting the crocodile to a degrading corporal punishment, and had simply expressed the desire that he should be opened and her husband released from his interior.

"What! You wish that my crocodile be perished!" the proprietor yelled, running in again. "No! let your husband be perished first, before my crocodile! . . . *Mein Vater* showed crocodile, *mein Grossvater* showed crocodile, *mein Sohn* will show crocodile, and I will show crocodile! All will show crocodile! I am known to *ganz Europa,* and you are not known to *ganz Europa,* and you must pay me a *Strafe!"*

"*Ja, ja,*" put in the vindictive German woman, "we shall not let you go. *Strafe,* since Karlchen is burst!"

"And, indeed, it's useless to flay the creature," I added calmly, anxious to get Elena Ivanovna away home as quickly as possible, "as our dear Ivan Matveitch is by now probably soaring somewhere in the empyrean."

"My dear"—we suddenly heard, to our intense amazement, the voice of Ivan Matveitch—"my dear, my advice is to apply direct to the superintendent's office, as without the assistance of the police the German will never be made to see reason."

These words, uttered with firmness and aplomb, and expressing an exceptional presence of mind, for the first minute so astounded us that we could not believe our ears. But, of course, we ran at once to the crocodile's tank, and with equal reverence and incredulity listened to the unhappy captive. His voice was muffled, thin and even squeaky, as though it came from a considerable distance. It reminded one of a jocose person who, covering his mouth with a pillow, shouts from an adjoining room, trying to mimic the sound of two peasants calling to one another in a deserted plain or across a wide ravine—a performance to which I once had the pleasure of listening in a friend's house at Christmas.

"Ivan Matveitch, my dear, and so you are alive!" faltered Elena Ivanovna.

"Alive and well," answered Ivan Matveitch, "and, thanks to the Almighty, swallowed without any damage whatever. I am only uneasy as to the view my superiors may take of the incident; for after getting a permit to go abroad I've got into a crocodile, which seems anything but clever."

"But, my dear, don't trouble your head about being clever; first of all we must somehow excavate you from where you are," Elena Ivanovna interrupted.

"Excavate!" cried the proprietor. "I will not let my crocodile be excavated. Now the *publicum* will come many more, and I will *fünfzig* kopecks ask and Karlchen will cease to burst."

"*Gott sei Dank!*" put in his wife.

"They are right," Ivan Matveitch observed tranquilly; "the principles of economics before everything."

"My dear! I will fly at once to the authorities and lodge a complaint, for I feel that we cannot settle this mess by ourselves."

"I think so too," observed Ivan Matveitch; "but in our age of industrial crisis it is not easy to rip open the belly of a crocodile without economic compensation, and meanwhile the inevitable question presents itself: What will the German take for his crocodile? And with it another: How will it be paid? For, as you know, I have no means . . ."

"Perhaps out of your salary . . ." I observed timidly, but the proprietor interrupted me at once.

"I will not the crocodile sell; I will for three thousand the crocodile sell! I will for four thousand the crocodile sell! Now the *publicum* will come very many. I will for five thousand the crocodile sell!"

In fact he gave himself insufferable airs. Covetousness and a revolting greed gleamed joyfully in his eyes.

"I am going!" I cried indignantly.

"And I! I too! I shall go to Andrey Osipitch himself. I will soften him with my tears," whined Elena Ivanovna.

"Don't do that, my dear," Ivan Matveitch hastened to interpose. He had long been jealous of Andrey Osipitch on his wife's account, and he knew she would enjoy going to weep before a gentleman of refinement, for tears suited her.

"And I don't advise you to do so either, my friend," he added, addressing me. "It's no good plunging headlong in that slap-dash way; there's no knowing what it may lead to. You had much better go today to Timofey Semyonitch, as though to pay an ordinary visit; he is an old-fashioned and by no means brilliant man, but he is trustworthy, and what matters most of all, he is straightforward. Give him my greetings and describe the circumstances of the case. And since I owe him seven roubles over our last game of cards, take the opportunity to pay him the money; that will soften the stern old man. In any case his advice may serve as a guide for us. And meanwhile take Elena Ivanovna home. . . . Calm yourself my dear," he continued, addressing her. "I am weary of these outcries and feminine squabblings, and should like a nap. It's soft and warm in here, though I have hardly had time to look round in this unexpected haven."

"Look round! Why, is it light in there?" cried Elena Ivanovna in a tone of relief.

"I am surrounded by impenetrable night," answered the poor captive; "but I can feel and, so to speak, have a look round with my hands. . . . Good-bye; set your mind at rest and don't deny yourself recreation and diversion. Till to-morrow! And you, Semyon Semyonitch, come to me in the evening, and as you are absent-minded and may forget it, tie a knot in your handkerchief."

I confess I was glad to get away, for I was overtired and somewhat bored. Hastening to offer my arm to the disconsolate Elena Ivanovna, whose charms were only enhanced by her agitation, I hurriedly led her out of the crocodile room.

"The charge will be another quarter-rouble in the evening," the proprietor called after us.

"Oh, dear, how greedy they are!" said Elena Ivanovna, looking at herself in every mirror on the walls of the Arcade, and evidently aware that she was looking prettier than usual.

"The principles of economics," I answered with some emotion, proud that passers-by should see the lady on my arm.

"The principles of economics," she drawled in a touching little voice. "I did not in the least understand what Ivan Matveitch said about those horrid economics just now."

"I will explain to you," I answered, and began at once telling her of the beneficial effects of the introduction of foreign capital into our country, upon which I had read an article in the *Petersburg News* and the *Voice* that morning.

"How strange it is," she interrupted, after listening for some time. "But do leave off, you horrid man. What nonsense you are talking. . . . Tell me, do I look purple?"

"You look perfect, and not purple!" I observed, seizing the opportunity to pay her a compliment.

"Naughty man!" she said complacently. "Poor Ivan Matveitch," she added a minute later, putting her little head on one side coquettishly. "I am really sorry for him. Oh, dear!" she cried suddenly, "how is he going to have his dinner . . . and . . . and . . . what will he do . . . if he wants anything?"

"An unforeseen question," I answered, perplexed in my turn. To tell the truth, it had not entered my head, so much more practical are women than we men in the solution of the problems of daily life!

"Poor dear! how could he have got into such a mess . . . nothing to amuse him, and in the dark. . . . How vexing it is that I have no photograph of him. . . . And so now I am a sort of widow," she added, with a seductive smile, evidently interested in her new position. "Hm! . . . I am sorry for him, though."

It was, in short, the expression of the very natural and intelligible grief of a young and interesting wife for the loss of her husband. I took her home at last, soothed her, and after dining with her and drinking a cup of aromatic coffee, set off at six o'clock to Timofey Semyonitch, calculating that at that hour all married people of settled habits would be sitting or lying down at home.

Having written this first chapter in a style appropriate to the incident recorded, I intend to proceed in a language more natural though less elevated, and I beg to forewarn the reader of the fact.

II

The venerable Timofey Semyonitch met me rather nervously, as though somewhat embarrassed. He led me to his tiny study and shut the door carefully, "that the children may not hinder us," he added with evident uneasiness. There he made me sit down on a chair by the writing-table, sat down himself in an easy chair, wrapped round him the skirts of his old wadded dressing-gown, and assumed an official and even severe air, in readiness for anything, though he was not my chief nor Ivan Matveitch's, and had hitherto been reckoned as a colleague and even a friend.

"First of all," he said, "take note that I am not a person in authority, but just such a subordinate official as you and Ivan Matveitch. . . . I have nothing to do with it, and do not intend to mix myself up in the affair."

I was surprised to find that he apparently knew all about it already. In spite of that I told him the whole story over in detail. I spoke with positive excitement, for I was at that moment fulfilling the obligations of a true friend. He listened without special surprise, but with evident signs of suspicion.

"Only fancy," he said, "I always believed that this would be sure to happen to him."

"Why, Timofey Semyonitch? It is a very unusual incident in itself . . ."

"I admit it. But Ivan Matveitch's whole career in the service was leading up to this end. He was flighty—conceited indeed. It was always 'progress' and ideas of all sorts, and this is what progress brings people to!"

"But this is a most unusual incident and cannot possibly serve as a general rule for all progressives."

"Yes, indeed it can. You see, it's the effect of over-education, I assure you. For over-education leads people to poke their noses into all sorts of places, especially where they are not invited. Though perhaps you know best," he added, as though offended. "I am an old man and not of much education. I began as a soldier's son, and this year has been the jubilee of my service."

"Oh, no, Timofey Semyonitch, not at all. On the contrary, Ivan Matveitch is eager for your advice; he is eager for your guidance. He implores it, so to say, with tears."

"So to say, with tears! Hm! Those are crocodile's tears and one cannot quite believe in them. Tell me, what possessed him to want to go abroad? And how could he afford to go? Why, he has no private means!"

"He had saved the money from his last bonus," I answered plaintively. "He only wanted to go for three months —to Switzerland . . . to the land of William Tell."

"William Tell? Hm!"

"He wanted to meet the spring at Naples, to see the museums, the customs, the animals . . ."

"Hm! The animals! I think it was simply from pride. What animals? Animals, indeed! Haven't we animals enough? We have museums, menageries, camels. There are bears quite close to Petersburg! And here he's got inside a crocodile himself . . ."

"Oh, come, Timofey Semyonitch! The man is in trouble, the man appeals to you as to a friend, as to an older relation, craves for advice—and you reproach him. Have pity at least on the unfortunate Elena Ivanovna!"

"You are speaking of his wife? A charming little lady," said Timofey Semyonitch, visibly softening and taking a pinch of snuff with relish. "Particularly prepossessing. And so plump, and always putting her pretty little head on one side. . . . Very agreeable. Andrey Osipitch was speaking of her only the other day."

"Speaking of her?"

"Yes, and in very flattering terms. Such a bust, he said, such eyes, such hair. . . . A sugar-plum, he said, not a lady—and then he laughed. He is still a young man, of course." Timofey Semyonitch blew his nose with a loud noise. "And yet, young though he is, what a career he is making for himself."

"That's quite a different thing, Timofey Semyonitch."

"Of course, of course."

"Well, what do you say then, Timofey Semyonitch?"

"Why, what can I do?"

"Give advice, guidance, as a man of experience, a relative! What are we to do? What steps are we to take? Go to the authorities and . . ."

"To the authorities? Certainly not," Timofey Semyonitch replied hurriedly. "If you ask my advice, you had better, above all, hush the matter up and act, so to speak, as a private person. It is a suspicious incident, quite unheard of. Unheard of, above all; there is no precedent for it, and it is far from creditable. . . . And so discretion above all. . . . Let him lie there a bit. We must wait and see . . ."

"But how can we wait and see, Timofey Semyonitch? What if he is stifled there?"

"Why should he be? I think you told me that he made himself fairly comfortable there?"

I told him the whole story over again. Timofey Semyonitch pondered.

"Hm!" he said, twisting his snuff-box in his hands. "To my mind it's really a good thing he should lie there a bit, instead of going abroad. Let him reflect at his leisure. Of course he mustn't be stifled, and so he must take measures to preserve his health, avoiding a cough, for instance, and so on. . . . And as for the German, it's my personal opinion he is within his rights, and even more so than the other side, because it was the other party who got into *his* crocodile without asking permission, and not *he* who got into Ivan Matveitch's crocodile without asking permission, though, so far as I recollect, the latter has no crocodile. And a crocodile is private property, and so it is impossible to slit him open without compensation."

"For the saving of human life, Timofey Semyonitch."

"Oh, well, that's a matter for the police. You must go to them."

"But Ivan Matveitch may be needed in the department. He may be asked for."

"Ivan Matveitch needed? Ha-ha! Besides, he is on leave, so that we may ignore him—let him inspect the countries of Europe! It will be a different matter if he doesn't turn up when his leave is over. Then we shall ask for him and make inquiries."

"Three months! Timofey Semyonitch, for pity's sake!"

"It's his own fault. Nobody thrust him there. At this rate we should have to get a nurse to look after him at government expense, and that is not allowed for in the regulations. But the chief point is that the crocodile is private property, so that the principles of economics apply in this question. And principles of economics are paramount. Only the other evening, at Luka Andreitch's, Ignaty Prokofyitch was saying so. Do you know Ignaty Prokofyitch? A capitalist, in a big way of business, and he speaks so fluently. 'We need industrial development,' he said; 'there is very little development among us. We must create it. We must create capital, so we must create a middle-class, the so-called bourgeoisie.

And as we haven't capital we must attract it from abroad. We must, in the first place, give facilities to foreign companies to buy up lands in Russia as is done now abroad. The communal holding of land is poison, is ruin.' And, you know, he spoke with such heat; well, that's all right for him—a wealthy man, and not in the service. 'With the communal system,' he said, 'there will be no improvement in industrial development or agriculture. Foreign companies,' he said, 'must as far as possible buy up the whole of our land in big lots, and then split it up, split it up, split it up, in the smallest parts possible'—and do you know he pronounced the words 'split it up' with such determination—'and then sell it as private property. Or rather, not sell it, but simply let it. 'When,' he said, 'all the land is in the hands of foreign companies they can fix any rent they like. And so the peasant will work three times as much for his daily bread and he can be turned out at pleasure. So that he will feel it, will be submissive and industrious, and will work three times as much for the same wages. But as it is, with the commune, what does he care? He knows he won't die of hunger, so he is lazy and drunken. And meanwhile money will be attracted into Russia, capital will be created and the bourgeoisie will spring up. The English political and literary paper, *The Times*, in an article the other day on our finances stated that the reason our financial position was so unsatisfactory was that we had no middle class, no big fortunes, no accommodating proletariat.' Ignaty Prokofyitch speaks well. He is an orator. He wants to lay a report on the subject before the authorities, and then to get it published in the *News*. That's something very different from verses like Ivan Matveitch's . . ."

"But how about Ivan Matveitch?" I put in, after letting the old man babble on.

Timofey Semyonitch was sometimes fond of talking and showing that he was not behind the times, but knew all about things.

"How about Ivan Matveitch? Why, I am coming to that. Here we are, anxious to bring foreign capital into the country—and only consider: as soon as the capital of a foreigner, who has been attracted to Petersburg, has been doubled through Ivan Matveitch, instead of protecting the foreign capitalist, we are proposing to rip open the belly of his original capital—the crocodile. Is it consistent? To my mind, Ivan Matveitch, as the true son of his fatherland, ought to rejoice and to be proud that through him the value of a foreign crocodile has been doubled and possibly even trebled. That's just what is wanted to attract capital. If one man succeeds, mind you, another will come with a crocodile, and a third will bring two or three of them at once, and capital will grow up about them—there you have a bourgeoisie. It must be encouraged."

"Upon my word, Timofey Semyonitch!" I cried, "you are demanding almost supernatural self-sacrifice from poor Ivan Matveitch."

"I demand nothing, and I beg you, before everything—as I have said already—to remember that I am not a person in authority and so cannot demand anything of any one. I am speaking as a son of the fatherland, that is, not as the *Son of the Fatherland,* but as a son of the fatherland. Again, what possessed him to get into the crocodile? A respectable man, a man of good grade in the service, lawfully married—and then to behave like that! Is it consistent?"

"But it was an accident."

"Who knows? And where is the money to compensate the owner to come from?"

"Perhaps out of his salary, Timofey Semyonitch?"

"Would that be enough?"

"No, it wouldn't, Timofey Semyonitch," I answered sadly. "The proprietor was at first alarmed that the crocodile would burst, but as soon as he was sure that it was all right, he began to bluster and was delighted to think that he could double the charge for entry."

"Treble and quadruple perhaps! The public will simply stampede the place now, and crocodile owners are smart people. Besides, it's not Lent yet, and people are keen on diversions, and so I say again, the great thing is that Ivan Matveitch should preserve his incognito, don't let him be in a hurry. Let everybody know, perhaps, that he is in the crocodile, but don't let them be officially informed of it. Ivan Matveitch is in particularly favourable circumstances for that, for he is reckoned to be abroad. It will be said he is in the crocodile, and we will refuse to believe it. That is how it can be managed. The great thing is that he should wait; and why should he be in a hurry?"

"Well, but if . . ."

"Don't worry, he has a good constitution . . ."

"Well, and afterwards, when he has waited?"

"Well, I won't conceal from you that the case is exceptional in the highest degree. One doesn't know what to think of it, and the worst of it is there is no precedent. If we had a precedent we might have something to go by. But as it is, what is one to say? It will certainly take time to settle it."

A happy thought flashed upon my mind.

"Cannot we arrange," I said, "that if he is destined to remain in the entrails of the monster and it is the will of Providence that he should remain alive, that he should send in a petition to be reckoned as still serving?"

"Hm! . . . Possibly as on leave and without salary . . ."

"But couldn't it be with salary?"

"On what grounds?"

"As sent on a special commission."

"What commission and where?"

"Why, into the entrails, the entrails of the crocodile. . . . So to speak, for exploration, for investigation of the facts on the spot. It would, of course, be a novelty, but that is progressive and would at the same time show zeal for enlightenment."

Timofey Semyonitch thought a little.

"To send a special official," he said at last, "to the inside of a crocodile to conduct a special inquiry is, in my personal opinion, an absurdity. It is not in the regulations. And what sort of special inquiry could there be there?"

"The scientific study of nature on the spot, in the living subject. The natural sciences are all the fashion nowadays, botany. . . . He could live there and report his observations. . . . For instance, concerning digestion or simply habits. For the sake of accumulating facts."

"You mean as statistics. Well, I am no great authority on that subject, indeed I am no philosopher at all. You say 'facts'—we are overwhelmed with facts as it is, and don't know what to do with them. Besides, statistics are a danger."

"In what way?"

"They are a danger. Moreover, you will admit he will report facts, so to speak, lying like a log. And, can one do one's official duties lying like a log? That would be another novelty and a dangerous one; and again, there is no precedent for it. If we had any sort of precedent for it, then, to my thinking, he might have been given the job."

"But no live crocodiles have been brought over hitherto, Timofey Semyonitch."

"Hm . . . yes," he reflected again. "Your objection is a just one, if you like, and might indeed serve as a ground for carrying the matter further; but consider again, that if with the arrival of living crocodiles government clerks begin to disappear, and then on the ground that they are warm and comfortable there, expect to receive the official sanction for their position, and then take their ease there . . . you must admit it would be a bad example. We should have every one trying to go the same way to get a salary for nothing."

"Do your best for him, Timofey Semyonitch. By the way, Ivan Matveitch asked me to give you seven roubles he had lost to you at cards."

"Ah, he lost that the other day at Nikifor Nikiforitch's. I remember. And how gay and amusing he was—and now!"

The old man was genuinely touched.

"Intercede for him, Timofey Semyonitch!"

"I will do my best. I will speak in my own name, as a private person, as though I were asking for information. And meanwhile, you find out indirectly, unofficially, how much would the proprietor consent to take for his crocodile?"

Timofey Semyonitch was visibly more friendly.

"Certainly," I answered. "And I will come back to you at once to report."

"And his wife . . . is she alone now? Is she depressed?"

"You should call on her, Timofey Semyonitch."

"I will. I thought of doing so before; it's a good opportunity. . . . And what on earth possessed him to go and look at the crocodile. Though, indeed, I should like to see it myself."

"Go and see the poor fellow, Timofey Semyonitch."

"I will. Of course, I don't want to raise his hopes by doing so. I shall go as a private person. . . . Well, good-bye, I am going to Nikifor Nikiforitch's again; shall you be there?"

"No, I am going to see the poor prisoner."

"Yes, now he is a prisoner! . . . Ah, that's what comes of thoughtlessness!"

I said good-bye to the old man. Ideas of all kinds were straying through my mind. A good-natured and most honest man, Timofey Semyonitch, yet, as I left him, I felt pleased at the thought that he had celebrated his fiftieth year of service, and that Timofey Semyonitchs are now a rarity among us. I flew at once, of course, to the Arcade to tell poor Ivan Matveitch all the news. And, indeed, I was moved by curiosity to know how he was getting on in the crocodile and how it was possible to live in a crocodile. And, indeed, was it possible to live in a crocodile at all? At times it really seemed to me as though it were all an outlandish, monstrous dream, especially as an outlandish monster was the chief figure in it.

III

And yet it was not a dream, but actual, indubitable fact. Should I be telling the story if it were not? But to continue.

It was late, about nine o'clock, before I reached the Arcade, and I had to go into the crocodile room by the back entrance, for the German had closed the shop earlier than usual that evening. Now in the seclusion of domesticity he was walking about in a greasy old frock-coat, but he seemed three times as pleased as he had been in the morning. It was evidently that he had no apprehensions now, and that the public had been coming "many more." The *Mutter* came out later, evidently to keep an eye on me. The German and the *Mutter* frequently whispered together. Although the shop was closed he charged me a quarter-rouble. What unnecessary exactitude!

"You will every time pay; the public will one rouble, and

you one quarter pay; for you are the good friend of your good friend; and I a friend respect . . ."

"Are you alive, are you alive, my cultured friend?" I cried, as I approached the crocodile, expecting my words to reach Ivan Matveitch from a distance and to flatter his vanity.

"Alive and well," he answered, as though from a long way off or from under the bed, though I was standing close beside him. "Alive and well; but of that later. . . . How are things going?"

As though purposely not hearing the question, I was just beginning with sympathetic haste to question him how he was, what it was like in the crocodile, and what, in fact, there was inside a crocodile. Both friendship and common civility demanded this. But with capricious annoyance he interrupted me.

"How are things going?" he shouted, in a shrill and on this occasion particularly revolting voice, addressing me peremptorily as usual.

I described to him my whole conversation with Timofey Semyonitch down to the smallest detail. As I told my story I tried to show my resentment in my voice.

"The old man is right," Ivan Matveitch pronounced as abruptly as usual in his conversation with me. "I like practical people, and can't endure sentimental milk-sops. I am ready to admit, however, that your idea about a special commission is not altogether absurd. I certainly have a great deal to report, both from a scientific and from an ethical point of view. But now all this has taken a new and unexpected aspect, and it is not worth while to trouble about mere salary. Listen attentively. Are you sitting down?"

"No, I am standing up."

"Sit down on the floor if there is nothing else, and listen attentively."

Resentfully I took a chair and put it down on the floor with a bang, in my anger.

"Listen," he began dictatorially. "The public came today in masses. There was no room left in the evening, and the police came in to keep order. At eight o'clock, that is, earlier than usual, the proprietor thought it necessary to close the shop and end the exhibition to count the money he had taken and prepare for tomorrow more conveniently. So I know there will be a regular fair tomorrow. So we may assume that all the most cultivated people in the capital, the ladies and the best society, the foreign ambassadors, the leading lawyers and so on, will all be present. What's more, people will be flowing here from the remotest provinces of our vast and interesting empire. The upshot of it is that I am the cynosure of all eyes, and though hidden to sight, I am eminent. I shall teach the idle crowd. Taught by experience, I shall be an example of greatness and resignation to fate! I shall be, so to say, a pulpit from which to instruct mankind. The mere biological details I can furnish about the monster I am inhabiting are of priceless value. And so, far from repining at what has happened, I confidently hope for the most brilliant of careers."

"You won't find it wearisome?" I asked sarcastically.

What irritated me more than anything was the extreme pomposity of his language. Nevertheless, it all rather disconcerted me. "What on earth, what, can this frivolous blockhead find to be so cocky about?" I muttered to myself. "He ought to be crying instead of being cocky."

"No!" he answered my observation sharply, "for I am full of great ideas, only now can I at leisure ponder over the amelioration of the lot of humanity. Truth and light will come forth now from the crocodile. I shall certainly develop a new economic theory of my own and I shall be proud of it —which I have hitherto been prevented from doing by my official duties and by trivial distractions. I shall refute everything and be a new Fourier. By the way, did you give Timofey Semyonitch the seven roubles?"

"Yes, out of my own pocket," I answered, trying to emphasise that fact in my voice.

"We will settle it," he answered superciliously. "I confidently expect my salary to be raised, for who should get a raise if not I? I am of the utmost service now. But to business. My wife?"

"You are, I suppose, inquiring after Elena Ivanovna?"

"My wife?" he shouted, this time in a positive squeal.

There was no help for it! Meekly, though gnashing my

teeth, I told him how I had left Elena Ivanovna. He did not even hear me out.

"I have special plans in regard to her," he began impatiently. "If I am celebrated *here*, I wish her to be celebrated *there*. Savants, poets, philosophers, foreign mineralogists, statesmen, after conversing in the morning with me, will visit her *salon* in the evening. From next week onwards she must have an 'At Home' every evening. With my salary doubled, we shall have the means for entertaining, and as the entertainment must not go beyond tea and hired footmen—that's settled. Both here and there they will talk of me. I have long thirsted for an opportunity for being talked about, but could not attain it, fettered by my humble position and low grade in the service. And now all this has been attained by a simple gulp on the part of the crocodile. Every word of mine will be listened to, every utterance will be thought over, repeated, printed. And I'll teach them what I am worth! They shall understand at last what abilities they have allowed to vanish in the entrails of a monster. 'This man might have been Foreign Minister or might have ruled a kingdom,' some will say. 'And that man did not rule a kingdom,' others will say. In what way am I inferior to a Garnier-Pagesishky or whatever they are called? My wife must be a worthy second—I have brains, she has beauty and charm. 'She is beautiful, and that is why she is his wife,' some will say. 'She is beautiful *because* she is his wife,' others will amend. To be ready for anything let Elena Ivanovna buy tomorrow the Encyclopædia edited by Andrey Kraevsky, that she may be able to converse on any topic. Above all, let her be sure to read the political leader in the *Petersburg News*, comparing it every day with the *Voice*. I imagine that the proprietor will consent to take me sometimes with the crocodile to my wife's brilliant *salon*. I will be in a tank in the middle of the magnificent drawing-room, and I will scintillate with witticisms which I will prepare in the morning. To the statesmen I will impart my projects; to the poet I will speak in rhyme; with the ladies I can be amusing and charming without impropriety, since I shall be no danger to their husbands' peace of mind. To all the rest I shall serve as a pattern of resignation to fate and the will of Providence. I shall make my wife a brilliant literary lady; I shall bring her forward and explain her to the public; as my wife she must be full of the most striking virtues; and if they are right in calling Andrey Alexandrovitch our Russian Alfred de Musset, they will be still more right in calling her our Russian Yevgenia Tour."

I must confess that although this wild nonsense was rather in Ivan Matveitch's habitual style, it did occur to me that he was in a fever and delirious. It was the same, everyday Ivan Matveitch, but magnified twenty times.

"My friend," I asked him, "are you hoping for a long life? Tell me, in fact, are you well? How do you eat, how do you sleep, how do you breathe? I am your friend, and you must admit that the incident is most unnatural, and consequently my curiosity is most natural."

"Idle curiosity and nothing else," he pronounced sententiously, "but you shall be satisfied. You ask how I am managing in the entrails of the monster? To begin with, the crocodile, to my amusement, turns out to be perfectly empty. His inside consists of a sort of huge empty sack made of gutta-percha, like the elastic goods sold in the Gorohovy Street, in the Morskaya, and, if I am not mistaken, in the Voznesensky Prospect. Otherwise, if you think of it, how could I find room?"

"Is it possible?" I cried, in a surprise that may well be understood. "Can the crocodile be perfectly empty?"

"Perfectly," Ivan Matveitch maintained sternly and impressively. "And in all probability, it is so constructed by the laws of Nature. The crocodile possesses nothing but jaws furnished with sharp teeth, and besides the jaws, a tail of considerable length—that is all, properly speaking. The middle part between these two extremities is an empty space enclosed by something of the nature of gutta-percha, probably really gutta-percha."

"But the ribs, the stomach, the intestines, the liver, the heart?" I interrupted quite angrily.

"There is nothing, absolutely nothing of all that, and probably there never has been. All that is the idle fancy of frivolous travellers. As one inflates an air-cushion, I am now with my person inflating the crocodile. He is incredibly elastic. Indeed, you might, as the friend of the family, get in with me if you were generous and self-sacrificing enough —and even with you here there would be room to spare. I even think that in the last resort I might send for Elena Ivanovna. However, this void, hollow formation of the crocodile is quite in keeping with the teachings of natural science. If, for instance, one had to construct a new crocodile, the question would naturally present itself. What is the fundamental characteristic of the crocodile? The answer is clear: to swallow human beings. How is one, in constructing the crocodile, to secure that he should swallow people? The answer is clearer still: construct him hollow. It was settled by physics long ago that Nature abhors a vacuum. Hence the inside of the crocodile must be hollow so that it may abhor the vacuum, and consequently swallow and so fill itself with anything it can come across. And that is the sole rational cause why every crocodile swallows men. It is not the same in the constitution of man: the emptier a man's head is, for instance, the less he feels the thirst to fill it, and that is the one exception to the general rule. It is all as clear as day to me now. I have deduced it by my own observation and experience, being, so to say, in the very bowels of Nature, in its retort, listening to the throbbing of its pulse. Even etymology supports me, for the very word crocodile means voracity. Crocodile—*crocodillo*—is evidently an Italian word, dating perhaps from the Egyptian Pharaohs, and evidently derived from the French verb *croquer,* which means to eat, to devour, in general to absorb nourishment. All these remarks I intend to deliver as my first lecture in Elena Ivanovna's *salon* when they take me there in the tank."

"My friend, oughtn't you at least to take some purgative?" I cried involuntarily.

"He is in a fever, a fever, he is feverish!" I repeated to myself in alarm.

"Nonsense!" he answered contemptuously. "Besides, in my present position it would be most inconvenient. I knew, though, you would be sure to talk of taking medicine."

"But, my friend, how . . . how do you take food now? Have you dined today?"

"No, but I am not hungry, and most likely I shall never take food again. And that, too, is quite natural; filling the whole interior of the crocodile I make him feel always full. Now he need not be fed for some years. On the other hand, nourished by me, he will naturally impart to me all the vital juices of his body; it is the same as with some accomplished coquettes who embed themselves and their whole persons for the night in raw steak, and then, after their morning bath, are fresh, supple, buxom and fascinating. In that way nourishing the crocodile, I myself obtain nourishment from him, consequently we mutually nourish one another. But as it is difficult even for a crocodile to digest a man like me, he must, no doubt, be conscious of a certain weight in his stomach—an organ which he does not, however, possess—and that is why, to avoid causing the creature suffering, I do not often turn over, and although I could turn over I do not do so from humanitarian motives. This is the one drawback of my present position, and in an allegorical sense Timofey Semyonitch was right in saying I was lying like a log. But I will prove that even lying like a log—nay, that only lying like a log—one can revolutionise the lot of mankind. All the great ideas and movements of our newspapers and magazines have evidently been the work of men who were lying like logs; that is why they called them divorced from the realities of life—but what does it matter, their saying that! I am constructing now a complete system of my own, and you wouldn't believe how easy it is! You have only to creep into a secluded corner or into a crocodile, to shut your eyes, and you immediately devise a perfect millennium for mankind. When you went away this afternoon I set to work at once and have already invented three systems, now I am preparing the fourth. It is true that at first one must refute everything that has gone before, but from the crocodile it is so easy to refute it; besides, it all becomes clearer, seen from the inside of the crocodile. . . . There are some drawbacks, though small ones, in my position, however; it is somewhat damp here and covered with a sort of slime; moreover, there is a smell of india-rubber like the smell of my old goloshes. That is all, there are no other drawbacks.

"Ivan Matveitch," I interrupted, "all this is a miracle in which I can scarcely believe. And can you, can you intend never to dine again?"

"What trivial nonsense you are troubling about, you thoughtless, frivolous creature! I talk to you about great ideas, and you . . . Understand that I am sufficiently nourished by the great ideas which light up the darkness in which I am enveloped. The good-natured proprietor has, however, after consulting the kindly *Mutter,* decided with her that they will every morning insert into the monster's jaws a bent metal tube, something like a whistle pipe, by means of which I can absorb coffee or broth with bread soaked in it. The pipe has already been bespoken in the neighbourhood, but I think this is superfluous luxury. I hope to live at least a thousand years, if it is true that crocodiles live so long, which, by the way—good thing I thought of it—you had better look up in some natural history tomorrow and tell me, for I may have been mistaken and have mixed it up with some excavated monster. There is only one reflection rather troubles me: as I am dressed in cloth and have boots on, the crocodile can obviously not digest me. Besides, I am alive, and so am opposing the process of digestion with my whole will power; for you can understand that I do not wish to be turned into what all nourishment turns into, for that would be too humiliating for me. But there is one thing I am afraid of: in a thousand years the cloth of my coat, unfortunately of Russian make, may decay, and then, left without clothing, I might perhaps, in spite of my indignation, begin to be digested; and though by day nothing would induce me to allow it, at night, in my sleep, when a man's will deserts him, I may be overtaken by the humiliating destiny of a potato, a pancake, or veal. Such an idea reduces me to fury. This alone is an argument for the revision of the tariff and the encouragement of the importation of English cloth, which is stronger and so will withstand Nature longer when one is swallowed by a crocodile. At the first opportunity I will impart this idea to some statesman and at the same time to the political writers on our Petersburg dailies. Let them publish it abroad. I trust this will not be the only idea they will borrow from me. I foresee that every morning a regular crowd of them, provided with quarter-roubles from the editorial office, will be flocking round me to seize my ideas on the telegrams of the previous day. In brief, the future presents itself to me in the rosiest light."

"Fever, fever!" I whispered to myself.

"My friend, and freedom?" I asked, wishing to learn his views thoroughly. "You are, so to speak, in prison, while every man has a right to the enjoyment of freedom."

"You are a fool," he answered. "Savages love independence, wise men love order; and if there is no order . . ."

"Ivan Matveitch, spare me, please!"

"Hold your tongue and listen!" he squealed, vexed at my interrupting him. "Never has my spirit soared as now. In my narrow refuge there is only one thing that I dread—the literary criticisms of the monthlies and the hiss of our satirical papers. I am afraid that thoughtless visitors, stupid and envious people and nihilists in general, may turn me into ridicule. But I will take measures. I am impatiently awaiting the response of the public tomorrow, and especially the opinion of the newspapers. You must tell me about the papers tomorrow."

"Very good; tomorrow I will bring a perfect pile of papers with me."

"Tomorrow it is too soon to expect reports in the newspapers, for it will take four days for it to be advertised. But from today come to me every evening by the back way through the yard. I am intending to employ you as my secretary. You shall read the newspapers and magazines to me, and I will dictate to you my ideas and give you commissions. Be particularly careful not to forget the foreign telegrams. Let all the European telegrams be here every day. But enough; most likely you are sleepy by now. Go home, and do not think of what I said just now about criticisms: I am not afraid of it, for the critics themselves are in critical position. One has only to be wise and virtuous and one will certainly get on to a pedestal. If not Socrates, then Diogenes, or perhaps both of them together— that is my future rôle among mankind."

So frivolously and boastfully did Ivan Matveitch hasten

to express himself before me, like feverish weak-willed women who, as we are told by the proverb, cannot keep a secret. All that he told me about the crocodile struck me as most suspicious. How was it possible that the crocodile was absolutely hollow? I don't mind betting that he was bragging from vanity and partly to humiliate me. It is true that he was an invalid and one must make allowances for invalids; but I must frankly confess, I never could endure Ivan Matveitch. I have been trying all my life, from a child up, to escape from his tutelage and have not been able to. A thousand times over I have been tempted to break with him altogether, and every time I have been drawn to him again, as though I were still hoping to prove something to him or to revenge myself on him. A strange thing, this friendship! I can positively assert that nine-tenths of my friendship for him was made up of malice. On this occasion, however, we parted with genuine feeling.

"Your friend a very clever man!" the German said to me in an undertone as he moved to see me out; he had been listening all the time attentively to our conversation.

"*À propos,*" I said, "while I think of it: how much would you ask for your crocodile in case any one wanted to buy it?"

Ivan Matveitch, who heard the question, was waiting with curiosity for the answer; it was evident that he did not want the German to ask too little; anyway, he cleared his throat in a peculiar way on hearing my question.

At first the German would not listen—was positively angry.

"No one will dare my own crocodile to buy!" he cried furiously, and turned as red as a boiled lobster. "Me not want to sell the crocodile! I would not for the crocodile a million thalers take. I took a hundred and thirty thalers from the public today, and I shall tomorrow ten thousand take, and then a hundred thousand every day I shall take. I will not him sell."

Ivan Matveitch positively chuckled with satisfaction. Controlling myself—for I felt it was a duty to my friend— I hinted coolly and reasonably to the crazy German that his calculations were not quite correct, that if he makes a hundred thousand every day, all Petersburg will have visited him in four days, and then there will be no one left to bring him roubles, that life and death are in God's hands, that the crocodile may burst or Ivan Matveitch may fall ill and die, and so on and so on.

The German grew pensive.

"I will him drops from the chemist's get," he said, after pondering, "and will save your friend that he die not."

"Drops are all very well," I answered, "but consider, too, that the thing may get into the law courts. Ivan Matveitch's wife may demand the restitution of her lawful spouse. You are intending to get rich, but do you intend to give Elena Ivanovna a pension?"

"No, me not intend," said the German in stern decision.

"No, we not intend," said the *Mutter,* with positive malignancy.

"And so would it not be better for you to accept something now, at once, a secure and solid though moderate sum, than to leave things to chance? I ought to tell you that I am inquiring simply from curiosity."

The German drew the *Mutter* aside to consult with her in a corner where there stood a case with the largest and ugliest monkey of his collection.

"Well, you will see!" said Ivan Matveitch.

As for me, I was at that moment burning with the desire, first, to give the German a thrashing, next, to give the *Mutter* an even sounder one, and, thirdly, to give Ivan Matveitch the soundest thrashing of all for his boundless vanity. But all this paled beside the answer of the rapacious German.

After consultation with the *Mutter* he demanded for his crocodile fifty thousand roubles in bonds of the last Russian loan with lottery voucher attached, a brick house in Gorohovy Street with a chemist's shop attached, and in addition the rank of Russian colonel.

"You see!" Ivan Matveitch cried triumphantly. "I told you so! Apart from this last senseless desire for the rank of a colonel, he is perfectly right, for he fully understands the present value of the monster he is exhibiting. The economic principle before everything!"

"Upon my word!" I cried furiously to the German. "But what should you be made a colonel for? What exploit have you performed? What service have you done? In what way have you gained military glory? You are really crazy!"

"Crazy!" cried the German, offended. "No, a person very sensible, but you very stupid! I have a colonel deserved for that I have a crocodile shown and in him a live *Hofrath* sitting! And a Russian can a crocodile not show and a live *Hofrath* in him sitting! Me extremely clever man and much wish colonel to be!"

"Well, good-bye, then, Ivan Matveitch!" I cried, shaking with fury, and I went out of the crocodile room almost at a run.

I felt that in another minute I could not have answered for myself. The unnatural expectations of these two blockheads were insupportable. The cold air refreshed me and somewhat moderated my indignation. At last, after spitting vigorously fifteen times on each side, I took a cab, got home, undressed and flung myself into bed. What vexed me more than anything was my having become his secretary. Now I was to die of boredom there every evening, doing the duty of a true friend! I was ready to beat myself for it, and I did, in fact, after putting out the candle and pulling up the bedclothes, punch myself several times on the head and various parts of my body. That somewhat relieved me, and at last I fell asleep fairly soundly, in fact, for I was very tired. All night long I could dream of nothing but monkeys, but towards morning I dreamt of Elena Ivanovna.

IV

The monkeys I dreamed about, I surmise, because they were shut up in the case at the German's; but Elena Ivanovna was a different story.

I may as well say at once, I loved the lady, but I make haste—post-haste—to make a qualification. I loved her as a father, neither more nor less. I judge that because I often felt an irresistible desire to kiss her little head or her rosy cheek. And although I never carried out this inclination, I would not have refused even to kiss her lips. And not merely her lips, but her teeth, which always gleamed so charmingly like two rows of pretty, well-matched pearls when she laughed. She laughed extraordinarily often. Ivan Matveitch in demonstrative moments used to call her his "darling absurdity"—a name extremely happy and appropriate. She was a perfect sugar-plum, and that was all one could say of her. Therefore I am utterly at a loss to understand what possessed Ivan Matveitch to imagine his wife as a Russian Yevgenia Tour? Anyway, my dream, with the exception of the monkeys, left a most pleasant impression upon me, and going over all the incidents of the previous day as I drank my morning cup of tea, I resolved to go and see Elena Ivanovna at once on my way to the office— which, indeed, I was bound to do as the friend of the family.

In a tiny little room out of the bedroom—the so-called little drawing-room, though their big drawing-room was little too—Elena Ivanovna was sitting, in some half-transparent morning wrapper, on a smart little sofa before a little tea-table, drinking coffee out of a little cup in which she was dipping a minute biscuit. She was ravishingly pretty, but struck me as being at the same time rather pensive.

"Ah, that's you, naughty man!" she said, greeting me with an absent-minded smile. "Sit down, feather-head, have some coffee. Well, what were you doing yesterday? Were you at the masquerade?"

"Why, were you? I don't go, you know. Besides, yesterday I was visiting our captive. . . ." I sighed and assumed a pious expression as I took the coffee.

"Whom? . . . What captive? . . . Oh, yes! Poor fellow! Well, how is he—bored? Do you know . . . I wanted to ask you . . . I suppose I can ask for a divorce now?"

"A divorce!" I cried in indignation and almost spilled the coffee. "It's that swarthy fellow," I thought to myself bitterly.

There was a certain swarthy gentleman with little moustaches who was something in the architectural line, and

who came far too often to see them, and was extremely
skillful in amusing Elena Ivanovna. I must confess I hated
him and there was no doubt that he had succeeded in seeing Elena Ivanovna yesterday either at the masquerade or
even here, and putting all sorts of nonsense into her head.

"Why," Elena Ivanovna rattled off hurriedly, as though
it were a lesson she had learnt, "if he is going to stay on
in the crocodile, perhaps not come back all his life, while I
sit waiting for him here. A husband ought to live at home,
and not in a crocodile. . . ."

"But this was an unforeseen occurrence," I was beginning, in very comprehensible agitation.

"Oh, no, don't talk to me, I won't listen, I won't listen,"
she cried, suddenly getting quite cross. "You are always
against me, you wretch! There's no doing anything with
you, you will never give me any advice! Other people tell
me that I can get a divorce because Ivan Matveitch will
not get his salary now."

"Elena Ivanovna! is it you I hear!" I exclaimed pathetically. "What villain could have put such an idea into your
head? And divorce on such a trivial ground as a salary is
quite impossible. And poor Ivan Matveitch, poor Ivan Matveitch is, so to speak, burning with love for you even in
the bowels of the monster. What's more, he is melting
away with love like a lump of sugar. Yesterday while you
were enjoying yourself at the masquerade, he was saying
that he might in the last resort send for you as his lawful
spouse to join him in the entrails of the monster, especially
as it appears the crocodile is exceedingly roomy, not only
able to accommodate two but even three persons. . . ."

And then I told her all that interesting part of my conversation the night before with Ivan Matveitch.

"What, what!" she cried, in surprise. "You want me to
get into the monster too, to be with Ivan Matveitch? What
an idea! And how am I to get in there, in my hat and crin-
oline? Heavens, what foolishness! And what should I look
like while I was getting into it, and very likely there would
be some one there to see me! It's absurd! And what should
I have to eat there? And . . . and . . . and what should I
do there when . . . Oh, my goodness, what will they think

of next . . . And what should I have to amuse me there?
. . . You say there's a smell of gutta-percha? And what
should I do if we quarrelled—should we have to go on
staying there side by side? Foo, how horrid!"

"I agree, I agree with all those arguments, my sweet
Elena Ivanovna," I interrupted, striving to express myself
with that natural enthusiasm which always overtakes a
man when he feels the truth is on his side. "But one thing
you have not appreciated in all this, you have not realised
that he cannot live without you if he is inviting you there;
that is a proof of love, passionate, faithful, ardent love.
. . . You have thought too little of his love, dear Elena
Ivanovna!"

"I won't, I won't, I won't hear anything about it!" waving me off with her pretty little hand with glistening pink
nails that had just been washed and polished. "Horrid man!
You will reduce me to tears! Get into it yourself, if you
like the prospect. You are his friend, get in and keep him
company, and spend your life discussing some tedious science. . . ."

"You are wrong to laugh at this suggestion"—I checked
the frivolous woman with dignity—"Ivan Matveitch has
invited me as it is. You, of course, are summoned there by
duty; for me, it would be an act of generosity. But when
Ivan Matveitch described to me last night the elasticity of
the crocodile, he hinted very plainly that there would be
room not only for you two, but for me also as a friend of
the family, especially if I wished to join you, and therefore . . ."

"How so, the three of us?" cried Elena Ivanovna, looking at me in surprise. "Why, how should we . . . are we
going to be all three there together? Ha-ha-ha! How silly
you both are! Ha-ha-ha! I shall certainly pinch you all
the time, you wretch! Ha-ha-ha! Ha-ha-ha!"

And falling back on the sofa, she laughed till she cried.
All this—the tears and the laughter—were so fascinating
that I could not resist rushing eagerly to kiss her hand,
which she did not oppose, though she did pinch my ears
lightly as a sign of reconciliation.

Then we both grew very cheerful, and I described to her

in detail all Ivan Matveitch's plans. The thought of her evening receptions and her *salon* pleased her very much.

"Only I should need a great many new dresses," she observed, "and so Ivan Matveitch must send me as much of his salary as possible and as soon as possible. Only . . . only I don't know about that," she added thoughtfully. "How can he be brought here in the tank? That's very absurd. I don't want my husband to be carried about in a tank. I should feel quite ashamed for my visitors to see it. . . . I don't want that, no, I don't."

"By the way, while I think of it, was Timofey Semyonitch here yesterday?"

"Oh, yes, he was; he came to comfort me, and do you know, we played cards all the time. He played for sweetmeats, and if I lost he was to kiss my hands. What a wretch he is! And only fancy, he almost came to the masquerade with me, really!"

"He was carried away by his feelings!" I observed. "And who would not be with you, you charmer?"

"Oh, get along with your compliments! Stay, I'll give a pinch as a parting present. I've learnt to pinch awfully well lately. Well, what do you say to that? By the way, you say Ivan Matveitch spoke several times of me yesterday?"

"No-no, not exactly. . . . I must say he is thinking more now of the fate of humanity, and wants . . ."

"Oh, let him! You needn't go on! I am sure it's fearfully boring. I'll go and see him some time. I shall certainly go tomorrow. Only not today; I've got a headache, and besides, there will be such a lot of people there today. . . . They'll say, 'That's his wife,' and I shall feel ashamed. . . . Good-bye. You will be . . . there this evening, won't you?"

"To see him, yes. He asked me to go and take him the papers."

"That's capital. Go and read to him. But don't come and see me today. I am not well, and perhaps I may go and see some one. Good-bye, you naughty man."

"It's that swarthy fellow is going to see her this evening," I thought.

At the office, of course, I gave no sign of being consumed by these cares and anxieties. But soon I noticed some of the most progressive papers seemed to be passing particularly rapidly from hand to hand among my colleagues, and were being read with an extremely serious expression of face. The first one that reached me was the *News-sheet*, a paper of no particular party but humanitarian in general, for which it was regarded with contempt among us, though it was read. Not without surprise I read in it the following paragraph:

"Yesterday strange rumours were circulating among the spacious ways and sumptuous buildings of our vast metropolis. A certain well-known *bon-vivant* of the highest society, probably weary of the *cuisine* at Borel's and at the X. Club, went into the Arcade, into the place where an immense crocodile recently brought to the metropolis is being exhibited, and insisted on its being prepared for his dinner. After bargaining with the proprietor he at once set to work to devour him (that is, not the proprietor, a very meek and punctilious German, but his crocodile), cutting juicy morsels with his penknife from the living animal, and swallowing them with extraordinary rapidity. By degrees the whole crocodile disappeared into the vast recesses of his stomach, so that he was even on the point of attacking an ichneumon, a constant companion of the crocodile, probably imagining that the latter would be as savoury. We are by no means opposed to that new article of diet with which foreign *gourmands* have long been familiar. We have, indeed, predicted that it would come. English lords and travellers make up regular parties for catching crocodiles in Egypt, and consume the back of the monster cooked like beefsteak, with mustard, onions and potatoes. The French who followed in the train of Lesseps prefer the paws baked in hot ashes, which they do, however, in opposition to the English, who laugh at them. Probably both ways would be appreciated among us. For our part, we are delighted at a new branch of industry, of which our great and varied fatherland stands pre-eminently in need. Probably before a year is out crocodiles will be brought in hundreds to replace this first one, lost in the stomach of a Petersburg *gourmand*. And why should not the crocodile be acclimatised among us in Russia' If the water of the Neva is too cold for these interesting strangers, there are ponds in the capital and rivers and lakes outside it. Why not breed crocodiles at Pargolovo, for instance, or at Pavlovsk, in the Presensky Ponds and in Samoteka in Moscow? While providing agreeable, wholesome nourishment for our fastidious *gourmands*, they might at the same time entertain the ladies who walk about these ponds and instruct the children in natural history. The crocodile skin might be used for making jewel-cases, boxes, cigar-cases, pocket-books, and possibly more than one thousand saved up in the greasy notes that are peculiarly beloved of merchants might be laid by in crocodile skin. We hope to return more than once to this interesting topic."

Though I had foreseen something of the sort, yet the reckless inaccuracy of the paragraph overwhelmed me. Finding no one with whom to share my impression, I turned to Prohor Savvitch who was sitting opposite to me, and noticed that the latter had been watching me for some time, while in his hand he held the *Voice* as though he were on the point of passing it to me. Without a word he took the *News-sheet* from me, and as he handed me the *Voice* he drew a line with his nail against an article to which he probably wished to call my attention. This Prohor Savvitch was a very queer man; a taciturn old bachelor, he was not on intimate terms with any of us, scarcely spoke to any one in the office, always had an opinion of his own about everything, but could not bear to impart it to any one. He lived alone. Hardly any one among us had ever been in his lodging.

This was what I read in the *Voice*.

"Every one knows that we are progressive and humanitarian and want to be on a level with Europe in this respect. But in spite of all our exertions and the efforts of our paper we are still far from maturity, as may be judged from the shocking incident which took place yesterday in the Arcade and which we predicted long ago. A foreigner arrives in the capital bringing with him a crocodile which he begins exhibiting in the Arcade. We immediately hasten to welcome a new branch of useful industry such as our powerful and varied fatherland stands in great need. Suddenly yesterday at four o'clock in the afternoon a gentleman of exceptional stoutness enters the foreigner's shop in an intoxicated condition, pays his entrance money, and immediately without any warning leaps into the jaws of the crocodile, who was forced, of course, to swallow him, if only from an instinct of self-preservation, to avoid being crushed. Tumbling into the inside of the crocodile, the stranger at once dropped asleep. Neither the shouts of the foreign proprietor, nor the lamentations of his terrified family, nor threats to send for the police made the slightest impression. Within the crocodile was heard nothing but laughter and a promise to flay him (*sic*), though the poor mammal, compelled to swallow such a mass, was vainly shedding tears. An uninvited guest is worse than a Tartar. But in spite of the proverb the insolent visitor would not leave. We do not know how to explain such barbarous incidents which prove our lack of culture and disgrace us in the eyes of foreigners. The recklessness of the Russian temperament has found a fresh outlet. It may be asked what was the object of the uninvited visitor? A warm and comfortable abode? But there are many excellent houses in the capital with very cheap and comfortable lodgings, with the Neva water laid on, and a staircase lighted by gas, frequently with a hall-porter maintained by the proprietor. We would call our readers' attention to the barbarous treatment of domestic animals: it is difficult, of course, for the crocodile to digest such a mass all at once, and now he lies swollen out to the size of a mountain, awaiting death in insufferable agonies. In Europe persons guilty of inhumanity towards domestic animals have long been punished by law. But in spite of our European enlightenment, in spite of our European pavements, in spite of the European architecture of our houses, we are still far from shaking off our time-honoured traditions.

'Though the houses are new, the conventions are old.'

"And, indeed, the houses are not new, at least the staircases in them are not. We have more than once in our paper alluded to the fact that in the Petersburg Side in the house of the merchant Lukyanov the steps of the wooden staircase have decayed, fallen away, and have long been a danger for Afimya Skapidarov, a soldier's wife who works in the house, and is often obliged to go up the stairs with water or armfulls of wood. At last our predictions have come true: yesterday evening at half-past eight Afimya Skapidarov fell down with a basin of soup and broke her leg. We do not know whether Lukyanov will mend his staircase now, Russians are often wise after the event, but the victim of Russian carelessness has by now been taken to the hospital. In the same way we shall never cease to maintain that the house-porters who clear away the mud from the wooden pavement in the Viborgsky Side ought not to spatter the legs of passers-by, but should throw the mud up into heaps as is done in Europe," and so, and so on.

"What's this?" I asked in some perplexity, looking at Prohor Savvitch. "What's the meaning of it?"

"How do you mean?"

"Why, upon my word! Instead of pitying Ivan Matveitch, they pity the crocodile!"

"What of it? They have pity even for a beast, a *mammal*. We must be up to Europe, mustn't we? They have a very warm feeling for crocodiles there too. He-he-he!"

Saying this, queer old Prohor Savvitch dived into his papers and would not utter another word.

I stuffed the *Voice* and the *News-sheet* into my pocket and collected as many old copies of the newspapers as I could find for Ivan Matveitch's diversion in the evening, and though the evening was far off, yet on this occasion I slipped away from the office early to go to the Arcade and look, if only from a distance, at what was going on there, and to listen to the various remarks and currents of opinion. I foresaw that there would be a regular crush there, and turned up the collar of my coat to meet it. I somehow felt rather shy—so unaccustomed are we to publicity. But I feel that I have no right to report my own prosaic feelings when faced with this remarkable and original incident.

Leo Tolstoy
1828 – 1910

WHAT MEN LIVE BY

"We know that we have passed out of death into life, because we love the brethren. He that loveth not abideth in death."—1 EPISTLE OF ST. JOHN, iii. 14.

"But whoso hath the world's goods, and beholdeth his brother in need, and shutteth up his compassion from him, how doth the love of God abide in him?

"My little children, let us not love in word, neither with the tongue, but in deed and truth."—iii. 17, 18.

"Love is of God; and every one that loveth is begotten of God and knoweth God.

"He that loveth not knoweth not God; for God is love."—iv. 7, 8.

"No man hath beheld God at any time: if we love one another, God abideth in us."—iv. 12.

"God is love; and he that abideth in love abideth in God, and God abideth in him."—iv. 16.

"If a man say, I love God, and hateth his brother, he is a liar; for he that loveth not his brother whom he hath seen cannot love God whom he hath not seen."—iv. 20.

A cobbler and his wife and children had lodgings with a peasant. He owned neither house nor land, and he supported himself and his family by shoemaking.

Bread was dear and labor was poorly paid, and whatever he earned went for food.

The cobbler and his wife had one shuba [1] between them,

[1] Fur or sheepskin outside garment.

and this had come to tatters, and for two years the cobbler had been hoarding in order to buy sheepskins for a new shuba.

When autumn came, the cobbler's hoard had grown; three paper rubles lay in his wife's box, and five rubles and twenty kopeks more were due the cobbler from his customers.

One morning the cobbler betook himself to the village to get his new shuba. He put on his wife's wadded nankeen jacket over his shirt, and outside of all a woolen kaftan. He put the three-ruble note in his pocket, broke off a staff, and after breakfast he set forth.

He said to himself, "I will get my five rubles from the peasants, and that with these three will buy pelts for my shuba."

The cobbler reached the village and went to one peasant's; he was not at home, but his wife promised to send her husband with the money the next week, but she could not give him any money. He went to another, and this peasant swore that he had no money at all; but he paid him twenty kopeks for cobbling his boots.

The cobbler made up his mind to get the pelts on credit. But the fur-dealer refused to sell on credit.

"Bring the money," said he; "then you can make your choice; but we know how hard it is to get what is one's due."

And so the cobbler did not do his errand, but he had the twenty kopeks for cobbling the boots, and he took from a peasant an old pair of felt boots to mend with leather.

At first the cobbler was vexed at heart; then he spent the twenty kopeks for vodka, and started to go home. In the morning he had felt cold, but after having drunk the brandy he was warm enough even without the shuba.

The cobbler was walking along the road, striking the frozen ground with the staff which he had in one hand, and swinging the felt boots in the other, and thus he talked to himself.

"I am warm even without a shuba," said he. "I drank a glass, and it dances through all my veins. And so I don't need a sheepskin coat. I walk along, and all my vexation is forgotten. What a fine fellow I am! What do I need? I can get along without the shuba. I don't need it at all. There's one thing: the wife will feel bad. Indeed, it is too bad; here I have been working for it, and now to have missed it! You just wait now! if you don't bring the money, I will take your hat, I vow I will! What a way of doing things! He pays me twenty kopeks at a time! Now what can you do with twenty kopeks? Get a drink; that's all! You say, 'I am poor!' But if you are poor, how is it with me? You have a house and cattle and everything; I have nothing but my own hands. You raise your own grain, but I have to buy mine, when I can, and it costs me three rubles a week for food alone. When I get home now, we shall be out of bread. Another ruble and a half of outgo! So you must give me what you owe me."

By this time the cobbler had reached the chapel at the cross-roads, and he saw something white behind the chapel.

It was already twilight, and the cobbler strained his eyes, but he could not make out what the object was.

"There never was any such stone there," he said to himself. "A cow? But it does not look like a cow! The head is like a man's; but what is that white? And why should there be any man there?"

He went nearer. Now he could see plainly. What a strange thing! It was indeed a man, but was he alive or dead? sitting there stark naked, leaning against the chapel, and not moving.

The cobbler was frightened. He said to himself, "Some one has killed that man, stripped him, and flung him down there. If I go near, I may get into trouble."

And the cobbler hurried by.

In passing the chapel he could no longer see the man; but after he was fairly beyond it, he looked back, and saw that the man was no longer leaning against the chapel, but was moving, and apparently looking after him.

The cobbler was still more scared by this, and he said to himself, "Shall I go back to him or go on? If I go back to him, there might something unpleasant happen; who knows what sort of a man he is? He can't have gone there for any good purpose. If I went to him, he might spring on me and choke me, and I could not get away from him; and even if he did not choke me, why should I try to make his acquaintance? What could be done with him, naked as he is? I can't take him with me, and give him my own clothes! That would be absurd."

And the cobbler hastened his steps. He had already gone some distance beyond the chapel, when his conscience began to prick him.

He stopped short.

"What is this that you are doing, Semyon?" he asked himself. "A man is perishing of cold, and you are frightened, and hurry by! Are you so very rich? Are you afraid of losing your money? Aï, Sema! That is not right!"

Semyon turned and went back to the man.

II

Semyon went back to the man, looked at him, and saw that it was a young man in the prime of life; there were no bruises visible on him, but he was evidently freezing and afraid; he was sitting there, leaning back, and he did not look at Semyon; apparently he was so weak that he could not lift his eyes.

Semyon went up close to him, and suddenly the man seemed to revive; he lifted his head and fastened his eyes on Semyon.

And by this glance the man won Semyon's heart.

He threw the felt boots down on the ground, took off his belt and laid it on the boots, and pulled off his kaftan.

"There's nothing to be said," he exclaimed. "Put these on! There now!"

Semyon put his hand under the man's elbow, to help him, and tried to lift him. The man got up.

And Semyon saw that his body was graceful and clean, that his hands and feet were comely, and that his face was agreeable. Semyon threw the kaftan over his shoulders. He could not get his arms into the sleeves. Semyon found the place for him, pulled the coat up, wrapped it around him, and fastened the belt.

He took off his tattered cap, and was going to give it to

the stranger, but his head felt cold, and he said to himself, "The whole top of my head is bald, but he has long curly hair."

So he put his hat on again.

"I had better let him put on my boots."

He made him sit down and put the felt boots on him.

After the cobbler had thus dressed him, he said: "There now, brother, just stir about, and you will get warmed up. All these things are in other hands than ours. Can you walk?"

The man stood up, looked affectionately at Semyon, but was unable to speak a word.

"Why don't you say something? We can't spend the winter here. We must get to shelter. Now, then, lean on my stick, if you don't feel strong enough. Bestir yourself!"

And the man started to move. And he walked easily, and did not lag behind. As they walked along the road Semyon said, "Where are you from, if I may ask?"

"I do not belong hereabouts."

"No; I know all the people of this region. How did you happen to come here and get to that chapel?"

"I cannot tell you."

"Some one must have treated you outrageously."

"No one has treated me outrageously. God has punished me."

"God does all things, but you must have been on the road bound for somewhere. Where do you want to go?"

"It makes no difference to me."

Semyon was surprised. The man did not look like a malefactor, and his speech was gentle, but he seemed reticent about himself.

And Semyon said to himself, "Such things as this do not happen every day." And he said to the man, "Well, come to my house, though you will find it very narrow quarters."

As Semyon approached the yard, the stranger did not lag behind, but walked abreast of him. The wind had arisen, and searched under Semyon's shirt, and as the effect of the wine had now passed away, he began to be chilled to the bone. He walked along, and began to snuffle, and he muffled his wife's jacket closer around him, and he said to himself, "That's the way you get a shuba! You go after a shuba, and you come home without your kaftan! yes, and you bring with you a naked man—besides, Matriona won't take kindly to it!"

And as soon as the thought of Matriona occurred to him, he began to feel downhearted.

But as soon as his eyes fell on the stranger, he remembered what a look he had given him behind the chapel, and his heart danced with joy.

III

Semyon's wife had finished her work early. She had chopped wood, brought water, fed the children, taken her own supper, and was now deliberating when it would be best to mix some bread, "today or tomorrow?"

A large crust was still left. She said to herself, "If Semyon gets something to eat in town, he won't care for much supper, and the bread will last till tomorrow."

Matriona contemplated the crust for some time, and said, "I am not going to mix any bread. There's just enough flour to make one more loaf. We shall get along till Friday."

Matriona put away the bread, and sat down at the table to sew a patch on her husband's shirt.

She sewed, and thought how her husband would be buying sheepskins for the shuba.

"I hope the fur-dealer will not cheat him. For he is as simple as he can be. He, himself, would not cheat anybody, but a baby could lead him by the nose. Eight rubles is no small sum. You can get a fine shuba with it. Perhaps not one tanned, but still a good one. How we suffered last winter without any shuba! Could not go to the river nor anywhere! And whenever he went outdoors, he put on all the clothes, and I hadn't anything to wear. He is late in getting home. He ought to be here by this time. Can my sweetheart have got drunk?"

Just as these thoughts were passing through her mind the door-steps creaked: some one was at the door. Matriona stuck in the needle, and went to the entry. There she saw that two men had come in,—Semyon, and with him a strange peasant, without a cap and in felt boots.

Matriona perceived immediately that her husband's breath smelt of liquor.

"Now," she said to herself, "he has gone and got drunk."

And when she saw that he had not his kaftan on, and wore only her jacket, and had nothing in his hands, and said nothing, but only simpered, Matriona's heart failed within her.

"He has drunk up the money, he has been on a spree with this miserable beggar; and, worse than all, he has gone and brought him home!"

Matriona let them pass by her into the cottage; then she herself went in; she saw that the stranger was young, and that he had on their kaftan. There was no shirt to be seen under the kaftan; and he wore no cap.

As soon as he went in, he paused, and did not move and did not raise his eyes.

And Matriona thought, "He is not a good man; his conscience troubles him."

Matriona scowled, went to the oven, and watched to see what they would do.

Semyon took off his cap and sat down on the bench good-naturedly.

"Well," said he, "Matriona, can't you get us something to eat?"

Matriona muttered something under her breath.

She did not offer to move, but as she stood by the oven she looked from one to the other and kept shaking her head.

Semyon saw that his wife was out of sorts and would not do anything, but he pretended not to notice it, and took the stranger by the arm.

"Sit down, brother," said he; "we'll have some supper."

The stranger sat down on the bench.

"Well," said Semyon, "haven't you cooked anything?"

Matriona's anger blazed out.

"I cooked," said she, "but not for you. You are a fine man! I see you have been drinking! You went to get a shuba, and you have come home without your kaftan.

And, then, you have brought home this naked vagabond with you. I haven't any supper for such drunkards as you are!"

"That'll do, Matriona; what is the use of letting your tongue run on so? If you had only asked first: 'What kind of a man . . .'"

"You just tell me what you have done with the money!"

Semyon went to his kaftan, took out the bill, and spread it out.

"Here's the money, but Trifonof did not pay me; he promised it tomorrow."

Matriona grew still more angry, "You didn't buy the new shuba, and you have given away your only kaftan to this naked vagabond whom you have brought home!"

She snatched the money from the table, and went off to hide it away, saying "I haven't any supper. I can't feed all your drunken beggars!"

"Hey there! Matriona, just hold your tongue! First you listen to what I have to say . . ."

"Much sense should I hear from a drunken fool! Good reason I had for not wanting to marry such a drunkard as you are. Mother gave me linen, and you have wasted it in drink; you went to get a shuba, and you spent it for drink."

Semyon was going to assure his wife that he had spent only twenty kopeks for drink; he was going to tell her where he had found the man; but Matriona would not give him a chance to speak a word; it was perfectly marvelous, but she managed to speak two words at once! Things that had taken place ten years before—she called them all up.

Matriona scolded and scolded; then she sprang at Semyon, and seized him by the sleeve.

"Give me back my jacket! It's the only one I have, and you took it from me and put it on yourself. Give it here, you miserable dog! bestir yourself, you villain!"

Semyon began to strip off the jacket. As he was pulling his arms out of the sleeves, his wife gave it a twitch and split the jacket up the seams. Matriona snatched the garment away, threw it over her head, and started for the door. She intended to go out, but she paused, and her heart was pulled in two directions,—she wanted to vent her spite, and she wanted to find what kind of a man the stranger was.

IV

Matriona paused, and said, "If he were a good man, then he would not have been naked; why, even now, he hasn't any shirt on; if he had been engaged in decent business, you would have told where you discovered such an elegant fellow!"

"Well, I was going to tell you. I was walking along, and there, behind the chapel, this man was sitting, stark naked, and half frozen to death. It is not summer, mind you, for a naked man! God brought me to him, else he would have perished. Now what could I do? Such things don't happen every day. I took and dressed him, and brought him home with me. Calm your anger. It's a sin, Matriona; we must all die."

Matriona was about to make a surly reply, but her eyes fell on the stranger, and she held her peace.

The stranger was sitting motionless on the edge of the bench, just as he had sat down. His hands were folded on his knees, his head was bent on his breast, his eyes were shut, and he kept frowning, as if something stifled him.

Matriona made no reply.

Semyon went on to say, "Matriona, can it be that God is not in you?"

Matriona heard his words, and glanced again at the stranger, and suddenly her anger vanished. She turned from the door, went to the corner where the oven was, and brought the supper.

She set a bowl on the table, poured out the kvas,[2] and put on the last of the crust. She gave them the knife and the spoons.

"Have some victuals," she said.

Semyon touched the stranger.

"Draw up, young man," said he.

Semyon cut the bread and crumbled it into the bowl, and

[2] Fermented drink made of rye meal or soaked bread-crumbs.

they began to eat their supper. And Matriona sat at the end of the table, leaned on her hand, and gazed at the stranger. And Matriona began to feel sorry for him, and she took a fancy to him.

And suddenly the stranger brightened up, ceased to frown, lifted his eyes to Matriona, and smiled.

After they had finished their supper, the woman cleared off the things, and began to question the stranger "Where are you from?"

"I do not belong hereabouts."

"How did you happen to get into this road?"

"I cannot tell you."

"Who maltreated you?"

"God punished me."

"And you were lying there stripped?"

"Yes; there I was lying all naked, freezing to death, when Semyon saw me, had compassion on me, took off his kaftan, put it on me, and bade me come home with him. And here you have fed me, given me something to eat and to drink, and have taken pity on me. May the Lord require you!"

Matriona got up, took from the window Semyon's old shirt which she had been patching, and gave it to the stranger; then she found a pair of drawers and gave them also to him.

"There now," said she, "I see that you have no shirt. Put these things on, and then lie down wherever you please, in the loft or on the oven."

The stranger took off the kaftan, put on the shirt, and went to bed in the loft. Matriona put out the light, took the kaftan, and lay down beside her husband.

Matriona covered herself up with the skirt of the kaftan, but she lay without sleeping; she could not get the thought of the stranger out of her mind.

When she remembered that he had eaten her last crust, and that there was no bread for the morrow, when she remembered that she had given him the shirt and the drawers, she felt disturbed; but then came the thought of how he had smiled at her, and her heart leaped within her.

Matriona lay a long time without falling asleep, and

when she heard that Semyon was also awake, she pulled up the kaftan, and said, "Semyon!"

"Ha?"

"You ate up the last of the bread, and I did not mix any more. I don't know how we shall get along tomorrow. Perhaps I might borrow some of neighbor Malanya."

"We shall get along; we shall have enough."

The wife lay without speaking. Then she said, "Well, he seems like a good man; but why doesn't he tell us about himself?"

"It must be because he can't."

"Siom!" [3]

"Ha?"

"We are always giving; why doesn't some one give to us?"

Semyon did not know what reply to make. He said, "You have talked enough!"

Then he turned over and went to sleep.

V

In the morning Semyon woke up.

His children were still asleep; his wife had gone to a neighbor's to get some bread. The stranger of the evening before, dressed in the old shirt and drawers, was sitting alone on the bench, looking up. And his face was brighter than it had been the evening before. And Semyon said, "Well, my dear, the belly asks for bread, and the naked body for clothes. You must earn your own living. What do you know how to do?"

"There is nothing that I know how to do."

Semyon was amazed, and he said, "If one has only the mind to, men can learn anything."

"Men work, and I will work."

"What is your name?"

"Mikhaïla."

"Well, Mikhaïla, if you aren't willing to tell about yourself, that is your affair; but you must earn your own living. If you will work as I shall show you, I will keep you."

[3] Diminutive of Semyon, or Simon.

"The Lord requite you! I am willing to learn; only show me what to do."

Semyon took a thread, drew it through his fingers, and showed him how to make a waxed end.

"It does not take much skill . . . look . . ."

Mikhaïla looked, and then he also twisted the thread between his fingers; he instantly imitated him, and finished the point.

Semyon showed him how to make the welt. This also Mikhaïla immediately understood. The shoemaker likewise showed him how to twist the bristle into the thread, and how to use the awl; and these things also Mikhaïla immediately learned to do.

Whatever part of the work Semyon showed him he imitated him in, and in two days he was able to work as if he had been all his life a cobbler. He worked without relaxation, he ate little, and when his work was done he would sit silent, looking up. He did not go on the street, he spoke no more than was absolutely necessary, he never jested, he never laughed.

The only time that he was seen to smile was on the first evening, when the woman got him his supper.

VI

Day after day, week after week, rolled by for a whole year.

Mikhaïla lived on in the same way, working for Semyon. And the fame of Semyon's apprentice went abroad; no one, it was said, could make such neat, strong boots as Semyon's apprentice, Mikhaïla. And from all around people came to Semyon to have boots made, and Semyon began to lay up money.

One winter's day, as Semyon and Mikhaïla were sitting at their work, a sleigh drawn by a troïka drove up to the cottage, with a jingling of bells.

They looked out of the window; the sleigh stopped in front of the cottage; a footman jumped down from the box and opened the door. A barin [4] in a fur coat got out of the

[4] The ordinary title of any landowner or noble.

sleigh, walked up to Semyon's cottage, and mounted the steps. Matriona hurried to throw the door wide open.

The barin bent his head and entered the cottage; when he drew himself up to his full height, his head almost touched the ceiling; he seemed to take up nearly all the room.

Semyon rose and bowed; he was surprised to see the barin. He had never before seen such a man.

Semyon himself was thin, the stranger was spare, and Matriona was like a dry chip; but this man seemed to be from a different world. His face was ruddy and full, his neck was like a bull's; it seemed as if he were made out of cast-iron.

The barin got his breath, took off his shuba, sat down on the bench, and said, "Which is the master shoemaker?"

Semyon stepped out, saying, "I, your honor."

The barin shouted to his footman, "Hey, Fedka,[5] bring me the leather."

The young fellow ran out and brought back a parcel. The barin took the parcel and laid it on the table.

"Open it," said he.

The footman opened it.

The barin touched the leather with his finger, and said to Semyon, "Now listen, shoemaker. Do you see this leather?"

"I see it, your honor," said he.

"Well, do you appreciate what kind of leather it is?"

Semyon felt of the leather, and said, "That's good leather."

"Indeed it's good! Fool that you are! you never in your life saw such before! German leather. It cost twenty rubles."

Semyon was startled. He said, "Where, indeed, could we have seen anything like it?"

"Well, that's all right. Can you make from this leather a pair of boots that will fit me?"

"I can, your honour."

The barin shouted at him, " 'Can' is a good word. Now just realize whom you are making those boots for, and out of what kind of leather. You must make a pair of boots, so

[5] Diminutive of Feodor, Theodore.

that when the year is gone they won't have got out of shape, or ripped. If you can, then take the job and cut the leather; but if you can't, then don't take it and don't cut the leather. I will tell you beforehand, if the boots rip or wear out of shape before the year is out, I will have you locked up; but if they don't rip or get out of shape before the end of the year, then I will give you ten rubles for your work."

Semyon was frightened, and was at a loss what to say. He glanced at Mikhaïla. He nudged him with his elbow, and whispered, "Had I better take it?"

Mikhaïla nodded his head, meaning, "You had better take the job."

Semyon took Mikhaïla's advice; he agreed to make a pair of boots that would not rip or wear out of shape before the year was over.

The barin shouted to his footman, ordered him to take the boot from his left foot; then he stretched out his leg, "Take the measure!"

Semyon cut off a piece of paper seventeen inches long, smoothed it out, knelt down, wiped his hands nicely on his apron, so as not to soil the barin's stockings, and began to take the measure.

Semyon took the measure of the sole, he took the measure of the instep; then he started to measure the calf of the leg, but the paper was not long enough. The leg at the calf was as thick as a beam.

"Look out; don't make it too tight around the calf!"

Semyon was going to cut another piece of paper. The barin sat there, rubbing his toes together in his stockings, and looking at the inmates of the cottage; he caught sight of Mikhaïla.

"Who is that yonder?" he asked; "does he belong to you?"

"He is a master workman. He will make the boots."

"Look here," says the barin to Mikhaïla, "remember that they are to be made so as to last a whole year."

Semyon also looked at Mikhaïla; he saw that Mikhaïla was paying no attention, but was standing in the corner, as if he saw some one there behind the barin. Mikhaïla gazed and gazed, and suddenly smiled, and his whole face lighted up.

"What a fool you are, showing your teeth that way! You had better see to it that the boots are ready in time."

And Mikhaïla replied, "They will be ready as soon as they are needed."

"Very well."

The barin drew on his boot, wrapped his shuba round him, and went to the door. But he forgot to stoop, and so struck his head against the lintel.

The barin stormed and rubbed his head; then he got into his sleigh and drove off. After the barin was gone Semyon said, "Well, he's as solid as a rock! You could not kill him with a mallet. His head almost broke the doorpost, but it did not seem to hurt him much."

And Matriona said, "How can they help getting fat, living as they do? Even death does not carry off such a nail as he is."

VII

And Semyon said to Mikhaïla, "Now, you see, we have taken this work, and we must do it as well as we can. The leather is expensive, and the barin gruff. We must not make any blunder. Now, your eye has become quicker, and your hand is more skilful, than mine; there's the measure. Cut out the leather, and I will be finishing up those vamps."

Mikhaïla did not fail to do as he was told; he took the barin's leather, stretched it out on the table, doubled it over, took the knife, and began to cut.

Matriona came and watched Mikhaïla as he cut, and she was amazed to see what he was doing. For she was used to cobbler's work, and she looked and saw that Mikhaïla was not cutting the leather for boots, but in rounded fashion.

Matriona wanted to speak, but she thought in her own mind, "Of course I can't be expected to understand how to make boots for gentlemen; Mikhaïla must understand it better than I do; I will not interfere."

After he had cut out the work, he took his waxed ends and began to sew, not as one does in making boots, with double threads, but with one thread, just as slippers are made.

Matriona wondered at this also, but still she did not like to interfere. And Mikhaïla kept on steadily with his work.

It came time for the nooning; Semyon got up, looked, and saw that Mikhaïla had been making slippers out of the barin's leather. Semyon groaned.

"How is this?" he asked himself. "Mikhaïla has lived with me a whole year, and never made a mistake, and now he has made such a blunder! The barin ordered thick-soled boots, and he has been making slippers without soles! He has ruined the leather. How can I make it right with the barin? We can't find such leather."

And he said to Mikhaïla, "What is this you have been doing? . . . My dear fellow, you have ruined me! You know the barin ordered boots, and what have you made?"

He was in the midst of his talk with Mikhaïla when a knock came at the rapper; some one was at the door. They looked out of the window, some one had come on horseback, and was fastening the horse. They opened the door. The same barin's footman came walking in.

"Good-day."

"Good-day to you; what is it?"

"My mistress sent me in regard to a pair of boots."

"What about the boots?"

"It is this. My barin does not need the boots; he has gone from this world."

"What is that you say?"

"He did not live to get home from your house; he died in the sleigh. When the sleigh reached home, we went to help him out, but there he had fallen over like a bag, and there he lay stone dead, and it took all our strength to lift him out of the sleigh. And his lady has sent me, saying: 'Tell the shoemaker of whom your barin just ordered boots from leather which he left with him—tell him that the boots are not needed, and that he is to make a pair of slippers for the corpse out of that leather just as quick as possible.' And I was to wait till they were made, and take them home with me. And so I have come."

Mikhaïla took the rest of the leather from the table and

rolled it up; he also took the slippers, which were all done, slapped them together, wiped them with his apron, and gave them to the young man. The young man took them.

"Good-by, friends! Good luck to you!"

VIII

Still another year, and then two more passed by, and Mikhaïla had now been living five years with Semyon. He lived in just the same way as before. He never went anywhere, he kept his own counsels, and in all that time he smiled only twice—once when Matriona gave him something to eat, and the other time when he smiled on the barin.

Semyon was more than contented with his workman, and he no longer asked him where he came from; his only fear was lest Mikhaïla should leave him.

One time they were all at home. The mother was putting the iron kettles on the oven, and the children were playing on the benches and looking out of the window. Semyon was pegging away at one window, and Mikhaïla at the other was putting lifts on a heel.

One of the boys ran along the bench toward Mikhaïla, leaned over his shoulder, and looked out of the window.

"Uncle Mikhaïla, just look! a merchant's wife is coming to our house with some little girls. And one of the little girls is a cripple."

The words were scarcely out of the boy's mouth before Mikhaïla threw down his work, leaned over toward the window, and looked out-of-doors. And Semyon was surprised. Never before had Mikhaïla cared to look out, but now his face seemed soldered to the window; he was looking at something very intently.

Semyon also looked out of the window: he saw a woman coming straight through his yard; she was neatly dressed; she had two little girls by the hand; they wore shubkas,[6] and kerchiefs over their heads. The little girls looked so much alike that it was hard to tell them apart, except that one of the little girls was lame in her foot; she limped as she walked.

[6] Little fur garments.

The woman came into the entry, felt about in the dark, lifted the latch, and opened the door. She let the two little girls go before her into the cottage, and then she followed.

"How do you do, friends?"

"Welcome! What can we do for you?"

The woman sat down by the table; the two little girls clung to her knee; they were bashful.

"These little girls need to have some goatskin shoes made for the spring."

"Well, it can be done. We don't generally make such small ones; but it's perfectly easy, either with welts or lined with linen. This here is Mikhaïla; he's my master workman."

Semyon glanced at Mikhaïla and saw that he had thrown down his work, and was sitting with his eyes fastened on the little girls.

And Semyon was amazed at Mikhaïla. To be sure the little girls were pretty; they had dark eyes, they were plump and rosy, and they wore handsome shubkas and kerchiefs; but still Semyon could not understand why he gazed so intently at them, as if they were friends of his.

Semyon was amazed, and he began to talk with the woman, and to make his bargain. After he had made his bargain, he began to take the measures. The woman lifted on her lap the little cripple, and said, "Take two measures from this one; make one little shoe from the twisted foot, and three from the well one. Their feet are alike; they are twins."

Semyon took his tape, and said in reference to the little cripple, "How did this happen to her? She is such a pretty little girl. Was she born so?"

"No; her mother crushed it."

Matriona joined the conversation; she was anxious to learn who the woman and children were, and so she said, "Then you aren't their mother?"

"No, I am not their mother; I am no relation to them, good wife, and they are no relation to me at all; I adopted them."

"If they are not your children, you take good care of them."

"Why shouldn't I take good care of them? I nursed them both at my own breast. I had a baby of my own, but God took him. I did not take such good care of him as I do of these."

"Whose children are they?"

IX

The woman became confidential, and began to tell them about it.

"Six years ago," said she, "these little ones were left orphans in one week; the father was buried on Tuesday, and the mother died on Friday. Three days these little ones remained without their father, and then their mother followed him. At that time I was living with my husband in the country: we were neighbors; we lived in adjoining yards. Their father was a peasant, and worked in the forest at wood-cutting. And they were felling a tree, and it caught him across the body. It hurt him all inside. As soon as they got him out, he gave his soul to God, and that same week his wife gave birth to twins—these are the little girls here. There they were, poor and alone, no one to take care of them, either grandmother or sister.

"She must have died soon after the children were born. For when I went in the morning to look after my neighbor, as soon as I entered the cottage, I found the poor thing dead and cold. And when she died she must have rolled over on this little girl. . . . That's the way she crushed it, and spoiled this foot.

"The people got together, they washed and laid out the body, they had a coffin made, and buried her. The people were always kind. But the two little ones were left alone. What was to be done with them? Now I was the only one of the women who had a baby. For eight weeks I had been nursing my firstborn, a boy. So I took them for the time being. The peasants got together; they planned and planned what to do with them, and they said to me, 'Marya, you just keep the little girls for a while, and give us a chance to decide.'

"So I nursed the well one for a while, but did not think

it worth while to nurse the deformed one. I did not expect that she was going to live. And, then, I thought to myself, why should the little angel's soul pass away? and I felt sorry for it. I tried to nurse her, and so I had my own and these two besides; yes, I had three children at the breast. But I was young and strong, and I had good food! And God gave me so much milk in my breasts that I had enough and to spare. I used to nurse two at once and let the third one wait. When one had finished, I would take up the third. And so God let me nurse all three; but when my boy was in his third year, I lost him. And God never gave me any more children. But we began to be in comfortable circumstances. And now we are living with the trader at the mill. We get good wages and live well. But we have no children of our own. And how lonely it would be, if it were not for these two little girls! How could I help loving them? They are to me like the wax in the candle!"

And the woman pressed the little lame girl to her with one arm, and with the other hand she tried to wipe the tears from her cheeks.

And Matriona sighed, and said, "The old saw isn't far wrong, 'Men can live without father and mother, but without God one cannot live.'"

While they were thus talking together, suddenly a flash of lightning seemed to irradiate from that corner of the cottage where Mikhaïla was sitting. All looked at him; and, behold! Mikhaïla was sitting there with his hands folded in his lap, and looking up and smiling.

x

The woman went away with the children, and Mikhaïla arose from the bench and laid down his work; he took off his apron, made a low bow to the shoemaker and his wife, and said, "Farewell, friends; God has forgiven me. Do you also forgive me?"

And Semyon and Matriona perceived that it was from Mikhaïla that the light had flashed. And Semyon arose, bowed low before Mikhaïla, and said to him, "I see, Mikhaïla, that you are not a mere man, and I have no right to detain you nor to ask questions of you. But tell me one thing: when I had found you and brought you home, you were sad; but when my wife gave you something to eat, you smiled on her, and after that you became more cheerful. And then when the barin ordered the boots, why did you smile a second time, and after that become still more cheerful; and now when this woman brought these two little girls, why did you smile for the third time and become perfectly radiant? Tell me, Mikhaïla, why was it that such a light streamed from you, and why you smiled three times?"

And Mikhaïla said, "The light blazed from me because I had been punished, but now God has forgiven me. And I smiled the three times because it was required of me to learn three of God's truths, and I have now learned the three truths of God. One truth I learned when your wife had pity on me, and so I smiled; the second truth I learned when the rich man ordered the boots, and I smiled for the second time; and now that I have seen the little girls, I have learned the third and last truth, and I smiled for the third time."

And Semyon said, "Tell me, Mikhaïla, why God punished you, and what were the truths of God, that I, too, may know them."

And Mikhaïla said, "God punished me because I disobeyed Him. I was an angel in heaven, and I was disobedient to God. I was an angel in heaven, and the Lord sent me to bring back the soul of a certain woman. I flew down to earth and I saw the woman lying alone—she was sick—she had just borne twins, two little girls. The little ones were sprawling about near their mother, but their mother was unable to lift them to her breast. The mother saw me; she perceived that God had sent me after her soul; she burst into tears, and said, 'Angel of God, I have just buried my husband; a tree fell on him in the forest and killed him. I have no sister, nor aunt, nor mother to take care of my little ones; do not carry off my soul; let me bring up my children myself, and nurse them and put them on their feet. It is impossible for children to live without father or mother.'

"And I heeded what the mother said; I put one child to her breast, and laid the other in its mother's arms, and I returned to the Lord in heaven. I flew back to the Lord, and I said, 'I cannot take the mother's soul. The father has been killed by a tree, the mother has given birth to twins, and begs me not to take her soul; she says, ' "Let me bring up my little ones; let me nurse them and put them on their feet. It is impossible for children to live without father and mother." I did not take the mother's soul.'

"And the Lord said, 'Go and take the mother's soul, and thou shalt learn three lessons: Thou shalt learn *what is in men*, and *what is not given unto men*, and *what men live by*. When thou shalt have learned these three lessons, then return to heaven.'

"And I flew down to earth and took the mother's soul. The little ones fell from her bosom. The dead body rolled over on the bed, and fell on one of the little girls and crushed her foot. I rose above the village and was going to give the soul to God, when a wind seized me, my wings ceased to move and fell off, and the soul arose alone to God, and I fell back to earth."

XI

And Semyon and Matriona now knew whom they had clothed and fed, and who it was that had been living with them, and they burst into tears of dismay and joy; and the angel said, "I was there in the field naked and alone. Hitherto I had never known what human poverty was; I had known neither cold nor hunger, and now I was a man. I was famished, I was freezing, and I knew not what to do. And I saw across the field a chapel made for God's service. I went to God's chapel, thinking to get shelter in it. But the chapel was locked, and I could not enter. And I crouched down behind the chapel, so as to get shelter from the wind. Evening came; I was hungry and chilled, and ached all over. Suddenly I hear a man walking along the road, with a pair of boots in his hand, and talking to himself. I now saw for the first time since I had become a man the face of a mortal man, and it filled me with dismay, and

I tried to hide from him. And I heard this man asking himself how he should protect himself from cold during the winter, and how get food for his wife and children. And I thought, 'I am perishing with cold and hunger, and here is a man whose sole thought is to get a shuba for himself and his wife and to furnish bread for their sustenance. It is impossible for him to help me.'

"The man saw me and scowled; he seemed even more terrible than before; then he passed on. And I was in despair. Suddenly I heard the man coming back. I looked up, and did not recognize that it was the same man as before; then there was death in his face, but now it had suddenly become alive, and I saw that God was in his face. He came to me, put clothes on me, and took me home with him.

"When I reached his house, a woman came out to meet us, and she began to scold. The woman was even more terrible to me than the man; a dead soul seemed to proceed forth from her mouth, and I was suffocated by the stench of death. She wanted to drive me out into the cold, and I knew that she would die if she drove me out. And suddenly her husband reminded her of God. And instantly a change came over the woman. And when she had prepared something for me to eat, and looked kindly on me, I looked at her, and there was no longer anything like death about her; she was now alive, and in her also I recognized God.

"And I remembered God's first lesson: *'Thou shalt learn what is in men.'*

"And I perceived that Love was in men. And I was glad because God had begun to fulfil His promise to me, and I smiled for the first time. But I was not yet ready to know the whole. I could not understand what was not given to men, and what men lived by.

"I began to live in your house, and after I had lived with you a year the man came to order the boots which should be strong enough to last him a year without ripping or wearing out of shape. And I looked at him, and suddenly perceived behind his back my comrade, the Angel of Death. No one besides myself saw this angel; but I knew him, and I knew that before the sun should go down he would take the rich man's soul. And I said to myself: 'This man is lay-ing his plans to live another year, and he knows not that ere evening comes he will be dead.'

"And I realized suddenly the second saying of God: *'Thou shalt know what is not given unto men.'*

"And now I knew what was in men. And now I knew also what was not given unto men. It is not given unto men to know what is needed for their bodies. And I smiled for the second time. I was glad because I saw my comrade, the angel, and because God had revealed unto me the second truth.

"But I could not yet understand all. I could not understand what men live by, and so I lived on, and waited until God should reveal to me the third truth also. And now in the sixth year the little twin girls have come with the woman, and I recognized the little ones, and I remembered how they had been left. And after I had recognized them, I thought, 'The mother besought me in behalf of her children, because she thought that it would be impossible for children to live without father and mother, but another woman, a stranger, has nursed them and brought them up.'

"And when the woman caressed the children that were not her own, and wept over them, then I saw in her the living God, and knew *what people live by.* And I knew that God had revealed to me the last truth, and had pardoned me, and I smiled for the third time."

XII

And the angel's body became manifest, and he was clad with light so bright that the eyes could not endure to look on him, and he spoke in clearer accents, as if the voice proceeded not from him, but came from heaven.

And the angel said, "I have learned that every man lives, not through care of himself, but by love.

"It was not given to the mother to know what her children needed to keep them alive. It was not given the rich man to know what he himself needed, and it is not given to any man to know whether he will need boots for daily living, or slippers for his burial.

"When I became a man, I was kept alive, not by what

thought I took for myself, but because a stranger and his wife had love in their hearts, and pitied and loved me. The orphans were kept alive, not because other people deliberated about what was to be done with them, but because a strange woman had love for them in her heart, and pitied them and loved them. And all men are kept alive, not by their own forethought, but because there is LOVE IN MEN.

"I knew before that God gave life to men, and desired them to live; but now I know something above and beyond that.

"I have learned that God does not wish men to live each for himself, and therefore He has not revealed to them what they each need for themselves, but He wishes them to live in union, and therefore He has revealed to them what is necessary for each and for all together.

"I have now learned that it is only in appearance that they are kept alive through care for themselves, but that in reality they are kept alive through love. *He who dwelleth in love, dwelleth in God, and God in him, for God is Love.*"

And the angel sang a hymn of praise to God, and the cottage shook with the sound of his voice.

And the ceiling parted, and a column of fire reached from earth to heaven. And Semyon and his wife and children fell prostrate on the ground. And pinions appeared on the angel's shoulders, and he soared away to heaven.

And when Semyon opened his eyes, the cottage was the same as it had ever been, and there was no one in it save himself and his family.

Leo Tolstoy

KHOLSTOMER
The Story of a Horse

Ever higher and higher rose the sky, wider spread the dawn,
whiter grew the pallid silver of the dew, more lifeless the
sickle of the moon, more vocal the forest. . . .

People were beginning to arise; and at the stables belonging to the barin were heard with increasing frequency the
whinnying of the horses, the stamping of hoofs on the
straw, and also the angry, shrill neighing of the animals
collecting together, and even disputing with one another
over something.

"We-e-ll! you've got time enough; half-starved, ain't
you?" said the old drover, quickly opening the creaking
gates. "Where you going?" he shouted, waving his hands
at a mare which tried to run through the gate.

Nester, the drover, was dressed in a *kazakin,* or Cossack
coat, with a decorated leather belt around his waist; his
knout was slung over his shoulder, and a handkerchief,
containing some bread, was tied into his belt. In his arms
he carried a saddle and halter.

The horses were not in the least startled, nor did they
show any resentment, at the drover's sarcastic tone; they
made believe that it was all the same to them, and leisurely
moved away from the gate—all except one old dark bay
mare, with a long flowing mane, who laid back her ears
and quickly turned around. At this opportunity a young
mare, who was standing behind, and had nothing at all to

do with this, whinnied, and began to kick at the first horse she fell in with.

"No!" shouted the drover, still more loudly and fiercely, and turned to the corner of the yard.

Out of all the horses—there must have been nearly a hundred—that were moving off toward their breakfast, none manifested so little impatience as a piebald gelding, which stood alone in one corner under the shed, and gazed with half-shut eyes, and licked the oak stanchion of the shed.

It is hard to say what enjoyment the piebald gelding got from this, but his expression while doing so was solemn and thoughtful.

"Wake up!" again cried the drover, in the same tone, turning to him; and, going up to him, he laid the saddle and shiny saddle-cloth on a pile of manure near him.

The piebald gelding ceased licking the stanchion, and looked long at Nester without moving. He did not manifest any sign of mirth or anger or sullenness, but only drew in his whole belly and sighed heavily, heavily, and then turned away. The drover took him by the neck, and gave him his breakfast.

"What are you sighing for?" asked Nester.

The horse switched his tail as if to say, "Well, it's all right, Nester."

Nester put on the saddle-cloth and saddle, whereupon the horse pricked up his ears, expressing as plainly as could be his disgust; but he received nothing but execrations for this "rot," and then the saddle-girth was pulled tight.

At this the gelding tried to swell out; but his mouth was thrust open, and a knee was pressed into his side, so that he was forced to let out his breath. Notwithstanding this, when they got the bit between his teeth, he once more pricked back his ears, and even looked round. Though he knew that this was of no avail, yet he seemed to reckon it essential to express his displeasure, and that he always would show it. When he was saddled, he pawed with his swollen right leg, and began to champ the bit—here also for some special reason, because it was time for him to know that there could be no taste in bits.

Nester mounted the gelding by the short stirrups, un-
wound his knout, freed his Cossack coat from under his
knee, settled down in the saddle in the position peculiar
to coachmen, hunters, and drovers, and twitched on the
reins.

The gelding lifted his head, showing a disposition to go
where he should be directed, but he stirred not from the
spot. He knew that before he went there would be much
shouting on the part of him who sat on his back, and
many orders to be given to Vaska, the other drover, and to
the horses. In fact, Nester began to shout, "Vaska! ha,
Vaska! have you let out any of the mares—hey? Where
are you, you old devil? No-o! Are you asleep? Open the
gate. Let the mares go first," and so on.

The gates creaked. Vaska, morose, and still full of sleep,
holding a horse by the bridle, stood at the gate-post and
let the horses out. The horses, one after the other, gingerly
stepping over the straw and snuffing it, began to pass
out—the young fillies, the yearlings, the little colts; while
the mares, heavy with young, stepped along heedfully, one
at a time, lifting their bellies. The young fillies sometimes
crowded in two at once, three at once, throwing their heads
across one another's backs, and hitting their hoofs against
the gates, each time receiving a volley of abuse from the
drovers. The colts sometimes kicked the mares they did
not know, and whinnied loudly in answer to the short
neighing of their mothers.

A young filly, full of wantonness, as soon as she got
outside the gate, tossed her head and shook it, began to
back, and whinnied, but nevertheless did not venture to
dash ahead of the old gray, grain-bestrewed Zhulduiba,
who, with a gentle but solid step, swinging her belly from
side to side, marched along, as always the dignified leader
of the other horses.

After a few moments the yard but now so lively was
left in melancholy loneliness; the posts stood out in sadness under the empty sheds, and only the sodden straw,
soiled with dung, was to be seen.

Familiar as this picture of emptiness was to the piebald
gelding, it seemed to have a melancholy effect on him.

Slowly, as if making a bow, he lowered and lifted his head, sighed as deeply as the tightly drawn girth permitted, and, dragging his somewhat bent and decrepit legs, he started off after the herd, carrying the old Nester on his bony back.

"I know now. As soon as we get out on the road, he will go to work to make a light, and smoke his wooden pipe with its copper mounting and chain," thought the gelding. "I am glad of this, because it is early in the morning and the dew is on the grass, and this odor is agreeable to me, and brings up many pleasant recollections. I am sorry only that when the old man has his pipe in his mouth he always becomes excited, gets to imagining things, and sits on one side, infallibly on one side, and on that side it hurts. However, God be with him. It's no new thing for me to suffer for the sake of others. I have even come to find some equine satisfaction in this. Let him play that he's cock of the walk, poor fellow; but it's for his own pleasure that he looks so big, since no one sees him at all. Let him ride sidewise," said the horse to himself; and, stepping gingerly on his crooked legs, he walked along the middle of the road.

II

After driving the herd down to the river, near which the horses were to graze, Nester dismounted and took off the saddle. Meantime the herd began slowly to scatter over the as yet untrodden field, covered with dew and with vapor rising alike from the damp meadow and the river that encircled it.

Taking off the bridle from the piebald gelding, Nester scratched him under his neck; and the horse in reply expressed his happiness and satisfaction by shutting his eyes.

"The old dog likes it," said Nester.

The gelding really did not like this scratching very much, and only out of delicacy pretended that it was agreeable to him. He nodded his head as a sign of assent. But suddenly, unexpectedly, and without any reason, Nester, imagining perhaps that too great familiarity might give the gelding false ideas about what he meant—Nester, without any warning, pushed away his head, and swinging the bridle, struck the horse very severely with the buckle on his lean leg, and, without saying anything, went up the hillock to a stump, near which he sat down as if nothing had happened.

Though this proceeding incensed the gelding, he showed no sign of it; and, leisurely switching his thin tail, and, sniffing at something, and merely for recreation cropping at the grass, he wandered down toward the river.

Not paying any heed to the antics played around him by the young fillies, the colts, and the yearlings, and knowing that the health of every one, and especially at his age, was subserved by getting a good drink of water on an empty stomach, and not eating till afterward, he turned his steps to where the bank was less steep and slippery; and, wetting his hoofs and gambrels, he thrust his snout into the river, and began to suck the water through his lips drawn back, to puff with his distending sides, and out of pure satisfaction to switch his thin, piebald tail with its leathery stump.

A chestnut filly, full of mischief, always nagging the old horse, and causing him manifold unpleasantnesses, came down to the water as if for her own necessities, but really merely for the sake of roiling the water in front of his nose.

But the piebald gelding had already drunk enough, and apparently giving no thought to the impudent mare, calmly put one miry leg before the other, shook his head, and, turning aside from the wanton youngster, began to eat. Dragging his legs in a peculiar manner, and not tramping down the abundant grass, the horse grazed for nearly three hours, scarcely stirring from the spot. Having eaten so much that his belly hung down like a bag from his thin, sharp ribs, he stood solidly on his four weak legs, so that as little strain as possible might come on any one of them— at least on the right fore leg, which was weaker than all —and went to sleep.

There is an honorable old age, there is an odious old age, there is a pitiable old age; there is also an old age that is both honorable and odious. The old age which the piebald gelding had reached was of this latter sort.

The old horse was of a great size—more than nineteen hands high. His color was white, spotted with black; at least, it used to be so, but now the black spots had changed to a dirty brown. There were three of these spots: one on the head including an irregular-shaped star which ran down the side of the nose and half of the neck; the long mane, tangled with burrs, was partly white and partly brownish. The second spotted place ran along the right side, and covered half the belly; the third was on the flank, including the upper part of the tail and half of the loins; the rest of the tail was whitish, variegated.

The big bony head, with deep hollows under the eyes, and with pendent black lip, somewhat lacerated, hung heavily and low on the neck, which bent from its leanness, and seemed to be made of wood. From behind the pendent lip could be seen the dark-red tongue protruding on one side, and the yellow, worn tusks of his lower teeth. His ears, one of which was slit, fell over sidewise, and only occasionally he twitched them lazily to scare away the sticky flies. One long tuft still remaining of the forelock hung behind the ears; the broad forehead was hollowed and rough; the skin hung loose on the big cheekbones. On the neck and head the veins stood out in knots, trembling and twitching whenever a fly touched them. The expression of his face was sternly patient, deeply thoughtful, and expressive of pain.

His fore legs were crooked at the knees. On both hoofs were swellings; and on the one which was half covered by the marking, there was near the knee at the back a sore boil. The hind legs were in better condition, but there had been severe bruises long before on the haunches, and the hair did not grow on those places. His legs seemed disproportionately long, because his body was so emaciated. His ribs, though also thick, were so exposed and drawn that the hide seemed dried in the hollows between them.

The back and withers were variated with old scars, and behind was still a freshly galled and purulent slough. The black stump of the tail, where the vertebræ could be

counted, stood out long and almost bare. On the brown
flank near the tail, where it was overgrown with white hairs,
was a scar as big as one's hand, that must have been from
a bite. Another cicatrice was to be seen on the front shoulder. The houghs of the hind legs and the tail were foul
from a recent bowel disorder. The hair all over the body,
though short, stood out straight.

But in spite of the loathsome old age to which this horse
had come, any one looking at him would have involuntarily
thought, and an expert would have said immediately, that
he must have been in his day a remarkably fine horse. The
expert would have said also that there was only one breed
in Russia that could give such broad bones, such huge
joints, such hoofs, such slender leg-bones, such an arched
neck, and, most of all, such a skull—eyes large, black,
and brilliant, and such a thoroughbred network of nerves
over his head and neck, and such delicate skin and hair.

In reality there was something noble in the form of this
horse, and in the terrible union in him of the repulsive signs
of decrepitude, the increased variegatedness of his hide,
and his actions, and the expression of self-dependence, and
the calm consciousness of beauty and strength.

Like a living ruin he stood in the middle of the dewy
field, alone; while not far away from him were heard the
galloping, the neighing, the lively whinnying, the snorting,
of the scattered herd.

III

The sun was now risen above the forest and shone brightly
on the grass and the winding river. The dew dried away
and fell off in drops. Like smoke the last of the morning
mist rolled up. Little curly clouds made their appearance,
but as yet there was no wind. On the other side of the
gleaming river stood the verdant rye, bending on its stalks,
and the air was fragrant with fresh verdure and flowers.
The cuckoo cooed from the forest with echoing voice; and
Nester, lying flat on his back, was reckoning up how many
years of life lay before him. The larks arose from the rye
and the meadow. The belated hare, overtaken by the

horses, went leaping across the field, and when it reached the copse it sat up and cocked its ears to listen.

Vaska went to sleep, burying his head in the grass; the mares, making wide circuits around him, scattered over the field below. The older ones, neighing, traced a shining track across the dewy grass, and kept trying to find some place where they might be undisturbed. They no longer grazed, but only nibbled on the succulent grass-blades. The whole herd was imperceptibly moving in one direction.

And again the old Zhulduiba, stately stepping before the others, showed that it was possible to keep going farther. The young Mushka, who had cast her first foal, kept hinnying, and, lifting her tail, was scolding her violet-colored colt. The young Atlasnaya, with smooth and shining skin, dropping her head so that her black and silken forelock hid her forehead and eyes, was playing with the grass, nipping it and tossing it, and stamping her leg, with its furry fetlock. One of the older little colts—he must have been imagining some kind of game—lifting, for the twenty-sixth time, his rather short and tangled tail, like a plume, gamboled around his dam, who calmly picked at the herbage, having evidently already summed up her son's character, and only occasionally stopped to look askance at him out of her big black eye.

One of these same young colts—black as a coal, with a large head with a marvelous top-knot rising above his ears, and his tail still inclining to the side on which he had lain in his mother's belly—pricked up his ears, and opened his stupid eyes, as he stood motionless in his place, either out of jealousy or indignation, looking steadily at the colt jumping and dancing, and seemed not to understand at all why he did it.

Some suckled, butting with their noses; others, for some unknown reason, notwithstanding their mothers' invitation, would move along in a short, awkward trot, in a diametrically opposite direction, as if seeking something, and then, no one knows why, would stop short and hinny in a desperately penetrating voice. Some were lying on their sides in a row; some were taking lessons in grazing; some trying to scratch themselves with their hind legs behind the ear.

Two mares, still with young, went off by themselves, and, slowly moving their legs, continued to graze. Evidently their condition was respected by the others, and none of the young colts ventured to go near or disturb them. If any saucy young steed took it into his head to approach too near to them, then merely a motion of an ear or tail would be sufficient to show him all the impropriety of his behavior.

The yearlings and the young fillies pretend to be full-grown and dignified, and rarely indulge in pranks, or join their gay companions. They ceremoniously nibble at the blades of grass, bending their swanlike, short-shorn necks, and, as if they also were blessed with tails, switch their little brushes. Just like the big horses, some of them lie down, roll over, and scratch one another's backs.

The jolliest band consists of the two-year-old and the three-year-old mares who have never foaled. They almost all wander off by themselves, and make a specially jolly virgin throng. Among them is heard a great tramping and stamping, hinnying and whinnying. They gather together, lay their heads over one another's shoulders, snuff the air, leap; and sometimes, lifting the tail like an oriflamme, proudly and coquettishly, in a half-trot, half-gallop, cara-cole in front of their companions.

Conspicuous for beauty and sprightly dashing ways, among all this young throng, was the wanton bay mare. Whatever she set on foot the others also did; wherever she went, there in her track followed also the whole throng of beauties.

The wanton was in a specially playful frame of mind this morning. The spirit of mischief was in her, just as it sometimes comes on men. Even at the riverside, playing her pranks on the old gelding, she had galloped along in the water, pretending that something had scared her, snorting, and then dashed off at full speed across the field; so that Vaska was constrained to gallop after her, and after the others who were at her heels. Then, after grazing a little while, she began to roll, then to tease the old mares, by dashing in front of them. Then she separated a suckling colt from its dam, and began to chase after it, pretending that she wanted to bite it. The mother was frightened, and ceased to graze; the little colt squealed in piteous tones. But the wanton young mare did not touch it, but only scared it, and made a spectacle for her comrades, who looked with sympathy on her antics.

Then she set out to turn the head of the roan horse which a muzhik, far away on the other side of the river, was driving with a *sokha,* or wooden plow, in the rye-field. She stood proudly, somewhat on one side, lifting her head high, shook herself, and neighed in a sweet, significant, and alluring voice. And frolic, gayety, and sentiment, and a touch of melancholy, were expressed in the sound of her neighing. In it were also desire and the promise of love and the melancholy that is born of love.

'Twas the time when the rail-bird, running from place to place among the thick reeds, passionately calls his mate; when also the cuckoo and the quail sing of love; and the flowers send to one another, on the breeze, their aromatic dust.

"And I am young and beautiful and strong," said the jolly wanton's neighing, "and till now it has not been given to me to experience the sweetness of this feeling, never yet has it been given me to feel it; and no lover, no not one, has yet come to woo me."

And the significant neighing rang with youthful melancholy over lowland and field, and it came to the ears of the roan horse far away. He pricked up his ears, and stopped. The muzhik kicked him with his wooden shoe; but the roan was bewitched by the silver sound of the distant neighing, and whinnied in reply. The muzhik grew angry, twitched him with the reins, and again kicked him in the belly with his bast shoe, so that he did not have a chance to complete all that he had to say in his neighing, but was forced to go on his way. And the roan horse felt a sweet sadness in his heart; and the sounds from the far-off rye-field, of that unfinished and passionate neigh, and the angry voice of the muzhik, long echoed in the ears of the herd.

If through one sound of her voice the roan horse could become so captivated as to forget his duty, what would

have become of him if he had had full view of the beautiful wanton, as she stood pricking up her ears, inflating
her nostrils, breathing in the air, and filled with longing,
while her young and beauteous body trembled as she called
to him?

But the wanton did not long ponder over her novel
sensations. When the voice of the roan was still, she whinnied scornfully, and, sinking her head, began to paw the
ground; and then she trotted off to wake up and tease the
piebald gelding. The piebald gelding was a long-suffering
butt for the amusement of this happy young wanton. She
made him suffer more than men did. But in neither case
did he give way to wrath. He was useful to men, but why
should these young horses torment him?

IV

He was old, they were young; he was lean, they were fat;
he was sad, they were happy. So he was thoroughly strange,
alien, an absolutely different creature; and it was impossible
for them to have compassion on him. Horses have pity
only on themselves, and only occasionally on those in whose
skin they may easily imagine themselves. But, indeed, was
not the piebald gelding himself to blame, in that he was
old and gaunt and ugly? . . .

One would think that he was not to blame. But in equine
ethics he was, and only those were right who were strong,
young, and happy; those who had all life before them;
those whose every muscle was tense with superfluous energy, and who curled their tails up into the air.

Maybe the piebald gelding himself understood this, and
in tranquil moments was agreed that he was to blame
because he had lived out all his life, that he must pay for
his life; but he was after all only a horse, and he could
not restrain himself often from feeling hurt, melancholy,
and discontented, when he looked on all these young horses
who tormented him for the very thing to which they
would be subjected when they came to the end of their
lives.

The reason for the heartlessness of these horses was a

peculiarly aristocratic feeling. Every one of them was related, either on the side of father or mother, to the celebrated Smetanka; but it was not known from what stock the piebald gelding sprang. The gelding was a chance comer, bought at the market three years before for eighty paper rubles.

The young chestnut mare, as if accidentally wandering about, came up to the piebald gelding's very nose, and brushed against him. He knew beforehand what it meant, and did not open his eyes, but laid back his ears and showed his teeth. The mare wheeled around, and made believe that she was going to let fly at him with her heels. He opened his eyes, and wandered off to another part. He had no desire as yet to go to sleep, and began to eat.

Again the wanton young mare, accompanied by her confederates, went to the gelding. A two-year-old mare with a star on her forehead, very silly, always in mischief, and always ready to imitate the chestnut mare, trotted along with her, and, as imitators always do, began to play the same trick that the instigator had done.

The brown mare would march along at an ordinary gait, apparently bent on her own affairs, and would pass by the gelding's very nose, not looking at him, so that he really did not know whether to be angry or not; and this was really ridiculous.

This was what she did now; but the starred mare, following in her steps, and feeling very gay, hit the gelding on the chest. He showed his teeth once more, whinnied, and, with a quickness of motion unexpected on his part, sprang at the mare, and bit her on the flank. The young mare with the star flew out with her hind legs, and kicked the old horse heavily on his thin bare ribs. The old horse uttered a hoarse noise, and was about to make another lunge, but thought better of it, and, sighing deeply, turned away.

It must have been that all the young horses of the drove regarded as a personal insult the boldness which the piebald gelding permitted himself to show toward the starred mare; for all the rest of the day they gave him no chance to graze, and left him not a moment of peace, so that the drover several times rebuked them, and could not comprehend what they were doing.

The gelding was so abused that he himself walked up to Nester when it was time for the old man to drive back the drove, and he showed greater happiness and content than usual when Nester saddled him and mounted him.

God knows what the old gelding's thoughts were as he bore on his back the old man Nester. Did he think with bitterness of these importunate and merciless youngsters? or, with a scornful and silent pride peculiar to old age, did he pardon his persecutors? At all events, he did not make manifest any of his thoughts till he reached home.

That evening some cronies had come to see Nester; and, as the horses were driven by the cottages of the domestics, he noticed a horse and telyega standing at his doorstep. After he had driven in the horses, he was in such haste that he did not take the saddle off; he left the gelding in the yard, and shouted to Vaska to unsaddle the animal, then shut the gate, and hurried to his friends.

Perhaps, owing to the affront put on the starred mare, the descendant of Smetanka, by that "low trash" bought for a horse, and not knowing father or mother, and therefore offending the aristocratic sentiment of the whole community; or because the gelding with the high saddle without a rider presented a strangely fantastic spectacle for the horses—at all events, that night something extraordinary took place in the paddock. All the horses, young and old, showing their teeth, tagged after the gelding, and drove him from one part of the yard to the other; the trampling of their hoofs echoed around him as he sighed and drew in his thin sides.

The gelding could not longer endure this, could not longer avoid their kicks. He halted in the middle of the paddock; his face expressed the repulsive, weak anger of helpless old age, and despair besides. He laid back his ears, and suddenly something happened that caused all the horses suddenly to become quiet. A very old mare, Viazopurikha, came up and sniffed the gelding, and sighed. The gelding also sighed. . . .

In the middle of the paddock, flooded with the moonlight, stood the tall, gaunt figure of the gelding, still wearing the high saddle with its prominent pommel. The horses, motionless and in deep silence, stood around him, as if they were learning something new and extraordinary from him. And, indeed, something new and extraordinary they learned from him.

This is what they learned from him. . . .

FIRST NIGHT

Yes, I was sired by Liubezni I. Baba was my dam. According to the geneology my name is Muzhik I. Muzhik I., I am according to my pedigree; but generally I am known as Kholstomer, on account of a long and glorious gallop, the like of which never took place in Russia. In lineage no horse in the world stands higher than I, for good blood. I would never have told you this. Why should I? You would never have known me, for not even Viazopurikha knew me, though she and I used to be together at Khrenovo, and it is only just now that she recognized me. You would not have believed me had it not been for Viazopurikha's witness, and I should never have told you this. I do not need the pity of my kind. But you insisted upon it. Well, I am that Kholstomer whom the amateurs are seeking for and cannot find, that Kholstomer whom the count himself named, and whom he let go from his stud because I outran his favorite "Lebedi." . . .

When I was born I did not know what they meant when they called me a piebald: I thought that I was a horse. The first remark made about my hide, I remember, deeply surprised me and my dam.

I must have been foaled in the night. In the morning, licked clean by my dam's tongue, I stood on my legs. I remember I kept wanting something, and that everything seemed to me perfectly wonderful, and, at the same time, perfectly simple. Our stalls were in a long, warm corridor, with latticed gates, through which everything could be seen.

My dam tempted me to suckle; but I was so innocent as yet that I bunted her with my nose, now under her fore legs, now under her udder. Suddenly my dam gazed at the latticed gate, and, throwing her leg over me, stepped to one side. The groom on duty was looking in at us through the lattice.

"See, Baba has foaled!" he exclaimed, and began to draw the bolt. He came in over the straw bed, and took me up in his arms. "Come and look, Taras!" he cried; "see what a piebald colt, a perfect magpie!"

I tore myself away from him, and fell on my knees.

"See, a perfect little devil!" he said.

My dam became disquieted; but she did not take my part, and merely drew a long, long breath, and stepped to one side. The grooms came, and began to look at me. One ran to tell the equerry.

All laughed as they looked at my spotting, and gave me various odd names. I did not understand these names, nor did my dam either. Up to that time in all my family there had never been a single piebald known. We had no idea that there was anything disgraceful in it. And then all extolled my structure and strength.

"See what a lively one!" said the hostler. "You can't hold him."

In a little while came the equerry, and began to marvel at my coloring. He also seemed disgusted.

"What a nasty beast!" he cried. "The general will not keep him in the stud. Ekh! Baba, you have caused me much trouble," he said, addressing my dam. "You ought to have foaled a colt with a star, but this is completely piebald."

My dam made no reply, and, as always in such circumstances, merely sighed again.

"What kind of a devil was his sire? A regular muzhik!" he went on to say. "It is impossible to keep him in the stud; it's a shame! But we'll see, we'll see," said he; and all said the same as they looked at me.

After a few days the general himself came. He took a look at me, and again all seemed horror-struck, and scolded me and my mother also on account of my hide. "But we'll see, we'll see," said every one, as soon as they caught sight of me.

Until spring we young colts lived in separate stalls with our dams; only occasionally, when the snow on the roof of the sheds began to melt in the sun, they would let us out into the wide yard, spread with fresh straw. There for the first time I became acquainted with all my kin, near and remote. There I saw how from different doors issued all the famous mares of that time with their colts. There was the old Holland mare, Mushka, sired by Smetanka, Krasnukha, the saddle-horse Dobrokhotikha, all celebrities at that time. All, gathered together there with their colts, walked up and down in the sunshine, rolled over on the fresh straw, and sniffed at each other like ordinary horses.

I cannot even now forget the sight of that paddock, full of the beauties of that day. It may seem strange to you to think of me as ever having been young and frisky, but I used to be. This very same Viazopurikha was there then, a yearling, whose mane had just been cut—a kind, jolly, frolicsome little horse. But let it not be taken as unkindly meant when I say that, though she is now considered a rarity among you on account of her pedigree, then she was only one of the meanest horses of that stud. She herself will corroborate this.

Though my piebald coat displeased the men, it was exceedingly attractive to all the horses. They all came round me, expressing their delight, and frisking with me. I even began to forget the words of the men about my hide, and felt happy. But I soon experienced the first sorrow of my life, and the cause of it was my dam. As soon as it began to thaw, and the swallows chirped under the eaves, and the spring made itself felt more and more in the air, my dam began to change in her behavior toward me.

Her whole nature was transformed. Suddenly, without any reason, she began to frisk, galloping around the yard, which certainly did not accord with her dignified growth; then she would pause and consider, and begin to whinny;

then she would bite and kick her sister mares; then she began to smell of me, and neigh with dissatisfaction, then, trotting out into the sun she would lay her head across the shoulder of my two-year-old sister Kupchika, and long and earnestly scratch her back, and push me away from nursing her. One time the equerry came, commanded the halter to be put on her, and they led her out of the paddock. She whinnied; I replied to her, and darted after her, but she would not even look at me. The groom Taras seized me in both arms, just as they shut the door on my mother's retreating form.

I struggled, threw the groom on the straw; but the door was closed, and I only heard my mother's whinnying growing fainter and fainter. And in this whinnying I perceived that she called not for me, but I perceived a very different expression. In reply to her voice, there was heard in the distance a mighty voice, as I afterward learned, the voice of Dobrui I., who, with two grooms in attendance, was about to be united once more with my dam.

I don't remember how Taras got out of my stall; it was too grievous for me. I felt that I had forever lost my mother's love, and wholly because I was a piebald, I said to myself, remembering what the people said of my hide; and such passionate anger came over me, that I began to pound the sides of the stall with my head and feet, and I pounded them until the sweat poured from me, and I could not stand up from exhaustion.

After some time my dam returned to me. I heard her as she came along the corridor in a prancing trot, wholly unusual to her, and entered our stall. The door was opened for her. I did not recognize her, so much younger and handsomer had she grown. She snuffed at me, neighed, and began to snort. But in her whole expression I could see that she did not love me.

She told me about the beauty of Dobrui and her love for him. These meetings continued, and the relations between my dam and me kept growing cooler and cooler.

Soon they led us to pasture. I now began to experience new pleasures which consoled me for the loss of my mother's love. I had friends and companions. We learned together to eat grass, to neigh like the old horses, and to lift our tails and gallop in wide circles around our dams. This was a happy time. Everything was forgiven to me; all loved me and were loved by me, and looked indulgently on all that I did. This did not last long.

Very soon something terrible happened to me.

The gelding sighed deeply, deeply, and moved aside from the horses.

The dawn was already far advanced. The gates creaked. Nester came. The horses scattered. The drover straightened the saddle on the gelding's back, and drove away the horses.

VI

SECOND NIGHT

As soon as the horses were driven in, they once more gathered around the piebald.

In the month of August, continued the piebald horse, I was separated from my mother, and I did not experience any unusual grief. I saw that she was already suckling a small brother—the famous Usan—and I was no longer what I had been before. I was not jealous, but I felt that I had become more than ever cool toward her. Besides, I knew that on leaving my mother I should be transferred to the general division of young horses, where we were stalled in twos and threes, and every day the whole herd went out to exercise.

I was in one stall with Milui. Milui was a saddle-horse, and afterward the emperor himself used to ride him, and he was represented in pictures and statuary. At that time he was a mere colt, with a shiny soft coat, a swanlike neck, and slender, straight legs. He was always lively, good-natured, and lovable; was always ready to frisk, and be caressed, and sport with either horse or man. He and I could not help being good friends, living together as we did; and our friendship lasted all the days of our youth.

He was gay, and inclined to be giddy. Even then he began to feel the tender passion to disport with the fillies, and he used to make sport of my guilelessness. To my unhappiness, I myself, out of egotism, tried to follow his example, and very soon was in love. And this early inclination of mine was the cause, in great measure, of my fate. It happened that I was enamored. . . . Viazopurikha was older than I by a year; she and I were good friends, but toward the end of autumn I noticed that she began to avoid me. . . .

But I am not going to relate all the story of my unhappy first love; she herself remembers my senseless passion, which ended for me in the most important change in my life.

The hostlers came along, drove her away, and pounded me. In the evening they led me into a special stall. I whinnied the whole night long, as if with a presentiment of what was coming on the morrow.

In the morning the general, the equerry, the under grooms, and the hostlers came into the corridor where my stall was, and set up a terrible screaming. The general screamed to the head groom; the groom justified himself, saying that he had not given orders to send me away, but that the under grooms had done it of their own free will. The general said that it had spoiled everything, but that it was impossible to keep young stallions. The head groom replied that he would have it attended to. They calmed down and went out. I did not understand it at all, but I perceived that something concerning me was under consideration. . . .

On the next day I had ceased forever to whinny; I became what I am now. All the light of my eyes was quenched. Nothing seemed sweet to me; I became self-absorbed, and began to be pensive. At first I felt indifferent to everything. I ceased even to eat, to drink, and to run; and all thought of sprightly sport was gone. Then it nevermore came into my mind to kick up my heels, to roll over, to whinny, without bringing up the terrible question, "Why? for what purpose?" And my vigor died away.

Once they led me out at eventide, at the time when they

were driving the stud home from the field. From afar I saw already the cloud of dust in which could be barely distinguished the familiar lineaments of all of our dams. I heard the cheerful snorting, and the trampling of hoofs. I stopped short, though the halter-rope by which the groom held me cut my neck; and I gazed at the approaching drove as one gazes at a happiness which is lost forever and will never return again. They drew near, and my eyes fell upon forms so well known to me—beautiful, grand, plump, full of life every one. Who among them all deigned to glance at me? I did not feel the pain which the groom in pulling the rope inflicted. I forgot myself, and involuntarily tried to whinny as of yore, and to gallop off; but my whinnying sounded melancholy, ridiculous, and unbecoming. Not one in the stud made sport of me, but I noticed that many of them from politeness turned away from me.

It was evident that in their eyes I was despicable and pitiable, and worst of all, ridiculous. My slender, weakly neck, my big head—I had become thin—my long, thick legs, and the awkward gait that I struck up, in my old fashion, around the groom, all must have seemed absurd to them. No one heeded my attempted whinnying, all turned away from me.

Suddenly I comprehended it all, comprehended how I was forever sundered from them, every one; and I know not how I stumbled home behind the groom.

I had already shown a tendency toward gravity and thoughtfulness; but now a decided change came over me. My spotted coat, which occasioned such a strange prejudice in men, my terrible and unexpected misfortune, and, moreover, my peculiarly isolated position in the stud—which I felt, but could never explain to myself—compelled me to turn my thoughts inward on myself. I pondered on the disgust that people showed when they berated me for being a piebald; I pondered on the inconstancy of maternal and of female affection in general, and its dependence on physical conditions; and, above all, I pondered on the characteristics of that strange race of mortals with whom we are so closely bound, and whom we call men—those characteristics which were the source of the peculiarity of my position in the stud, felt by me but incomprehensible.

The significance of this peculiarity, and of the human characteristics on which it was based, was discovered to me by the following incident:

It was winter, at Christmas-tide. All day long no fodder had been given to me, nor had I been led out to water. I afterward learned that this arose from our groom being drunk. On this day the equerry came to me, saw that I had no food, and began to use hard language about the missing groom, and went away.

On the next day, the groom with his mates came out to our stalls to give us some hay. I noticed that he was especially pale and depressed, and in the expression of his long back there was a something significant and demanding sympathy.

He angrily flung the hay behind the grating. I laid my head over his shoulder; but he struck me such a hard blow with his fist on the nose, that I started back. Then he kicked me in the belly with his boots.

"If it hadn't been for this scurvy beast," said he, "there wouldn't have been any trouble."

"Why?" asked another groom.

"Mind you, he doesn't come to inquire about the count's! But twice a day he comes out to look after his own."

"Have they given him the piebald?" inquired another.

"Whether they've given it to him or sold it to him, the dog only knows! The count's might all die o' starvation—it wouldn't make any difference; but see how it upset him when I didn't give his horse his fodder! 'Lie down!' says he, and then such a basting I got! No Christianity in it. More pity on the cattle than on a man. I don't believe he's ever been christened; he himself counted the blows, the barbarian! The general did not use the whip so. He made my back all welts. There's no soul of a Christian in him!"

Now, what they said about whips and Christianity, I understood well enough; but it was perfectly dark to me as to the meaning of the words, my horse, his horse, by which I perceived that men understood some sort of bond between me and the groom. Wherein consisted this bond, I could not then understand at all. Only long afterward, when I was separated from the other horses, I came to learn what it meant. At that time I could not understand at all that it meant that they considered *me* the property of a man. To say *my* horse in reference to me, a live horse, seemed to me as strange as to say, *my earth, my atmosphere, my water*.

But these words had a monstrous influence on me. I pondered on them ceaselessly; and only after long and varied relations with men did I come at last to comprehend the meaning that men find in these strange words.

The meaning is this: Men rule in life, not by deeds, but by words. They love not so much the possibility of doing or not doing anything, as the possibility of talking about different objects in words agreed on between them. Such words, considered very important among them, are the words, *my, mine, ours*, which they employ for various things, beings, and objects; even for the earth, people, and horses. In regard to any particular thing, they agree that only one person shall say, "It is *mine.*"

And he who in this play, which they engage in, can say *mine* in regard to the greatest number of things, is considered the most fortunate among them. Why this is so, I know not; but it is so. Long before, I had tried to explain this to my satisfaction, by some direct advantage; but it seemed that I was wrong.

Many of the men who, for instance, called me their horse, did not ride on me, but entirely different men rode on me. They themselves did not feed me, but entirely different people fed me. Again, it was not those who called me their horse who treated me kindly, but the coachman, the veterinary, and, as a general thing, outside men.

Afterward, as I widened the sphere of my experiences, I became convinced that the concept *my,* as applied not only to us horses, but to other things, has no other foundation than a low and animal, a human instinct, which they call the sentiment or right of property. Man says, *my house,* and never lives in it, but is only cumbered with the building and maintenance of it. The merchant says, *my shop*—my clothing-shop, for example—and he does not even wear clothes made of the best cloth in his shop.

There are people who call land theirs, and have never seen their land, and have never been on it. There are men who call other people theirs, but have never seen these people; and the whole relationship of these owners, to these people, consists in doing them harm.

There are men who call women theirs—their wives or mistresses; but these women live with other men. And men struggle in life not to do what they consider good, but to call as many things as possible their own.

I am convinced now that herein lies the substantial difference between men and us. And, therefore, not speaking of other things where we are superior to men, we are able boldly to say that in this one respect at least we stand, in the scale of living beings, higher than men. The activity of men—at all events, of those with whom I have had to do—is guided by words; ours, by deeds.

And here the equerry obtained this right to say about me, *my horse;* and hence he lashed the hostler. This discovery deeply disturbed me; and these thoughts and opinions which my variegated coat aroused in men, and the thoughtfulness aroused in me by the change in my dam, together subserved to make me into that solemn and contemplative gelding that I am.

I was threefold unhappy: I was piebald; I was a gelding; and men imagined that I did not belong to God and myself, as is the prerogative of every living thing, but that I belonged to the equerry.

The consequences of their imagining this about me were many. The first was that they kept me apart from the others, fed me better, led me with a thong more frequently, and harnessed me up earlier. They harnessed me first when I was in my third year. I remember the first time; the equerry himself, who imagined that I was his, began, with a crowd of grooms, to harness me, expecting from me some ebullition of temper or contrariness. They put leather straps on me, and conducted me into the stalls. They laid on my back a wide leather cross, and attached it to the thills, so that I should not kick; but I was only waiting an opportunity to show my gait, and my love for work.

They marveled because I went like an old horse. They began to drive me, and I began to practise trotting. Every day I had greater and greater success, so that in three months the general himself, and many others, praised my gait. But this was a strange thing: for the very reason that they imagined that I was the equerry's, and not theirs, my gait had for them an entirely different significance.

The stallions, my brothers, were put through their paces; their time was reckoned; people came to see them; they were driven in gilded drozhskies. Costly saddles were put upon them. But I was driven in the equerry's simple drozhskies, when he had business at Chesmenko and other manor-houses. All this resulted from the fact that I was piebald, but more than all from the fact that I was, according to their idea, not the property of the count, but of the equerry.

Tomorrow, if we are alive, I will tell you what a serious influence on me was exercised by this right of proprietor-ship which the equerry arrogated to himself.

All that day the horses treated Kholstomer with great consideration. But Nester's behavior toward him was as rough as ever. The muzhik's gray stallion, coming toward the drove, whinnied; and again the chestnut filly coquettishly replied to him.

VII

THIRD NIGHT

The new moon was in the sky, and her narrow sickle poured a mild light on Kholstomer, standing in the middle of the yard; the horses had clustered around him.

The principal and most surprising consequence to me of the fact that I was not the count's property nor God's, but was the equerry's, continued the piebald, was that what constitutes our chief activity—the mettlesome race—was made the cause of my banishment. They were driving Lebedi around the ring; and a jockey from Chesmenko was riding me, and entered the course. Lebedi dashed past us. He trotted well, but he seemed to want to show off. He had not that skill which I had cultivated in myself; that is, of compelling one leg instantly to follow on the motion of the other, and not to waste the least degree of energy, but use it all in pressing forward. Lebedi dashed by us. I dashed into the ring; the jockey did not hold me back.

"Say, will you time my piebald?" he cried; and, when Lebedi came abreast of us a second time, he let me out. Lebedi had the advantage of his momentum, and so I was left behind in the first heat; but in the second I began to gain on him; came up to him—he was in a drozhsky—caught up with him, passed beyond him, and won the race. They tried it a second time—the same thing. I was the swifter. And this filled them all with dismay. The general begged them to send me away as soon as possible, so that I might not be heard of again. "Otherwise the count will know about it, and there will be trouble," said he. And they sent me to the horse-dealer. I did not remain there long. A hussar, who came along to get a remount, bought me. All this had been so unfair, so cruel, that I was glad when they took me from Khrenovaya, and forever separated me from all that had been near and dear to me. It was too hard for me among them. Before *them* stood love, honor, freedom; before me labor, humiliation—humiliation, labor, to the end of my days. Why? Because I was piebald, and because I was compelled to be somebody's horse. . . ."

Kholstomer could not tell any more of his story that evening. In the paddock an event took place which filled all the horses with dismay. Kupchikha, a mare who had been overlong with foal and had at first been listening to Kholstomer's story, got up and went slowly over to the shelter of the shed, and there began to scream so piercingly that she attracted the attention of all the horses; then she lay down, then she got up again, then she lay down again. The old dams all understood what was her trouble, but the younger horses became greatly excited, and, leaving the gelding by himself, they went and stood around her.

By morning there was a new colt born, and it stood unsteadily on its legs. Nester shouted to the groom, and they took the dam and her little one to the stall, and separated them from the other horses.

VIII

FOURTH NIGHT

The next evening, when the gates were closed and all was still, the piebald continued thus:

I had many experiences, both among men and among my own kind, while changing about from hand to hand. I stayed with two masters the longest: with a prince, an officer of hussars, and then with an old man who lived at Nikola Yavlennui Church.

I spent the happiest days of my life with the hussar.

Though he was the cause of my destruction, though he loved nothing and nobody, yet I loved him, and still love him, for this very reason.

He pleased me precisely because he was handsome, fortunate, rich, and therefore loved no one.

You understand this lofty equine sentiment of ours. His coldness, and my dependence on him, added greatly to the strength of my affection for him. "Beat me, drive me to death," I used to think in those happy days; "for that very reason I shall be all the happier."

He bought me of the horse-dealer to whom the equerry had sold me, for eight hundred rubles. He bought me because there was no demand for piebald horses. Those were my happiest days.

He had a mistress. I knew it because every day I took him to her; and I took her out driving, and sometimes took them together.

His mistress was a handsome woman, and he was handsome, and his coachman was handsome; and I loved them all because they were. And life was worth living then.

This is the way my life was spent: In the morning the groom came to rub me down—not the coachman, but the groom. The groom was a young lad, taken from among the muzhiks. He would open the door, let the wind drive out the steam from the horses, shovel out the manure, take off the blanket, begin to flourish the brush over my body, and with the currycomb to brush out the rolls of sweaty hair on the floor of the stall, marked by the stamping of hoofs. I would make believe bite his sleeves, would push him with my leg.

Then we were led out, one after the other, to drink from a tub of cold water; and the youngster admired my sleek, spotted coat, which he had polished, my legs straight as an arrow, my broad hoofs, my glossy flank, and back wide enough to sleep on. Then he would throw the hay behind the broad rack, and pour the oats into the oaken cribs. Then Feofan and the old coachman would come.

The master and the coachman were alike. Neither the one nor the other feared any one or loved any one except themselves, and therefore everybody loved them. Feofan came in a red shirt, plush breeches, and coat. I used to like to hear him when, all pomaded for a holiday, he would come to the stable in his coat, and cry, "Well, you beast, are you asleep?" and poke me in the loin with the handle of his fork; but never so as to hurt, only in fun. I could instantly take a joke, and I would lay back my ears and show my teeth.

We had a chestnut stallion which belonged to a pair. Sometimes at night they would harness us together. This Polkan could not understand a joke, and was simply ugly as the devil. I used to stand in the next stall to him, and seriously quarrel. Feofan was not afraid of him. He used to go straight up to him, shout to him—it seemed as if he were going to kick him—but no, straight by, and put on the halter.

Once we ran away together, in a pair, down over the Kuznetskoye. Neither the master nor the coachman was frightened; they laughed, they shouted to the people, and they sawed on the reins and pulled up, and so I did not run over anybody.

In their service I wasted my best qualities, and half of my life. There they gave me too much water to drink, and spoilt my legs. . . .

But, in spite of everything, that was the best part of my life. At twelve o'clock they would come, harness me, oil my hoofs, moisten my forelock and mane, and put me between the thills.

The sledge was of cane, plaited, upholstered in velvet. The harness had little silver buckles, the reins were of silk, and once I wore a fly-net. The whole business was such that, when all the straps and belts were put on and drawn, it was impossible to make out where the harness ended and the horse began. They would finish harnessing in the shed. Feofan would come out, his middle wider that his shoulders, with his red girdle up under his arms. He would inspect the harness, take his seat, straighten his kaftan, put his foot in the stirrup, get off some joke, always crack his whip, though he scarcely ever touched me with it—merely for form's sake—and cry, "Now off with you!" And, frisking at every step, I would prance out of the gate; and the cook, coming out to empty her dishwater, would pause in the road; and the muzhik, bringing in his firewood, would open his eyes. We would drive up and down, occasionally stopping. The lackeys come out, the coachmen drive up. And conversation would not flag. Always kept waiting. Sometimes for three hours we were kept at the door; occasionally we take a turn around, and talk awhile, and again we would halt.

At last there would be a tumult in the hallway; out would come the gray-haired Tikhon, with his paunch, in his dress-coat—"Drive on"; then there was none of that feeble way of saying, "Go ahead," as if I did not know that we were going forward and not backward. Feofan would cluck and drive up to the door, and the prince would come out quickly, unconcernedly, as if there was nothing wonderful either in this sledge or the horses, or Feofan himself, as he bends his back and holds out his hands in such a way that it would seem impossible to keep it up long.

The prince comes out in his shako and cloak, with a gray beaver collar concealing his ruddy face, with its black brows, a handsome face, which ought never to be covered. He would come out with clanking saber, jingling spurs, and copper-heeled boots; stepping over the carpet appar-

ently in a hurry, and not paying any heed to me or to Feofan, whom everybody except himself looked at and admired.

Feofan clucks. I tug at the reins, and with a respectable
rapid trot we are off and away. I glance round at the
prince, and toss my aristocratic head and delicate top-
knot. . . .

The prince is in good spirits; he sometimes jests with
Feofan. Feofan replies, half turning round to the prince
his handsome face, and, not dropping his hands, makes
an almost imperceptible motion with the reins which I
understand: and on, on, on, with ever wider and wider
strides, straining every muscle, and sending the muddy
snow over the dasher, off I go! Then there was none of
the absurd way that obtains today of crying "Oh!" as if the
coachman were in pain, and couldn't speak. "G'long! Look
out there! G'long! Look out there," shouts Feofan; and
the people clear the way, and stand craning their necks to
see the handsome gelding, the handsome coachman, and
the handsome barin. . . .

I loved specially to outstrip some racer. When Feofan
and I would see in the distance some team worthy of our
mettle, flying like a whirlwind, we would gradually come
nearer and nearer to him. And soon, tossing the mud over
the dasher, I would be even with the passenger, and would
snort over his head, then even with the saddle, with the
bell-bow; then I would already see him and hear him behind me, gradually getting farther and farther away. But
the prince and Feofan and I, we all kept silent, and made
believe that we were merely out for a drive, and by our
actions that we did not notice those with slow horses
whom we overtook on our way. I loved to race, but I
loved also to meet a good racer. One wink, sound, glance,
and we would be off, and would fly along, each on his
own side of the road. . . .

Here the gates creaked, and the voices of Nester and
Vaska were heard.

IX

FIFTH NIGHT

The weather began to change. The sky was overcast; and in the morning there was no dew, but it was warm, and the flies were sticky. As soon as the herd was driven in, the horses gathered around the piebald, and thus he finished his story:

The happy days of my life were soon ended. I lived so only two years. At the end of the second winter, there happened an event which was most delightful to me, and immediately after came my deepest sorrow. It was at Shrovetide. I took the prince to the races. Atlasnui and Buichok also ran in the race.

I don't know what they were doing in the summer-house; but I know that he came, and ordered Feofan to enter the ring. I remember they drove me into the ring, stationed me, and stationed Atlasnui. Atlasnui was in racing gear, but I was harnessed in a city sleigh. At the turning stake I left him behind. A laugh and a cry of victory greeted my achievement.

When they began to lead me around, a crowd followed after, and a man offered the prince five thousand. He only laughed, showing his white teeth.

"No," said he, "this isn't a horse, it's a friend. I wouldn't sell him for a mountain of gold. Good day, gentlemen!"

He threw open the fur robes, and got in.

"To Ostozhenko."

That was where his mistress lived. And we flew. . . .

It was our last happy day. We reached her home. He called her *his*. But she loved some one else, and had gone off with him. The prince ascertained this at her room. It was five o'clock; and, not letting me be unharnessed, he started in pursuit of her. It had never happened before; they applied the knout to me, and made me gallop. For the first time, I began to flag, and, I am ashamed to say, I wanted to rest.

But suddenly I heard the prince himself shouting in an unnatural voice, "Hurry up!" and the knout whistled and cut me; and I dashed ahead again, my leg hitting against the iron of the dasher. We overtook her, after going twenty-five versts. I got him there; but I trembled all night, and could not eat anything. In the morning they gave me water. I drank it, and forever ceased to be the horse that I had been. I was sick. They tortured me and maimed me—treated me as men are accustomed to do. My hoofs came off. I had abscesses, and my legs grew bent. I had no strength in my chest. Laziness and weakness were everywhere apparent. I was sent to the horse-dealer. He fed me on carrots and other things, and made me something quite unlike my old self, but yet capable of deceiving one who did not know. But there was no strength and no swiftness in me.

Moreover, the horse-dealer tormented me, by coming to my stall when customers were on hand, and beginning to stir me up, and torture me with a great knout so that it drove me to madness. Then he would wipe the bloody foam off the whip, and lead me out.

An old lady bought me of the dealer. She used to keep coming to Nikola Yavlennui, and she used to whip the coachman. The coachman would come and weep in my stall. And I knew that his tears had an agreeable salt taste. Then the old woman died. Her overseer took me into the country, and sold me to a peddler; then I was fed on wheat, and grew sicker still. I was sold to a muzhik. There I had to plow, had almost nothing to eat, and I cut my leg with a plowshare. I became sick again. A gipsy got possession of me. He tortured me horribly, and at last I was sold to the overseer here. And here I am. . . .

All were silent. The rain began to fall.

X

As the herd returned home the following evening, they met the master and a guest. Zhulduiba, leading the way, cast her eyes on two men's figures: one was the young master in a straw hat; the other a tall, stout, military man with wrinkled face. The old mare gazed at the man, and swerving went near to him; the rest, the younger ones, were thrown into some confusion, huddled together, especially when the master and his guest came directly into the midst of the horses, making gestures to each other, and talking.

"Here's this one. I bought it of Voyeïkof—the dapplegray horse," said the master.

"And that young black mare, with the white legs—where did you get her? Fine one," said the guest.

They examined many of the horses as they walked around, or stood on the field. They remarked also the chestnut mare. "That's one of the saddle-horses—the breed of Khrenovsky."

They quietly gazed at all the horses as they went by. The master shouted to Nester; and the old man, hastily digging his heels into the sides of the piebald, trotted out. The piebald horse hobbled along, limping on one leg; but his gait was such that it was evident that in other circumstances he would not have complained, even if he had been compelled to go in this way, as long as his strength held out, to the world's end. He was ready even to go at full gallop, and at first even broke into one.

"I have no hesitation in saying that there isn't a better horse in Russia than that one," said the master, pointing to one of the mares. The guest corroborated this praise. The master, full of satisfaction, walked up and down, made observations, and told the story and pedigree of each of the horses.

It was apparently somewhat of a bore to the guest to listen to the master; but he devised questions to make it seem as if he were interested in it.

"Yes, yes," said he, in some confusion.

"Look," said the host, not replying to the questions, "look at those legs, look. . . . She cost me dear, but I shall have a three-year-old from her that'll go!"

"Does she trot well?" asked the guest.

Thus they scrutinized almost all the horses, and there was nothing more to show. And they were silent.

"Well, shall we go?"

"Yes, let us go."

They went out through the gate. The guest was glad that the exhibition was over, and that he was going home, where he would eat, drink, smoke, and have a good time. As they went by Nester, who was sitting on the piebald and waiting for further orders, the guest struck his big fat hand on the horse's side.

"Here's good blood," said he. "He's like the piebald horse, if you remember, that I told you about."

The master perceived that it was not of his horses that the guest was speaking; and he did not listen, but, looking around, continued to gaze at his stud.

Suddenly, at his very ear, was heard a dull, weak, senile neigh. It was the piebald horse that began to neigh, but could not finish it. Becoming, as it were, confused, he broke short off.

Neither the guest nor the master paid any attention to this neigh, but went home. Kholstomer had recognized in the wrinkled old man his beloved former master, the once brilliant, handsome, and wealthy Sierpukhovskoï.

XI

The rain continued to fall. In the paddock it was gloomy, but at the manorhouse it was quite the reverse. The luxurious evening meal was spread in the luxurious dining-room. At the table sat master, mistress, and the guest who had just arrived.

The mistress of the house, in a delicate condition, as any one could see by her shape, and by the way she sat, by her plumpness, and especially by her eyes, which had a sweet introspection and serious look in them, was in her place behind the samovar.

The master held in his hand a box of specially fine decennial cigars, such as no one else had, according to his story, and proceeded to offer them to the guest. The master was a handsome young man of twenty-five, fresh, neatly dressed, smoothly brushed. He was dressed in a fresh, loosely fitting suit of clothes, made in London. On his watch-chain were big expensive charms. His cuff-buttons were of gold, large, even massive, set with turquoises. His beard was *à la Napoléon III.*; and his mustaches were waxed, and stood out in the way that is acquired nowhere else than in Paris.

The lady wore a silk-muslin dress, brocaded with large variegated flowers; on her head, large gold hairpins in her thick auburn hair, which was beautiful, though not entirely her own. Her hands were adorned with many bracelets and rings, all expensive.

The samovar was silver, the service exquisite. The lackey, magnificent in his dress-coat and white waistcoat and necktie, stood like a statue at the door, awaiting orders. The furniture was of bent wood, and bright; the wall-papers dark with large flowers. Around the table tinkled a cunning little dog, with a silver collar bearing an extremely hard English name, which neither of them could pronounce because they knew not English.

In the corner, among the flowers, stood the pianoforte, inlaid with mother-of-pearl. Everything breathed of newness, luxury, and rarity. Everything was extremely fine; but it all bore a peculiar impress of profusion, wealth, and an absence of intellectual interests.

The master was a great lover of racing, strong and hotheaded; one of those whom one meets everywhere, who drive out in sable furs, send costly bouquets to actresses, drink the most expensive wine, of the very latest brand, at the most expensive restaurant, offer prizes in their own names, and entertain the most expensive of . . .

The newcomer, Nikita Sierpukhovskoï, was a man of forty years, tall, stout, bald, with huge mustaches and side-whiskers. He ought to have been very handsome; but it was evident that he had wasted his forces—physical and moral and pecuniary.

He was so deeply in debt that he was obliged to go into the service so as to escape the sponging-house. He had now come to the government city as chief of the imperial stud. His influential relations had obtained this for him.

He was dressed in an army kittel and blue trousers. His kittel and trousers were such as only those who are rich can afford to wear; so with his linen also. His watch was

English. His boots had peculiar soles, as thick as a finger. Nikita Sierpukhovskoï had squandered a fortune of two millions, and was still in debt to the amount of one hundred and twenty thousand rubles. From such a course there always remains a certain momentum of life, giving credit, and the possibility of living almost luxuriously for another ten years.

The ten years had already passed, and the momentum was finished; and it had become hard for him to live. He had already begun to drink too much; that is, to get fuddled with wine, which had never been the case with him before. Properly speaking, he had never begun and never finished drinking.

More noticeable in him than all else was the restlessness of his eyes (they had begun to wander), and the uncertainty of his intonations and motions. This restlessness was surprising, from the fact that it was evidently a new thing in him, because it could be seen that he had been accustomed, all his life long, to fear nothing and nobody, and that now he endured severe sufferings from some dread which was thoroughly alien to his nature.

The host and hostess remarked this, exchanged glances, showing that they understood each other, postponed until they should get to bed the consideration of this subject, and, evidently, merely endured poor Sierpukhovskoï.

The sight of the young master's happiness humiliated Nikita, and compelled him to painful envy, as he remembered his own irrevocable past.

"You don't object to cigars, Marie?" he asked, addressing the lady in that peculiar tone, acquired only by practice, full of urbanity and friendliness, but not wholly satisfactory—such as men who know the world use addressing women who are mistresses rather than wives. Not that he could have wished to insult her; on the contrary, he was much more anxious to gain her good-will and that of the host, though he would not for anything have acknowledged it to himself. But he had long been used to talking thus with such women. He knew that she would have been astonished, even affronted, if he had behaved to her as toward a lady. Moreover, it was necessary for him to preserve that peculiar shade of deference for the acknowledged wife of his friend. He treated such women always with consideration, not because he shared those so-called convictions that are promulgated in newspapers (he never read such trash), about esteem as the prerogative of every man, about the absurdity of marriage, etc., but because all well-bred men act thus, and he was a well-bred man, though inclined to drink.

He took a cigar. But his host awkwardly seized a handful of cigars, and placed them before the guest.

"No, just see how good these are! try them."

Nikita pushed away the cigars with his hand, and in his eyes flashed something like resentment and shame.

"Thanks"—he took out his cigar-case—"try mine."

The lady had tact. She perceived how it affected him. She began hastily to talk with him.

"I am very fond of cigars. I should smoke myself if everybody about me did not smoke."

And she gave him one of her bright, kindly smiles. He half smiled in reply. Two of his teeth were gone.

"No, take this," continued the host, who had not tact. "Those others are not so strong. *Fritz, bringen Sie noch einen Kasten,*" he said, "*dort zwei.*"

The German lackey brought another box.

"Do you like these larger ones? They are stronger. This is a very good kind. Take them all," he added, continuing to force them upon his guest.

He was evidently glad that there was some one on whom he could lavish his rarities, and he saw nothing out of the way in it. Sierpukhovskoï began to smoke, and hastened to take up the subject that had been dropped.

"How much did you have to go on Atlasnui?" he asked.

"He cost me dear—not less than five thousand, but at all events I am secured. Plenty of colts, I tell you!"

"Do they trot?" inquired Sierpukhovskoï.

"First-rate. Today Atlasnui's colts took three prizes: one at Tula, one at Moscow, and one at Petersburg. He raced with Voyeïkof's Voronui. The rascally jockey made four abatements, and almost put him out of the race."

"He was rather raw; too much Dutch stock in him, I should say," said Sierpukhovskoï.

"Well, but the mares are finer ones. I will show you to-morrow. I paid three thousand for Dobruina, two thousand for Laskovaya."

And again the host began to enumerate his wealth. The mistress saw that this was hard for Sierpukhovskoï, and that he only pretended to listen.

"Won't you have some more tea?" asked the hostess.

"I don't care for any more," said the host, and he went on with his story. She got up; the host detained her, took her in his arms, and kissed her.

Sierpukhovskoï smiled at first, as he looked at them, but his smile seemed to them unnatural; but when his host got up, and threw his arms around her, and went out with her as far as the *portière*, his face suddenly changed; he sighed deeply, and an expression of despair took possession of his wrinkled face. There was also wrath in it.

The host returned, and smiled as he sat down opposite Nikita. Neither of them spoke.

XII

"Yes, you said that you bought him of Voyeïkof," said Sierpukhovskoï, with assumed indifference.

"Oh, yes! I was speaking of Atlasnui. I had a great mind to buy the mares of Dubovitsky. Nothing but rubbish was left."

"He was *burned* out," said Sierpukhovskoï, and suddenly stood up and looked around. He remembered that he owed this ruined man twenty thousand rubles, and that, if *burned* out were said of any one, it might by good rights be said about himself. He began to laugh.

Both preserved a long silence. The host was revolving in his mind how he might boast a little before his guest. Sierpukhovskoï was cogitating how he might show that he did not consider himself burned out. But the thoughts of both moved with difficulty, in spite of the fact that they tried to enliven themselves with cigars.

"Well, when shall we have something to drink, I wonder?" said Sierpukhovskoï to himself.

"At all events, we must have something to drink, else I shall die of the blues with him," said the host to himself.

"How is it? are you going to stay here long?" asked Sierpukhovskoï.

"About a month longer. Shall we have a little lunch? What say you? Fritz, is everything ready?"

They went back to the dining-room. There, under a hanging lamp, stood the table loaded with candles and very extraordinary things: siphons, and bottles with fancy stoppers, extraordinary wine in decanters, extraordinary liqueurs and vodka. They drank, sat down, drank again, sat down, and tried to talk. Sierpukhovskoï grew flushed and began to speak unreservedly.

They talked about women: who kept such and such a one; the gipsy, the ballet-girl, the *soubrette*.[1]

"Why, you left Mathieu, didn't you?" asked the host.

This was the mistress who had caused Sierpukhovskoï's ruin.

"No, she left me. Oh, brother, how one remembers what one has squandered in life! Now I am glad, fact, when I get a thousand rubles; glad, fact, when I get out of everybody's way. I cannot in Moscow. Ah! what's to be said!"

The host was bored to listen to Sierpukhovskoï. He wanted to talk about himself—to brag. But Sierpukhovskoï also wanted to talk about himself—about his brilliant past. The host poured out some more wine, and waited till he had finished, so as to tell him about his affairs—how he was going to arrange his stud as no one ever had before; and how Marie loved him, not for his money, but for himself.

"I was going to tell you that in my stud . . ." he began. But Sierpukhovskoï interrupted him.

"There was a time, I may say," he began, "when I loved, and knew how to live. You were talking just now about racing; please tell me what is your best racer."

The host was glad of the chance to tell some more about his stud, but Sierpukhovskoï again interrupted him.

[1] *Frantsuzhenka,* the little Frenchwoman.

"Yes, yes," said he. "But the trouble with you breeders is that you do it only for ostentation, and not for pleasure, for life. It wasn't so with me. I was telling you this very day that I used to have a piebald racer, with just such spots as I saw among your colts. Oh! what a horse he was! You can't imagine it; this was in '42. I had just come to Moscow. I went to a dealer, and saw a piebald gelding. All in best form. He pleased me. Price? Thousand rubles. He pleased me. I took him, and began to ride him. I never had, and you never had, and never will have, such a horse. I never knew a better horse, either for gait, or strength, or beauty. You were a lad then. You could not have known, but you may have heard, I suppose. All Moscow knew him."

"Yes, I heard about him," said the host, reluctantly. "But I was going to tell you about my . . ."

"So you heard about him. I bought him just as he was, without pedigree, without proof; but then I knew Voyeïkof, and I traced him. He was sired by Liubeznuï I. He was called Kholstomer.[2] He'd measure linen for you! On account of his spotting, he was given to the equerry at the Khrenovski stud; and he had him gelded and sold him to the dealer. There aren't horses like him any more, friend! Ah! what a time that was! Ah! vanished youth!" he said, quoting the words of a gipsy song. He began to get wild. "Eh! that was a golden time! I was twenty-five. I had eighty thousand a year income; then I hadn't a gray hair; all my teeth like pearls. . . . Whatever I undertook prospered. And yet all came to an end." . . .

"Well, you didn't have such lively races then," said the host, taking advantage of the interruption. "I tell you that my first horses began to run without . . ."

"Your horses! Horses were more mettlesome then . . ."

"How more mettlesome?"

"Yes, more mettlesome. I remember how one time I was at Moscow at the races. None of my horses were in it. I did not care for racing; but I had blooded horses, General

---

[2] *Kholstomer* means a cloth-measurer; suggesting the greatest distance from finger to finger of the outstretched arms, and rapidity in accomplishing the motion.

Chaulet, Mahomet. I had my piebald with me. My coachman was a splendid young fellow. I liked him. But he was rather given to drink, so I drove. 'Sierpukhovskoï' said they, 'when are you going to get some trotters?'—'I don't care for your low-bred beasts, the devil take 'em! I have a hack-driver's piebald that's worth all of yours.'—'Yes, but he doesn't race.'—'I'll bet you a thousand rubles.' They took me up. He went round in five seconds, won the wager of a thousand rubles. But that was nothing. With my blooded horses I went in a troïka a hundred versts in three hours. All Moscow knew about it."

And Sierpukhovskoï began to brag so fluently and steadily that the host could not get in a word, and sat facing him with dejected countenance. Only, by way of diversion, he would fill up his glass and that of his companion.

It began already to grow light, but still they sat there. It became painfully tiresome to the host. He got up.

"Sleep—let's go to sleep, then," said Sierpukhovskoï, as he got up, and went staggering and puffing to the room that had been assigned to him.

The master of the house rejoined his mistress.

"Oh, he's unendurable. He got drunk, and lied faster than he could talk."

"And he made love to me, too."

"I fear that he's going to beg some money of me."

Sierpukhovskoï threw himself on the bed without undressing, and drew a long breath.

"I must have talked a good deal of nonsense," he thought. "Well, it's all the same. Good wine, but he's a big hog. Something cheap about him. And I am a great hog myself," he remarked, and laughed aloud. "Well, I used to support others; now it's my turn. Perhaps the Winkler girl will help me. I'll borrow some money of her. He may come to it. I suppose I've got to undress. Can't get my boot off. Hey, hey!" he cried; but the man who had been ordered to wait on him had long before gone to bed.

He sat up, took off his kittel and his vest, and somehow managed to crawl out of his trousers; but it was long before his boots would stir; with his stout belly it was hard work to stoop over. He got one off; he struggled and struggled with the other, got out of breath, and gave it up. And so with one leg in the boot he threw himself down, and began to snore, filling the whole room with the odor of wine, tobacco, and vile old age.

XIII

If Kholstomer remembered anything that night, it was the frolic that Vaska gave him. He threw over him a blanket, and galloped off. He was left till morning at the door of a tavern, with a muzhik's horse. They licked each other. In the morning he went back to the herd, and itched all over.

"Something makes me itch fearfully," he thought.

Five days passed. They brought a veterinary. He said cheerfully, "The mange. You'll have to dispose of him to the gipsies."

"Better have his throat cut; only have it done today."

The morning was calm and clear. The herd had gone to pasture. Kholstomer remained behind. A strange man came along, thin, dark, dirty, in a kaftan spotted with something black. This was the knacker. He took Kholstomer by the halter, and without looking at him started off. The horse followed quietly, not looking round, and, as always, dragging his legs and kicking up the straw with his hind legs.

As he went out of the gate, he turned his head toward the well; but the knacker twitched the halter, and said, "It's not worth while."

The knacker and Vaska, who followed, proceeded to a depression behind the brick barn, and stopped, as if there was something peculiar in this most ordinary place; and the knacker, handing the halter to Vaska, took off his kaftan, rolled up his sleeves, and produced a knife and whetstone from his boot-leg.

The piebald pulled at the halter, and out of sheer *ennui* tried to bite it, but it was too far off. He sighed, and closed his eyes. His lip hung down, showing his worn yellow teeth, and he began to drowse, lulled by the sound of the knife on the stone. Only his sick and swollen leg trembled a little.

Suddenly he felt that he was grasped by the lower jaw, and that his head was lifted up. He opened his eyes. Two dogs were in front of him. One was snuffing in the direction of the knacker, the other sat looking at the gelding as if he were expecting something especially from him. The gelding looked at them, and began to rub his jaw against the hand that held him.

"Of course they want to cure me," he said; "let it come!"

And the thought had hardly passed through his mind, before they did something to his throat. It hurt him; he started back, stamped his foot, but restrained himself, and waited for what was to follow. . . . What followed, was some liquid pouring in a stream down his neck and breast. He drew a deep breath, lifting his sides. And it seemed easier, much easier, to him.

The whole burden of his life was taken from him.

He closed his eyes, and began to droop his head—no one held it. Then his legs quivered, his whole body swayed. He was not so much terrified as he was astonished. . . .

Everything was so new. He was astonished; he tried to run ahead, up the hill . . . but, instead of this, his legs, moving where he stood, interfered. He began to roll over on his side, and, while expecting to make a step, he fell forward, and on his left side.

The knacker waited till the death-struggle was over, drove away the dogs which were creeping nearer, and then seized the horse by the legs, turned him over on the back, and, commanding Vaska to hold his leg, began to take off the hide.

"That was a horse indeed!" said Vaska.

"If he'd been fatter, it would have been a fine hide," said the knacker.

That evening the herd passed by the hill; and those who were on the left wing saw a red object below them, and around it some dogs busily romping, and crows and hawks flying over it. One dog, with his paws on the carcass, and shaking his head, was growling over what he was tearing with his teeth. The brown filly stopped, lifted her head and neck, and long sniffed the air. It took force to drive her away.

At sunset, in a ravine of the ancient forest, in the bottom of an overgrown glade, some large-headed wolf-whelps were beside themselves with joy. There were five of them —four about of a size, and one little one with a head bigger than his body. A lean, hairless she-wolf, her belly with hanging dugs almost touching the ground, crept out of the bushes, and sat down in front of the wolves. The wolves sat in a semicircle in front of her. She went to the smallest, and, lowering her stumpy tail, and bending her snout to the ground, made a few convulsive motions, and opening her jaws filled with teeth, she struggled, and disgorged a great piece of horse-flesh.

The larger whelps made a movement to seize it; but she restrained them with a threatening growl, and let the little one have it all.

The little one, as if in anger, seized the morsel, hiding it under him, and began to devour it. Then the she-wolf disgorged for the second, and the third, and in the same way for all five, and finally lay down in front of them to rest.

At the end of a week there lay behind the brick barn only the great skull, and two shoulder-blades; all the rest had disappeared. In the summer a muzhik who gathered up the bones carried off also the skull and shoulder-blades, and put them to use.

The dead body of Sierpukhovskoï, who had been about in the world, and had eaten and drunk, was buried long after. Neither his skin nor his flesh nor his bones were of any use.

And just as his dead body, which had been about in the world, had been a great burden to others for twenty years, so the disposal of this body became only an additional charge on men. Long it had been useless to every one, long it had been only a burden. But still the dead who bury their dead found it expedient to dress this soon-to-be-decaying, swollen body in a fine uniform, in fine boots; to place it in a fine new coffin, with new tassels on the four corners; then to place this new coffin in another, made of lead, and carry it to Moscow; and there to dig up the bones of people long buried, and then to lay away this malodorous body devoured by worms, in its new uniform and polished boots, and to cover the whole with earth.

Anton Chekhov
1860 – 1904

THE LADY WITH THE DOG

It was said that a new person had appeared on the sea-front: a lady with a little dog. Dmitri Dmitritch Gurov, who had by then been a fortnight at Yalta, and so was fairly at home there, had begun to take an interest in new arrivals. Sitting in Verney's pavilion, he saw, walking on the sea-front, a fair-haired young lady of medium height, wearing a *béret;* a white Pomeranian dog was running behind her.

And afterwards he met her in the public gardens and in the square several times a day. She was walking alone, always wearing the same *béret,* and always with the same white dog; no one knew who she was, and every one called her simply "the lady with the dog."

"If she is here alone without a husband or friends, it wouldn't be amiss to make her acquaintance," Gurov reflected.

He was under forty, but he had a daughter already twelve years old, and two sons at school. He had been married young, when he was a student in his second year, and by now his wife seemed half as old again as he. She was a tall, erect woman with dark eyebrows, staid and dignified, and, as she said of herself, intellectual. She read a great deal, used phonetic spelling, called her husband, not Dmitri, but Dimitri, and he secretly considered her unintelligent, narrow, inelegant, was afraid of her, and did not like to be at home. He had begun being unfaithful to her long ago—had been unfaithful to her often, and, probably on that account, almost always spoke ill of women, and when they were talked about in his presence, used to call them "the lower race."

It seemed to him that he had been so schooled by bitter experience that he might call them what he liked, and yet he could not get on for two days together without "the lower race." In the society of men he was bored and not himself, with them he was cold and uncommunicative; but when he was in the company of women he felt free, and knew what to say to them and how to behave; and he was at ease with them even when he was silent. In his appearance, in his character, in his whole nature, there was something attractive and elusive which allured women and disposed them in his favour; he knew that, and some force seemed to draw him, too, to them.

Experience often repeated, truly bitter experience, had taught him long ago that with decent people, especially Moscow people—always slow to move and irresolute—every intimacy, which at first so agreeably diversifies life and appears a light and charming adventure, inevitably grows into a regular problem of extreme intricacy, and in the long run the situation becomes unbearable. But at every fresh meeting with an interesting woman this experience seemed to slip out of his memory, and he was eager for life, and everything seemed simple and amusing.

One evening he was dining in the gardens, and the lady in the *béret* came up slowly to take the next table. Her expression, her gait, her dress, and the way she did her hair told him that she was a lady, that she was married, that she was in Yalta for the first time and alone, and that she was dull there. . . . The stories told of the immorality in such places as Yalta are to a great extent untrue; he despised them, and knew that such stories were for the most part made up by persons who would themselves have been glad to sin if they had been able; but when the lady sat down at the next table three paces from him, he remembered these tales of easy conquests, of trips to the mountains, and the tempting thought of a swift, fleeting love affair, a romance with an unknown woman, whose name he did not know, suddenly took possession of him.

He beckoned coaxingly to the Pomeranian, and when the dog came up to him he shook his finger at it. The Pomeranian growled: Gurov shook his finger at it again.

The lady looked at him and at once dropped her eyes.

"He doesn't bite," she said, and blushed.

"May I give him a bone?" he asked; and when she nodded he asked courteously, "Have you been long in Yalta?"

"Five days."

"And I have already dragged out a fortnight here."

There was a brief silence.

"Time goes fast, and yet it is so dull here!" she said, not looking at him.

"That's only the fashion to say it is dull here. A provincial will live in Belyov or Zhidra and not be dull, and when he comes here it's 'Oh, the dullness! Oh, the dust!' One would think he came from Grenada."

She laughed. Then both continued eating in silence, like strangers, but after dinner they walked side by side; and there sprang up between them the light jesting conversation of people who are free and satisfied, to whom it does not matter where they go or what they talk about. They walked and talked of the strange light on the sea: the water was of a soft warm lilac hue, and there was a golden streak from the moon upon it. They talked of how sultry it was after a hot day. Gurov told her that he came from Moscow, that he had taken his degree in Arts, but had a post in a bank; that he had trained as an opera-singer, but had given it up, that he owned two houses in Moscow. . . . And from her he learnt that she had grown up in Petersburg, but had lived in S—— since her marriage two years before, that she was staying another month in Yalta, and that her husband, who needed a holiday too, might perhaps come and fetch her. She was not sure whether her husband had a post in a Crown Department or under the Provincial Council—and was amused by her own ignorance. And Gurov learnt, too, that she was called Anna Sergeyevna.

Afterwards he thought about her in his room at the hotel —thought she would certainly meet him next day; it would be sure to happen. As he got into bed he thought how lately she had been a girl at school, doing lessons like his own daughter; he recalled the diffidence, the angularity, that was still manifest in her laugh and her manner of talking with a stranger. This must have been the first time in her life she had been alone in surroundings in which she was followed, looked at, and spoken to merely from a secret motive which she could hardly fail to guess. He recalled her slender, delicate neck, her lovely grey eyes.

"There's something pathetic about her, anyway," he thought, and fell asleep.

II

A week had passed since they had made acquaintance. It was a holiday. It was sultry indoors, while in the street the wind whirled the dust round and round, and blew people's hats off. It was a thirsty day, and Gurov often went into the pavilion, and pressed Anna Sergeyevna to have syrup and water or an ice. One did not know what to do with oneself.

In the evening when the wind had dropped a little, they went out on the groyne to see the steamer come in. There were a great many people walking about the harbour; they had gathered to welcome some one, bringing bouquets. And two peculiarities of a well-dressed Yalta crowd were very conspicuous: the elderly ladies were dressed like young ones, and there were great numbers of generals.

Owing to the roughness of the sea, the steamer arrived late, after the sun had set, and it was a long time turning about before it reached the groyne. Anna Sergeyevna looked through her lorgnette at the steamer and the passengers as though looking for acquaintances, and when she turned to Gurov her eyes were shining. She talked a great deal and asked disconnected questions, forgetting next moment what she had asked; then she dropped her lorgnette in the crush.

The festive crowd began to disperse; it was too dark to

see people's faces. The wind had completely dropped, but Gurov and Anna Sergeyevna still stood as though waiting to see some one else come from the steamer. Anna Sergeyevna was silent now, and sniffed the flowers without looking at Gurov.

"The weather is better this evening," he said. "Where shall we go now? Shall we drive somewhere?"

She made no answer.

Then he looked at her intently, and all at once put his arm round her and kissed her on the lips, and breathed in the moisture and the fragrance of the flowers; and he immediately looked round him, anxiously wondering whether any one had seen them.

"Let us go to your hotel," he said softly. And both walked quickly.

The room was close and smelt of the scent she had bought at the Japanese shop. Gurov looked at her and thought: "What different people one meets in the world!" From the past he preserved memories of careless, good-natured women, who loved cheerfully and were grateful to him for the happiness he gave them, however brief it might be; and of women like his wife who loved without any genuine feeling, with superfluous phrases, affectedly, hysterically, with an expression that suggested that it was not love nor passion, but something more significant; and of two or three others, very beautiful, cold women, on whose faces he had caught a glimpse of a rapacious expression—an obstinate desire to snatch from life more than it could give, and these were capricious, unreflecting, domineering, unintelligent women not in their first youth, and when Gurov grew cold to them their beauty excited his hatred, and the lace on their linen seemed to him like scales.

But in this case there was still the diffidence, the angularity of inexperienced youth, an awkward feeling; and there was a sense of consternation as though some one had suddenly knocked at the door. The attitude of Anna Sergeyevna—"the lady with the dog"—to what had happened was somehow peculiar, very grave, as though it were her fall—so it seemed, and it was strange and inappropriate. Her face dropped and faded, and on both sides of it her long hair hung down mournfully; she mused in a dejected attitude like "the woman who was a sinner" in an old-fashioned picture.

"It's wrong," she said. "You will be the first to despise me now."

There was a watermelon on the table. Gurov cut himself a slice and began eating it without haste. There followed at least half an hour of silence.

Anna Sergeyevna was touching; there was about her the purity of a good, simple woman who had seen little of life. The solitary candle burning on the table threw a faint light on her face, yet it was clear that she was very unhappy.

"How could I despise you?" asked Gurov. "You don't know what you are saying."

"God forgive me," she said, and her eyes filled with tears. "It's awful."

"You seem to feel you need to be forgiven."

"Forgiven? No. I am a bad, low woman; I despise myself and don't attempt to justify myself. It's not my husband but myself I have deceived. And not only just now; I have been deceiving myself for a long time. My husband may be a good, honest man, but he is a flunkey! I don't know what he does there, what his work is, but I know he is a flunkey! I was twenty when I was married to him. I have been tormented by curiosity; I wanted something better. 'There must be a different sort of life,' I said to myself. I wanted to live! To live, to live! . . . I was fired by curiosity . . . you don't understand it, but, I swear to God, I could not control myself; something happened to me: I could not be restrained. I told my husband I was ill, and came here. . . . And here I have been walking about as though I were dazed, like a mad creature; . . . and now I have become a vulgar, contemptible woman whom any one may despise."

Gurov felt bored already, listening to her. He was irritated by the naïve tone, by this remorse, so unexpected and inopportune; but for the tears in her eyes, he might have thought she was jesting or playing a part.

"I don't understand," he said softly. "What is it you want?"

She hid her face on his breast and pressed close to him.

"Believe me, believe me, I beseech you . . ." she said. "I love a pure, honest life, and sin is loathsome to me. I don't know what I am doing. Simple people say: 'The Evil One has beguiled me.' And I may say of myself now that the Evil One has beguiled me."

"Hush, hush! . . ." he muttered.

He looked at her fixed, scared eyes, kissed her, talked softly and affectionately, and by degrees she was comforted, and her gaiety returned; they both began laughing.

Afterwards when they went out there was not a soul on the sea-front. The town with its cypresses had quite a death-like air, but the sea still broke noisily on the shore; a single barge was rocking on the waves, and a lantern was blinking sleepily on it.

They found a cab and drove to Oreanda.

"I found out your surname in the hall just now: it was written on the board—Von Diderits," said Gurov. "Is your husband a German?"

"No; I believe his grandfather was a German, but he is an Orthodox Russian himself."

At Oreanda they sat on a seat not far from the church, looked down at the sea, and were silent. Yalta was hardly visible through the morning mist; white clouds stood motionless on the mountain-tops. The leaves did not stir on the trees, grasshoppers chirruped, and the monotonous hollow sound of the sea rising up from below, spoke of the peace, of the eternal sleep awaiting us. So it must have sounded when there was no Yalta, no Oreanda here; so it sounds now, and it will sound as indifferently and monotonously when we are all no more. And in this constancy, in this complete indifference to the life and death of each of us, there lies hid, perhaps, a pledge of our eternal salvation, of the unceasing movement of life upon earth, of unceasing progress towards perfection. Sitting beside a young woman who in the dawn seemed so lovely, soothed and spellbound in these magical surroundings—the sea, mountains, clouds, the open sky—Gurov thought how in reality everything is beautiful in this world when one reflects: everything except what we think or do ourselves when we forget our human dignity and the higher aims of our existence.

A man walked up to them—probably a keeper—looked at them and walked away. And this detail seemed mysterious and beautiful, too. They saw a steamer come from Theodosia, with its lights out in the glow of dawn.

"There is dew on the grass," said Anna Sergeyevna, after a silence.

"Yes. It's time to go home."

They went back to the town.

Then they met every day at twelve o'clock on the sea-front, lunched and dined together, went for walks, admired the sea. She complained that she slept badly, that her heart throbbed violently; asked the same questions, troubled now by jealousy and now by the fear that he did not respect her sufficiently. And often in the square or gardens, when there was no one near them, he suddenly drew her to him and kissed her passionately. Complete idleness, these kisses in broad daylight while he looked round in dread of some one's seeing them, the heat, the smell of the sea, and the continual passing to and fro before him of idle, well-dressed, well-fed people, made a new man of him; he told Anna Sergeyevna how beautiful she was, how fascinating. He was impatiently passionate, he would not move a step away from her, while she was often pensive and continually urged him to confess that he did not respect her, did not love her in the least, and thought of her as nothing but a common woman. Rather late almost every evening they drove somewhere out of town, to Oreanda or to the waterfall; and the expedition was always a success, the scenery invariably impressed them as grand and beautiful.

They were expecting her husband to come, but a letter came from him, saying that there was something wrong with his eyes, and he entreated his wife to come home as quickly as possible. Anna Sergeyevna made haste to go.

"It's a good thing I am going away," she said to Gurov. "It's the finger of destiny!"

She went by coach and he went with her. They were driving the whole day. When she had got into a compartment of the express, and when the second bell had rung, she said, "Let me look at you once more . . . look at you once again. That's right."

She did not shed tears, but was so sad that she seemed ill, and her face was quivering.

"I shall remember you . . . think of you," she said. "God be with you; be happy. Don't remember evil against me. We are parting forever—it must be so, for we ought never to have met. Well, God be with you."

The train moved off rapidly, its lights soon vanished from sight, and a minute later there was no sound of it, as though everything had conspired together to end as quickly as possible that sweet delirium, that madness. Left alone on the platform, and gazing into the dark distance, Gurov listened to the chirrup of the grasshoppers and the hum of the telegraph wires, feeling as though he had only just waked up. And he thought, musing, that there had been another episode or adventure in his life, and it, too, was at an end, and nothing was left of it but a memory. . . . He was moved, sad, and conscious of a slight remorse. This young woman whom he would never meet again had not been happy with him; he was genuinely warm and affectionate with her, but yet in his manner, his tone, and his caresses there had been a shade of light irony, the coarse condescension of a happy man who was, besides, almost twice her age. All the time she had called him kind, exceptional, lofty; obviously he had seemed to her different from what he really was, so he had unintentionally deceived her. . . .

Here at the station was already a scent of autumn; it was a cold evening.

"It's time for me to go north," thought Gurov as he left the platform. "High time!"

III

At home in Moscow everything was in its winter routine; the stoves were heated, and in the morning it was still dark when the children were having breakfast and getting ready for school, and the nurse would light the lamp for a short time. The frosts had begun already. When the first snow had fallen, on the first day of sledge-driving it is pleasant to see the white earth, the white roofs, to draw soft, delicious breath, and the season brings back the days of one's youth. The old limes and birches, white with hoar-frost, have a good-natured expression; they are nearer to one's heart than cypresses and palms, and near them one doesn't want to be thinking of the sea and the mountains.

Gurov was Moscow born; he arrived in Moscow on a fine frosty day, and when he put on his fur coat and warm gloves, and walked along Petrovka, and when on Saturday evening he heard the ringing of the bells, his recent trip and the places he had seen lost all charm for him. Little by little he became absorbed in Moscow life, greedily read three newspapers a day, and declared he did not read the Moscow papers on principle! He already felt a longing to go to restaurants, clubs, dinner-parties, anniversary celebrations, and he felt flattered at entertaining distinguished lawyers and artists, and at playing cards with a professor at the doctors' club. He could already eat a whole plateful of salt fish and cabbage. . . .

In another month, he fancied, the image of Anna Sergeyevna would be shrouded in a mist in his memory, and only from time to time would visit him in his dreams with a touching smile as others did. But more than a month passed, real winter had come, and everything was still clear in his memory as though he had parted with Anna Sergeyevna only the day before. And his memories glowed more and more vividly. When in the evening stillness he heard from his study the voices of his children, preparing their lessons, or when he listened to a song or the organ at the restaurant, or the storm howled in the chimney, suddenly everything would rise up in his memory: what had happened on the groyne, and the early morning with the mist on the mountains, and the steamer coming from Theodosia, and the kisses. He would pace a long time about his room, remembering it all and smiling; then his memories passed into dreams, and in his fancy the past was mingled with what was to come. Anna Sergeyevna did not visit him in dreams, but followed him about everywhere like a shadow and haunted him. When he shut his eyes he saw her as though she were living before him, and she seemed to him lovelier, younger, tenderer than she was; and he imagined himself finer than he had been in Yalta. In the evenings she peeped out at him from the bookcase, from the fireplace, from the corner—he heard her breathing, the caressing rustle of her dress. In the street he watched the women, looking for someone like her.

He was tormented by an intense desire to confide his memories to some one. But in his home it was impossible to talk of his love, and he had no one outside; he could not talk to his tenants nor to any one at the bank. And what had he to talk of? Had he been in love, then? Had there been anything beautiful, poetical, or edifying or simply interesting in his relations with Anna Sergeyevna? And there was nothing for him but to talk vaguely of love, of woman, and no one guessed what it meant; only his wife twitched her black eyebrows, and said: "The part of a lady-killer does not suit you at all, Dimitri."

One evening, coming out of the doctors' club with an official with whom he had been playing cards, he could not resist saying, "If only you knew what a fascinating woman I made the acquaintance of in Yalta!"

The official got into his sledge and was driving away, but turned suddenly and shouted, "Dmitri Dmitritch!"

"What?"

"You were right this evening: the sturgeon was a bit too strong!"

These words, so ordinary, for some reason moved Gurov to indignation, and struck him as degrading and unclean. What savage manners, what people! What senseless nights, what uninteresting, uneventful days! The rage for card-playing, the gluttony, the drunkenness, the continual talk always about the same thing. Useless pursuits and conversations always about the same things absorb the better part of one's time, the better part of one's strength, and in the end there is left a life grovelling and curtailed, worthless and trivial, and there is no escaping or getting away from it—just as though one were in a madhouse or a prison.

Gurov did not sleep all night, and was filled with indignation. And he had a headache all next day. And the next night he slept badly; he sat up in bed, thinking, or paced up and down his room. He was sick of his children, sick of the bank; he had no desire to go anywhere or to talk of anything.

In the holidays in December he prepared for a journey, and told his wife he was going to Petersburg to do something in the interests of a young friend—and he set off for S——. What for? He did not very well know himself. He wanted to see Anna Sergeyevna and to talk with her—to arrange a meeting, if possible.

He reached S—— in the morning, and took the best room at the hotel, in which the floor was covered with grey army cloth, and on the table was an inkstand, grey with dust and adorned with a figure on horseback, with its hat in its hand and its head broken off. The hotel porter gave him the necessary information; Von Diderits lived in a house of his own in old Gontcharny Street—it was not far from the hotel: he was rich and lived in good style, and had his own horses; every one in the town knew him. The porter pronounced the name "Dridirits."

Gurov went without haste to Old Gontcharny Street and found the house. Just opposite the house stretched a long grey fence adorned with nails.

"One would run away from a fence like that," thought Gurov, looking from the fence to the windows of the house and back again.

He considered: today was a holiday, and the husband would probably be at home. And in any case it would be tactless to go into the house and upset her. If he were to send her a note it might fall into her husband's hands, and then it might ruin everything. The best thing was to trust to chance. And he kept walking up and down the street by the fence, waiting for the chance. He saw a beggar go in at the gate and the dogs fly at him; then an hour later he heard a piano, and the sounds were faint and indistinct. Probably it was Anna Sergeyevna playing. The front door suddenly opened, and an old woman came out, followed by the familiar white Pomeranian. Gurov was on the point of calling to the dog, but his heart began beating violently, and in his excitement he could not remember the dog's name.

He walked up and down, and loathed the grey fence more and more, and by now he thought irritably that Anna Sergeyevna had forgotten him, and was perhaps already amusing herself with some one else, and that that was very natural in a young woman who had nothing to look at from morning till night but that confounded fence. He went back to his hotel room and sat for a long while on the sofa, not knowing what to do, then he had dinner and a long nap.

"How stupid and worrying it is!" he thought when he woke and looked at the dark windows: it was already evening. "Here I've had a good sleep for some reason. What shall I do in the night?"

He sat on the bed, which was covered by a cheap grey blanket, such as one sees in hospitals, and he taunted himself in his vexation, "So much for the lady with the dog ... so much for the adventure. . . . You're in a nice fix. . . ."

That morning at the station a poster in large letters had caught his eye. "The Geisha" was to be performed for the first time. He thought of this and went to the theatre.

"It's quite possible she may go to the first performance," he thought.

The theatre was full. As in all provincial theatres, there was a fog above the chandelier, the gallery was noisy and restless; in the front row the local dandies were standing up before the beginning of the performance, with their hands behind them; in the Governor's box the Governor's daughter, wearing a boa, was sitting in the front seat, while the Governor himself lurked modestly behind the curtain with only his hands visible; the orchestra was a long time tuning up; the stage curtain swayed. All the time the audience were coming in and taking their seats Gurov looked at them eagerly.

Anna Sergeyevna, too, came in. She sat down in the third row, and when Gurov looked at her his heart contracted, and he understood clearly that for him there was in the whole world no creature so near, so precious, and so important to him; she, this little woman, in no way remarkable, lost in a provincial crowd, with a vulgar lorgnette in her hand, filled his whole life now, was his sorrow and his joy, the one happiness that he now desired for himself, and to the sounds of the inferior orchestra, of the wretched provincial violins, he thought how lovely she was. He thought and dreamed.

A young man with small side-whiskers, tall and stooping, came in with Anna Sergeyevna and sat down beside her; he bent his head at every step and seemed to be continually bowing. Most likely this was the husband whom at Yalta, in a rush of bitter feeling, she had called a flunkey. And there really was in his long figure, his side-whiskers, and the small bald patch on his head, something of the flunkey's obsequiousness; his smile was sugary, and in his buttonhole there was some badge of distinction like the number on a waiter.

During the first interval the husband went away to smoke; she remained alone in her stall. Gurov, who was sitting in the stalls, too, went up to her and said in a trembling voice, with a forced smile, "Good evening."

She glanced at him and turned pale, then glanced again with horror, unable to believe her eyes, and tightly gripped the fan and the lorgnette in her hands, evidently struggling with herself not to faint. Both were silent. She was sitting, he was standing, frightened by her confusion and not venturing to sit down beside her. The violins and the flute began tuning up. He felt suddenly frightened; it seemed as though all the people in the boxes were looking at them. She got up and went quickly to the door; he followed her, and both walked senselessly along passages, and up and down stairs, and figures in legal, scholastic, and civil service uniforms, all wearing badges, flitted before their eyes. They caught glimpses of ladies, of fur coats hanging on pegs; the draughts blew on them, bringing a smell of stale tobacco. And Gurov, whose heart was beating violently, thought, "Oh, heavens! Why are these people here and this orchestra! . . ."

And at that instant he recalled how when he had seen Anna Sergeyevna off at the station he had thought that everything was over and they would never meet again. But how far they were still from the end!

On the narrow, gloomy staircase over which was written "To the Amphitheatre," she stopped.

"How you have frightened me!" she said, breathing hard, still pale and overwhelmed. "Oh, how you have frightened me! I am half dead. Why have you come? Why?"

"But do understand, Anna, do understand . . ." he said hastily in a low voice. "I entreat you to understand. . . ."

She looked at him with dread, with entreaty, with love; she looked at him intently, to keep his features more distinctly in her memory.

"I am so unhappy," she went on, not heeding him. "I have thought of nothing but you all the time; I live only in the thought of you. And I wanted to forget, to forget you; but why, oh, why, have you come?"

On the landing above them two schoolboys were smoking and looking down, but that was nothing to Gurov; he drew Anna Sergeyevna to him, and began kissing her face, her cheeks, and her hands.

"What are you doing, what are you doing!" she cried in horror, pushing him away. "We are mad. Go away today; go away at once. . . . I beseech you by all that is sacred, I implore you. . . . There are people coming this way!"

Some one was coming up the stairs.

"You must go away," Anna Sergeyevna went on in a whisper. "Do you hear, Dmitri Dmitritch? I will come and see you in Moscow. I have never been happy; I am miserable now, and I never, never shall be happy, never! Don't make me suffer still more! I swear I'll come to Moscow. But now let us part. My precious, good, dear one, we must part!"

She pressed his hand and began rapidly going downstairs, looking round at him, and from her eyes he could see that she really was unhappy. Gurov stood for a little while, listened, then, when all sound had died away, he found his coat and left the theatre.

IV

And Anna Sergeyevna began coming to see him in Moscow. Once in two or three months she left S——, telling her husband that she was going to consult a doctor about an internal complaint—and her husband believed her, and did not believe her. In Moscow she stayed at the Slaviansky Bazaar hotel, and at once sent a man in a red cap to Gurov. Gurov went to see her, and no one in Moscow knew of it.

Once he was going to see her in this way on a winter morning (the messenger had come the evening before when he was out). With him walked his daughter, whom he wanted to take to school: it was on the way. Snow was falling in big wet flakes.

"It's three degrees above freezing-point, and yet it is snowing," said Gurov to his daughter. "The thaw is only on the surface of the earth; there is quite a different temperature at a greater height in the atmosphere."

"And why are there no thunderstorms in the winter, father?"

He explained that, too. He talked, thinking all the while that he was going to see *her,* and no living soul knew of it, and probably never would know. He had two lives: one, open, seen and known by all who cared to know, full of relative truth and of relative falsehood, exactly like the lives of his friends and acquaintances; and another life running its course in secret. And through some strange, perhaps accidental, conjunction of circumstances, everything that was essential, of interest and of value to him, everything in which he was sincere and did not deceive himself, everything that made the kernel of his life, was hidden from other people; and all that was false in him, the sheath in which he hid himself to conceal the truth—such, for instance, as his work in the bank, his discussions at the club, his "lower race," his presence with his wife at anniversary festivities—all that was open. And he judged of others by himself, not believing in what he saw, and always believing that every man had his real, most interesting life under the cover of secrecy and under the cover of night. All personal life rested on secrecy, and possibly it was partly on that account that civilised man was so nervously anxious that personal privacy should be respected.

After leaving his daughter at school, Gurov went on to the Slaviansky Bazaar. He took off his fur coat below, went upstairs, and softly knocked at the door. Anna Sergeyevna, wearing his favourite grey dress, exhausted by the journey and the suspense, had been expecting him since the evening before. She was pale; she looked at him, and did not smile, and he had hardly come in when she fell on his breast. Their kiss was slow and prolonged, as though they had not met for two years.

"Well, how are you getting on there?" he asked. "What news?"

"Wait; I'll tell you directly. . . . I can't talk."

She could not speak; she was crying. She turned away from him, and pressed her handkerchief to her eyes.

"Let her have her cry out. I'll sit down and wait," he thought, and he sat down in an arm-chair.

Then he rang and asked for tea to be brought him, and while he drank his tea she remained standing at the window with her back to him. She was crying from emotion, from the miserable consciousness that their life was so hard for them; they could only meet in secret, hiding themselves from people, like thieves! Was not their life shattered?

"Come, do stop!" he said.

It was evident to him that this love of theirs would not soon be over, that he could not see the end of it. Anna Sergeyevna grew more and more attached to him. She adored him, and it was unthinkable to say to her that it was bound to have an end some day; besides, she would not have believed it!

He went up to her and took her by the shoulders to say something affectionate and cheering, and at that moment he saw himself in the looking-glass.

His hair was already beginning to turn grey. And it seemed strange to him that he had grown so much older, so much plainer during the last few years. The shoulders on which his hands rested were warm and quivering. He felt compassion for this life, still so warm and lovely, but probably already not far from beginning to fade and wither like his own. Why did she love him so much? He always seemed to women different from what he was, and they loved in him not himself, but the man created by their imagination, whom they had been eagerly seeking all their lives; and afterwards, when they noticed their mistake, they loved him all the same. And not one of them had been happy with him. Time passed, he had made their acquaintance, got on with them, parted, but he had never once loved; it was anything you like, but not love.

And only now when his head was grey he had fallen properly, really in love—for the first time in his life.

Anna Sergeyevna and he loved each other like people very close and akin, like husband and wife, like tender friends; it seemed to them that fate itself had meant them for one another, and they could not understand why he had a wife and she a husband; and it was as though they were a pair of birds of passage, caught and forced to live in different cages. They forgave each other for what they were ashamed of in their past, they forgave everything in the present, and felt that this love of theirs had changed them both.

In moments of depression in the past he had comforted himself with any arguments that came into his mind, but now he no longer cared for arguments; he felt profound compassion, he wanted to be sincere and tender. . . .

"Don't cry, my darling," he said. "You've had your cry; that's enough. . . . Let us talk now, let us think of some plan."

Then they spent a long while taking counsel together, talked of how to avoid the necessity for secrecy, for deception, for living in different towns and not seeing each other for long at a time. How could they be free from the intolerable bondage?

"How? How?" he asked, clutching his head. "How?"

And it seemed as though in a little while the solution would be found, and then a new and splendid life would begin; and it was clear to both of them that they had still a long, long road before them, and that the most complicated and difficult part of it was only just beginning.

Anton Chekhov

ANNA ON THE NECK

After the wedding they had not even light refreshments;
the happy pair simply drank a glass of champagne,
changed into their travelling things, and drove to the station. Instead of a gay wedding ball and supper, instead of
music and dancing, they went on a journey to pray at a
shrine a hundred and fifty miles away. Many people com-
mended this, saying that Modest Alexeitch was a man
high up in the service and no longer young, and that a
noisy wedding might not have seemed quite suitable; and
music is apt to sound dreary when a government official
of fifty-two marries a girl who is only just eighteen. People said, too, that Modest Alexeitch, being a man of principle, had arranged this visit to the monastery expressly
in order to make his young bride realize that even in
marriage he put religion and morality above everything.

The happy pair were seen off at the station. The crowd
of relations and colleagues in the service stood, with
glasses in their hands, waiting for the train to start to
shout "Hurrah!" and the bride's father, Pyotr Leontyitch,
wearing a top-hat and the uniform of a teacher, already
drunk and very pale, kept craning towards the window,
glass in hand and saying in an imploring voice, "Anyuta!
Anya, Anya! one word!"

Anna bent out of the window to him, and he whispered
something to her, enveloping her in a stale smell of alco-
hol, blew into her ear—she could make out nothing—and
made the sign of the cross over her face, her bosom, and

her hands; meanwhile he was breathing in gasps and tears were shining in his eyes. And the schoolboys, Anna's brothers, Petya and Andrusha, pulled at his coat from behind, whispering in confusion, "Father, hush! . . . Father, that's enough. . . ."

When the train started, Anna saw her father run a little way after the train, staggering and spilling his wine, and what a kind, guilty, pitiful face he had.

"Hurra—ah!" he shouted.

The happy pair were left alone. Modest Alexeitch looked about the compartment, arranged their things on the shelves, and sat down, smiling, opposite his young wife. He was an official of medium height, rather stout and puffy, who looked exceedingly well nourished, with long whiskers and no moustache. His clean-shaven, round, sharply defined chin looked like the heel of a foot. The most characteristic point in his face was the absence of moustache, the bare, freshly shaven place, which gradually passed into the fat cheeks, quivering like jelly. His deportment was dignified, his movements were deliberate, his manner was soft.

"I cannot help remembering now one circumstance," he said, smiling. "When, five years ago, Kosorotov received the order of St. Anna of the second grade, and went to thank His Excellency, His Excellency expressed himself as follows: 'So now you have three Annas: one in your buttonhole and two on your neck.' And it must be explained that at that time Kosorotov's wife, a quarrelsome and frivolous person, had just returned to him, and that her name was Anna. I trust that when I receive the Anna of the second grade His Excellency will not have occasion to say the same thing to me."

He smiled with his little eyes. And she, too, smiled, troubled at the thought that at any moment this man might kiss her with his thick damp lips, and that she had no right to prevent his doing so. The soft movements of his fat person frightened her; she felt both fear and disgust. He got up, without haste took off the order from his neck, took off his coat and waistcoat, and put on his dressing-gown.

"That's better," he said, sitting down beside Anna.

Anna remembered what agony the wedding had been, when it had seemed to her that the priest, and the guests, and every one in church had been looking at her sorrowfully and asking why, why was she, such a sweet, nice girl, marrying such an elderly, uninteresting gentleman. Only that morning she was delighted that everything had been satisfactorily arranged, but at the time of the wedding, and now in the railway carriage, she felt cheated, guilty, and ridiculous. Here she had married a rich man and yet she had no money, her wedding-dress had been bought on credit, and when her father and brothers had been saying good-bye, she could see from their faces that they had not a farthing. Would they have any supper that day? And tomorrow? And for some reason it seemed to her that her father and the boys were sitting tonight hungry without her, and feeling the same misery as they had the day after their mother's funeral.

"Oh, how unhappy I am!" she thought. "Why am I so unhappy?"

With the awkwardness of a man with settled habits, unaccustomed to deal with women, Modest Alexeitch touched her on the waist and patted her on the shoulder, while she went on thinking about money, about her mother and her mother's death. When her mother died, her father, Pyotr Leontyitch, a teacher of drawing and writing in the high school, had taken to drink, impoverishment had followed, the boys had not had boots or goloshes, their father had been hauled up before the magistrate, the warrant officer had come and made an inventory of the furniture. . . . What a disgrace! Anna had had to look after her drunken father, darn her brothers' stockings, go to market, and when she was complimented on her youth, her beauty, and her elegant manners, it seemed to her that every one was looking at her cheap hat and the holes in her boots that were inked over. And at night there had been tears and a haunting dread that her father would soon, very soon, be dismissed from the school for his weakness, and that he would not survive it, but would die, too, like their mother. But ladies of their acquaintance had taken the matter in hand and looked about for a good match for Anna. This Modest Alexeitch, who was neither young nor good-looking but had money, was soon found. He had a hundred thousand in the bank and the family estate, which he had let on lease. He was a man of principle and stood well with His Excellency; it would be nothing to him, so they told Anna, to get a note from His Excellency to the directors of the high school, or even to the Education Commissioner, to prevent Pyotr Leontyitch from being dismissed.

While she was recalling these details, she suddenly heard strains of music which floated in at the window, together with the sound of voices. The train was stopping at a station. In the crowd beyond the platform an accordion and a cheap squeaky fiddle were being briskly played, and the sound of a military band came from beyond the villas and the tall birches and poplars that lay bathed in the moonlight; there must have been a dance in the place. Summer visitors and townspeople, who used to come out here by train in fine weather for a breath of fresh air, were parading up and down on the platform. Among them was the wealthy owner of all the summer villas—a tall, stout, dark man called Artynov. He had prominent eyes and looked like an Armenian. He wore a strange costume; his shirt was unbuttoned, showing his chest; he wore high boots with spurs, and a black cloak hung from his shoulders and dragged on the ground like a train. Two boarhounds followed him with their sharp noses to the ground.

Tears were still shining in Anna's eyes, but she was not thinking now of her mother, nor of money, nor of her marriage; but shaking hands with schoolboys and officers she knew, she laughed gaily and said quickly, "How do you do? How are you?"

She went out on to the platform between the carriages into the moonlight, and stood so that they could all see her in her new splendid dress and hat.

"Why are we stopping here?" she asked.

"This is a junction. They are waiting for the mail train to pass."

Seeing that Artynov was looking at her, she screwed up her eyes coquettishly and began talking aloud in French;

and because her voice sounded so pleasant, and because she heard music and the moon was reflected in the pond, and because Artynov, the notorious Don Juan and spoiled child of fortune, was looking at her eagerly and with curiosity, and because every one was in good spirits—she suddenly felt joyful, and when the train started and the officers of her acquaintance saluted her, she was humming the polka the strains of which reached her from the military band playing beyond the trees; and she returned to her compartment feeling as though it had been proved to her at the station that she would certainly be happy in spite of everything.

The happy pair spent two days at the monastery, then went back to town. They lived in a rent-free flat. When Modest Alexeitch had gone to the office, Anna played the piano, or shed tears of depression, or lay down on a couch and read novels or looked through fashion papers. At dinner Modest Alexeitch ate a great deal and talked about politics, about appointments, transfers, and promotions in the service, about the necessity of hard work, and said that, family life not being a pleasure but a duty, if you took care of the kopecks the roubles would take care of themselves, and that he put religion and morality before everything else in the world. And holding his knife in his fist as though it were a sword, he would say, "Every one ought to have his duties!"

And Anna listened to him, was frightened, and could not eat, and she usually got up from the table hungry. After dinner her husband lay down for a nap and snored loudly, while Anna went to see her own people. Her father and the boys looked at her in a peculiar way, as though just before she came in they had been blaming her for having married for money a tedious, wearisome man she did not love; her rustling skirts, her bracelets, and her general air of a married lady, offended them and made them uncomfortable. In her presence they felt a little embarrassed and did not know what to talk to her about; but yet they still loved her as before, and were not used to having dinner without her. She sat down with them to cabbage soup, porridge, and fried potatoes, smelling of mutton dripping. Pyotr Leontyitch filled his glass from the decanter with a trembling hand and drank it off hurriedly, greedily, with repulsion, then poured out a second glass and then a third. Petya and Andrusha, thin, pale boys with big eyes, would take the decanter and say desperately, "You mustn't, father. . . . Enough, father. . . ."

And Anna, too, was troubled and entreated him to drink no more; and he would suddenly fly into a rage and beat the table with his fists, "I won't allow any one to dictate to me!" he would shout. "Wretched boys! wretched girl! I'll turn you all out!"

But there was a note of weakness, of good-nature in his voice, and no one was afraid of him. After dinner he usually dressed in his best. Pale, with a cut on his chin from shaving, craning his thin neck, he would stand for half an hour before the glass, prinking, combing his hair, twisting his black moustache, sprinkling himself with scent, tying his cravat in a bow; then he would put on his gloves and his top-hat, and go off to give his private lessons. Or if it was a holiday he would stay at home and paint, or play the harmonium, which wheezed and growled; he would try to wrest from it pure harmonious sounds and would sing to it; or would storm at the boys, "Wretches! Good-for-nothing boys! You have spoiled the instrument!"

In the evening Anna's husband played cards with his colleagues, who lived under the same roof in the government quarters. The wives of these gentlemen would come in—ugly, tastelessly dressed women, as coarse as cooks—and gossip would begin in the flat as tasteless and unattractive as the ladies themselves. Sometimes Modest Alexeitch would take Anna to the theatre. In the intervals he would never let her stir a step from his side, but walked about arm in arm with her through the corridors and the foyer. When he bowed to some one, he immediately whispered to Anna: "A civil councillor . . . visits at His Excellency's"; or, "A man of means . . . has a house of his own." When they passed the buffet Anna had a great longing for something sweet; she was fond of chocolate and apple cakes, but she had no money, and she did not like to ask her husband. He would take a pear, pinch it with his fingers, and ask uncertainly, "How much?"

"Twenty-five kopecks!"

"I say!" he would reply, and put it down; but as it was awkward to leave the buffet without buying anything, he would order some seltzer-water and drink the whole bottle himself, and tears would come into his eyes. And Anna hated him at such times.

And suddenly flushing crimson, he would say to her rapidly, "Bow to that old lady!"

"But I don't know her."

"No matter. That's the wife of the director of the local treasury! Bow, I tell you," he would grumble insistently. "Your head won't drop off."

Anna bowed and her head certainly did not drop off, but it was agonizing. She did everything her husband wanted her to, and was furious with herself for having let him deceive her like the veriest idiot. She had only married him for his money, and yet she had less money now than before her marriage. In old days her father would sometimes give her twenty kopecks, but now she had not a farthing. To take money by stealth or ask for it, she could not; she was afraid of her husband, she trembled before him. She felt as though she had been afraid of him for years. In her childhood the director of the high school had always seemed the most impressive and terrifying force in the world, sweeping down like a thunderstorm or a steam-engine ready to crush her; another similar force of which the whole family talked, and of which they were for some reason afraid, was His Excellency; then there were a dozen others, less formidable, and among them the teachers at the high school, with shaven upper lips, stern, implacable; and now finally there was Modest Alexeitch, a man of principle, who even resembled the director in the face. And in Anna's imagination all these forces blended together into one, and, in the form of a terrible, huge white bear, menaced the weak and erring such as her father. And she was afraid to say anything in opposition to her husband, and gave a forced smile, and tried to make a show

of pleasure when she was coarsely caressed and defiled
by embraces that excited her terror.

Only once Pyotr Leontyitch had the temerity to ask for
a loan of fifty roubles in order to pay some very irksome
debt, but what an agony it had been!

"Very good; I'll give it to you," said Modest Alexeitch
after a moment's thought; "but I warn you I won't help
you again till you give up drinking. Such a failing is disgraceful in a man in the government service! I must remind you of the well-known fact that many capable people have been ruined by that passion, though they might
possibly, with temperance, have risen in time to a very
high position."

And long-winded phrases followed: "inasmuch as . . .,"
"following upon which proposition . . .," "in view of the
aforesaid contention . . ."; and Pyotr Leontyitch was in
agonies of humiliation and felt an intense craving for al-
cohol.

And when the boys came to visit Anna, generally in
broken boots and threadbare trousers, they, too, had to
listen to sermons.

"Every man ought to have his duties!" Modest Alexeitch
would say to them.

And he did not give them money. But he did give Anna
bracelets, rings, and brooches, saying that these things
would come in useful for a rainy day. And he often un-
locked her drawer and made an inspection to see whether
they were all safe.

II

Meanwhile winter came on. Long before Christmas there
was an announcement in the local papers that the usual
winter ball would take place on the twenty-ninth of December in the Hall of Nobility. Every evening after cards
Modest Alexeitch was excitedly whispering with his colleagues' wives and glancing at Anna, and then paced up
and down the room for a long while, thinking. At last, late
one evening, he stood still, facing Anna, and said, "You
ought to get yourself a ball dress. Do you understand?

Only please consult Marya Grigoryevna and Natalya Kuz-minishna."

And he gave her a hundred roubles. She took the money, but she did not consult any one when she ordered the ball dress; she spoke to no one but her father, and tried to imagine how her mother would have dressed for a ball. Her mother had always dressed in the latest fashion and had always taken trouble over Anna, dressing her elegantly like a doll, and had taught her to speak French and dance the mazurka superbly (she had been a governess for five years before her marriage). Like her mother, Anna could make a new dress out of an old one, clean gloves with benzine, hire jewels; and, like her mother, she knew how to screw up her eyes, lisp, assume graceful attitudes, fly into raptures when necessary, and throw a mournful and enigmatic look into her eyes. And from her father she had inherited the dark colour of her hair and eyes, her highly-strung nerves, and the habit of always making herself look her best.

When, half an hour before setting off for the ball, Mod-est Alexeitch went into her room without his coat on, to put his order round his neck before her pier-glass, dazzled by her beauty and the splendour of her fresh, ethereal dress, he combed his whiskers complacently and said, "So that's what my wife can look like . . . so that's what you can look like! Anyuta!" he went on, dropping into a tone of solemnity, "I have made your fortune, and now I beg you to do something for mine. I beg you to get introduced to the wife of His Excellency! For God's sake, do! Through her I may get the post of senior reporting clerk!"

They went to the ball. They reached the Hall of No-bility, the entrance with the hall porter. They came to the vestibule with the hat-stands, the fur coats; footmen scurrying about, and ladies with low necks putting up their fans to screen themselves from the draughts. There was a smell of gas and of soldiers. When Anna, walking upstairs on her husband's arm, heard the music and saw herself full length in the looking-glass in the full glow of the lights, there was a rush of joy in her heart, and she felt the same presentiment of happiness as in the moonlight at the station. She walked in proudly, confidently, for the first time feeling herself not a girl but a lady, and unconsciously imitating her mother in her walk and in her manner. And for the first time in her life she felt rich and free. Even her husband's presence did not oppress her, for as she crossed the threshold of the hall she had guessed instinctively that the proximity of an old husband did not detract from her in the least, but, on the contrary, gave her that shade of piquant mystery that is so attractive to men. The orchestra was already playing and the dances had begun. After their flat Anna was overwhelmed by the lights, the bright colours, the music, the noise, and looking round the room, thought, "Oh, how lovely!" She at once distinguished in the crowd all her acquaintances, every one she had met before at parties or on picnics—all the officers, the teachers, the lawyers, the officials, the landowners, His Excellency, Artynov, and the ladies of the highest standing, dressed up and very *décolletées*, handsome and ugly, who had already taken up their positions in the stalls and pavilions of the charity bazaar, to begin selling things for the benefit of the poor. A huge officer in epaulettes—she had been introduced to him in Staro-Kievsky Street when she was a schoolgirl, but now she could not remember his name—seemed to spring from out of the ground, begging her for a waltz, and she flew away from her husband, feeling as though she were floating away in a sailing-boat in a violent storm, while her husband was left far away on the shore. She danced passionately, with fervour, a waltz, then a polka and a quadrille, being snatched by one partner as soon as she was left by another, dizzy with music and the noise, mixing Russian with French, lisping, laughing, and with no thought of her husband or anything else. She excited great admiration among the men—that was evident, and indeed it could not have been otherwise; she was breathless with excitement, felt thirsty, and convulsively clutched her fan. Pyotr Leontyitch, her father, in a crumpled dress-coat that smelt of benzine, came up to her, offering her a plate of pink ice.

"You are enchanting this evening," he said, looking at her rapturously, "and I have never so much regretted that you were in such a hurry to get married. . . . What was it for? I know you did it for our sake, but . . ." With a shaking hand he drew out a roll of notes and said: "I got the money for my lessons today, and can pay your husband what I owe him."

She put the plate back into his hand, and was pounced upon by some one and borne off to a distance. She caught a glimpse over her partner's shoulder of her father gliding over the floor, putting his arm round a lady and whirling down the ballroom with her.

"How sweet he is when he is sober!" she thought.

She danced the mazurka with the same huge officer; he moved gravely, as heavily as a dead carcase in a uniform, twitched his shoulders and his chest, stamped his feet very languidly—he felt fearfully disinclined to dance. She fluttered round him, provoking him by her beauty, her bare neck; her eyes glowed defiantly, her movements were passionate, while he became more and more indifferent, and held out his hands to her as graciously as a king.

"Bravo, bravo!" said people watching them.

But little by little the huge officer, too, broke out; he grew lively, excited, and, overcome by her fascination, was carried away and danced lightly, youthfully, while she merely moved her shoulders and looked slyly at him as though she were now the queen and he were her slave; and at that moment it seemed to her that the whole room was looking at them, and that everybody was thrilled and envied them. The huge officer had hardly had time to thank her for the dance, when the crowd suddenly parted and the men drew themselves up in a strange way, with their hands at their sides. His Excellency, with two stars on his dress-coat, was walking up to her. Yes, His Excellency was walking straight towards her, for he was staring directly at her with a sugary smile, while he licked his lips as he always did when he saw a pretty woman.

"Delighted, delighted . . ." he began. "I shall order your husband to be clapped in a lock-up for keeping such a treasure hidden from us till now. I've come to you with a message from my wife," he went on, offering her his arm. "You must help us. . . . M-m-yes. . . . We ought to

give you the prize for beauty as they do in America. . . .
M-m-yes. . . . The Americans. . . . My wife is expecting
you impatiently."

He led her to a stall and presented her to a middle-aged
lady, the lower part of whose face was disproportionately
large, so that she looked as though she were holding a
big stone in her mouth.

"You must help us," she said through her nose in a sing-
song voice. "All the pretty women are working for our
charity bazaar, and you are the only one enjoying yourself.
Why won't you help us?"

She went away, and Anna took her place by the cups
and the silver samovar. She was soon doing a lively trade.
Anna asked no less than a rouble for a cup of tea, and
made the huge officer drink three cups. Artynov, the rich
man with prominent eyes, who suffered from asthma, came
up, too; he was not dressed in the strange costume in
which Anna had seen him in the summer at the station,
but wore a drcss-coat like every one else. Keeping his
eyes fixed on Anna, he drank a glass of champagne and
paid a hundred roubles for it, then drank some tea and
gave another hundred—all this without saying a word, as
he was short of breath through asthma. . . . Anna invited
purchasers and got money out of them, firmly convinced
by now that her smiles and glances could not fail to afford these people great pleasure. She realized now that
she was created exclusively for this noisy, brilliant, laughing life, with its music, its dancers, its adorers, and her
old terror of a force that was sweeping down upon her
and menacing to crush her seemed to her ridiculous: she
was afraid of no one now, and only regretted that her
mother could not be there to rejoice at her success.

Pyotr Leontyitch, pale by now but still steady on his
legs, came up to the stall and asked for a glass of brandy.
Anna turned crimson, expecting him to say something inappropriate (she was already ashamed of having such a
poor and ordinary father); but he emptied his glass, took
ten roubles out of his roll of notes, flung it down, and
walked away with dignity without uttering a word. A
little later she saw him dancing in the grand chain, and

by now he was staggering and kept shouting something, to the great confusion of his partner; and Anna remembered how at the ball three years before he had staggered and shouted in the same way, and it had ended in the police-sergeant's taking him home to bed, and next day the director had threatened to dismiss him from his post. How inappropriate that memory was!

When the samovars were put out in the stalls and the exhausted ladies handed over their takings to the middle-aged lady with the stone in her mouth, Artynov took Anna on his arm to the hall where supper was served to all who had assisted at the bazaar. There were some twenty people at supper, not more, but it was very noisy. His Excellency proposed a toast. "In this magnificent dining-room it will be appropriate to drink to the success of the cheap dining-rooms, which are the object of today's bazaar."

The brigadier-general proposed the toast: "To the power by which even the artillery is vanquished," and all the company clinked glasses with the ladies. It was very, very gay.

When Anna was escorted home it was daylight and the cooks were going to market. Joyful, intoxicated, full of new sensations, exhausted, she undressed, dropped into bed, and at once fell asleep. . . .

It was past one in the afternoon when the servant waked her and announced that M. Artynov had called. She dressed quickly and went down into the drawing-room. Soon after Artynov, His Excellency called to thank her for her assistance in the bazaar. With a sugary smile, chewing his lips, he kissed her hand, and asking her permission to come again, took his leave, while she remained standing in the middle of the drawing-room, amazed, enchanted, unable to believe that this change in her life, this marvellous change, had taken place so quickly; and at that moment Modest Alexeitch walked in . . . and he, too, stood before her now with the same ingratiating, sugary, cringingly respectful expression which she was accustomed to see on his face in the presence of the great and powerful; and with rapture, with indignation, with contempt, convinced that no harm would come to her from it, she said, articulating distinctly each word, "Be off, you blockhead!"

From this time forward Anna never had one day free, as she was always taking part in picnics, expeditions, performances. She returned home every day after midnight, and went to bed on the floor in the drawing-room, and afterwards used to tell every one, touchingly, how she slept under flowers. She needed a very great deal of money, but she was no longer afraid of Modest Alexeitch, and spent his money as though it were her own; and she did not ask, did not demand it, simply sent him in the bills. "Give bearer two hundred roubles," or "Pay one hundred roubles at once."

At Easter Modest Alexeitch received the Anna of the second grade. When he went to offer his thanks, His Excellency put aside the paper he was reading and settled himself more comfortably in his chair.

"So now you have three Annas," he said, scrutinizing his white hands and pink nails—"one on your buttonhole and two on your neck."

Modest Alexeitch put two fingers to his lips as a precaution against laughing too loud and said, "Now I have only to look forward to the arrival of a little Vladimir. I make bold to beg your Excellency to stand godfather."

He was alluding to Vladimir of the fourth grade, and was already imagining how he would tell everywhere the story of this pun, so happy in its readiness and audacity, and he wanted to say something equally happy, but His Excellency was buried again in his newspaper, and merely gave him a nod.

And Anna went on driving about with three horses, going out hunting with Artynov, playing in one-act dramas, going out to supper, and was more and more rarely with her own family; they dined now alone. Pyotr Leontyitch was drinking more heavily than ever; there was no money, and the harmonium had been sold long ago for debt. The boys did not let him go out alone in the street now, but looked after him for fear he might fall down; and whenever they met Anna driving in Staro-Kievsky Street with a pair of horses and Artynov on the box instead of a coach-man, Pyotr Leontyitch took off his top-hat, and was about to shout to her, but Petya and Andrusha took him by the arm, and said imploringly, "You mustn't, father. Hush, father!"

Alexander Kuprin
1870 – 1938

THE OUTRAGE
A True Story

It was five o'clock on a July afternoon. The heat was terrible. The whole of the huge stone-built town breathed out heat like a glowing furnace. The glare of the white-walled house was insufferable. The asphalt pavements grew soft and burned the feet. The shadows of the acacias spread over the cobbled road, pitiful and weary. They too seemed hot. The sea, pale in the sunlight, lay heavy and immobile as one dead. Over the streets hung a white dust.

In the foyer of one of the private theatres a small committee of local barristers who had undertaken to conduct the cases of those who had suffered in the last pogrom against the Jews was reaching the end of its daily task. There were nineteen of them, all juniors, young, progressive and conscientious men. The sitting was without formality, and white suits of duck, flannel and alpaca were in the majority. They sat anywhere, at little marble tables, and the chairman stood in front of an empty counter where chocolates were sold in the winter.

The barristers were quite exhausted by the heat which poured in through the windows, with the dazzling sunlight and the noise of the streets. The proceedings went lazily and with a certain irritation.

A tall young man with a fair moustache and thin hair was in the chair. He was dreaming voluptuously how he would be off in an instant on his new-bought bicycle to the bungalow. He would undress quickly, and without waiting to cool, still bathed in sweat, would fling himself into the clear, cold, sweet-smelling sea. His whole body was enervated and tense, thrilled by the thought. Impatiently moving the papers before him, he spoke in a drowsy voice.

"So, Joseph Moritzovich will conduct the case of Rubinchik. . . . Perhaps there is still a statement to be made on the order of the day?"

His youngest colleague, a short, stout Karaite, very black and lively, said in a whisper so that every one could hear: "On the order of the day, the best thing would be iced *kvas*. . . ."

The chairman gave him a stern side-glance, but could not restrain a smile. He sighed and put both his hands on the table to raise himself and declare the meeting closed, when the doorkeeper, who stood at the entrance to the theatre, suddenly moved forward and said: "There are seven people outside, sir. They want to come in."

The chairman looked impatiently round the company.

"What is to be done, gentlemen?"

Voices were heard.

"Next time. *Basta!*"

"Let 'em put it in writing."

"If they'll get it over quickly. . . . Decide it at once."

"Let 'em go to the devil. Phew! It's like boiling pitch."

"Let them in." The chairman gave a sign with his head, annoyed. "Then bring me a Vichy, please. But it must be cold."

The porter opened the door and called down the corridor: "Come in. They say you may."

Then seven of the most surprising and unexpected individuals filed into the foyer. First appeared a full-grown, confident man in a smart suit, of the colour of dry sea-sand, in a magnificent pink shirt with white stripes and a crimson rose in his buttonhole. From the front his head looked like an upright bean, from the side like a horizontal bean. His face was adorned with a strong, bushy, martial moustache. He wore dark blue pince-nez on his nose, on his hands straw-coloured gloves. In his left hand he held a black walking stick with a silver mount, in his right a light blue handkerchief.

The other six produced a strange, chaotic, incongruous impression, exactly as though they had all hastily pooled not merely their clothes, but their hands, feet and heads as well. There was a man with the splendid profile of a Roman senator, dressed in rags and tatters. Another wore an elegant dress waistcoat, from the deep opening of which a dirty Little-Russian shirt leapt to the eye. Here were the unbalanced faces of the criminal type, but looking with a confidence that nothing could shake. All these men, in spite of their apparent youth, evidently possessed a large experience of life, an easy manner, a bold approach, and some hidden, suspicious cunning.

The gentleman in the sandy suit bowed just his head, neatly and easily, and said with a half-question in his voice: "Mr. Chairman?"

"Yes. I am the chairman. What is your business?"

"We—all whom you see before you," the gentleman began in a quiet voice and turned round to indicate his companions, "we come as delegates from the United Rostov-Kharkov-and-Odessa-Nikolayev Association of Thieves."

The barristers began to shift in their seats.

The chairman flung himself back and opened his eyes wide. "Association of *what?*" he said, perplexed.

"The Association of Thieves," the gentleman in the sandy suit coolly repeated. "As for myself, my comrades did me the signal honour of electing me as the spokesman of the deputation."

"Very . . . pleased," the chairman said uncertainly.

"Thank you. All seven of us are ordinary thieves—naturally of different departments. The Association has authorised us to put before your esteemed Committee"—the gentleman again made an elegant bow—"our respectful demand for assistance."

"I don't quite understand . . . quite frankly . . . what is the connection. . . ." The chairman waved his hands helplessly. "However, please go on."

"The matter about which we have the courage and the honour to apply to you, gentlemen, is very clear, very simple, and very brief. It will take only six or seven minutes. I consider it my duty to warn you of this beforehand, in view of the late hour and the 15 degrees that Fahrenheit marks in the shade." The orator expectorated slightly and glanced at his superb gold watch. "You see, in the reports that have lately appeared in the local papers of the melancholy and terrible days of the last pogrom, there have very often been indications that among the instigators of the pogrom who were paid and organised by the police—the dregs of society, consisting of drunkards, tramps, souteneurs, and hooligans from the slums—thieves were also to be found. At first we were silent, but finally we considered ourselves under the necessity of protesting against such an unjust and serious accusation, before the face of the whole of intellectual society. I know well that in the eye of the law we are offenders and enemies of society. But imagine only for a moment, gentlemen, the situation of this enemy of society when he is accused wholesale of an offence which he not only never committed, but which he is ready to resist with the whole strength of his soul. It goes without saying that he will feel the outrage of such an injustice more keenly than a normal, average, fortunate citizen. Now, we declare that the accusation brought against us is utterly devoid of all basis, not merely of fact but even of logic. I intend to prove this in a few words if the honourable committee will kindly listen."

"Proceed," said the chairman.

"Please do . . . Please . . ." was heard from the barristers, now animated.

"I offer you my sincere thanks in the name of all my comrades. Believe me, you will never repent your attention to the representatives of our . . . well, let us say, slippery, but nevertheless difficult, profession. 'So we begin,' as Giraldoni sings in the prologue to *Pagliacci*.

"But first I would ask your permission, Mr. Chairman, to quench my thirst a little. . . . Porter, bring me a lemonade and a glass of English bitter, there's a good fellow. Gentlemen, I will not speak of the moral aspect of our profession nor of its social importance. Doubtless you know better than I the striking and brilliant paradox of

Proudhon: *La propriété c'est le vol*—a paradox if you like, but one that has never yet been refuted by the sermons of cowardly bourgeois or fat priests. For instance: a father accumulates a million by energetic and clever exploitation, and leaves it to his son—a rickety, lazy, ignorant, degenerate idiot, a brainless maggot, a true parasite. Potentially a million rubles is a million working days, the absolutely irrational right to labour, sweat, life, and blood of a terrible number of men. Why? What is the ground of reason? Utterly unknown. Then why not agree with the proposition, gentlemen, that our profession is to some extent as it were a correction of the excessive accumulation of values in the hands of individuals, and serves as a protest against all the hardships, abominations, arbitrariness, violence, and negligence of the human personality, against all the monstrosities created by the bourgeois capitalistic organisation of modern society? Sooner or later, this order of things will assuredly be overturned by the social revolution. Property will pass away into the limbo of melancholy memories and with it, alas! we will disappear from the face of the earth, we, *les braves chevaliers d'industrie.*"

The orator paused to take the tray from the hands of the porter, and placed it near to his hand on the table.

"Excuse me, gentlemen. . . . Here, my good man, take this, . . . and by the way, when you go out shut the door close behind you."

"Very good, your Excellency!" the porter bawled in jest.

The orator drank off half a glass and continued: "However, let us leave aside the philosophical, social, and economic aspects of the question. I do not wish to fatigue your attention. I must nevertheless point out that our profession very closely approaches the idea of that which is called art. Into it enter all the elements which go to form art—vocation, inspiration, fantasy, inventiveness, ambition, and a long and arduous apprenticeship to the science. From it is absent virtue alone, concerning which the great Karamzin wrote with such stupendous and fiery fascination. Gentlemen, nothing is further from my intention than to trifle with you and waste your precious time with idle paradoxes; but I cannot avoid expounding my idea briefly. To an outsider's ear it sounds absurdly wild and ridiculous to speak of the vocation of a thief. However, I venture to assure you that this vocation is a reality. There are men who possess a peculiarly strong visual memory, sharpness and accuracy of eye, presence of mind, dexterity of hand, and above all a subtle sense of touch, who are as it were born into God's world for the sole and special purpose of becoming distinguished card-sharpers. The pickpockets' profession demands extraordinary nimbleness and agility, a terrific certainty of movement, not to mention a ready wit, a talent for observation and strained attention. Some have a positive vocation for breaking open safes: from their tenderest childhood they are attracted by the mysteries of every kind of complicated mechanism—bicycles, sewing machines, clock-work toys and watches. Finally, gentlemen, there are people with an hereditary animus against private property. You may call this phenomenon degeneracy. But I tell you that you cannot entice a true thief, and thief by vocation, into the prose of honest vegetation by any gingerbread reward, or by the offer of a secure position, or by the gift of money, or by a woman's love: because there is here a permanent beauty of risk, a fascinating abyss of danger, the delightful sinking of the heart, the impetuous pulsation of life, the ecstasy! You are armed with the protection of the law, by locks, revolvers, telephones, police and soldiery; but we only by our own dexterity, cunning and fearlessness. We are the foxes, and society—is a chicken-run guarded by dogs. Are you aware that the most artistic and gifted natures in our villages become horse-thieves and poachers? What would you have? Life is so meagre, so insipid, so intolerably dull to eager and high-spirited souls!

"I pass on to inspiration. Gentlemen, doubtless you have had to read of thefts that were supernatural in design and execution. In the headlines of the newspapers they are called 'An Amazing Robbery,' or 'An Ingenious Swindle,' or again 'A Clever Ruse of the Gangsters.' In such cases our bourgeois paterfamilias waves his hands and exclaims: 'What a terrible thing! If only their abilities were turned to good—their inventiveness, their amazing knowledge of human psychology, their self-possession, their fearlessness, their incomparable histrionic powers! What extraordinary benefits they would bring to the country!' But it is well known that the bourgeois paterfamilias was specially devised by Heaven to utter commonplaces and trivialities. I myself sometimes—we thieves are sentimental people, I confess—I myself sometimes admire a beautiful sunset in Aleksandra Park or by the sea-shore. And I am always certain beforehand that some one near me will say with infallible *aplomb*: 'Look at it. If it were put into a picture no one would ever believe it!' I turn round and naturally I see a self-satisfied, full-fed paterfamilias, who delights in repeating some one else's silly statement as though it were his own. As for our dear country, the bourgeois paterfamilias looks upon it as though it were a roast turkey. If you've managed to cut the best part of the bird for yourself, eat it quietly in a comfortable corner and praise God. But he's not really the important person. I was led away by my detestation of vulgarity and I apologise for the digression. The real point is that genius and inspiration, even when they are not devoted to the service of the Orthodox Church, remain rare and beautiful things. Progress is a law—and theft too has its creation.

"Finally, our profession is by no means as easy and pleasant as it seems to the first glance. It demands long experience, constant practice, slow and painful apprenticeship. It comprises in itself hundreds of supple, skilful processes that the cleverest juggler cannot compass. That I may not give you only empty words, gentlemen, I will perform a few experiments before you now. I ask you to have every confidence in the demonstrators. We are all at present in the enjoyment of legal freedom, and though we are usually watched, and every one of us is known by face, and our photographs adorn the albums of all detective departments, for the time being we are not under the necessity of hiding ourselves from anybody. If any one of you should recognise any of us in the future under different circumstances, we ask you earnestly always to act in accordance with your professional duties and your obligations as citizens. In grateful return for your kind attention we have decided to declare your property inviolable, and to invest it with a thieves' taboo. However, I proceed to business."

The orator turned round and gave an order: "Sesoi the Great, will you come this way!"

An enormous fellow with a stoop, whose hands reached to his knees, without a forehead or a neck, like a big, fair Hercules, came forward. He grinned stupidly and rubbed his left eyebrow in his confusion.

"Can't do nothin' here," he said hoarsely.

The gentleman in the sandy suit spoke for him, turning to the committee.

"Gentlemen, before you stands a respected member of our association. His specialty is breaking open safes, iron strong boxes, and other receptacles for monetary tokens. In his night work he sometimes avails himself of the electric current of the lighting installation for fusing metals. Unfortunately he has nothing on which he can demonstrate the best items of his repertoire. He will open the most elaborate lock irreproachably. . . . By the way, this door here, it's locked, is it not?"

Every one turned to look at the door, on which a printed notice hung: "Stage Door. Strictly Private."

"Yes, the door's locked, evidently," the chairman agreed.

"Admirable. Sesoi the Great, will you be so kind?"

" 'Tain't nothin' at all," said the giant leisurely.

He went close to the door, shook it cautiously with his hand, took out of his pocket a small bright instrument, bent down to the keyhole, made some almost imperceptible movements with the tool, suddenly straightened and flung the door wide in silence. The chairman had his watch in his hands. The whole affair took only ten seconds.

"Thank you, Sesoi the Great," said the gentleman in the sandy suit politely. "You may go back to your seat."

But the chairman interrupted in some alarm: "Excuse me. This is all very interesting and instructive, but . . . is it included in your esteemed colleague's profession to be able to lock the door again?"

"Ah, *mille pardones.*" The gentleman bowed hurriedly.

"It slipped my mind. Sesoi the Great, would you oblige?"

The door was locked with the same adroitness and the same silence. The esteemed colleague waddled back to his friends, grinning.

"Now I will have the honour to show you the skill of one of our comrades who is in the line of picking pockets in theatres and railway-stations," continued the orator. "He is still very young, but you may to some extent judge from the delicacy of his present work of the heights he will attain by diligence. Yasha!" A swarthy youth in a blue silk blouse and long glacé boots, like a gipsy, came forward with a swagger, fingering the tassels of his belt, and merrily screwing up his big, impudent black eyes with yellow whites.

"Gentlemen," said the gentleman in the sandy suit persuasively, "I must ask if one of you would be kind enough to submit himself to a little experiment. I assure you this will be an exhibition only, just a game."

He looked round over the seated company.

The short plump Karaite, black as a beetle, came forward from his table.

"At your service," he said amusedly.

"Yasha!" The orator signed with his head.

Yasha came close to the solicitor. On his left arm, which was bent, hung a bright-coloured, figured scarf.

"Suppose yer in church or at the bar in one of the halls, —or watchin' a circus," he began in a sugary, fluent voice. "I see straight off—there's a toff. . . . Excuse me, sir. Suppose you're the toff. There's no offence—just means a rich gent, decent enough, but don't know his way about. First—what's he likely to have about 'im? All sorts. Mostly, a ticker and a chain. Whereabouts does he keep 'em? Somewhere in his top vest pocket—here. Others have 'em in the bottom pocket. Just here. Purse—most always in the trousers, except when a greeny keeps it in his jacket. Cigar case. Have a look first what it is—gold, silver—with a monogram. Leather—what decent man'd soil his hands? Cigar case. Seven pockets: here, here, here, up there, there, here and here again. That's right, ain't it? That's how you go to work."

As he spoke the young man smiled. His eyes shone straight into the barrister's. With a quick, dexterous movement of his right hand he pointed to various portions of his clothes.

"Then again you might see a pin here in the tie. However we do not appropriate. Such *gents* nowadays—they hardly ever wear a real stone. Then I comes up to him. I begin straight off to talk to him like a gent: 'Sir, would you be so kind as to give me a light from your cigarette' —or something of the sort. At any rate, I enter into conversation. What's next? I look him straight in the peepers, just like this. Only two of me fingers are at it—just this and this." Yasha lifted two fingers of his right hand on a level with the solicitor's face, the forefinger and the middle finger and moved them about.

"D'you see? With these two fingers I run over the whole pianner. Nothin' wonderful in it: one, two, three—ready. Any man who wasn't stupid could learn easily. That's all it is. Most ordinary business. I thank you."

The pickpocket swung on his heel as if to return to his seat.

"Yasha!" The gentleman in the sandy suit said with meaning weight. "Yasha!" he repeated sternly.

Yasha stopped. His back was turned to the barrister, but he evidently gave his representative an imploring look, because the latter frowned and shook his head.

"Yasha!" he said for the third time, in a threatening tone.

"Huh!" The young thief grunted in vexation and turned to face the solicitor. "Where's your little watch, sir?" he said in a piping voice.

"Oh!" the Karaite brought himself up sharp.

"You see—now you say 'Oh!'" Yasha continued reproachfully. "All the while you were admiring me right hand, I was operatin' yer watch with my left. Just with these two little fingers, under the scarf. That's why we carry a scarf. Since your chain's not worth anything—a present from some *mamselle* and the watch is a gold one, I've left you the chain as a keepsake. Take it," he added with a sigh, holding out the watch.

"But . . . That is clever," the barrister said in confusion. "I didn't notice it at all."

"That's our business," Yasha said with pride.

He swaggered back to his comrades. Meantime the orator took a drink from his glass and continued.

"Now, gentlemen, our next collaborator will give you an exhibition of some ordinary card tricks, which are worked at fairs, on steamboats and railways. With three cards, for instance, an ace, a queen, and a six, he can quite easily. . . . But perhaps you are tired of these demonstrations, gentlemen." . . .

"Not at all. It's extremely interesting," the chairman answered affably. "I should like to ask one question—that is if it is not too indiscreet—what is your own specialty?"

"Mine . . . H'm. . . . No, how could it be an indiscretion? . . . I work the big diamond shops . . . and my other business is banks," answered the orator with a modest smile. "Don't think this occupation is easier than others. Enough that I know four European languages, German, French, English, and Italian, not to mention Polish, Ukrainian and Yiddish. But shall I show you some more experiments, Mr. Chairman?"

The chairman looked at his watch.

"Unfortunately the time is too short," he said. "Wouldn't it be better to pass on to the substance of your business? Besides, the experiments we have just seen have amply convinced us of the talent of our esteemed associates. . . . Am I not right, Isaac Abramovich?"

"Yes, yes . . . absolutely," the Karaite barrister readily confirmed.

"Admirable," the gentleman in the sandy suit kindly agreed. "My dear Count"—he turned to a blond, curly-haired man, with a face like a billiard-maker on a bank-holiday—"put your instruments away. They will not be wanted. I have only a few words more to say, gentlemen. Now that you have convinced yourselves that our art, although it does not enjoy the patronage of high-placed individuals, is nevertheless an art; and you have probably come to my opinion that this art is one which demands many personal qualities besides constant labour, danger, and unpleasant misunderstandings—you will also, I hope, believe that it is possible to become attached to its practice and to love and esteem it, however strange that may appear at first sight. Picture to yourselves that a famous poet of talent, whose tales and poems adorn the pages of our best magazines, is suddenly offered the chance of writing verses at a penny a line, signed into the bargain, as an advertisement for 'Cigarettes Jasmine'—or that a slander was spread about one of you distinguished barristers, accusing you of making a business of concocting evidence for divorce cases, or of writing petitions from the cabmen to the governor in public-houses! Certainly your relatives, friends and acquaintances wouldn't believe it. But the rumour has already done its poisonous work, and you have to live through minutes of torture. Now picture to yourselves that such a disgraceful and vexatious slander, started by God knows whom, begins to threaten not only your good name and your quiet digestion, but your freedom, your health, and even your life!

"This is the position of us thieves, now being slandered by the newspapers. I must explain. There is in existence a class of scum—*passez-moi le mot*—whom we call their 'Mothers' Darlings.' With these we are unfortunately confused. They have neither shame nor conscience, a dissipated riff-raff, mothers' useless darlings, idle, clumsy drones, shop assistants who commit unskilful thefts. He thinks nothing of living on his mistress, a prostitute, like the male mackerel, who always swims after the female and lives on her excrements. He is capable of robbing a child with violence in a dark alley, in order to get a penny; he will kill a man in his sleep and torture an old woman. These men are the pests of our profession. For them the beauties and the traditions of the art have no existence. They watch us real, talented thieves like a pack of jackals after a lion. Suppose I've managed to bring off an important job—we won't mention the fact that I have to leave two-thirds of what I get to the receivers who sell the goods and discount the notes, or the customary subsidies to our incorruptible police—I still have to share out something to each one of these parasites, who have got wind of my job, by accident, hearsay, or a casual glance.

"So we call them *Motients,* which means 'half,' a corruption of *moitié* . . . Original etymology. I pay him only because he knows and may inform against me. And it mostly happens that even when he's got his share he runs off to the police in order to get another dollar. We honest thieves . . . Yes, you may laugh, gentlemen, but I repeat it: we honest thieves detest these reptiles. We have another name for them, a stigma of ignominy; but I dare not utter it here out of respect for the place and for my audience. Oh, yes, they would gladly accept an invitation to a pogrom. The thought that we may be confused with them is a hundred times more insulting to us even than the accusation of taking part in a pogrom.

"Gentlemen! While I have been speaking I have often noticed smiles on your faces. I understand you. Our presence here, our application for your assistance, and above all the unexpectedness of such a phenomenon as a systematic organisation of thieves, with delegates who are thieves, and a leader of the deputation, also a thief by profession—it is all so original that it must inevitably arouse a smile. But now I will speak from the depth of my heart. Let us be rid of our outward wrappings, gentlemen, let us speak as men to men.

"Almost all of us are educated, and all love books. We don't only read the adventures of Roqueambole, as the realistic writers say of us. Do you think our hearts did not bleed and our cheeks did not burn from shame, as though we had been slapped in the face, all the time that this unfortunate, disgraceful, accursed, cowardly war lasted? Do you really think that our souls do not flame with anger when our country is lashed with Cossack-whips, and trodden under foot, shot and spit at by mad, exasperated men? Will you not believe that we thieves meet every step towards the liberation to come with a thrill of ecstasy?

"We understand, every one of us—perhaps only a little less than you barristers, gentlemen—the real sense of the pogroms. Every time that some dastardly event or some ignominious failure has occurred, after executing a martyr in a dark corner of a fortress, or after deceiving public confidence, some one who is hidden and unapproachable gets frightened of the people's anger and diverts its vicious element upon the heads of innocent Jews. Whose diabolical mind invents these pogroms—these titanic blood-lettings, these cannibal amusements for the dark, bestial souls?

"We all see with certain clearness that the last convulsions of the bureaucracy are at hand. Forgive me if I present it imaginatively. There was a people that had a chief temple, wherein dwells a bloodthirsty deity, behind a curtain, guarded by priests. Once fearless hands tore the curtain away. Then all the people saw, instead of a god, a huge, shaggy, voracious spider, like a loathsome cuttlefish. They beat it and shoot at it: it is dismembered already; but still in the frenzy of its final agony it stretches over all the ancient temple its disgusting, clawing tentacles. And the priests, themselves under sentence of death, push into the monster's grasp all whom they can seize in their terrified, trembling fingers.

"Forgive me. What I have said is probably wild and incoherent. But I am somewhat agitated. Forgive me. I continue. We thieves by profession know better than any one else how these pogroms were organised. We wander everywhere: into public houses, markets, tea-shops, doss-houses, public places, the harbour. We can swear before God and man and posterity that we have seen how the police organise the massacres, without shame and almost without concealment. We know them all by face, in uniform or disguise. They invited many of us to take part; but there was none so vile among us as to give even the outward consent that fear might have extorted.

"You know, of course, how the various strata of Russian society behave towards the police? It is not even respected by those who avail themselves of its dark services. But we despise and hate it three, ten times more—not because many of us have been tortured in the detective departments, which are just chambers of horror, beaten almost to death, beaten with whips of ox-hide and of rubber in order to extort a confession or to make us betray a comrade. Yes, we hate them for that too. But we thieves, all of us who have been in prison, have a mad passion for freedom.

Therefore we despise our gaolers with all the hatred that
a human heart can feel. I will speak for myself. I have
been tortured three times by police detectives till I was
half dead. My lungs and liver have been shattered. In the
mornings I spit blood until I can breathe no more. But if
I were told that I will be spared a fourth flogging only by
shaking hands with a chief of the detective police, I would
refuse to do it!

"And then the newspapers say that we took from these
hands Judas-money, dripping with human blood. No, gentlemen, it is a slander which stabs our very soul, and in-
flicts insufferable pain. Not money, nor threats, nor promises will suffice to make us mercenary murderers of our
brethren, nor accomplices with them."

"Never . . . No . . . No . . . ," his comrades standing
behind him began to murmur.

"I will say more," the thief continued. "Many of us
protected the victims during this pogrom. Our friend,
called Sesoi the Great—you have just seen him, gentlemen—was then lodging with a Jewish braid-maker on the
Moldavanka. With a poker in his hands he defended his
landlord from a great horde of assassins. It is true,
Sesoi the Great is a man of enormous physical strength,
and this is well known to many of the inhabitants of the
Moldavanka. But you must agree, gentlemen, that in these
moments Sesoi the Great looked straight into the face of
death. Our comrade Martin the Miner—this gentleman
here"—the orator pointed to a pale, bearded man with
beautiful eyes who was holding himself in the background
—"saved an old Jewess, whom he had never seen before,
who was being pursued by a crowd of these *canaille*. They
broke his head with a crowbar for his pains, smashed his
arm in two places and splintered a rib. He is only just
out of hospital. That is the way our most ardent and determined members acted. The others trembled for anger
and wept for their own impotence.

"None of us will forget the horrors of those bloody days
and bloody nights lit up by the glare of fires, those sobbing women, those little children's bodies torn to pieces
and left lying in the street. But for all that not one of us

thinks that the police and the mob are the real origin of the evil. These tiny, stupid, loathsome vermin are only a senseless fist that is governed by a vile, calculating mind, moved by a diabolical will.

"Yes, gentlemen," the orator continued, "we thieves have nevertheless merited your legal contempt. But when you, noble gentlemen, need the help of clever, brave, obedient men at the barricades, men who will be ready to meet death with a song and a jest on their lips for the most glorious word in the world—Freedom—will you cast us off then and order us away because of an inveterate revulsion? Damn it all, the first victim in the French Revolution was a prostitute. She jumped up on to a barricade, with her skirt caught elegantly up into her hand and called out: 'Which of you soldiers will dare to shoot a woman?' Yes, by God." The orator exclaimed aloud and brought down his fist on to the marble table top: "They killed her, but her action was magnificent, and the beauty of her words immortal.

"If you should drive us away on the great day, we will turn to you and say: 'You spotless Cherubim—if human thoughts had the power to wound, kill, and rob man of honour and property, then which of you innocent doves would not deserve the knout and imprisonment for life?' Then we will go away from you and build our own gay, sporting, desperate thieves' barricade, and will die with such united songs on our lips that you will envy us, you who are whiter than snow!

"But I have been once more carried away. Forgive me. I am at the end. You now see, gentlemen, what feelings the newspaper slanders have excited in us. Believe in our sincerity and do what you can to remove the filthy stain which has so unjustly been cast upon us. I have finished."

He went away from the table and joined his comrades. The barristers were whispering in an undertone, very much as the magistrates of the bench at sessions. Then the chairman rose.

"We trust you absolutely, and we will make every effort to clear your association of this most grievous charge. At the same time my colleagues have authorised me, gentlemen, to convey to you their deep respect for your passionate feelings as citizens. And for my own part I ask the leader of the deputation for permission to shake him by the hand."

The two men, both tall and serious, held each other's hands in a strong, masculine grip.

The barristers were leaving the theatre; but four of them hung back a little beside the clothes rack in the hall. Isaac Abramovich could not find his new, smart grey hat anywhere. In its place on the wooden peg hung a cloth cap jauntily flattened in on either side.

"Yasha!" The stern voice of the orator was suddenly heard from the other side of the door. "Yasha! It's the last time I'll speak to you, curse you! . . . Do you hear?"

The heavy door opened wide. The gentleman in the sandy suit entered. In his hands he held Isaac Abramovich's hat; on his face was a well-bred smile.

"Gentlemen, for Heaven's sake forgive us—an odd little misunderstanding. One of our comrades exchanged his hat by accident. . . . Oh, it is yours! A thousand pardons. Doorkeeper! Why don't you keep an eye on things, my good fellow, eh? Just give me that cap, there. Once more, I ask you to forgive me, gentlemen."

With a pleasant bow and the same well-bred smile he made his way quickly into the street.

Maxim Gorky
1868 – 1936

IN THE STEPPES

We had left Perekop in the worst of moods, hungry as wolves and hating the whole world. For twelve whole hours we had vainly employed all our efforts and ingenuity to steal or to earn something, and when we were at last convinced that neither the one nor the other was possible, we decided to go on farther. Where? Just farther.

The decision was unanimous and communicated one to the other, but we were ready, too, in every respect, to travel farther along that path of life we had long followed; this decision was arrived at silently; it was not voiced by any of us, but was visibly reflected in the angry beam of our hungry eyes.

There were three of us. We had known one another for some time, having stumbled across each other in a public-house in Kherson on the banks of the Dniepr. One of us had been a soldier in a railway battalion and then a workman in one of the railways on the Vistula in Poland; he was a red-haired, sinewy man; he could speak German and possessed a detailed knowledge of prison life.

Men of our kind do not like to talk of their past, having always some more or less valid reason for not doing so, hence we believed what each said as a matter of course; that is, we believed outwardly, inwardly each had but a poor belief in himself.

When our comrade, a dry little man with thin sceptically compressed lips, informed us that he had been a student in the Moscow University, the soldier and I took it for granted that he had. At bottom, it was all the same to us whether he had been a student, a thief or a police-spy; the only thing that mattered was that when we met him he was our equal, in that he was hungry, enjoyed the special attention of the police, was suspiciously treated by the peasants in the villages, and hated the one and the other with the impotent hatred of a hunted, hungry animal, and dreamed of universal vengeance against everyone—in a word, his position among the kings of nature and the lords of life, and his mood, made him a bird of our feather.

Misfortune is the best of cement for making the most opposite of characters stick together, and we all felt that we had a right to regard ourselves as unfortunate.

The third was myself. In my innate modesty, which I have evinced since my earliest days, I will say nothing about my virtues; and having no desire to appear naïve, I will likewise be silent about my vices. Suffice it for a clue to my character to say that I have always regarded myself as better than others and continue to do so today.

Thus, we had left Perekop and went on farther. Our aim for that day was to reach one of the shepherds in the steppe; one could always beg a piece of bread from a shepherd; shepherds rarely refused to give to passing tramps.

I was walking beside the soldier, the "student" followed in the rear. On his shoulders hung something that had once resembled a jacket; on his head, which was sharp-pointed, angular and closely-cropped, rested the remains of a broad-brimmed hat; grey trousers with variegated patches encased his thin legs; tied to his feet with some string made out of the lining of his suit were the soles of some boots he had picked up on the road, which implements he called sandals. He walked in silence, raising much dust, his small green eyes shining brightly. The soldier wore a red fustian shirt, which, to use his own expression, he had "acquired with his own hands" in Kherson; over the shirt he wore a warm padded waistcoat; a military cap of an indefinite hue was "tilted over the right brow," according to army instruction; wide, rough trousers flapped about his legs; his feet were bare.

I, too, was barefoot.

We walked on. Around us on all sides in magnificent proportions stretched the steppe; canopied with the sultry blue dome of a cloudless summer sky, it lay round and black like a great dish. The grey dusty road cut across it in a broad line and burned our feet. Here and there were stubble tracts of cut corn, which bore a strange resemblance to the unshaven cheeks of the soldier.

The latter was singing as we walked, in a hoarse bass voice, "And Thy holy sabbath we praise and glorify. . . ."

When he was in the army he used to fulfil an office in the battalion church in the nature of chanter, and consequently he had an abundant knowledge of hymns and church music, a knowledge which he misused every time our conversation lagged.

Against the horizon in front of us forms of gentle line towered up, soft of hue, blending from purple to pale pink. "Those must be the Crimean mountains," said the "student" hoarsely.

"Mountains?" exclaimed the soldier. "Too soon to be seeing them, my friend! That's a cloud. . . . Simply a cloud. And what a cloud! Like cranberry-jelly and milk."

I observed that it would be agreeable if the cloud were really of jelly, which instantly aroused our hunger, the scourge of our days.

"Hell!" cursed the soldier, as he spat. "Not a living soul to be met. No one. . . . There's nothing to do but to suck your paws like the bears in winter."

"I told you that we ought to have made for the inhabited parts," said the "student," with a desire to improve the occasion.

"You told us!" the soldier rejoined. "It's your place to tell us, as you're educated. But where are the inhabited parts? The devil knows!"

The student said nothing, but compressed his lips. The sun sank and the clouds on the horizon danced in a myriad indescribable hues. There was a smell of earth and of salt, and this dry and savoury smell made our appetites the keener. The pain gnawed at our stomachs, a strange, unpleasant sensation; the sap seemed to be oozing slowly from all the muscles of the body; they were drying up and losing their living suppleness. A parched, stinging sensation filled the cavity of the mouth and the throat, the brain was muddled and small dark objects danced before the eyes; sometimes these took the form of steaming chunks of meat, or of hunks of milkbread; memory supplied these "ghosts of the past, dumb ghosts," with their natural odours, and then it seemed as if a knife were veritably turned in the stomach.

Still, we walked on, discussing our sensations and keeping a sharp look out on all sides for signs of sheep, or listening for the loud squeaking of a Tartar cart carrying fruit to the Armenian market.

But the steppe was solitary and silent.

On the eve of this hard day the three of us had eaten four pounds of rye bread and five melons, and had walked some forty versts—expenditure not commensurate with income—and having fallen asleep in the market-place of Perekop we had been awakened by our hunger.

The "student," in justice be it said, had advised us not to go to sleep, but to work during the night. . . . As projects for the outrage of private property are not mentioned in polite society, I will say no more about it. My desire was to be just, it is against my interest to be vulgar. I know that in our highly civilised days people are becoming more and more tender-hearted, and that when one seizes a neighbour by the throat with the object of strangling him, it is done with every possible kindness and the decorum appropriate to the occasion. The experience of my own throat has made me notice this progress in morality, so that I am able with a pleasant feeling of confidence to assert that everything in this world is developing and progressing. The progress may particularly be seen in the annual increase in the number of prisons, public-houses, and brothels. . . .

And so, swallowing our hungry saliva, and endeavouring by friendly conversation to still the pain in our stomachs, we walked across the deserted and silent steppe, walked towards the red glow of the sunset, filled with a vague kind of hope. In front of us the sun was sinking gently into the soft clouds, profusely painted with its rays, and behind us, on either side, the blue darkness which rose from the steppe to the sky narrowed the unfriendly horizon around us.

"Collect some stuff for a fire, brothers," said the soldier, picking up a piece of wood. "We've got to spend the night in the steppe, and there's a dew on. Anything will do, dried dung, twigs."

We separated to both sides of the road, and commenced to collect dry grass and any combustible material. Every time it became necessary to bend to the ground, the whole body was filled with a desire to fall on it, to lie still and to eat it, black and rich, to eat and eat, until one could eat no more, and then to sleep. What mattered it if it meant to sleep for ever, so long as one could eat and feel the warm, thick mess slowly descending from the mouth down the parched gullet to the hungry, gnawing stomach, hot with desire for something to digest.

"If only we could find a root or something," the soldier sighed. "There are roots you can eat. . . ."

But the black ploughed earth contained no roots. The southern night descended swiftly; the last rays of the sun were barely extinguished when the stars were shining in the dark blue sky and the shadows around us merged closer and closer together, shutting out the infinite flatness of the steppe. "Brother," the "student" whispered, "there's a man lying to the left of us."

"A man?" the soldier asked doubtfully. "Why should he be lying there?"

"Go and ask. He's probably got some bread if he can spread himself out in the steppe," the "student" ventured. The soldier looked in the direction indicated and, spitting resolutely, said, "Let us go to him."

Only the sharp green eyes of the "student" could have seen a man in the black heap some fifty sajens to the left of the road. We walked towards him, stepping quickly over the clods of ploughed earth, our newly awakened hope for food quickening the pangs of our hunger. We were quite close to him, but the man did not move.

"Perhaps it isn't a man." The soldier gloomily expressed the thought of all.

But our doubt was scattered that very instant. The heap on the ground suddenly moved, rose up, and we could see that it was a real, living man, kneeling, his hand out-stretched towards us.

"Stop, or I'll shoot!" he said in a hoarse, trembling voice.

A sharp click rent the turbid air.

We stopped as at a word of command, and for some seconds we were silent, overcome by the pleasant greeting.

"The villain!" the soldier muttered expressively.

"Um! Travelling with a revolver," the "student" said thoughtfully, "must be a fish rich in caviare."

"Hi!" shouted the soldier; he had evidently decided on some course.

The man did not change his posture, and did not speak.

"Hi, you! We won't harm you. . . . Give us some bread. . . . We are starving. Give us bread, brother, for Christ's sake! Be damned!"

The last words were uttered under his breath.

The man was silent.

"Can't you hear?" the soldier asked, trembling with rage and despair. "Give us some bread. We won't come near you. Throw it to us."

"All right," said the man abruptly.

Had he said "my dear brothers," and put into those words the most sacred and purest of feeling, they would not have roused us more or made us more human than that hoarsely spoken and abrupt "All right."

"Don't be afraid of us, good man," said the soldier kindly, with an ingratiating smile on his lips, though the man could not see the smile, being at a distance from us of at least twenty paces.

"We are peaceful folk. We are on our way from Russia to Kuban. We've lost our money and eaten everything we've got. It's two days since we've had a meal."

"Wait," said the man, flourishing his arm in the air. A black lump flew out and dropped near us on the ploughed earth. The "student," fell upon it.

"Wait, here's more and more. That's all. I haven't any more."

When the "student" had collected these original gifts, they were found to consist of about four pounds of stale black bread, covered with earth. The latter circumstance did not trouble us in the least, the former pleased us greatly, for stale bread is much more satisfying than new, containing less moisture. "There . . . and there . . . and there," the soldier gave us each our portions. "They are not equal. I must take a pinch more of yours, scholar, or there won't be enough for him."

The "student" obediently submitted to the loss of a fraction of an ounce of bread. I took the morsel and put it into my mouth, and commenced to chew it. I chewed it slowly, scarcely able to restrain the convulsive movement of my jaws, which were ready to chew stone. I had a keen sense of pleasure to feel the spasm in my gullet and satisfy it gradually, bit by bit. Warm, inexpressibly and indescribably sweet the bread penetrated mouthful by mouthful into the burning stomach and seemed instantly to be turned to blood and brain. Joy, a strange, peaceful, vivifying joy glowed in the heart in the measure in which the stomach was filled; the general condition was one of somnolence. I forgot the chronic hunger of these cursed days, I forgot my comrades, who were immersed in the enjoyment of sensations similar to my own. But when I threw the last crumbs into my mouth with the palm of my hand, I began to feel a deadly hunger.

"The devil's probably got some more, and I dare say he's got some meat, too," mumbled the soldier, sitting on the ground and rubbing his stomach.

"To be sure he has. The bread smelt of meat. I'm certain he's got more bread," the "student" added under his breath. "If it weren't for that revolver. . . ."

"Who is he, eh?"

"Our brother Isaac, evidently."

"The dog!" the soldier concluded.

We were sitting close together, looking askance in the direction where our benefactor sat with the revolver. No sound of life escaped him.

The night gathered its dark forces around us. A dead silence reigned in the steppe; we could hear each others' breathing. Now and again came the melancholy cry of a marmot. The stars, the living flowers of heaven, were shining above us. . . . We were hungry.

I will say with pride that I was no better and no worse than my casual comrades of that rather strange night. I suggested that we should go over to the man. We need do him no harm, but we could eat up all his food. If he shoots, let him. Out of the three only one of us might possibly be hit, and that very unlikely, and if any one were hit the wound might not be fatal.

"Come," said the soldier, jumping to his feet.

And we went, almost at a run, the "student" keeping behind us.

"Comrade!" the soldier called reproachfully.

A hoarse mumbling met us, the click of a catch, a flash, and a sharp report rang out.

"Missed!" the soldier exclaimed joyously, reaching the man at a bound. "Now, you devil, now you'll get it."

The "student" threw himself on the man's wallet. The "devil" rolled over on his back and began to moan, shielding himself with his hands.

"What the deuce!" exclaimed the soldier in his bewilderment. He had already raised his foot to kick the man. "He must have hit himself. Hi! you! Have you shot yourself?"

"Here's meat, pasties, and bread, lots of it, brothers," said the "student" exultantly.

"Oh, die and be damned. . . . Come and eat, friends!" the soldier cried.

I took the revolver from the man's hand. He had ceased to moan, and was lying quite still. The chamber contained one more bullet.

Again we were eating, eating in silence. The man, too, lay silent, without so much as moving a limb. We paid not the slightest heed to him.

"Have you really done this all for the bread, brothers?" a trembling, hoarse voice asked suddenly.

We all started. The "student" even choked and coughed, bending down to the ground.

The soldier cursed as he chewed a mouthful of food.

"You soul of a dog, may you burst like a rotten log! Did you think we wanted to skin you? What good would your skin be to us? You damned silly mug! Arms himself and shoots at people, the devil!"

As he was eating during all this, the invective was robbed of its force.

"Wait till we've done eating, we'll settle with you!" the "student" said threateningly.

At this the stillness of the night was broken by a wailing and sobbing that frightened us.

"Brothers . . . how was I to know? I fired because I was frightened. I'm on my way from New Athens . . . to the Smolensk province. . . . Oh, Lord! The fever's got hold of me. . . . It comes on when the sun sets. Miserable wretch that I am. . . . It was because of the fever that I left Athens. . . . I did carpentering there. . . . I am a carpenter by trade. . . . I've got a wife at home and two little girls. I haven't seen them for four years . . . Brothers . . . eat everything."

"We'll do that without your asking," the "student" said.

"Oh, God, had I only known that you were kind-hearted, quiet folk. . . . You don't think I'd have fired? But what would you have, brothers, in the steppe at night. . . . Am I to blame?"

He was crying as he spoke, or more correctly, emitting a trembling, frightened, wailing sound.

"There he goes whining now," the soldier said contemptuously.

"He's probably got some money on him," suggested the "student."

The soldier half closed his eyes, looked at him, and laughed.

"You're a good one at guessing. . . . Come, let us light a fire and go to sleep."

"And what about him?" the "student" inquired.

"Let him go to the devil. You don't want to roast him, eh?"

"He deserves it." The "student" shook his sharp-pointed head.

We went to fetch the materials we had collected, which we had dropped when the carpenter had stopped us by his menacing cry. We brought them over, and were soon sitting by a fire. It burned gently in the still night, lighting up the small space in which we sat. We felt sleepy, but could have supped all over again.

"Brothers!" called the carpenter. He was lying about three paces from us, and now and then it seemed to me that I could hear him whispering.

"Well?" asked the soldier.

"Can I come to you . . . to the fire? I am dying. . . . My bones are all aching. . . . Oh, God, I shall never get home."

"Crawl over here," the "student" said.

Slowly, as though fearing to lose a hand or a leg, the carpenter moved over the ground to the fire. He was a tall man, terribly emaciated. His clothing hung about him with a horrible looseness, and his large, troubled eyes reflected the pain that he suffered. His distorted face was haggard, and, even by the light of the fire, the colour of it was yellowish, earthy, and dead. He was trembling all over; we felt a scornful pity for him. Stretching out his long, thin arms to the fire, he rubbed his bony fingers, the joints bending slowly and feebly. When all is said and done he was a disgusting sight to look at.

"Why do you travel in this condition and on foot? Mean, eh?" the soldier asked sullenly.

"They advised me not to go . . . they said . . . by the water . . . but to come through Crimea . . . because of the air . . . they said. . . . And now, brothers . . . I can't go on. . . . I'm dying! I shall die alone in the steppe. . . . The birds will peck at me and no one will recognise me. . . . My wife . . . my little girls, are expecting me. . . . I wrote to them. . . . And my bones will be washed by the rains of the steppe. . . . Lord, Lord!"

He howled like a wounded wolf.

"Oh, hell!" exclaimed the soldier, enraged, and jumping

to his feet. "Stop your whining! Leave us in peace! Dying are you? Well, get on with it, and don't make so much row about it! You won't be missed."

"Give him a knock on the head," the "student" suggested.

"Let us go to sleep," I said. "And as for you, if you want to stop by the fire, you mustn't whine."

"Do you hear?" the soldier said angrily. "Mind you do what he says. You think we're going to pity you and nurse you because you threw us a piece of bread and fired at us! To hell with you! Others would. . . . Phu!"

The soldier ceased, and stretched himself out on the ground. The "student" was already lying down. I, too, lay down. The terrified carpenter, shrinking into a heap, moved over to the fire and stared into it silently. I was lying to the right of him and could hear the chattering of his teeth. The "student" was lying to the left, curled up and apparently asleep. The soldier was lying face upwards, his hands under his head, looking up at the sky.

"What a night, to be sure! What a lot of stars! It looks like heat." After a time he turned to me. "What a sky! Looks more like a blanket than a sky. I do like this wandering life, friend. . . . It may be a cold and hungry life, but it's free. . . . No one to lord it over you. . . . You are your own master. . . . If you want to bite your own head off, no one can say you nay. . . . How good! The hunger of these days made me vicious . . . but here I am now, looking up at the sky. . . . The stars are winking at me. They seem to say, 'Never mind, Lakatin, go over the earth, learn, but don't give in to anyone.' . . . Ha! . . . How comfortable the heart feels! And how are you, carpenter? You mustn't be angry with me, and there's no need to fear anything. . . . If we have eaten up your bread, what does it matter? You had bread and we hadn't, so we ate yours. . . . And you go and shoot bullets at us like a savage. You made me very angry, and if you hadn't fallen down, I'd have given it to you for your impudence. And as for the bread, you'll be getting to Perekop tomorrow, you can buy some there. . . . You've got money, I know. . . . How long have you had the fever?"

For a long time I could hear the droning of the soldier's deep voice and the trembling voice of the carpenter. The dark, almost black night descended lower and lower over the earth; the chest was filled with fragrant, juicy air. The fire emitted an even light and a vivifying warmth. The eyes closed, and through the drowsiness a soothing, purifying influence was borne.

"Get up! Quick! Let us go!"

With a feeling of apprehension I jumped to my feet, assisted by the soldier, who was tugging me up from the ground by my sleeve.

"Come, quick march!"

His face was grave and troubled. I looked about me. The sun was rising and its rosy rays fell on the still, blue face of the carpenter. His mouth was open; the eyes were bulging out of their sockets and stared with a glassy stare, expressive of horror. The clothing at his chest was torn; his posture was unnatural and convulsed.

"Seen enough? Come on, I say." The soldier tugged at my arm.

"Is he dead?" I asked, shuddering with the keenness of the morning air.

"I should say so. If I were to strangle you, you'd be dead, wouldn't you?" the soldier explained.

"Did . . . the 'student'?" I cried.

"Who else? You, perhaps? Or I? There's a scholar for you. . . . Did him in nicely and left his comrades in the lurch. If I'd only known this yesterday, I'd have killed that 'student' myself. I'd have killed him with a blow. One punch on the temple and one blackguard less in the world. Do you realise what he's done? We must be gone from here so that not a human eye sees us in the steppe. Understand? They'll discover the carpenter today, strangled and robbed. They'll be on the look out for the like of us. They'll ask where we've come from . . . where we've slept. And they'll catch us. . . . Although we've got nothing on us. . . . But here's that revolver of his in my bosom! What a kettle of fish!"

"Throw it away," I cautioned him.

"Why?" he said thoughtfully. "It's a thing of value. . . . They mightn't catch us, after all. . . . No, I shan't throw it away. It's worth three roubles. And it's got another bullet in it. I wonder how much money he robbed him of, the dirty devil!"

"So much for the carpenter's little daughters," I said.

"Daughters? What daughters? Oh, his. . . . Well, they'll grow up, and as it isn't us they'll marry, we needn't bother about them. . . . Come on, brother, quick. . . . Where shall we go?"

"I don't know. It makes no difference."

"And I don't know, and I know that it makes no difference. Let's go to the right. The sea must be there."

I turned back. A long way from us in the steppe a black hill towered up, and above it the sun was shining.

"Looking to see if he's come to life? Don't you fear, they won't catch us. A clever chap that scholar of ours was. Managed the thing well. A nice comrade, to be sure. . . . Left us well in the soup. Eh, brother, folk are getting more vicious. Year after year they get more and more vicious." The soldier spoke sadly.

The steppe, silent and solitary and bathed in the bright morning sunshine, unfolded before us, merging at the horizon with the sky. It was light with a gentle, kindly light; all dark and unjust deeds seemed impossible in that great expanse of uninterrupted plain with a blue dome for a sky.

"I'm hungry, brother," observed my comrade, rolling a cigarette from cheap tobacco.

"What shall we eat and where?"

"It's a problem."

With this the teller of the story, a man lying in the bed next to mine in a hospital, concluded, saying, "That is all. The soldier and I became great friends. We walked together as far as the Kara region. He was a kindly fellow, experienced, and a typical tramp. I had a great respect for him. We were together as far as Asia Minor and then we lost sight of each other. . . ."

"Do you ever remember the carpenter?" I asked.

"As you have seen, or rather, as you have heard."

"No more?"

He laughed.

"What do you expect me to feel about him? I wasn't to blame for what happened to him, any more than you are to blame for what happened to me. . . . No one is to blame for anything, because we are all alike—beasts."

Leonid Andreyev
1871 – 1919

THE SEVEN
WHO WERE HANGED

I AT ONE P.M. YOUR EXCELLENCY

As the minister was a very stout man, inclined to apoplexy,
all possible precautions were taken so that he should not
be dangerously excited by the news that a serious attempt
on his life was about to be made. On seeing, however, that
the minister took the information calmly, and even smiled,
he was given the details. The assassination was planned for
the following morning, when he would be due to leave the
house with his official report. A number of terrorists had
been denounced by an informer and were being kept under
vigilant watch by detectives. Armed with bombs and revolvers, they were to meet at one p.m. in front of the house
to await his coming out. There they were to be trapped.

"Wait a minute," said the minister in surprise. "How do
they know that I am to go with my report at one p.m.,
when I myself only knew it the day before yesterday?"

The chief of the secret service made a vague gesture
with his hands.

"Exactly at one p.m., your Excellency," he said.

The minister shook his head, half in surprise, half in
approval of the measures taken by the police, who had managed things so well; and a gloomy smile appeared on his
thick, dark lips. Then, obediently and still with the same

smile on his face, he got ready quickly, so as not to hamper the police, and drove off to spend the night in the hospitable mansion put at his disposal. His wife and two children were also removed from the dangerous house round which the bomb throwers were to gather next day.

While lights were on in the friend's mansion and polite, familiar faces bowed to him and smilingly expressed their indignation, the dignitary felt a kind of pleasant excitement —as if he had been given or was about to be given some great and unexpected prize. But people went away, the lights were put out and through the plate-glass windows a ghastly, lace-like light from the electric street lamps lay upon the ceiling and walls. Alien to the house, with its statues, and silence, the light entering from the street, quiet and undefined, evoked the agonising thought of the futility of bolts and guards and walls. It was then, in the stillness and solitude of the night in a strange bedroom, that the dignitary was overcome with unbearable fear.

He had been suffering from kidney trouble and any great agitation caused his face, feet and hands to swell, making him still heavier, fatter and more massive. Now, lying, a huge mass of bloated flesh on top of the pressed down bedsprings, he was aware, with a sick man's agony, of the swollen face, which seemed not his own, and could not stop thinking of the cruel fate that had been prepared for him. He recollected, one after the other, all the recent terrible cases when bombs had been thrown at people of his, or even of higher rank. He imagined the bombs tearing the bodies to pieces, spattering the brains against filthy brick walls and knocking out teeth from their roots. These imaginings made him feel as if his own fat, sick body, stretched out on the bed, belonged to someone else and had already undergone the fiery might of the explosion. He fancied that his arms had become detached from his shoulders, his teeth were knocked out, his brain scattered, and his feet numb and motionless, toes upward, like those of a dead man. He made a violent movement, breathed loudly and coughed, so that he should not have the remotest likeness to a corpse. He tried to surround himself with the live noise of grating springs and rustling blankets; and in order to prove that he was very much alive, not a bit dead and indeed far removed from death—just like anyone else, in fact—he spoke out in a loud, deep, abrupt voice in the quietness and loneliness of the bedroom.

"Brave fellows! Brave fellows! Brave fellows!"

He was praising the detectives, the police, the soldiers and all those who were guarding his life and had managed so skilfully and in such good time to avert his assassination. But even whilst he moved in bed, praised his preservers, and smiled with a forced, wry smile, indicating his contempt for those stupid, unsuccessful terrorists, he did not believe in his rescue and knew that life would be torn from him suddenly and at once. Death, which had been planned for him and which yet only existed in the thoughts and intentions of his would-be assassins, seemed to be already standing there in the room. It would remain there and not go away till those people had been caught, the bombs taken away from them and they themselves locked up behind strong bars. There, in that corner, stood Death, and would not go, could not go, like an obedient soldier placed on guard at the will and order of a superior.

"At one p.m., your Excellency." The phrase, modulated in a variety of tones, kept on sounding—now gaily mocking, now angry, now blunt and stubborn. As if there were hundreds of wound-up gramophones in the bedroom and they were all shouting, one after the other, with idiotic, mechanical persistence, the words commanded them:

"At one p.m., your Excellency."

And that one p.m. tomorrow, which only recently was no different from any other hour, but was only a steady movement of the hand across the dial of his golden watch, suddenly acquired an ominous importance. It jumped off the dial and began to live independently, stretching out till it was like a great black pillar cutting the whole of life in two; as if there were no other hours before or after, and this insolent, conceited hour alone had a right to some special existence.

"Well, what do you want?" asked the minister angrily, through his teeth.

The gramophones roared: "At one p.m., your Excellency!" and the black pillar grinned and bowed. Grinding his teeth, the minister raised himself in bed, sat up and leaned his face on the palm of his hand; it was quite impossible for him to find sleep on that hideous night.

Pressing his face with his swollen perfumed palms, he pictured to himself with terrifying clearness how on the next day he would have got up in the morning, knowing nothing, would have taken his coffee, knowing nothing, and then put on his things in the hall. Neither he, nor the butler, who would have helped him on with his fur coat, nor the footman, who would have brought him his coffee, would have known that it was quite futile to drink coffee or put on the fur coat, since in the next few minutes everything, the fur coat, his body and the coffee inside him, would have been annihilated, caught up by death. Then the butler would open the glass door . . . Yes, with his own hands, the nice, good, polite butler with the blue, soldierly eyes and medals across his chest, would open the terrible door, because he knew nothing. Everybody would smile, because they knew nothing.

"Oh," came suddenly and loudly from the minister and he slowly removed his hands from his face. Looking far into the darkness with a fixed strained glance, he stretched out his arm with the same slow movement, felt for the switch and turned on the light. Then he rose, and, without putting on his slippers, walked barefoot over the carpet of the unfamiliar, strange bedroom, found the switch of a wall lamp and turned it on. The room became light and pleasant and only the disordered bed with the blanket dropped on the floor witnessed to a terror not yet completely passed.

In his night attire, with beard ruffled by his restless movements, and angry eyes, the dignitary looked just like any other angry old man suffering from insomnia and asthma. It was as if the death which people were planning for him had laid him bare, tearing away the magnificence and imposing splendour by which he was surrounded. It was difficult to believe that he possessed great power and that his body, such an ordinary human body, was to perish terribly in the flame and crash of a monstrous explosion. He did not dress himself and, without feeling the cold, sat down on the nearest chair, propped his dishevelled beard on his hand, and fixed his eyes with the concentration of deep and calm reflexion upon the unfamiliar plaster ceiling.

So that was it! That was why he had trembled with fear and agitation! That was why Death stood in the corner and would not, could not, disappear!

"Fools!" he said with weighty contempt.

"Fools!" he repeated louder and turned his head slightly towards the door, so that those of whom he was speaking could hear him. He was speaking of those whom he had just now called brave fellows, but who in an excess of zeal had given him a detailed account of the forthcoming plot.

"Of course," he pondered deeply with sudden force and clearness of thought, "now, since they told me, I know and am terrified, but had I not known I should have drunk my coffee peacefully. Later, of course, this death . . . but am I really so much afraid of death? Here have I been suffering from kidney trouble and no doubt shall die of it one day, but I do not feel terrified, because I know nothing. But those idiots told me: 'At one p.m., your Excellency.' They thought, the fools, that I should be glad, instead of which *It* appeared in the corner and would not go. *It* will not go, because *It* is my thought. It is not death, but the knowledge of death, which is terrifying. Life would be impossible if man knew positively and precisely the day and hour of his death. Yet those idiots warned me: 'At one p.m., your Excellency.'"

He began to feel cheerful and relieved as if someone had told him that he was immortal and would never die. With a renewed sense of his own strength and cleverness amidst that bunch of idiots, who were so absurdly and imprudently invading the mystery of the future, he began to ponder the blissfulness of the unknown, arranging his thoughts with difficulty like an old, sick and greatly tried man. No living creature, neither man nor beast, was given to know the day and hour of its death. He, for instance, had been ill recently and his doctors told him that he was dying and ought to make his final arrangements. He had not believed them and actually he had lived. Something similar had happened in his youth. He had come to grief in life and decided to commit suicide. He got ready the revolver, wrote the last letters, even fixed the time for his suicide, and then, just before the end, he had suddenly changed his mind. Something may always change at the very last minute, an unforeseen accident may occur, and therefore nobody can tell when he will die.

"At one p.m., your Excellency," those amiable asses had told him, and, though they did so only because death had been averted, the very knowledge of the possible hour filled him with terror. It was quite likely that some day he would be assassinated, but it was not to happen tomorrow, and he might sleep confidently like an immortal. Fools, they did not realise what a great law they had tampered with, what an abyss they had opened, when they said with that idiotic amiability, "At one p.m., your Excellency."

"No, not at one p.m., your Excellency. It is not known when. Not known when. What?"

"Nothing," was the reply of the stillness, "nothing."

"No, you are saying something."

"No, nothing much. I am saying—tomorrow at one p.m."

With a sharp agony at his heart, he suddenly realised that there would be no sleep or peace or joy for him till that black, cursed hour, torn out of the clock-face, should have passed. It was only the shadow of the knowledge of what should be unknown to every living creature that stood there in the corner, and yet its presence sufficed to eclipse the light and cast on man an impenetrable darkness of horror. The terror of death, once aroused, spread throughout the body, penetrated the bones and looked palely out of each pore.

It was no longer the assassins of tomorrow that he feared; they had disappeared, were forgotten, swallowed up in a crowd of persons and happenings hostile to his everyday life. What he now feared was something sudden and inevitable—an apoplectic fit, heart failure or the weakness of some silly, thin artery, which might suddenly fail to bear the pressure of blood and burst like a lightly stretched glove on plump fingers.

His short, thick neck filled him with terror. It was unbearable to look at his short, swollen fingers and to feel how short they were and filled with the moisture of death.

If before, in the darkness, he had had to move so as not to feel like a dead man, now, in that bright, coldly-hostile, horrible light, it was terrifying, almost impossible to stir, even to get a cigarette or to ring for somebody. His nerves were on edge. And each nerve seemed like a rearing, bent-up wire, crowned by a small head, with eyes staring madly from fear and convulsively open, gasping, speechless mouth. He could not breathe.

Suddenly, in the darkness amidst dust and cobwebs, an electric bell came to life somewhere on the ceiling. The little metallic tongue struck convulsively in terror the edge of the tinkling cup. It stopped for a while, then again went on, moving in an unceasing, frightened ringing. It was his Excellency ringing from his room.

People began to run. Single little lamps flashed here and there in chandeliers and on walls. They did not give much light, but enough to create shadows. These appeared everywhere. They stood in corners, stretched across the ceiling, clung tremulously to every elevation, lay upon walls. It was really difficult to understand where they had been before—those numberless, ugly, silent shadows, the voiceless souls of voiceless objects.

A deep, trembling voice said something loudly. Then the doctor was summoned on the 'phone—the dignitary was in a bad way. His Excellency's wife was also summoned.

II   CONDEMNED TO DEATH BY HANGING

Everything happened as the police had foretold. Four terrorists, three men and a woman, armed with bombs, infernal machines and revolvers, were caught near the entrance of the house; the fifth was found and arrested in her own flat, where the conspiracy had been hatched. A great deal of dynamite, half-finished bombs and other weapons, were seized on the occasion. All the arrested persons were very young; the eldest of the men was twenty-eight, the younger of the women was only nineteen. They were sentenced in the same fortress in which they had been imprisoned after their arrest, and were tried quickly and secretly, as was the custom in those merciless days.

At their trial all five were calm, but very grave and thoughtful. Their contempt for the judges was so boundless that none of them felt like stressing their hardihood even by an unnecessary smile or any pretended expression of gaiety. They were calm in proportion to the need to screen their souls, caught up in the great agony of coming death, from the evil, hostile glances of strangers. Sometimes they refused, sometimes they consented, to answer questions; if the latter, they answered briefly, simply and precisely, as if addressing not judges, but statisticians, concerned in filling up some special forms. Three of them, one woman and two men, gave their real names. The other two refused to do so and remained unknown to the court. To all happenings in the court they showed that kind of mild, hazy curiosity, characteristic either of very sick people or of those who are absorbed in some all-engrossing idea. They would look up quickly, catch some specially interesting stray word and lapse again into their own thoughts at the point at which they had been diverted from them.

Nearest to the judges sat the prisoner who called himself Sergey Golovin. He was the son of a retired colonel and had himself been an officer. He was very young and broad-shouldered, with fair hair and such good health that neither prison nor the prospect of inevitable death had been able to take the vivid colour from his cheeks, nor the expression of youthful, happy naïvety from his blue eyes. He kept pulling energetically at his fair ruffled beard, to which he had not yet got accustomed. Screwing up his eyes and blinking incessantly, he looked out of the window.

All this took place at the end of winter when, in the midst of snowstorms and dim, frozen days, the approaching spring sent as forerunner a bright sunny day or single hour, which was so spring-like, so vividly young and glittering, that the sparrows in the street went mad with joy and people felt almost intoxicated. And now, through the dusty top window, uncleaned since last summer, a very strange, lovely sky could be seen. At first glance it seemed milky grey and dim, but, when you looked longer, blue began to appear and grew in depth, becoming ever brighter and more bound-less. And the fact that it did not disclose itself at once, but hid chastely behind the dimness of transparent clouds, made it sweet as a young girl one loves. Sergey Golovin looked at the sky, pulled his little beard, screwed up first one eye and then the other behind their long silken lashes, and pon-dered something intensely. At one moment he even moved his fingers quickly, whilst an expression of naïve joy ap-peared on his face, but he looked round and his smile was extinguished like a trodden-out spark. And almost instantly, through the red of his cheeks, which had scarcely grown pale, showed an earthy, deathly grey; and the downy hair, painfully plucked out by the roots, was pressed in his white-tipped fingers, as in a vice. But the joy of life and the spring were stronger—and in a few minutes the same young ingenuous face was turned again towards the spring sky.

A young pale unknown girl, with the nickname of Mousia, also looked out in the same direction at the sky. She was younger than Golovin, but she seemed older be-cause of her severity and the darkness of her direct proud eyes. Only her very thin and slender neck and her delicate, girlish arms revealed her age. Besides there was that some-thing intangible which is youth itself and which sounded so clearly in her pure harmonious voice, tuned to perfec-tion like a precious instrument, disclosing its musical rich-ness in every simple word and exclamation. She was very pale, but her pallor was not deathly but of that special burning whiteness characteristic of persons who are con-sumed by a powerful inward flame, when the body seems transparently illuminated like fine Sèvres porcelain. She sat almost motionless, only occasionally touching, with a scarcely visible movement, the circular mark on the third finger of her right hand left by a ring recently removed. The glance she turned to the sky was without tenderness or joyful recollections, and she only looked at it because, in that dirty official hall, the strip of blue sky was the one lovely, pure, true thing in sight—and did not try to learn secrets from her eyes.

The judges pitied Sergey Golovin, but they hated her.

Her neighbour, unknown, but nicknamed Werner, also

sat motionless in a somewhat affected posture, with hands folded between his knees. If a face can be bolted, as one bolts a heavy door, the unknown prisoner had bolted his face like an iron door and hung an iron lock on it. He stared down motionless at the dirty wooden floor, and it was impossible to tell whether he was calm or intensely excited, whether pondering something or listening to the informers giving evidence before the court. He was not tall; his features were subtle and noble. His beauty was so delicate that he reminded one of a moonlight night in the South, where cypresses throw their dark shadows on the seashore; whilst at the same time he inspired a feeling of great calm force, unconquerable determination and cold and daring courage. The very politeness of his brief and precise answers seemed somehow dangerous on his lips and given with his slight bow. Whilst on all the others the prisoners' dress looked like an awkward joke, one failed to notice it on him—so alien was the attire to the man. And though bombs and infernal machines had been found on the other terrorists and only a black revolver on Werner, the judges for some reason considered him the leader and addressed him with some respect as well as briefly and to the point.

The next prisoner to him, Vassily Kashirin, was absorbed in a great unbearable terror of death as well as in a desperate effort to suppress that terror and hide it from the judges. Since early morning, when they had brought him before the court, he had begun to choke from palpitation of the heart. Drops of sweat continually appeared on his forehead, his hands were moist and cold and his cold sweaty shirt clung to his body, hampering his movements. By the exercise of superhuman will-power he kept his fingers from trembling, his voice firm and clear and his eyes steady. He saw nothing around him and voices came to him as through a mist, into which he strained desperately—to answer firmly, to answer loudly. But having once answered, he immediately forgot both question and reply and resumed the silent desperate struggle with himself. Death was so apparent in him that the judges avoided looking at him, and it was almost as impossible to tell his age as that of a corpse which has begun to decompose. According to his papers he was only twenty-three. Once or twice Werner gently touched his knee with his hand and each time Vassily answered in the same phrase, "All right."

The most awful moments for him were when he was suddenly seized with the longing to shout aloud, without words, with the desperate yell of a beast. Then he would touch Werner gently and the latter, without raising his eyes, would answer softly, "It's all right, Vasia, it will soon be over."

Tanya Kovalchuk, the fifth terrorist, embraced them all with a motherly, solicitous glance and appeared devoured with anxiety. She had never had children; she was still very young and red-cheeked, like Sergey Golovin, but somehow seemed the mother of them all. The expression of her face, with its smiles and fears, was full of solicitude and boundless love. She paid no attention to the Court, as if it were something extraneous, but only listened to the way the others answered questions and tried to make out whether their voices trembled, whether they were afraid or needed water.

She could not look at Vasia without anguish and wrung her plump fingers silently; but Mousia and Werner she watched with pride and admiration, a grave and serious expression on her face, whilst with Sergey Golovin she tried to exchange smiles.

"The dear boy is looking at the sky. Look, look, my dear one," she said to herself whilst watching him.

"And Vasia? What is it? My God, my God. . . . What am I to do with him? To say something might make things still worse—supposing he burst into tears."

Like a quiet pool at dawn, reflecting every passing cloud, she reflected on her plump, dear, kind face every transient feeling and thought of each of those four. To the fact that she herself was also on trial and that she, too, would be hanged, she did not give a thought and was completely indifferent to the matter. It was in her flat that a store of bombs and dynamite had been discovered, and strangely enough it was she who had fired on the police and wounded one detective in the head.

The trial ended at eight p.m., when it was beginning to get dark. Gradually the blue sky faded away before the eyes of Mousia and Sergey Golovin; it did not flush and smile quietly, as on summer evenings, but thickened, grew grey, and suddenly became cold and wintry. Golovin heaved a sigh, stretched himself and looked once again out of the window but already there was only cold wintry gloom. Still pulling at his little beard, he began, with childlike curiosity, to observe the judges, the soldiers with their rifles, and to smile at Tanya Kovalchuk. But Mousia, after the sky had faded away, steadily, without lowering her eyes to the ground, directed them to a corner where a spider's web rocked slightly under the invisible current from the steam heating, and remained thus till the sentence was pronounced.

After the verdict, the condemned took leave of the frock-coated barristers, avoiding their disconcertingly pitying and guilty eyes, and crowded together in the doorway for a minute, exchanging short remarks.

"All right, Vasia, soon all will be over," said Werner.

"I am all right, brother," Kashirin replied loudly, calmly and even almost cheerfully. And indeed his face had a slight tinge of red and no longer resembled a decomposing corpse.

"The devil take them, they have hanged us all," naïvely cursed Golovin.

"That was only to be expected," retorted Werner calmly.

"Tomorrow the sentence will be formally pronounced and we shall all be placed together," said Kovalchuk reassuringly. "We shall remain together until the execution."

Mousia was silent. Then she resolutely moved forward.

III   I MUST NOT BE HANGED

A fortnight before the terrorists were tried, other judges of the same regional military court had tried and condemned to death by hanging, Ivan Yanson, a peasant.

This Ivan Yanson was a farm labourer, who worked for a well-to-do farmer and differed in no way from other such workmen. He was a native of Vesenberg in Estonia and as, in the course of a few years, he moved from one farm to another, he gradually drew nearer the capital. He spoke Russian very badly, and as his master was a Russian called Lazarev and there were no Estonians in the neighbourhood, Yanson scarcely spoke at all for nearly two years. Apparently he was not in general given to talkativeness and was silent with men as well as with beasts. He watered and harnessed a horse in silence, sauntering round it with slow uncertain steps; and when the horse, annoyed by his silence, began to rear and prance, he would beat it in silence with a huge whip. He beat it cruelly with cold wicked persistence, and if this happened when he had been drinking heavily, he worked himself up into a frenzy. On such occasions the hissing of the whip and the frightened broken anguished tapping of the hooves on the wooden floor of the barn could be heard in the house. When Yanson beat the horse in this way the master would beat him, but he could not change him, so he gave it up.

Once or twice a month Yanson got drunk. This happened on the occasions when he drove his master to the big railway station, where there was a bar. After having dropped his master at the station, he would drive off about half a mile, park his sledge and horse deep in the snow at the side of the road and wait there till the train had left. The sledge would lie on its side, almost upside down, and the horse, up to his belly in a snow-drift, would stand with legs astraddle and put down his nose every now and then to lick the soft friable snow. Yanson, meanwhile, half lay on the sledge in an awkward posture and seemed to slumber. The untied ear-flaps of his much-worn fur cap would hang down helplessly, like the ears of a spaniel, and his small red nose would run.

Then Yanson would go back to the station and quickly get drunk.

On the return journey he would gallop the whole ten versts to the farm. The mercilessly beaten little horse, mad with terror, would jump with all four legs at once, like a frenzied creature. The sledge rolled about, almost turned over, knocked into posts; and Yanson, dropping the reins and each moment in danger of being flung out, would yell something in jerky Estonian, which sounded half song, half shout. But usually he would not even sing. Silently, his teeth set firmly in an access of incomprehensible fury, suffering and delight, he would drive on like a blind man. Passers-by went unnoticed and unwarned, and he did not slow down his mad race round turnings or down hills. How he had failed not to kill someone or do himself an injury on one of these wild drives was a miracle.

He ought to have been sacked long ago, as he had been from other places, but he was cheap and other workmen were not much better, so he stayed there two years. There were no events in Yanson's life. One day he received a letter written in Estonian, but as he was illiterate and the others did not know Estonian, the letter remained unread; and, with a kind of savage, fanatical indifference, as if unaware of the fact that the letter might bring news from home, Yanson threw it on the manure heap. At one time, evidently longing for a woman, he tried to woo the cook, but he was unsuccessful and was repulsed and scorned. He was short and sickly, with a pitted freckled face, and his sleepy eyes were of a dirty greenish colour. Yanson took the rebuff with indifference and did not molest the cook again.

Though he spoke little, Yanson seemed always to be listening to something. He listened to the dismal plain with its hillocks of frozen manure, looking like rows of little snow-covered graves; he listened to the delicate blue distances, to the buzzing of telegraph poles and to people's talk. What the plain and the telegraph poles said to him, he alone knew, but people's talk was disquieting, full of rumours of murders, robberies and arson. And one night from the neighbouring village was heard the thin, helpless tinkling of the tiny church bell and the crackling of flames. Strangers from no one knew where had robbed a rich farm, murdered the farmer and his wife and set the house on fire.

On Yanson's farm, too, there was an uneasy feeling; the dogs were kept unchained by day as well as by night and the master slept with a gun by his side. He wanted to give Yanson a similar gun, though one-barrelled and old, but the latter turned it round in his hands, shook his head over it, and for some reason refused it. The master could not understand why Yanson would not have it and scolded him, but the servant had more faith in his Finnish knife than in the old rusty gun.

"It would be the death of me," he said, looking sleepily at his master with his glassy eyes. The master threw up his hands in despair.

"What a fool you are, Ivan! How is one to get anything done with such workmen?"

One winter evening, when the other workmen had been sent to the station, that same Ivan Yanson, who had refused to trust the gun, made an extremely complicated attempt at robbery, murder and rape. He did it in an amazingly simple way. He locked the cook in the kitchen, then, lazily, pretending to be almost dead with sleep, he approached his master from behind and stabbed him several times quickly in the back. The master fell unconscious to the ground, his wife began to run screaming round the room, and Yanson, grinning and brandishing his knife, started to ransack the trunks and chests of drawers. He found the money and then, as if noticing his mistress for the first time, and seemingly to his own surprise, rushed upon her to violate her. But as he happened to drop his knife at this moment, the mistress proved to be the stronger, and not only did not allow herself to be violated, but almost succeeded in strangling him. At this point the farmer on the floor began to show signs of life, whilst the cook thundered with the oven-fork in an effort to force the kitchen door, and Yanson ran off into the fields. He was caught an hour later squatting behind a corner of the barn, striking one dead match after the other in an attempt to set the farm on fire.

A few days later the farmer died from blood poisoning, and Yanson's turn having come, amongst the other robbers and murderers, he was tried and sentenced to death. In the court he looked as he always did; a small sickly man with a freckled face and sleepy, glassy little eyes. He did not quite seem to realise what was going on around him and appeared to be completely indifferent. He blinked his white eyelashes dully, gazed, without any curiosity at the unfamiliar, imposing court room and picked his nose with his rough, horny, stiff finger. Only those who had seen him on Sundays at church could have guessed that he had smartened himself up; he wore round his neck a knitted, dirty red scarf and had damped down his hair in places. Where the hair was moist it looked darker and lay smoothly, but where it was not it stuck up in fair thin tufts, like wisps of straw on a meadow laid waste by hail.

When the sentence was pronounced—death by hanging —Yanson suddenly became agitated. He turned deep red and began to tie and untie the scarf as though it were strangling him. Then he started to wave his arms about aimlessly and said, addressing the judge who had not read the sentence, whilst pointing to the one who had, *"She* said that I was to be hanged."

"Who is *she?"* asked, in a deep bass voice, the presiding judge who had pronounced the sentence. Everyone smiled, trying to conceal their smiles in their moustaches or papers, but Yanson, pointing with his finger at the presiding judge, answered frowningly and angrily, "You."

"Well?"

Yanson again turned his eyes to the silent, reticently smiling judge, in whom he sensed a friend and a person quite unconcerned in the sentence, and repeated, "She has said that I am to be hanged. I must not be hanged."

"Take the prisoner away."

But Yanson managed to repeat once more, weightily and with conviction, "I must not be hanged."

His little angry face and his attempt to be imposing with outstretched finger were so absurd that even the escorting soldier broke the rules by saying half aloud as he led him from the court, "What a fool you are, lad!"

"I must not be hanged," repeated Yanson stubbornly.

"They will hitch you up quickly, you won't have time to jerk."

"Keep quiet now," shouted another guard angrily. But he could not refrain from adding, "Another robber! Why did you take a human life, you fool? Now you will hang."

"They might pardon him," said the first soldier, who felt sorry for Yanson.

"What! Pardon the likes of him. . . . Now that's enough talking."

But Yanson was already silent. He was taken again to the same cell where he had spent more than a month and to which he had grown accustomed, as he had become accustomed to everything, to blows, to vodka, and to the gloomy snow-covered fields strewn with hillocks like a graveyard. Now he felt almost cheerful at the sight of his bed, and his window with the iron bars, and he was given something to eat, for he had had nothing since the morning. The only unpleasant thing was the occurrence in court, but he could not think, was incapable of thinking about it. And death by hanging he could not picture to himself at all.

Though Yanson was under sentence of death, there were many other prisoners of this kind, and the prison warders did not regard him as a dangerous criminal. They talked to him, therefore, without fear or respect, as they talked to the other prisoners who were not condemned to death. Actually, they did not consider his death as death. On hearing the sentence, his jailor said to him admonishingly, "Well, brother, so they are going to hang you?"

"When will they hang me?" asked Yanson incredulously.

"Well, you will have to wait, brother," was the reply, "till there are a number of you. They will not put themselves out for one man, especially a man like you. They want something bigger."

"So when?" asked Yanson insistently. He was not offended that he was not considered worth hanging alone, nor did he believe it. He thought it was only an excuse for postponing his execution in order to grant him a reprieve later on. He became cheerful; the dim terrible moment, about which he could not think, had moved far into the distance and become fantastic and impossible, as death always seems.

"When, when?" growled the jailor, a stupid old man. "It isn't like hanging a dog, which you take behind the barn and finish off in the twinkling of an eye. Or would you like it to be done that way, you fool?"

"I don't want to be hanged," said Yanson with a cheerful

grimace. "It was she who said I was to be hanged, but I don't want to be."

And that was perhaps the first time in his life that he had laughed. It was a grating, foolish, but extremely cheerful merry laugh, like the cackling of a goose—ga-ga-ga. The jailor looked at him with surprise and frowned sternly. The silly cheerfulness of a man condemned to death was an insult to the prison and the execution itself and made them appear in a strange light. Suddenly for a second, or rather the fraction of a second, that old jailor, who had spent all his life in prison and to whom its laws were laws of nature, saw the prison and all its life as something like a lunatic asylum, in which he, the jailor, was the chief madman.

"The devil take it," he said spitting. "Why are you grinning? This is not a public house!"

"I don't want to be hanged, ga-ga-ga," laughed Yanson.

"Satan!" cried the jailor, feeling he must make the sign of the cross.

Nothing could have been more unlike Satan, however, than this little man with the small, flabby face, but something in his goose cackle was destructive of the sanctity and might of the prison. If he went on laughing, the rotten walls might collapse and the rusty gratings fall to pieces and he, the jailor himself, might find himself bringing the prisoners to the gates and saying: "Please, gentlemen, take a walk in the town, or perhaps you would prefer the country?" Satan!

But Yanson had already stopped laughing and only screwed up his eyes cunningly.

"Well, take care," said the jailor in a vaguely threatening tone and went away with a backward glance.

All that evening Yanson was calm and even cheerful. He kept repeating to himself the phrase, "I must not be hanged," and it seemed to him so convincing, so wise and so irrefutable that there was nothing to worry about. He had long ago forgotten about his crime and only sometimes felt sorry that he had not succeeded in violating the farmer's wife. But even that he soon forgot.

Every morning Yanson would ask when he was to be hanged and every morning the jailor would answer angrily, "There is plenty of time, Satan. Wait." And he would hastily retreat before Yanson had time to burst out laughing.

Because of these monotonously reiterated words and because every day began, passed and ended in the most ordinary manner, Yanson became irretrievably convinced that there would be no execution. He began very quickly to forget about the trial and would loll all day long on his bunk day-dreaming vaguely and happily. His dreams were of the dismal snow-covered fields with their hillocks, the station bar and other still brighter and more distant things. He was well fed in prison, so that in a few days he became stouter and began to put on airs a little.

"She would have loved me now," he said to himself once, thinking of the master's wife. "Now I look fat, just like the master."

His only great longing was for vodka; to drink it and to drive a little horse, swiftly, swiftly, at a gallop.

When the news of the arrest of the terrorists reached the prison and Yanson asked the routine question, the jailor answered unexpectedly and roughly, "Now it won't be long."

Then he looked at Yanson calmly and pompously and repeated, "Now it won't be long. I should say in a week."

Yanson grew pale and so dim was the glance of his glassy eyes that he might have been falling asleep as he asked, "Are you joking?"

"First you could not wait, and now you say I am joking. We don't joke here. It is you who like to joke, but for us jokes are not fitting," said the jailor with dignity and walked out.

That very evening Yanson grew thinner. His skin, which had temporarily stretched and grown smooth, suddenly contracted into a number of tiny wrinkles and even seemed to hang down in places. His eyes became sleepy and all his movements were as slow and sluggish as if every turn of his head or movement of his fingers or feet had become a complicated and cumbersome undertaking, requiring great previous consideration. At night he lay down on his bed but did not close his eyes; though sleepy, they remained open till morning.

"Oho," said the jailor delightedly, on seeing him the next day. "This is no public house, you see, my fine fellow."

With great satisfaction, like a scientist whose experiment has been proved correct again, he surveyed the condemned man attentively and in detail from head to foot. Now all would go as it should. Satan was disgraced and the sanctity of prison and executions restored once more. Condescendingly, even with sincere sympathy, the old man enquired, "Do you want to see anyone or not?"

"Why should I?"

"Well, to say good-bye. Your mother or your brother?"

"I must not be hanged," said Yanson in a low voice and gave a sidelong glance at the jailor. "I don't want to be."

The jailor looked at him and silently made a gesture with his hand.

Towards evening Yanson had calmed down somewhat. The day had been as usual; the cloudy winter sky looked as it always did, footsteps and some business conversation in the corridor sounded just as usual, and the cabbage soup smelt so natural and ordinary that he began to disbelieve in the execution. But at night he was overcome by fear. Formerly night to him had been simply darkness, that special dark period when one had to sleep, but now he felt in it something mysterious and ominous. In order not to believe in death, one must be surrounded by customary sights and sounds—steps, voices, light, cabbage soup. But now everything had become strange and the very stillness and darkness were something like death.

And the longer the night dragged on, the more terrible it became. With the simplicity of a savage or a child, who thinks everything is possible, Yanson felt like shouting out to the sun—"Shine." He begged and implored the sun to shine, but the night drew its dark hours steadfastly over the earth and there was no power which could stop its course. This impossibility, which for the first time was clearly visualised by Yanson's weak brain, filled him with terror. Still without daring to face it clearly, he realised

the inevitability of approaching death, and placed his be-
numbed foot on the first step of the gallows.

Day soothed him again and night frightened him again,
and this went on until one night when he knew and felt
that death was unavoidable and that it would take place in
three days' time at dawn, with the sunrise.

He had never considered what death was and death had
no form for him, but now he felt distinctly, saw and knew
that it had entered the cell and was looking for him, grop-
ing with its hands. To save himself he began running round
the cell.

But the cell was so small that the corners seemed to be
all round instead of angular and they were all thrusting him
into the centre. And there was nothing behind which he
could hide. And the door was locked and it was light. His
body struck several times against the wall and bounced once
against the door—there was a hollow, empty sound. He
stumbled over something and fell face downwards and then
he felt that it was catching him. He lay on his stomach,
clinging to the floor, hiding his face in the dirty dark
asphalt, and began to yell in terror. He lay there and
shouted at the top of his voice till someone came. Even
after he had been lifted from the floor, placed on his bed
and cold water poured over his head, Yanson could not
bring himself to open his tightly closed eyes. He opened
one eye, saw the light, empty corner and someone's boot in
the emptiness and began to cry out again.

But the cold water began to have its effect. And several
blows on the head, administered as medicine by the jailor
on duty, that same old man, were also helpful. The sensation of life they produced really drove death away and Yanson opened his eyes and, his brain thoroughly muddled,
slept soundly the rest of the night. He lay on his back, his
mouth open, and snored loudly and furiously. The flat dead
white of the eye without pupil was visible between his half-
closed eyelids.

Later everything in the world, day, night, steps, voices
and cabbage soup, became one continual nightmare and put
him into a state of wild and indescribably confused bewilderment. His feeble mind could not combine two ideas

which so fantastically contradicted each other—the usual bright day and the taste and smell of cabbage soup with the fact that in two days, or a day, he must die. He did not think at all, he did not even count the hours, he simply stood there, numb with terror, faced with a contradiction that split his brain in two. His face became evenly pale, with no patches of white or red, and he appeared calm. But he took no food and stopped sleeping altogether. He either sat all night on a little stool, cross-legged and terrified, or walked about the cell with quiet, stealthy, sleepy glances. He kept his mouth half open all the time, as if he were in a state of continual amazement, and he scrutinised the most trivial thing before taking it up, and handled it distrustfully.

When he had reached this stage, the warders and the soldier, who had been watching him through the small grating, paid no more attention to him. That was the normal state of the condemned. It was, in the jailor's opinion, though he had never experienced it, similar to the state of cattle led to the slaughter, after they have been stunned by a blow on the forehead from the butt end of an axe.

"Now he is stunned, now he will feel nothing till death itself," said the jailor, looking at him with his experienced eyes. "Ivan, do you hear? Hallo, Ivan!"

"I must not be hanged," answered Yanson gloomily and his lower jaw dropped again.

"If you had not murdered someone, you would not be hanged," said the senior jailor in an admonitory tone. He was still young, but pompous, with medals on his breast. "But you have committed murder and yet don't want to be hanged."

"You wanted to kill a man without paying for it. He's stupid, stupid but cunning."

"I don't want . . ." began Yanson.

"Well, friend . . . you may want it or not, that's your business," said the senior jailor indifferently. "Instead of talking nonsense, however, you had better make arrangements about your belongings."

"He hasn't got any. One shirt and pants. Yes, and a fur cap, the dandy!"

So the time passed till Thursday. On Thursday at midnight a number of persons entered Yanson's cell and a gentleman with epaulettes said, "Well, get ready, we must be off."

Moving in the same slow way, Yanson put on all he had and tied his dirty red scarf about his neck. Watching him while he dressed, the man with the epaulettes smoked cigarettes and said to someone, "What a warm morning. Just like spring."

Yanson's little eyes were stuck together and he seemed to be falling asleep. He moved so slowly and stiffly that the jailor shouted at him, "Hurry up, are you dreaming?"

Yanson suddenly stood still.

"I don't want . . ." he said feebly.

They took him by the arms and led him away and he marched obediently, shrugging his shoulders. Outside he was fanned by a moist spring air and his small nose began to run. Although it was night, the thaw was increasing and from somewhere came the merry sound of quick drops falling on stone. As he waited while the police, clanking their sabres and bending their heads, got into the black, unlighted carriage, Yanson idly moved his finger under his running nose and adjusted his badly tied scarf.

IV   WE OF ORYOL

The same judges of the regional military court, who had tried Yanson, sentenced to execution by hanging a peasant from Eletz in the province of Oryol. This was Michael Golubetz, nicknamed Mishka Tziganok, a Tartar. His last crime, for which there was indubitable evidence, had been robbery with violence and included the murder of three people. Before that the trail of his dark past was shrouded in deep mystery. There were vague rumours of his having been implicated in a whole series of other robberies and murders; blood and fire and dark, drunken debauchery seemed to have accompanied his steps. With complete frankness and outspokenness he called himself a robber, and regarded with scorn those who adopted the modern title of "expropriators." Seeing that denial was of no avail, he voluntarily confessed his last crime down to the last detail. When questioned further about his past, however, he only grinned and whistled, saying, "Ask the wind that blows in the field."

When hard pressed with questions, Tziganok would assume a serious and dignified air.

"We of Oryol are all hot-heads," he remarked gravely and with deliberation. "The first-class thieves live in Oryol and Kromy. Karatshev and Livny are the best places for thieves; but Eletz is the head and front of all thieves. What more is there to say!"

He was nicknamed Tziganok, the Gipsy, because of his appearance and thievish ways. His hair was of most extraordinary blackness, he was lean and had spots from yellow fever on his sharp, Tartar-like cheek-bones. He rolled the whites of his eyes as horses do and was in a perpetual hurry. His glance was short and quick but terrifyingly direct and full of curiosity. When he looked quickly at an object, it was as if it lost something, gave him part of itself and became different. One did not easily or without an unpleasant feeling pick up a cigarette at which he had looked, for it was as if it had been in his mouth. He was possessed by a perpetual restlessness, which sometimes twisted him like a rope and sometimes sent him flying like a broad shower of scattering sparks. He drank water almost by the bucketful, like a horse.

When questioned in court, he jumped quickly to his feet and answered briefly, firmly and even with some satisfaction, "Right."

Sometimes he would stress the word, as, "R-r-right."

Once, suddenly, when some quite different point was under discussion, he jumped to his feet and asked the presiding judge, "Do you give me leave to whistle?"

"What for?" said the judge in surprise.

"Evidence has been given that I signalled to my comrades and I will show you how I did it. It is very interesting."

Though rather disconcerted, the judge agreed to the request. Tziganok quickly put four fingers in his mouth, two from each hand, and rolled his eyes savagely. A real wild robber's whistle rent the dead atmosphere of the court, a whistle which made the deafened horses leap and rear and people's faces involuntarily turn white. The mortal anguish of the victim, the wild joy of the murderer, the ominous warning, the summons, the darkness and loneliness of a stormy autumn night—all were heard in that piercing sound, which was neither quite human nor quite bestial.

The presiding judge shouted something and waved his hand at Tziganok, who stopped obediently. And like an artist, who has triumphantly performed a difficult but always successful aria, he sat down wiping his wet fingers on his prison dress, and looked round at the audience with a self-satisfied air.

"A real brigand!" said one of the judges, rubbing his ear. And another judge, who had a broad Russian beard and the eyes of a Tartar, like those of Tziganok, looked dreamily into space above the prisoner's head, smiled and remarked, "This is really interesting."

Light-heartedly, without the slightest pity or compunction, the judge pronounced the death sentence.

"Right," said Tziganok, when the verdict was given. "In the open field on a cross-beam. Right."

And turning to the guard, he said with bravado, "Well, let's go, sour-face. Keep a good hold of your gun or I'll have it from you!"

The soldier looked at him sternly and with fear, exchanging glances with the other guard and feeling the lock of his gun. The other did the same. All the way to the prison they seemed to fly rather than walk. So absorbed were they in the criminal, that they were unconscious of the ground they trod on, and forgot time and themselves.

Like Yanson, Mishka Tziganok had to spend seventeen days in prison before the execution. The whole seventeen days passed for him as quickly as if it were one, and was filled with a continuous inextinguishable dream of escape, liberty and life. The restlessness, which possessed him, and was now kept under by walls and gratings and the dead window through which nothing could be seen, turned all its rage inwards and burned Tziganok's mind like scattered coals. As in drunken dreams, bright unfinished pictures swarmed upon him, jostled each other and became confused, and were then borne along in an irresistible dazzling whirl. They all tended towards one end—escape, liberty and life. Sometimes, expanding his nostrils like a horse, Tziganok would inhale the air for hours on end. It seemed to him that he could smell hemp, the smoke of a fire and the faintly acrid odour of burning. Sometimes he would circle the cell like a wolf, quickly touching the walls, tapping, measuring, piercing the ceiling with his glance, sawing through the gratings. His restlessness wearied out the soldier, who watched him through the peephole, so that the fellow sometimes threatened to shoot him. Tziganok retorted rudely and with mockery, and if everything ended peacefully, it was because the quarrel soon took on the character of an ordinary inoffensive peasants' brawl, where shooting seemed quite out of place.

At night Tziganok slept soundly, almost without stirring, in the unchanging but living immobility of a spring temporarily out of action. But once on his feet he immediately resumed his circling, planning and touching. His hands were continually dry and hot, but his heart often turned suddenly cold, as if in his breast had been placed a piece of unmelting ice which sent a small dry shiver all over his body. Always swarthy, at such moments Tziganok would turn still darker and take on a bluish cast-iron colour. He developed a strange habit. He kept licking and smacking his lips, as if he had eaten something excessively and nauseatingly sweet, and spat out on the floor, hissing as he did so, the saliva which kept accumulating in his mouth. When speaking he left his words unfinished, for so quickly did his thoughts run that his tongue could not catch up with them.

One day the chief warder, accompanied by a guard, entered his cell. He looked askance at the bespattered floor and said gloomily, "Look how he has filthied the place!"

Tziganok retorted quickly, "You, fat face, have filthied the whole world and have I reproached you? What have you come here for?"

In the same gloomy way the warder offered him the job of executioner. Tziganok bared his teeth in a grin and then burst out laughing.

"So you cannot find anybody? I like that! Go ahead and do the hanging yourself, ha-ha. You have got the necks and the rope and nobody to do the job. By God, I like that!"

"Your life would be spared in return."

"I should say so! As a corpse I could scarcely do the hanging for you! What a fool!"

"Well, what do you say? Is it the same to you either way?"

"How do you do the hanging? I expect you strangle people secretly."

"No, to music," snarled the warder.

"What a fool he is! Of course it should be done to music—this way," and he began to sing something with bravado.

"You seem to have gone quite crazy, my friend," said the warder. "Well, what is your answer? Talk sense."

Tziganok grinned: "You're in too much of a hurry. You must come again, then I'll tell you."

And now, into the whirl of bright, unfinished pictures, which rushed past Tziganok, torturing him by their rapidity, came a new one. How splendid to become an executioner in a red shirt! He pictured vividly to himself a square with a big crowd, a high scaffold and himself, Tziganok, pacing up and down with an axe in his hand. The sun shone upon the heads of the people, and was gaily reflected in the axe, and everything was so cheerful and bright that even the victim whose head was to be chopped off smiled too. Carts and horses' heads were visible behind the crowd—the peasants had come in from the village. Beyond he could see the open fields.

"Tz-ah," exclaimed Tziganok, smacking and licking his lips, and spat out the accumulated saliva. Suddenly he felt as if a fur cap had been pulled over his head right down to his mouth; it was dark and stifling and his heart turned into a lump of unmelting ice, sending a slight shiver all over him.

The warder came twice again, but Tziganok grinned and said, "You seem to be in a hurry. It won't hurt you to come once more."

At last, however, the warder shouted casually through the peep-hole, "You have lost your chance, you crow! They have found someone else."

"The devil take you, go and hang them yourself," snapped Tziganok. And he dropped day-dreaming about the executioner's job.

But when, finally, the time of the execution drew near the rush of broken images became unbearable. Tziganok wanted to stop, to set his feet wide in order to come to a standstill, but the whirling current carried him away and there was nothing to hold on to—everything swam around him. His sleep now became restless too. He was visited by new dreams, heavy as coloured wooden blocks and even more violent than his thoughts. They no longer came in a stream, but in an endless fall from an endless mountain, in a whirling flight through the whole visible world of colours. Tziganok had had a rather dashing moustache, but in prison he grew a short black bristling beard, which gave him a terrifying, almost insane appearance. At times he was really out of his mind and senselessly circled the cell, still tapping the rough plastered walls. And he drank water like a horse.

One evening, when the lights were put on, Tziganok went on all fours in the middle of the cell and began to utter a trembling wolf-like howl. He did it with great seriousness, howling as if he were performing a most important and necessary rite. He breathed in deeply and out slowly in a prolonged and trembling howl, then, blinking his eyes, he listened attentively to the effect. The very tremor in his voice seemed somehow artificial. He did not howl at random but carefully produced each note in that animal cry full of terror and grief.

Suddenly he broke off the howling and remained silently on all fours for a few minutes. Then he whispered to the ground, "Dear good people, dear good people, have mercy. . . . Dear good people!"

And here, too, he seemed to listen to the effect of his words. After each word—he stopped and listened. Then he jumped to his feet and for an hour on end gave vent to the most terrible curses.

"You so-and-so," he shouted, rolling his blood-shot eyes, "if you hang me, you hang me, but for you there will be . . ."

Meanwhile the soldier on guard, white as chalk and weeping with anguish and terror, pounded on the door with the butt end of his rifle and shouted helplessly, "I'll shoot you, by God, I'll shoot you. Do you hear?"

But he dared not shoot; if there were no open mutiny, those sentenced to death were never shot. Tziganok ground his teeth, swore and spat. His human brain, placed on that marvellously narrow verge between life and death, was falling to pieces like a lump of dry weather-beaten clay.

On the night when they came into the cell to take Tziganok to execution, he bestirred himself and seemed to revive. The sweet taste in his mouth became still sweeter and the saliva was not to be held back, but his cheeks took on a little colour and some of his former savage cunning sparkled in his eyes. Whilst dressing he asked an official, "Who is going to do the hanging? The new man? He won't have got his hand in yet."

"You need not worry about that," said the official dryly.

"How can I help worrying, your Honour? They are going to hang me, not you. At least do not be sparing of the Government's soap on the loop."

"All right, all right, please keep quiet."

"This man has eaten up all your soap," said Tziganok, pointing at the warder. "Look how his face shines."

"Silence!"

"Do not be stingy!"

Tziganok burst out laughing, but the taste of sweetness in his mouth was increasing and his legs suddenly became strangely numb. When he came out into the yard, however, he managed to shout, "The carriage for the Count of Bengal!"

V   KISS HIM AND BE SILENT

The sentence on the five terrorists was pronounced in its final form and ratified the same day. The condemned were not told when they were to be executed, but, judging by what had been done on other occasions, they knew they would be hanged the same night or, at latest, the following. When they were offered an opportunity of seeing their relatives the next day, Thursday, they understood that the execution would take place on Friday at dawn.

Tanya Kovalchuk possessed no near relations, and those she had lived somewhere in a remote spot in Little Russia and probably knew nothing of the trial and imminent execution. Mousia and Werner, the unidentified prisoners, were presumed to have no relatives, and only two of them, Sergey Golovin and Vassily Kashirin, were to see their parents. They were both filled with anguish and terror at the thought of this meeting, but somehow could not bring themselves to refuse the old folks a last talk and embrace.

Sergey Golovin, especially, was perturbed by the forthcoming meeting. He was extremely fond of his father and mother, had seen them not long before and was now terrified as to what was going to happen. The execution itself, defeating thought by its monstrous strangeness and madness, was easier to imagine, and seemed less terrifying than these few short incomprehensible minutes, which were as if outside time, outside life itself. His human brain refused to contemplate how he was to look, or what he was to think and say. The simplest and most ordinary behaviour—to take his father's hand, to kiss him and say, "How are you, Father?"—seemed incredibly horrible, because of the monstrous, inhuman, insane lie concealed in it.

After the sentence the condemned were not placed together in one cell, as assumed by Kovalchuk. Each went back to solitary confinement. All the morning till eleven o'clock, when his parents came, Sergey Golovin paced furiously up and down the cell, plucking his little beard, frowning piteously and muttering. From time to time he stopped in full course to take breath and gasped like a man who has been too long under water. He was of such excellent physique, however, his youthful vitality was so great, that even in these moments of cruel suffering the blood pulsated vividly under his skin, giving colour to his cheeks, and his blue eyes shone brightly and innocently.

However, everything went off better than Sergey had anticipated.

Sergey's father, Nikolay Sergeevich Golovin, a retired colonel, was the first to enter the room. He was of an even white all over—face, beard, hair and hands—as if a white marble statue had been dressed in men's clothes. He wore the same old coat as ever, well cleaned and smelling of benzine, with new cross epaulettes. He entered with a firm military steady step and, stretching out his dry white hand, said in a loud voice, "How do you do, Sergey?"

The mother followed him with short steps, smiling strangely. She, too, shook his hand and repeated loudly, "How do you do, Seryoshenka?"

She kissed his lips and sat down in silence. She did not fall upon his neck, did not burst into tears, in short did none of those terrible things which Sergey had feared so much; she kissed him and sat down in silence. She even straightened her black silk frock with her trembling hands.

Sergey did not know that the whole of the preceding night the colonel, having locked himself in his little study, had given himself up entirely to working out the details of this meeting. We must strive not to make harder, but to ease, our son's last minutes, was the colonel's firm decision, and he weighed carefully every sentence and every movement of the next day's meeting. Now and then he became confused, forgot the sentence he had just prepared and wept bitterly, sitting on a corner of his oil-cloth-covered divan. Next morning he explained to his wife how to behave at the meeting.

"The main thing is to kiss him and be silent," he instructed her. "Later on you may speak, a little later, but when you kiss him, be silent. Do not speak soon after the kiss, do you understand? For you may say something better left unsaid."

"I understand, Nikolay Sergeevich," the mother answered, crying.

"And do not cry. For Heaven's sake, don't weep! You will kill him if you do that, old woman."

"And why do you weep yourself?"

"How can one help weeping with you! You must not weep, do you hear?"

"Very well, Nikolay Sergeevich."

Riding in the cab, he wanted to repeat his admonitions once more, but forgot them. So they both rode in silence, both of them bent, old and grey and lost in thought, while the city was full of gay sounds. It was Shrovetide and the streets were crowded and noisy.

They sat down. The colonel placed himself in his prepared pose with right hand in the lapel of his coat. Sergey sat down for a minute, looked close at his mother's wrinkled face and jumped up.

"Sit down, Seryoshenka," begged his mother.

"Sit down, Sergey," repeated his father.

There was silence. The mother smiled oddly.

"We have done everything in our power for you, Seryoshenka. Father . . ."

"It was no good, Mamma dear . . ."

The colonel said firmly, "We had to do it, Sergey, so that you should not think your parents had deserted you."

There was silence again. It was terrible to utter a word, for every spoken word seemed to have lost its real significance and meant only one thing—death. Sergey looked at his father's clean little overcoat, which smelt of benzine, and thought, "They have no servant now, so he has to clean it himself. How is it that I have never noticed when he cleans his coat? Probably in the mornings." And he asked suddenly, "How is my sister? Is she well?"

"Ninochka knows nothing," said his mother quickly.

But the colonel stopped her sternly, "Why tell a lie? The girl read it in the papers. Let Sergey know that everybody, that all his dearest . . . have been thinking of him at this time and . . ."

He could not go on and stopped. Suddenly the mother's face crumpled up all at once, ran down with tears, shook and became wet and wild. Her faded eyes stared frenziedly and her breathing became quicker, shorter and louder.

"Se . . . Ser . . . Se . . . Se . . ." she repeated without moving her lips.

"Mamma dear!"

The colonel stepped forward. He was trembling all over, in every fold of his coat and every wrinkle of his face, and, without realising how terrifying he looked in his deathly whiteness, in his heroic and desperate firmness, he said to his wife, "Be silent. Do not torment him. Do not torment him. He has to die. Do not torment him!"

She had already stopped in terror, but he still shook his clenched fist in front of his chest and repeated, "Do not torment him."

Then he stepped back and, putting his trembling arm behind his back, asked loudly with white lips and an expression of forced calm, "When?"

"Tomorrow morning," answered Sergey, whose lips were white also.

The mother looked at the ground, chewing her lips, as though she heard nothing. Still chewing her lips, she uttered, as if casually, the simple strange words, "Ninochka asked us to kiss you for her, Seryoshenka."

"Kiss her for me," said Sergey.

"We will. The Khvostovs also sent you their love."

"Which Khvostovs? Oh, yes."

The colonel interrupted, "Well, we must go. Get up, Mother, we must go."

They both helped the enfeebled mother to rise.

"Bid him farewell," ordered the colonel. "Make the sign of the cross."

She did everything she was told. But while making the sign of the cross and kissing her son with a brief kiss, she shook her head and repeated meaninglessly, "No, it's not so, no, not so. No, no. And afterwards, what shall I do, what shall I say? No, not so."

"Good-bye, Sergey," said his father. They shook hands and embraced each other firmly but briefly.

"You . . ." began Sergey.

"Well," asked his father abruptly.

"No, it is not so. No, no. What shall I say?" murmured his mother, shaking her head. Meanwhile she had sat down again and was rocking herself backwards and forwards.

"You . . ." began Sergey again. Suddenly his face crumpled up pathetically like a child's and his eyes all at once filled with tears. Through their shining gleams he saw his father's white face near him, with eyes also full of tears.

"You, Father, are a noble man."

"Don't, don't," said his father in terror, and suddenly, as if he had broken in two, his head fell upon his son's shoulder. He used to be taller than Sergey, but now he had shrunk and his dry downy head rested like a little white ball on his son's shoulder. They kissed each other eagerly and silently. Sergey kissed the fluffy white hair and his father the prisoner's dress.

"And what about me?" said a loud voice suddenly.

They turned round. Sergey's mother stood there, her head thrown back, and looked at them angrily, almost with hate.

"What is it, Mother?" asked the colonel.

"What about me?" said she, shaking her head, with extravagant emphasis. "You kiss each other, and what about me? You men kiss, and I? And I?"

"Mamma dear," and Sergey rushed to her.

What followed cannot and should not be described.

The colonel's last words were, "I bless you in your death, Seryosha. Die bravely as befits an officer."

And they left. Somehow they left. They had been there, stood there and spoken, and suddenly they were gone. It was here Mother sat, there stood Father—and suddenly, somehow, they were gone. On coming back to his cell Sergey lay down on his bed, his face turned to the wall to hide it from the soldiers, and he wept for a long time. Then, exhausted by his tears, he slept soundly.

Only his mother came to see Vassily Kashirin. His father, a well-to-do merchant, refused to visit him. When the old woman entered, Vassily was pacing up and down the cell, shivering all over with cold, though the day was warm, almost hot. And their conversation was brief and painful.

"You should not have come, Mamma. You are only giving pain to yourself and me."

"Why all this, Vasia? Why did you do it? Oh, Lord!" and the old woman began to weep, wiping her tears with the corner of her black woollen kerchief. As it had been his and his brothers' habit to shout at their mother, because she did not understand anything, Vassily stopped and, shivering with cold, said angrily, "There it is! I knew it! You do not understand a thing, Mamma. Not a thing!"

"All right, all right. What is the matter with you? Are you cold?"

"Cold!" Vassily cut her short and continued to pace the room, looking at her askance and angrily.

"Perhaps you have caught cold?"

"Ah, Mamma, what is a cold, when . . ." and he waved his hand hopelessly.

The old woman was about to say, "And our old man has ordered pancakes* to be served from Monday on," but she was frightened and began to wail, "I said to him—'Isn't he your son? Go and give him absolution.' But he was as obstinate as an old goat."

"To hell with him. What kind of a father has he been to me? He has been a scoundrel all his life and such he has remained."

"Vasenka, you are speaking of your father," said the old woman, drawing herself up disapprovingly.

"Certainly, of my father."

"Your own father."

"What kind of a father has he been to me?"

It was all absurd and dreadful. He was almost face to face with death, and here was this small, futile, unwanted something, which sprang up and made words sound like empty nut-shells cracking under one's feet. He almost wept for sorrow of that eternal misunderstanding which all his life had stood like a big wall between him and his family, and even now, in these last hours before death, peered at him with its small stupid eyes. Vassily shouted out, "Do take it in. I am going to be hanged! Hanged! Do you understand or not? Hanged!"

"You should have left people alone, then you would not . . ." cried the old woman.

"God above! How can this be! Even the beasts are better! Am I your son or not?"

*Translator's Note: Pancakes are served in Russia after funerals.

He began to cry and sat down in a corner. Sitting in her corner, the old woman burst into tears. Unable even for an instant to unite in a feeling of love, and so confront the horror of approaching death, they both shed cold tears of loneliness, which gave no solace to the heart. The mother said, "You asked whether I was your mother or not, you reproach me. And I have gone quite white these last days. I have become an old woman. And yet you talk and reproach me."

"All right, all right, Mamma. Forgive me. You must go now. Kiss my brothers for me."

"Am I not your mother? Do you think I do not pity you?"

At last she went away. She cried bitterly, wiping her eyes with the corner of her kerchief, and did not see the road. The farther she went from the prison, the more scalding her tears became. She turned back towards the prison, but somehow got hopelessly lost in the city in which she had been born, bred and grown old. She finally found herself in a little deserted garden with some old lopped trees and sat down upon a bench wet with thaw. Suddenly it flashed upon her—he was going to be hanged tomorrow.

The old woman jumped up and tried to run, but her head suddenly began to turn round and she fell to the ground. The little icy path was wet and slippery and the old woman could not get up. She turned around, tried to raise herself on her elbows, then on her knees, but she fell on her side. The black kerchief had slipped from her head, showing a bald patch on the back amidst dirty grey hair. She fancied for some reason that she was at a wedding feast, that her son was getting married and that she had drunk a great deal and was thoroughly intoxicated.

"No more, I cannot, really I cannot," she kept saying, shaking her head as she crawled over the wet icy snow crust and imagining they were pouring out more and more wine for her.

She felt sick at heart amidst the drunken laughter and the wild dancing and feasting. But they went on pouring out wine, ever more and more wine.

There was a bell tower with an old-fashioned clock in the fortress where the condemned prisoners were kept. Every hour, every half hour and every quarter of an hour the clock rang out, in a long-drawn sorrowful peal, which slowly faded away in the sky, like the distant mournful call of birds of passage. During the day that strange sorrowful music was lost in the bustle of the large and crowded city street which ran past the fortress. Trams clanged, the pavement rang with horse hooves, and swaying cars hooted in the distance. Special carnival peasant drivers had come up to town from the outskirts for the Shrovetide season, and the little bells on the necks of their stunted horses filled the air with tinkling. There was chatter, rather intoxicated, merry Shrovetide chatter; and the fresh spring thaw with its dirty pools on the pavement, and the trees grown suddenly dark in the square, seemed to go well with the discordant bustle. A warm wind blew from the sea in strong damp gusts. One could almost see with the naked eye the tiny fresh particles of air frolicking as they were borne along into boundless space.

At night the street became silent in the solitary light of its large electric suns. And then the big fortress with its flat walls, in which was no single light, disappeared into the darkness and stillness. Thus a deep dividing line of silence, immobility and obscurity was drawn between it and the ever living, bustling city. Then the striking of the clock became audible. The strange melody, alien to the earth, was slowly born and faded out high up. It was born again, deceiving the ear, and rang out mournfully and quietly. It stopped and rang again. The hours and minutes fell into a metallic, softly ringing bowl, like big transparent glass drops falling from an unknown height. Or as if birds of passage were flying by.

That was the only sound that was carried day and night into the cells where the condemned prisoners sat each alone. It penetrated the roof and the thickness of the stone walls, stirring the stillness. It disappeared unnoticed and returned just as unnoticed. Sometimes they would forget and not hear it; sometimes they waited for it in despair, living from one hour to the next, distrustful of the stillness. Only important criminals were kept in this fortress, and its regulations were especially stern and harsh, hard as a corner of the fortress wall. And if there be any nobility in cruelty, then this dull, dead, mutely majestic stillness, stifling the smallest rustle, the slightest breath, was noble.

In this majestic stillness, broken only by the sorrowful peal of the flying minutes, five people, two women and three men, separated from every living thing, awaited nightfall, dawn and the execution; and each of them prepared for it in his or her own way.

VII   THERE IS NO DEATH

Just as Tanya Kovalchuk had thought all her life of others and not of herself, so now she suffered and grieved deeply for her friends. She thought of death as something imminent and agonising for Seryosha Golovin, for Mousia and the others, but for her personally it seemed to have no concern.

And to make up for her enforced firmness in court, she now wept for hours on end—as old women weep, who have known great sorrow, or as those who are very pitiful and kind-hearted weep in youth. The thought that Seryosha might be short of tobacco and Werner deprived of his customary strong tea, when they were now to die, tormented her perhaps as much as the thought of the execution itself. The execution was something unavoidable and extraneous, and was not worth considering; but it was terrible that a prisoner on the eve of his execution should be deprived of tobacco. She recalled and relived in her memory pleasant details of their life together, and then grew numb with terror at the thought of Sergey's meeting with his parents.

She grieved especially over Mousia. For some time she had been under the impression that Mousia was in love with Werner, and although this was not so, she none the less longed ardently for something good and bright for both of them. When she was free Mousia used to wear a little silver ring engraved with a skull and bones, with a wreath of thorns around them. Tanya Kovalchuk regarded that ring as a symbol of doom and used to beg Mousia, sometimes seriously, sometimes in joke, to give it to her.

"Let me have it," she begged.

"No, Tanechka, I will not give it you. You will soon wear another ring on your finger."

They in their turn, for some reason, thought she would soon get married, which vexed her, for she did not want a husband. And as she remembered those half jesting conversations with Mousia, and knew that Mousia was now doomed, she choked with tears of motherly pity. Each time the clock struck she lifted her tear-stained face and listened—how did those others in their cells take this wearisome, obdurate summons of death?

But Mousia was happy.

Her hands folded behind her back, her prison dress, several sizes too large, making her look like a man or rather an adolescent boy, who had put on someone else's clothes, she paced the cell steadily and indefatigably. The sleeves of the dress were too long for her, so she tucked them up, and her thin arms, so emaciated that they were scarcely bigger than a child's, stuck out of its wide openings like flower stems appearing from a coarse dirty earthen pot. The rough material had rubbed and irritated her delicate white neck; and now and then, with a movement of both hands, Mousia freed her throat and carefully touched with her finger the spot where the skin was red and sore.

Mousia paced the cell and, reddening with excitement, thought out her exculpation before the world. She needed exculpation because she, so young and insignificant, who had achieved so little and was nothing of a heroine, was to be granted the same honourable and glorious death as real heroes and martyrs before her. Believing firmly in human kindness, pity and love, she pictured the sufferings of others on her account, their agony and distress, and blushed with shame. It was as if, in attaining the scaffold, she had committed some great blunder.

At her last meeting with her lawyer, she begged him to get her poison, but suddenly changed her mind. For what if he or others should think she was putting on airs, or was afraid; and, instead of dying modestly and unobtrusively, she made more fuss than was necessary. So she added hastily, "No, I don't think I want it after all."

Now she desired one thing only—to prove to people beyond a doubt that she was no heroine, and that death was not terrible, so that they should not worry or trouble about her. She wanted to explain that it was not her fault that she, so young and insignificant, should die such a death and have so much fuss made about her.

Like a person trying to clear himself from some real accusation, Mousia sought to exonerate herself by searching for something which would enhance her sacrifice and give it real value. She deliberated: "It is true that I am very young, that I might have lived for a long time, but . . ."

And as a candle fades in the glare of the rising sun, so her youth and life appeared dull and dark confronted by that great radiance which was about to shine around her modest head. There was no exoneration.

But perhaps that special gift she carried in her soul—boundless love, boundless readiness for danger, boundless disregard of herself? For indeed it was not her fault that she was not allowed to do all that she might and longed to have done. They had killed her on the threshold of the temple, at the foot of the altar.

But if a person's value is measured not only by what he has done, but by what he wishes to do, then . . . then she was worthy of the martyr's crown.

"Is it possible?" thought Mousia bashfully. "Am I really worthy of it? Worthy that people should weep and grieve over such a little, insignificant girl?"

An indescribable joy overcame her. There were no doubts or hesitations, she was accepted in their midst, she entered as an equal the ranks of those noble souls, who from time immemorial have attained high heaven by way of the stake, tortures and execution. She knew bright peace and rest and boundless, tranquil, radiant happiness. She felt as if she had already left life and soared bodiless in its light.

"And this is death? Can one call this death?" thought Mousia blissfully.

If scientists, philosophers and executioners from all over the world had assembled in her cell and spread out before her books, scalpels, axes and nooses in the effort to prove that death exists, that man dies and is killed and that there is no immortality—they would only have astonished her. How could there be no immortality, since she was already immortal? How could one speak of immortality and death, when she was already dead and immortal, as alive in death as she had been alive in life?

And if they were to bring a coffin containing her own decomposing body, filling the cell with stench, and say, "Look, that is you!"

She would have looked and answered, "No, that is not I."

And if they should try to convince her, through fear, that this ominous decaying body was she, she—Mousia—would have answered with a smile, "No, you think that *this* is I, but *this* is not I. I am she to whom you speak, how then could I be *this?*"

"But you will die and become like this."

"No, I shall not die."

"You will be executed. There's the noose."

"I shall be executed, but I shall not die. How can I die, since I am already immortal?"

And the scientists, philosophers and executioners would step back and say in trembling voices, "Do not touch this place. It is holy ground."

Of what else did Mousia think? Of many other things, for to her the thread of life was not broken by death, but ran on smoothly and evenly. She thought of her comrades; both of those far away, to whom her execution would cause grief and pain, and those near her, together with whom she would walk to the scaffold. She was astonished at Vassily's fear, for he had always been very brave and could even jest with death. On that Tuesday morning, for instance, when he with the rest of them were placing in their belts the explosives, which were to cause their ruin a few hours later, Tanya Kovalchuk's hand shook so that she had to be sent away; but Vassily joked, played the buffoon, whirled round and was so careless that Werner said sternly, "There is no need to take liberties with death."

Why was he afraid now? But this incomprehensible fear was so foreign to Mousia's soul that she soon ceased to think or try to find the cause of it. She suddenly had a desperate longing to see Seryosha Golovin and have a good laugh with him. After a few moments' thought, she longed still more desperately to see Werner and have a good argument with him. She imagined Werner to be pacing by her side with his even measured steps, digging his heels into the ground, and said, "No, Werner dear, that is all nonsense, it is of no importance whether you killed NN. or not. You are clever, but you reason as though you were playing chess—you make one move and then another, and then you have won. The important thing is, Werner, that we ourselves are ready to die. Do you understand? What do those people think? That there is nothing more terrible than death. Having invented death themselves, they are afraid of it and try to frighten us with it. But this is what I should like to do—step out all alone in front of a whole regiment of soldiers and fire at them with my Browning. I am alone, it is true, and there are thousands of them and I might kill no one. What matters is that they are thousands. When thousands kill one, it means that that one has conquered. It's true, Werner, my dear."

But this was so obvious that she did not feel like continuing the argument. No doubt Werner now realised it for himself. Perhaps, however, it was just that her mind refused to stay fixed on any one thing—like a lightly hovering bird that sees boundless horizons and is free of all the space and depth of the lovely tender blue sky. The clock rang out continually, stirring the mute stillness; and her thoughts mingled with the harmonious sound, made beautiful by distance, and also began to chime; as if the smoothly gliding images had turned into music. She seemed to herself to be riding along a broad smooth road; the night was quiet and dark and the springs of the carriage swayed whilst the little bells tinkled. All care and emotion had vanished; the tired body relaxed in the darkness, whilst the mind, weary but happy, created bright images and revelled in their colours and quiet peace. Mousia recalled the three comrades who had been hanged a short time ago, and their faces were bright and joyful and near, nearer than the faces of those who still lived. So does a man think with joy in the morning of his friends' home, which he will visit in the evening with greetings on his smiling lips.

Mousia had worn herself out with pacing. She lay down carefully on her plank bed and went on day-dreaming with her eyes lightly closed. The hours rang out continually, stirring the mute stillness, and bright singing images floated calmly in the wake of their chimes. Mousia thought, "Is this really death? My God, how glorious it is! Or is it life? I don't know. I don't know. I will look and listen."

For quite a time, since the first days of her imprisonment, she had begun to imagine sounds. Possessed of a very musical ear, rendered still more sensitive by the stillness, she invented whole musical patterns from a background of meagre grains of reality—the guards' footsteps in the corridor, the chimes of the clock, the rustling of the wind on the iron roof or the creaking of the lantern. At first this phenomenon frightened Mousia and she repelled it as an insane hallucination; later, when she realised that she was not crazy and that these sounds did not indicate any mental deterioration, she yielded to them tranquilly.

And now, suddenly, she seemed to hear quite distinctly the sound of military music. Bewildered, she opened her eyes and raised her head—there was night outside the window and the clock was striking. There it is again, she thought calmly, and shut her eyes. No sooner had she closed them than she heard the sound of music again. Soldiers, a whole regiment of them, were coming from the right of the building and passing by her window. Their feet beat time rhythmically upon the frozen ground, one—two, one—two. She could even hear the creaking of a leather boot, now and then, or a foot slip and regain the step. And the music came nearer; it was an unfamiliar, but very loud and cheerful festival march. They must be celebrating some special occasion in the fortress.

Now the band was just outside the window and the whole cell was filled with gay, rhythmic, harmonious sounds. One big brass trumpet was very much out of tune, now it was behind, now ran comically ahead. Mousia seemed to see the little soldier with that trumpet, his earnest face, and she laughed.

Then it all moved into the distance. The footsteps, one—two, one—two, died away. From afar the music sounded even gayer and more beautiful. Once or twice again the high-pitched brass voice of the trumpet was heard cheerfully out of tune, then everything was silent. Again the clock on the tower struck the hour, slowly, mournfully, scarcely stirring the stillness.

"They've gone," thought Mousia with faint regret. She missed the vanished sounds, so gay and amusing, she even missed the departed soldier boys, because they had brass trumpets and creaking boots and were quite different from those she wanted to shoot with her Browning.

"Please, once more," she begged gently. And they came again. They bent over her, enveloped her in a transparent cloud, lifted her high up, where birds of passage float and cry like heralds. To the right, to the left, up and down, they cry like heralds. They call, they proclaim, they announce their flight from afar. They spread their wings wide and the darkness supports them as does the light; and on their swelling breasts, cutting the air, is reflected from below the city shining blue. Mousia's heart beat more and more regularly, her breathing became more and more tranquil and low. She was falling asleep. Her face was tired and pale; there were circles under her eyes and her girlish arms· were thin to emaciation, but there was a smile on her lips. Tomorrow, when the sun rose, this human face would be distorted in an inhuman grimace, the brain would be covered with thick blood and the glassy eyes bulge from their sockets; but today she sleeps quietly and smiles in her great immortality.

Mousia was asleep.

But the life of the prison continued its accustomed way,

deaf and quick of hearing, blind and vigilant, like eternal
fear itself. Somewhere people walked, somewhere people
whispered, somewhere a gun clanked. Someone shrieked,
it seemed; or perhaps no one shrieked, and it was only
the stillness which made one think so.

The shutter in the door fell noiselessly, and in the black
opening appeared a dark whiskered face, which stared at
Mousia for a long time in astonishment, then disappeared
noiselessly as it had come. The bells rang and chimed,
slowly, poignantly; as if the wearied hours were climbing
a high mountain to midnight, and the ascent was becoming
ever more difficult. They slipped, they slid, they rushed
down with a moan, and again began climbing painfully
to their black summit.

Somewhere people talked. Somewhere people whispered.
And already the horses were being harnessed in the black
carriage without lights.

VIII   THERE IS DEATH AND LIFE ALSO

Sergey Golovin had never thought of death, which seemed
so alien as not to concern him at all. He was a cheerful
youth of excellent physique, endowed with a bright, even
temper and a capacity for enjoying life; and this quality
caused every thought and feeling detrimental to life to be
absorbed in his organism quickly and without trace. Just
as all his cuts, wounds and bites healed rapidly, so everything painfully affecting his soul was immediately ejected
and disappeared. He applied himself to everything with
the same even temper and zest, whether business or
pleasure, whether photography, cycling or the preparation
of a terrorist attempt. He found everything in life pleasant
and important and was under an equal necessity to do
everything well.

And he did do everything well. He was a splendid sailor,
an excellent shot, faithful in friendship as in love, and was
a fanatical believer in the "word of honour." His friends
laughed at him, saying that if a notorious informer, scoundrel or spy, should give him his word of honour that he
was not an informer, Sergey would believe him and give

him a friendly handshake. He had one failing, however. He was convinced that he sang well—though he had not the slightest ear for music, and sang abominably out of tune even in revolutionary songs; yet he took it amiss when his friends laughed at him.

"Either you are all asses or I am an ass," he would say seriously in an offended voice. After some thought, they would all agree, equally seriously, "It is you who are the ass. That is plain from your voice."

But, as often happens with charming people, his friends loved him more, perhaps, for this failing than for his virtues.

He was so fearless of death and regarded it so little, that on the fatal morning, before leaving Tanya Kovalchuk's flat, he was the only one who ate a good breakfast. He drank two glasses of tea and milk and ate a large white roll. Then, looking sadly at Werner's untouched bread, he said, "Why don't you eat anything? Eat and keep up your strength."

"I don't feel like it," was the answer.

"Well then, I'll have it. May I?"

"You certainly have a good appetite, Seryosha!"

Instead of replying, Sergey began, with his mouth full, to sing raucously and out of tune, "Terrible whirlwinds howl above us."

After the arrest, the thought that they had made a mess of it and done for themselves depressed him; but he went on to consider—"There is still one more thing to do well— to die"—and cheered up again. Strange as it may seem, he had not been in the fortress two days before he began to practise gymnastics according to the remarkably rational system of a certain German called Müller, about which he was an enthusiast. He stripped himself naked and, to the alarmed surprise of the watching warder, went conscientiously through all the prescribed eighteen exercises. As an enthusiast for Müller's system, it pleased him that the guard was looking on with astonishment; and, although he knew that there would be no reply, he remarked to the eye glued to the peep-hole, "It does you good, brother, makes you strong. This is what you need in your regiment."

His tone was persuasive and kind, so as not to frighten the warder, and he had no idea that the soldier simply thought him a lunatic.

The terror of death came on him gradually, in spasms as it were. It was as though someone gripped him and thrust a fist violently into his heart from below. The feeling was rather painful than terrible. It would pass off only to recur a few hours later, and each time the attack was longer and more violent. And it began to reveal itself as the dim shadow of a great, well-nigh unbearable fear.

"Is it possible I am afraid?" thought Sergey with astonishment. "What nonsense!"

But it was not he who was afraid, it was his young strong healthy body, which could not be deceived by the exercises of the German Müller or by rubbings with a wet towel. And the stronger and fresher it felt after the cold water, the sharper and more unbearable was the sensation of sudden fear. It was just at that time in the morning when, in freedom, he felt happiest and most vigorous, after a sound night's sleep and physical exercises, that he now experienced the onset of an acute and, as it were, alien fear. He realised this and thought to himself, "You're a fool, brother Sergey. To make it easier for the body to die, you should weaken it, not strengthen it. Fool!"

So he gave up physical exercises and cold rubs. And he shouted to the guard in explanation of the change, "No matter that I've given it up. It's a fine thing, brother, only no good for those who are to hang. For everybody else it's excellent."

And actually things became somehow easier. He also tried to eat less, so as to grow still weaker; but, in spite of the lack of fresh air and exercise, his appetite was still very good. It was difficult to check it and he ate everything that was brought to him. Then he began to try another way; before ever beginning to eat, he would pour out half the hot meal into the pail. This seemed to help—a dull sleepiness and weariness set in as a result.

"I'll teach you!" he exclaimed threateningly to his body, passing his hand sadly and tenderly over the flabby softened muscles.

The body soon, however, adapted itself to the new order of things, and the terror of death appeared once again. True, the acute burning pain had turned to a dull nauseating one. "That's because there is so long to wait," thought Sergey. "It would be a good idea to sleep through till the day of the execution," and he tried to sleep as much as possible. At first he succeeded in this, but later, either because he slept too much or for some other reason, insomnia set in. And with it came poignant far-sighted thoughts and a longing for life.

"Do I really fear that bugbear?" he thought to himself about death. "I regret my life. Life is a glorious thing, no matter what the pessimists say. And what if they hanged a pessimist? Ah, I regret life, I regret it very much. And why has my beard grown? For long it would not grow and now suddenly it has become long. Why?"

He shook his head sadly and heaved long-drawn painful sighs. He was silent, and then another long, deep sigh. Again a short silence followed by a still longer and heavier sigh.

And so it went on till the day of the trial and the last meeting with the old people. He awoke in his cell with the full consciousness that he had finished with life forever and that there were only a few hours left in that emptiness preceding death, and was overcome by a feeling of strangeness. It seemed as though he had been stripped of everything, stripped in a quite extraordinary way; not only had his clothes been taken from him, but he was bereft of the sun, noise and light, acts and speech. Death was not yet but life had already passed; and instead there was something new, something quite incomprehensible, which seemed now devoid of meaning, now full of meaning, but was so deep, mysterious and inhuman that it was impossible to understand.

"Damn it all," wondered Sergey painfully. "What is this? And where is this I? What is this I?"

He examined himself attentively and with interest, beginning with his large prison slippers and ending with his stomach, which stuck out beneath his prison dress. He walked across the cell with arms outspread, continuing to

examine himself, like a woman in a new dress too long
for her. He moved his head experimentally—it turned.
And this thing, which was rather terrible for some reason, was he, Sergey Golovin, and it would cease to be.

He was overcome by a sense of the strangeness of everything. He tried to walk across the cell—walking seemed
strange. He tried to sit down—sitting down seemed
strange. He tried to drink some water—it seemed strange to drink
or swallow or hold a cup in his fingers and strange that
those fingers trembled. He choked and began to cough,
and while coughing he thought—how strange to cough.

"What is the matter with me? Am I going mad?" thought
Sergey shuddering. "That would be the last straw, the devil
take it!"

He rubbed his forehead with his hand, but this action,
too, seemed strange. Then, scarcely breathing, he remained
perfectly motionless for hours on end, as it seemed to him,
suppressing every thought, holding his breath, avoiding
every movement; for every thought and movement was
madness. Time had disappeared, as if it had turned into
space, transparent, airless space, or a huge square on
which was everything, earth, life and people. And all was
visible at a glance, everything to the very end, to the mysterious abyss—death. And the agony was not in that death
was visible, but that life and death were visible together.
A sacrilegious hand had drawn aside the curtain which
for countless ages had hidden the mystery of life and the
mystery of death, and now they ceased to be mysteries,
and yet they were not intelligible; like a truth engraved
in an unknown language. There were no thoughts in his
human brain, no words in his human speech, which could
encompass what he saw. And the words "I am frightened"
came into his mind only because there were no other
words, because there did not and could not exist any other
conception corresponding to this new set of conditions, so
outside human experience. Thus might a human being feel
if, while remaining within the bounds of human understanding, feeling and experience, he should suddenly see
God himself. He would see and not understand, even
though he knew that the name of this being was God, and

he would shudderingly suffer the terrible torment of utter incomprehension.

"There's Müller for you!" he suddenly said loudly with extraordinary conviction, tossing up his head. And, with one of those unexpected emotional transitions so characteristic of the human soul, he burst into merry hearty laughter.

"Oh Müller, my dear Müller, my wonderful German! And yet you are right, Müller, and I am an ass, brother Müller."

He paced the cell quickly once or twice and then, once more greatly astonishing the soldier who watched him through the peep-hole, stripped himself naked and went through all the eighteen exercises gaily and most conscientiously. He stretched and expanded his young, rather thin body, squatted on his heels, stood on tiptoe and breathed in and breathed out, and flung out his legs and arms. And after each exercise he said with satisfaction, "That's right! That's something real, brother Müller!"

His cheeks glowed, drops of hot sweat came pleasantly from his pores, and his heart beat strongly and regularly.

"It's like this, Müller," reasoned Sergey, throwing out his chest so that his ribs were plainly visible beneath the thin stretched skin:—"It's like this, Müller; there is a nineteenth exercise—to be hanged by the neck in a motionless position. And that is called execution. Do you understand, Müller? They take a live man, say Sergey Golovin, bundle him up, as if he were a doll, and hang him by the neck till he is dead. It's a stupid business, Müller, but it cannot be helped, there is no way out."

He bent his body to the right and repeated, "There is no way out, brother Müller."

IX THE TERROR OF LONELINESS

Separated from Sergey and Mousia only by a few empty cells, but feeling as desperately lonely as if he were alone in the universe, the unhappy Vassily Kashirin was ending his life in terror and grief, to the same sound of the chimes of the clock.

Covered with sweat, his moist shirt clinging to his body, his naturally curly hair matted and tangled, he raced convulsively and hopelessly up and down the cell, like a man with unbearable toothache. He would sit for a while, then rush about once more, then stop and press his forehead against the wall or search for something with his eyes, as if he were looking for medicine. He had changed so much that he almost seemed to have two faces, the young one which was his formerly and had disappeared somewhere, and a new terrible one which had come out of darkness in place of it.

For him the terror of death had come all at once and taken complete and overwhelming possession. During the morning he had accustomed himself to the idea of going to certain death, but as evening came on and he remained still locked in his solitary cell, he was enveloped and swamped in a mad wave of terror. So long as by his own free will he exposed himself to danger and death, so long as he held in his own hands the choice of a fate, however terrible, he felt at ease and almost cheerful. His terror, which belonged to the mean, shrivelled, old-womanish side of him, was swamped in a feeling of complete freedom, of delight in the bold, firm and fearless assertion of his willpower. With an infernal machine at his belt, he himself seemed to have turned into an infernal machine, absorbed into himself the cruel force of dynamite and acquired its fiery death-dealing powers. And whilst walking in the street amidst ordinary bustling folk, immersed in their own affairs and in getting out of the way of cab-horses and trams, he had seemed to himself an emissary from another secret world, where death and fear were unknown.

Then suddenly came this abrupt, cruel and stupefying change. He could no longer move according to his own will, but must go where others took him. He could no longer choose his position, but was put into a stone cage and locked up like an inanimate object. He could no longer freely decide between life and death, like others, but was going to sure and inevitable extinction. He who had been the incarnation of will power, life and strength, had become in a moment an image of utter helplessness, a beast led to the slaughter, or a deaf and dumb object, which could be picked up and thrown into the fire or broken. No matter what he might say, no one would listen to him; if he attempted to shout, they would stop his mouth with a gag; wherever he might try to move on his own volition, they would take him away and hang him. If he resisted, struggled or lay down on the ground, they would overpower him, lift him up and bind him, and carry him bound to the scaffold. And the fact that this mechanical outrage would be carried through by people just like himself put them in a new, strange and evil light. Sometimes they seemed like phantoms, feigning to be people and appearing to him only for a special purpose; and sometimes like mechanical puppets on wires. They would seize hold of him, take him away, hang him, and jerk his legs. Then they would cut the rope, take him down, carry him away and bury him.

From the first day of his imprisonment people and life had been transformed for him into an incomprehensible and terrible world of apparitions and mechanical puppets. Almost frantic with fear he tried to bring to mind that people have tongues and speak, but he could not, for they seemed mute. He tried to remember their speech, the meaning of the words they used in intercourse, but he could not. Their mouths opened, sounds came, then they went away, moving their feet, and nothing was left.

Thus might a person feel if one night, when he was alone in the house, all the things came to life, moved and acquired unlimited power over him, the man; if the cupboard, the chair, the writing-table and the sofa should all suddenly sit in judgement on him. He would cry out and rush about, beseech them and shout for help, and they would speak to each other in their own language and then —the cupboard, the chair, the desk and the sofa—take him away to be hanged. And the rest of the furniture would look on.

And all things began to seem unreal, like so many toys, to Vassily Kashirin, the man who was sentenced to death by hanging; his cell, the door with the peep-hole, the strokes of the wound-up clock, the neatly moulded fortress, and especially that mechanical doll with the gun who stamped with his feet in the corridor, and the others who frightened him by peeping through the hole in the door and silently brought him food. What he felt was not the fear of death; rather did he wish for death. For with all its eternal, mysterious incomprehensibility, it was more accessible to his reason than this wildly and fantastically changed world. Moreover, death seemed to be completely annihilated in this mad world of ghosts and puppets; it had been deprived of its hugeness and mystery, becoming also a piece of mechanism, and terrible only for that reason. They would seize hold of him, take him away, hang him and jerk his legs. Then they would cut the rope, take him down, carry him away and bury him.

Human beings had disappeared from the world.

At the trial the proximity of his friends had brought Kashirin to himself, and once more, for an instant, he was capable of seeing people. They sat and passed judgement, said something in human speech, listened and seemed to understand. But already at the meeting with his mother, he felt clearly, with the terror of a man who is going out of his mind and realises it, that this old woman in the little black kerchief was just a well-contrived mechanical doll like those which say "pa-pa, ma-ma," only better constructed. As he tried to talk to her, he thought, shuddering.

"Oh, Lord, this is a doll. A mother doll. And out there is a soldier doll and at home there is a father doll and I am the doll Vassily Kashirin."

It seemed to him that in a moment he would hear somewhere the working of machinery, the creaking of unoiled wheels. When his mother began to cry, something human again flashed up for an instant, but no sooner did she begin to speak than it disappeared and his feeling became one of curiosity and terror at seeing tears flowing from the doll's eyes.

Later on, in his cell, when his terror became unbearable, Vassily Kashirin made an attempt to pray. Of all that, under the guise of religion, had surrounded his youthful years in the house of his father, a shop-keeper, there remained only the bitter dregs, which repelled and annoyed him. He had no faith. Once, however, perhaps in early childhood, he had heard a few words, which made him tremble with emotion and all his life sounded in his memory like quiet poetry. These words were, "The joy of all that mourn."

At difficult moments he would whisper to himself, not in prayer and without being definitely conscious of what he said, "The joy of all that mourn"—and suddenly he would feel better and long to complain in a low voice to someone he loved, "Our life . . . is it life at all? Oh, my dearest, is this really life?"

And suddenly life would become amusing and he would feel like ruffling his hair, kicking out his limbs, and crying: "Strike me," as he offered his chest to the world's blows.

He told no one, not even his closest friends, of his "joy of all that mourn," and so deep was it buried in his soul, that he himself was scarcely conscious of it. It was only on rare occasions and with caution that he brought it to mind.

And now, when the terror of the insoluble mystery was before him, covering him completely, as water at springtide submerges the willow twigs on the bank, he wanted to pray. He would have liked to go down on his knees, but he was ashamed to do so before the soldier, so, folding his arms across his chest, he whispered low, "Oh, joy of all that mourn."

He repeated imploringly and with anguish, "Oh, joy of all that mourn, come to me, help Vaska Kashirin!"

A long time ago, whilst he was in his first year at the university and still led a dissipated life, and before he met Werner and joined the revolutionary organisation, he used to call himself pathetically and in bravado, "Vaska Kashirin." Now, for some reason, he felt like calling himself that again. But the words of his prayer came out sounding dead, as if unable to arouse response, "Oh, joy of all that mourn."

Something stirred. Far away a silent and sorrowful image seemed to float and quietly disappear without irradiating the gloom of death. The wound-up clock on the tower struck the hour. The soldier in the corridor knocked with his sabre, or was it a gun? Then he began to yawn lengthily with pauses between the yawns.

"Oh, joy of all that mourn! And are you silent? You will not say a word to Vaska Kashirin?"

He smiled imploringly and waited. But in his soul and around him there was emptiness. The gentle sorrowful image did not reappear. Unwanted and painful memories came back to him. He remembered the burning wax candles, the priest in his cassock, the ikon painted on the wall, his father bending and straightening himself as he bowed to the ground in prayer, whilst throwing a glance sideways at Vaska to see whether he was praying or up to mischief. And his terror became even greater than before the prayer.

Everything became a blank.

Madness crept on him painfully. Consciousness was going out like the cooling ashes of a scattered and dying bonfire, or like the corpse of a man just dead, whose heart is still warm whilst his feet and hands are already stiff. Once again a spark of his dying reason flared up redly and told him that he, Vassily Kashirin, might go mad here, experience agony for which there is no name, reach such limits of pain and suffering as no earthly being had ever before felt; he knew that he might beat his head against the wall, put out his eyes with his own fingers, talk and shout as much as he liked, or declare weeping that he could bear no more, and all would be of no good. Nothing would happen.

And nothing did happen. The feet, which have their own life and consciousness, continued to walk and carry the damp, trembling body. The arms, which have their own consciousness, tried in vain to wrap closer the cloak across his chest, and to warm the trembling moist body. The body shook and shivered; the eyes stared. And that was almost calmness.

But there was still one more moment of wild terror. That was when people entered the cell. His mind did not even take in what that meant—that it was time to go to execution; he simply saw people and was frightened with an almost child-like terror.

"I will not, I will not," he whispered inaudibly with livid lips, and retreated silently into the cell, as in childhood when his father had lifted his hand to strike him.

"You must come," they said.

They talked and walked about and handed over something. He shut his eyes, swayed and started to get ready slowly. Apparently he began to come to himself, for suddenly he asked an official for a cigarette. The latter obligingly opened his cigarette case on which was engraved a decadent figure.

X   THE WALLS FALL DOWN

The unknown prisoner, nicknamed Werner, was a man who was tired of life and of struggle. There was a time when he had felt a great love for life and enjoyed the theatre, literature and intercourse with his fellows. Endowed with a splendid memory and a strong will, he had mastered to perfection several European languages and could easily pass as a German, Frenchman, or Englishman. He spoke German as a rule with a Bavarian accent, but could when he wished talk like a real Berliner born. He liked to dress well, had beautiful manners, and was the only one of his confederates who could, without risk of detection, make an appearance at fashionable balls.

But for a long time now, unknown to his comrades, a grim disdain for people had grown up in his soul; he was filled with despair and a heavy, almost mortal weariness. By nature more of a mathematician than a poet, he had up till now known no moments of inspiration or ecstasy, and sometimes felt like a madman who tries to square the circle in pools of human blood. The enemy with whom he carried on a daily warfare could not inspire him with any respect. He found a closely woven net of stupidity, treachery, lies, filth and rotten deceit. The final thing, which, it seemed, had for ever destroyed in him the will to live, was the murder of an informer, carried out by

him at the bidding of the Organisation. He did the killing
calmly, but when he saw the dead face, false but all the
same pitiful and now so peaceful, all respect for himself
and his cause left him. Not that he felt remorse, but
suddenly his own personality simply ceased to have any
value for him, became a thoroughly insignificant, uninteresting, boring stranger. Being a man of single and in-
tegrated will, he did not leave the Organisation and outwardly remained the same; only deep down in his eyes
was something cold and terrible. But he said nothing to
anyone.

He possessed still another rare characteristic. As there
are people who have never had a headache, so he did not
know what fear was. And his attitude to the fear of others,
though not censorious, was not specially sympathetic—as
to a fairly widespread disease from which he, himself, had
never suffered. He pitied his comrades, especially Vassily
Kashirin; but it was a chilly, almost official pity, such as
some of the judges might probably have felt.

Werner realised that execution is not only death but
something else. But in any case he had determined to meet
it calmly, as something purely extraneous; to live to the
end as if nothing had happened or would happen. Only in
this way could he express his complete disdain for the
execution and preserve intact his inalienable freedom of
soul. At the trial (although this, perhaps, even his own
comrades, who well knew his cold indifference and disdain, would not have believed) he thought neither of life
nor death. With concentration, with the closest and most
tranquil attention, he was playing a difficult game of chess.
An excellent player, he had begun this game on the first
day of his imprisonment, and continued it without interruption. Nor did the verdict which sentenced him to death
by hanging displace one figure on the unseen board.

Even the fact that he would not, apparently, be able to
finish the game did not stop him; and he began the morning of the last day left to him on earth by correcting a
not altogether successful move made the day before. He
sat for a long time motionless with his hands pressed
between his knees; then got up and began to walk about,

considering. He had an individual gait; he bent the upper part of his body slightly forward and struck the ground with his heels firmly and decidedly, so that even on dry ground his feet left a deep, perceptible track. Quietly, on one breath, he whistled a simple Italian aria; it helped him to think.

But this time, for some reason, the game went badly. With the unpleasant feeling that he was making some big and even obvious mistake, he turned back more than once and checked the game almost from the beginning. He did not find any mistakes, but the feeling that he had made one not only did not disappear but became stronger and more unpleasant. And suddenly an unexpected and vexing thought came into his mind: did not his mistake consist in the fact that he was trying to distract his mind from the execution and shield it from that fear of death which was unavoidable for the condemned?

"No, why?" he answered coldly, and quietly closed the unseen board. And with the same concentrated attention with which he had played, and as if answering a stiff examination, he tried to realise the terror and hopelessness of his situation. Looking round the cell, and trying to leave nothing out of account, he calculated the hours that remained before the execution, and drew for himself an approximate and fairly accurate picture of the execution itself. He shrugged his shoulders.

"Well?" he remarked to someone half enquiringly— "That's all. What is there to be afraid of?"

He was certainly not afraid. And not only had he no fear, but, as if in opposition to fear, he found within himself a feeling of vague but great and daring joy. And the still undiscovered mistake no longer bothered or irritated him, but also seemed clearly to indicate something good and unexpected; as if a near and dear friend, whom he had thought dead, appeared alive and unhurt and laughed.

Werner once more shrugged his shoulders and felt his pulse; his heart was beating fast, but strongly and regularly with a certain resonant strength. Again, like a novice imprisoned for the first time, he looked attentively at the walls, the bolts, the chair screwed to the floor, and thought,

"Why do I feel so easy, happy and free? Yes, free. I think of the execution tomorrow, and it is as if it did not exist. I look at the walls, and there seem to be no walls. And I feel as free as if I were not only not in prison, but had just come out of a prison in which I had been all my life. What is the meaning of this?"

His hands began to tremble, which was an unheard-of phenomenon for Werner. His mind beat about more and more furiously. Tongues of flame seemed to flare up in his head; the fire was trying to force its way out and illumine a wide distance, which was still under the darkness of night. And then it forced its way out and the light flashed over a wide prospect.

The dull weariness, which had exhausted Werner for the last two years, fell from his heart like a dead, cold and heavy serpent with closed eyes and ghastly shut mouth. Before the face of death his gay, splendid youth had returned. But this was more than splendid youthfulness. With that astonishing illumination of the soul, which at rare moments flashes on a person and raises him to the highest peaks of consciousness, Werner suddenly saw both life and death and was amazed by the vastness of the unknown spectacle. It was as if he had come by a path, narrow as a knife-blade, to the highest point of a mountain range, and on one side saw life and on the other death, like two gleaming, deep, beautiful seas mingling on the horizon in one limitless broad expanse.

"What is this? What a divine sight!" he said slowly, involuntarily half-rising and straightening himself, as if in the presence of a higher being. His eager and piercing glance annihilated walls, space and time, and he looked deeply and widely into his past life.

And he saw life afresh. He did not try as before to express what he saw in words, nor are such words to be found in human speech, which is after all poor and meagre. All that was mean, dirty and evil and had aroused in him disdain for his fellows, at times even making the sight of a human face distasteful to him, had completely disappeared. So, for a person who mounts in a balloon, disappear the rubbish and dirt of the crowded streets of the town he has left, and ugliness becomes beauty.

With an unconscious movement, Werner stepped to the table and leaned on it with his right hand. By nature proud and forceful, he had never yet assumed such a proud, free and forceful pose, never turned his neck with such dignity, never looked thus; for never yet had he felt so free and full of power as here in prison, separated by a few hours only from execution and death.

He saw people afresh and they seemed to his illuminated sight dear and delightful and not as of old. Soaring above time, he saw clearly how young humanity is, only yesterday howling like a beast in the woods. And what had seemed horrible in people, unforgivable and disgusting, suddenly became lovable; as a child's inability to walk like a grown-up is lovable, or his disconnected prattle sparkling with gems of genius, or his amusing blunders and faults, or his cruel bruises.

"My dear ones," suddenly and unexpectedly came from Werner with a smile; and at once he lost all the dignity of his pose and became once more a convict, who feels the closeness and discomfort of being under lock and key and is rather bored by the annoying, searching eye glued to the panel of the door. Strange to say, he almost immediately forgot what he had just seen so vividly and clearly, and, still more strangely, he did not even try to remember it. He simply sat down as comfortably as possible without his customary stiffness of posture, and looked round at the walls and gratings with a strangely weak and tender smile, quite unlike himself. And something else took place, which had never before happened to Werner; he suddenly began to cry.

"My dear comrades," he whispered and wept bitterly. "My dear comrades!"

By what secret paths had he journeyed from a feeling of proud and boundless freedom to that tender and passionate pity? He did not know and did not think about it. And whether his pity was for his dear comrades, or whether his tears concealed something in him still loftier and more passionate—this, too, his suddenly resurrected and youthful heart did not know. He wept and whispered, "My dear comrades! Oh, my dear comrades!"

In this man, who wept so bitterly and smiled through his tears, no one would have recognised the cold, haughty, weary and arrogant Werner—neither the judges, nor his comrades, nor he himself.

XI   THEY ARE TAKEN AWAY

Before putting the condemned prisoners in carriages, all five of them were assembled in a big, cold room with a vaulted ceiling, which looked like a disused office or empty waiting-room. Here they were allowed to talk to each other.

But Tanya Kovalchuk was the only one who at once availed herself of that permission. The others silently and closely pressed each other's hands, some of which were cold as ice, others hot as fire, and in silence, trying not to look at each other, crowded together in an awkward distracted bunch. Now, when they were together, they were somehow ashamed of what each had felt when alone; and they were afraid to look at each other, not wishing to see or to show that each had passed through or suspected in himself, a certain new rather shameful experience.

But after having glanced at each other once or twice and smiled, they suddenly felt natural and at ease with one another as before. No change seemed to have taken place, or if there was one, it had been so evenly distributed among all that it was not noticeable in each individual. They all moved and spoke strangely; abruptly and in spurts, and either too slowly or too quickly. Sometimes they swallowed their words and repeated them several times, and sometimes they did not finish the sentence they had begun or thought they had finished it. But all this they did not notice. They all blinked and looked at ordinary objects with curiosity, as if they did not recognise them, like people who usually wore eye-glasses and had suddenly taken them off. They all kept turning round suddenly, as though someone from behind were calling and wished to show them something. But this, too, they did not realise. Mousia's and Tanya Koval-chuk's cheeks and ears were burning. Sergey looked rather pale at first, but quickly got better and seemed as usual.

Only Vassily attracted everyone's attention. Even amongst them he looked different and ghastly. Werner was roused to tender anxiety and said to Mousia in a low voice, "What is it, Mousechka? Is it possible that he . . . What? Let's go to him."

Vassily looked at Werner from far away, as if he did not recognise him, and dropped his eyes.

"Vasia, what's wrong with your hair? What's the matter with you? All right, brother, it's all right, it will soon be over. You must bear up, you know."

Vassily was silent. But when it almost seemed that he would say nothing, there came a dull, belated, terribly distant reply—so might the grave itself answer after many calls.

"I'm all right. I'm bearing up."

And he repeated, "I'm bearing up."

Werner was delighted.

"That's right. That's a brave fellow. Good, good!"

But he met a dark, leaden glance, which seemed to come from remote depths, and thought with momentary anguish —"Where is he speaking from?" And with deep tenderness, as to one already in the grave, he said, "Vasia, do you hear me? I love you very much."

"And I love you, too," came from the tongue which moved with difficulty.

Mousia suddenly took Werner's arm and, with an expression of astonishment, said intensely, like an actress on the stage, "Werner, what's the matter with you? You said—'I love you.' Never before did you say to anybody 'I love you.' Why are you altogether so . . . bright and gentle? Why?"

"Why?"

And expressing his feelings, like an actor, with similar intensity, Werner pressed Mousia's hand close and said, "Yes, now I love people very much. Don't tell the others, I'm ashamed, but I feel great love."

Their glances met and burst into flame, whilst everything

around seemed to go dark; so in a sudden flash of lightning all other lights are extinguished and the intensely yellow, brilliant flame casts its shadow upon the earth.

"Yes," said Mousia. "Yes, Werner."

"Yes," he answered. "Yes, Mousia."

Something had been made clear and irrevocably settled between them. And Werner, his glance bright, roused himself again and quickly stepped up to Sergey.

"Seryosha!"

But it was Tanya Kovalchuk who answered. Full of delight, almost weeping with maternal pride, she pulled Sergey violently by the sleeve and said, "Werner, listen! I have been crying my eyes out about him, grieving for him, and he—does gymnastics."

"According to Müller?" smiled Werner.

Sergey frowned in some confusion.

"You should not laugh, Werner. I have become thoroughly convinced . . ."

They all burst out laughing. They had drawn strength and courage from being together and had gradually become as they used to be; but this, too, they had not noticed and thought they had not changed. Werner suddenly stopped laughing and said to Sergey with great seriousness, "You are right, Seryosha. You are quite right."

"But you should understand . . ." began Golovin delightedly. "Of course we . . ."

But at that moment they were requested to set off. The guards were so obliging as to allow them to seat themselves in pairs according to their own choice. They were on the whole extraordinarily kind; they tried, on the one hand, to express their human attitude to them, and on the other, to efface themselves as much as possible as if the whole proceeding was automatic. But they were pale.

"You, Mousia, go with him," said Werner pointing at Vassily, who stood motionless.

"I understand," nodded Mousia. "And you?"

"I? Tanya with Sergey, you with Vasia . . . I alone. It's all right, I can do it, you know."

When they went outside, the damp darkness struck with soft but warm force against their faces and eyes; it took their breath away and immediately refreshed and tenderly enveloped their trembling bodies. It was difficult to believe that this astonishing thing was just a spring wind, a warm moist wind. It was a real spring night, astonishing in its loveliness, and smelling of melted snow and the purity of boundless space; one heard the tinkle of falling drops. The drops fell rapidly, chasing each other busily and quickly, uniting to beat out a harmonious song. Then one drop would suddenly get out of time and all the rest would entangle themselves in a merry splash and hasty confusion. Then a big stern drop would fall firmly and again the rapid spring song would strike up clearly and sonorously. A pale glow from the electric lights lay over the city and the fortress roofs.

"A-ah," came in a deep sigh from Sergey Golovin, and he held his breath for a while, as if unwilling to exhale from his lungs the fresh and lovely air.

"Has this weather been going on for long?" enquired Werner. "It is real spring."

"This is only the second day of it," was the obliging reply, made with politeness. "Before that we had nothing but frosts."

One after the other, the dark carriages rolled softly along. Each took up two people and disappeared in the darkness towards a small lantern which swung at the gates. Each carriage was surrounded by the dark silhouettes of the guards, and the hooves of their horses struck the ground rhythmically or floundered in the wet snow.

When Werner, bending, was about to enter the carriage, the guard said rather vaguely, "There is someone else riding with you."

Werner was astonished.

"Where to? Where is he going? Oh yes. Another one? Who is he?"

The soldier was silent. Indeed, something small and motionless, but alive, was pressed against the dark corner of the carriage, and an oblique ray from the lamp fell upon an open eye. In sitting down, Werner jolted the man's knee with his leg and said, "Excuse me, comrade."

There was no reply. Only after the carriage had begun to

move, a stammering voice asked suddenly in broken Russian, "Who are you?"

"I am Werner," was the answer, "condemned to be hanged for an attempt on the life of NN. And who are you?"

"I am Yanson. I must not be hanged."

They were travelling to where they would stand, two hours later, before the face of the great insoluble mystery, to pass from life into death; and they made friends. Life and death were moving simultaneously on two planes and life, in all its stupid, funny trivialities, remained life until the very end.

"What have you done, Yanson?"

"I cut my master's throat with a knife. I stole money."

Judging by his voice, Yanson seemed to be falling asleep. In the darkness, Werner found his limp hand and pressed it. Yanson took away his hand with an equally limp movement.

"Are you frightened?" asked Werner.

"I don't want to be hanged."

They lapsed into silence. Werner again found the Estonian's hand and pressed it closely between his dry hot palms. It lay there as motionless as a piece of wood, but Yanson did not attempt to remove it again.

It was close and stuffy in the carriage. There was a smell of soldiers' clothes, fustiness, manure and the leather of wet boots. The young guard who sat opposite Werner breathed heavily upon him with a mixed odour of onions and cheap tobacco. The keen fresh air, however, penetrated through crevices and filled that stuffy moving box with a sensation of spring, still stronger than was to be felt outside. The carriage turned now right, now left, and sometimes appeared to have turned right round and be going back. At times they seemed, for some reason, to be circling for hours on end in the same spot. At first a bluish electric light pierced the thick curtains at the windows; then, after they had turned a corner, it suddenly grew dark, and only by this could they guess that they had reached the deserted streets in the outskirts and were approaching the Northern railway station. Sometimes, when the carriage turned sharply, Werner's live bent knee jolted in a friendly way against the similar live bent knee of the guard and it was difficult to believe in the approaching execution.

"Where are we going?" asked Yanson suddenly. His head swam slightly from constant turning in the dark box and he felt rather sick.

Werner answered, pressing the Estonian's hand still closer. He wanted to say something specially friendly and caressing to this sleepy little man, whom he already loved as he had never loved anyone before.

"My dear, you don't seem to be comfortable. Move this way, towards me."

After a pause, Yanson answered, "Thank you. I am all right. Are they going to hang you, too?"

"Yes," answered Werner with unexpected cheerfulness, almost laughingly, and waved his hand in a particularly free and light-hearted manner. It almost seemed as if the subject under discussion were an absurd, nonsensical joke, which some nice but extremely funny people were trying to play on him.

"Have you a wife?" asked Yanson.

"No. What should I do with a wife?" was the reply. "I am alone."

"I also am alone. Singly," corrected Yanson after a pause.

Werner's head also began to swim. It seemed at times as if they were riding to a festival; for it is a strange fact that almost everyone taken to execution has had this feeling, and experienced, together with anguish and terror, a vague rejoicing at the unusual event about to take place. Reality becomes intoxicated with fantasy, and death, hand in hand with life, brings forth visions. It seemed quite possible that flags would wave from the houses.

"We've arrived!" said Werner merrily and with interest, as the carriage stopped, and he sprang out lightly. But with Yanson the business took longer; resisting silently and very limply, he tried not to get out. He clung to the handle, and the guard opened the helpless fingers and tore the hand away. Then he clung to the corner, the door, and the high wheel, but loosened his hold at once at the slightest effort on the part of the guard. Or, rather, the taciturn Yanson did not cling but sleepily stuck to every object, and was taken off easily and without effort. At last he stood on the ground.

There were no flags. As always at night, the station was dark, deserted and lifeless. There were no more passenger trains, and as for the train which awaited these passengers silently outside the station, there was no need for bright lights or bustle.

Werner was suddenly seized by boredom; not by fear or anguish, but by a feeling of enormously wearisome, tedious boredom, from which he longed to escape by going off somewhere, lying down, or closing his eyes tightly. He stretched himself and gave a prolonged yawn. Yanson also stretched himself and yawned quickly several times.

"I wish they would get it over quickly," said Werner wearily. Yanson said nothing and shrank into himself.

When the condemned prisoners were moving along the deserted platform, ringed round by the guard, to the dimly lit carriages, Werner found himself next Sergey Golovin. The latter pointed sideways and began to say something, but only the word "lamp" was clearly audible, the rest was drowned in his slow and weary yawns.

"What do you say?" asked Werner with an answering yawn.

"The lamp. The flame in the lamp is smoking," said Sergey.

Werner looked round. Indeed, the flame in the lamp was smoking thickly and the top of the glass had already turned black.

"Yes, it is smoking," he said. And then came the sudden thought, "What does it matter to me that the lamp is smoking, when . . ." The same thought, apparently, came to Sergey, for he threw a quick glance at Werner and turned away. But they stopped yawning, both of them.

They all walked unaided to the carriages, except Yanson, who had to be taken by the arms. First he resisted with his feet, as if gluing his soles to the boards of the platform, then bent his knees and hung on the arms of the guards, whilst his legs dragged like those of a drunkard and his toes scratched the boards. The business of pushing him through the door took some time, but was done in silence.

Vassily Kashirin, too, walked unaided, dimly imitating the movements of his comrades; he did everything they did. But as he mounted the platform of the carriage he stumbled and a guard took him by the elbows to support him. Vassily shuddered and gave a piercing shriek, tearing his arm away, "Ai!"

"Vasia, what's the matter?" asked Werner, dashing towards him. Vasia was silent and shook all over. The bewildered guard seemed rather hurt and explained, "I wanted to help him, but he . . ."

"Let's come along, Vasia, I'll help you," said Werner, and tried to take his arm. But Vassily again withdrew it and cried out even louder than before.

"Ai!"

"Vasia, it is I, Werner."

"I know. Do not touch me. By myself."

Still shaking, he entered the carriage by himself and sat down in a corner. Bending towards Mousia, Werner asked in a low voice, indicating Vassily with his eyes, "How goes it?"

"Badly," answered Mousia just as low. "He is already dead. Werner, tell me, is there such a thing as death?"

"I don't know, Mousia, but I think not," answered Werner, seriously and thoughtfully.

"So I thought. But he? I feel worn out after being with him in the carriage. It was like travelling with a corpse."

"I don't know, Mousia. Perhaps for some people there is death. For a time, and afterwards it will vanish. For me, too, there was death, but now it has gone."

Mousia's somewhat pale cheeks flushed, "For you, too, there was death, Werner? Truly?"

"There was, but now it has gone. As happened with you."

A noise was heard at the door of the carriage. Stamping loudly with his heels, breathing heavily and spitting with disgust, in came Mishka Tziganok. He threw a glance around him and stood still obstinately, "There's no room here, guard!" he shouted to the tired angry-looking soldier.

"Give me a place or I won't go, you can hang me here on the lamp-post. What a carriage they have given us, those scoundrels! Is this a carriage? It's the devil's belly, not a carriage!"

Suddenly, however, he bent his head, stretched out his neck, and in that posture went forward to the others. Framed in his dishevelled hair and beard, his black eyes looked out wildly and piercingly with a rather insane expression.

"Ah, gentlemen," he drawled. "So that's how it is! How do you do, sir?"

He gave Werner a poke with his hand and sat down opposite him. Bending close to him, he winked one eye and made a quick movement of his hand over his throat.

"You, too? Ah?"

"Yes," smiled Werner.

"Are all of them to be hanged?"

"All of them."

"Oho!" Tziganok grinned and quickly probed all of them with his glance, which rested a little longer on Mousia and Yanson. Then he winked at Werner again, "Was it a minister?"

"Yes, a minister. And you?"

"I, sir, am here for something else. A minister is too big game for me. I am a brigand, sir, that's what I am. A murderer. No matter, sir, press closer, it's not of my own free will that I'm crowding you. There will be plenty of room for everybody in the other world."

He looked round at everyone wildly, from under his ruffled hair, with a swift, distrustful glance. But they all regarded him silently, seriously and even with obvious sympathy. He grinned, struck Werner several times on the knee, and said, "That's it, sir! As in the song—'Don't rustle, Mother oak grove so green.'"

"Why do you call me sir, when we all . . ."

"That's true," agreed Tziganok with satisfaction. "A queer sort of gentleman when you are going to be hanged by my side! There's a gentleman for you," he added, prodding with his fingers at the silent guard. "But that one of yours is no worse than the likes of us," indicating Vassily with his eyes. "Sir, I say, sir, are you afraid?"

"It's all right," came from the stiffly moving tongue.

"Why say all right? Do not be ashamed, there's nothing to be ashamed of. Only a dog wags its tail and grins when it is taken to be hanged, but you are a human being. And who is that lop-eared fellow? He is not one of you?"

His eyes skipped about rapidly and he kept hissing and spitting out the sweet saliva which collected in his mouth.

The flaps of Yanson's worn-out fur cap stirred slightly as he sat pressed against the corner in a small motionless lump, but he did not answer. Werner replied for him, "He cut his master's throat."

"Oh, Lord," said Tziganok in astonishment, "why do they let the likes of him commit murder?"

For some time Tziganok had been casting sidelong glances at Mousia, and now, turning round quickly, he fixed her with his straight, rough glance.

"Miss, I say, miss! How is this? Her little cheeks are rosy and she laughs. Look, she is really laughing!" And he caught Werner's knee with fingers that clutched like iron. "Look, look!"

Blushing and with a rather embarrassed smile, Mousia gave him a look as straight as his own and caught the sad wild appeal in his piercing half-frenzied eyes.

Everybody was silent.

The wheels went on rattling fast and busily, the little carriages leapt along the narrow rails and ran forward persistently. When the little engine came to a bend or crossing, it gave a shrill eager whistle, for the driver was anxious not to run over anybody. And it was preposterous to think that human beings were expending so much of their customary care, effort and capability in order to hang people; that such simple sensible means were being applied to accomplish the maddest act on earth. The carriages ran and people sat in them as they always sat, and travelled as they usually travel; there would be the customary halt when "the train stops for a few minutes."

Then follows death, eternity, the great mystery.

The little carriages ran on persistently.

Several years running Sergey Golovin had lived with his relatives in a country house on this same line. He used often to travel on it both by day and night and knew the line well. When he shut his eyes he could fancy that now, too, he was going home, having stayed in town late with friends and taken the last train back.

"It won't be long now," he said, opening his eyes, and looked at the dark mute window covered by a grating.

Nobody stirred or answered and only Tziganok quickly and repeatedly spat out sweet saliva. His eyes began to run over the carriage, probing the windows and doors, scanning the soldiers.

"Cold," said Vassily Kashirin with lips as stiff as if they were frozen, and he pronounced it co-o-d.

Tanya bestirred herself, "Here is a scarf, tie it round your neck. It is a very warm one."

"Round his neck?" asked Sergey unexpectedly, and was frightened at his own question. But, as the same thought had occurred to all of them, nobody heard him. It was as though no one had said anything or as if all of them had said the same thing at the same time.

"Never mind, Vasia, tie it on, tie it on, you will be much warmer," advised Werner. Then he turned to Yanson and asked him in a tender voice, "My dear, aren't you cold?"

"Werner, perhaps he would like to smoke? Comrade, wouldn't you like to smoke?" asked Mousia. "We have some cigarettes."

"Yes, I would," was the answer.

"Seryosha, give him a cigarette," said Werner delightedly, but Sergey had already got one out. All watched with affection as Yanson's fingers took the cigarette, the match burned up and blue smoke came from Yanson's lips.

"Thank you," said Yanson. "It's good."

"How extraordinary!" said Sergey.

"What is extraordinary?" said Werner, turning round. "What is extraordinary?"

"Just that—the cigarette."

He held a cigarette, an ordinary cigarette, between his two live fingers and, pale with astonishment, regarded it almost with terror. They all stared at the thin little tube, out of which curled a blue ribbon of smoke, blown to one side by the draught, whilst the gathering ash at the tip grew dark. It went out.

"It has gone out," said Tanya.

"Yes, it has gone out."

"The devil take it," said Werner frowning, and looked uneasily at Yanson, whose hand with the cigarette hung down as if dead. Suddenly Tziganok turned round quickly and bent close above Werner till their faces almost touched; rolling the whites of his eyes like a horse, he whispered, "Sir, what about doing the escort in . . . Well? Shall I try?"

"You must not," replied Werner, also in a whisper. "Drink the cup to the dregs."

"But why not? A fight is much jollier. I go for him and he goes for me, and you yourself don't notice that you've been killed. As though you hadn't died."

"No, it won't do," said Werner and turned to Yanson. "My dear, why aren't you smoking?"

Yanson's flabby face suddenly crumpled up pathetically, as if someone had suddenly pulled a string setting all his wrinkles in motion and they had all gone criss-cross. As though in a dream, Yanson began to whimper without tears, in a dry almost affected voice, "I don't want to smoke. Akha. Ak-ha. Ak-ha. I must not be hanged. Ak-ha. Ak-ha. Ak-ha."

They fussed around him. Tanya Kovalchuk, weeping profusely, stroked his arm and adjusted the hanging flaps of his worn-out cap, as she said, "My own dear! Do not cry, my poor one! My poor unhappy fellow!"

Mousia looked sideways. Tziganok caught her glance and grinned, baring his teeth. "His Honour is a queer fellow! He drinks tea and yet has a cold belly," he said with a short laugh. But his own face had turned blue-black, like cast iron, and his big yellow teeth were chattering.

Suddenly the little carriages shook and the pace perceptibly slackened. All, except Yanson and Kashirin, half rose and sat down again as quickly.

"The station!" said Sergey.

All the air seemed suddenly to have been pumped out of the carriages, so difficult had it become to breathe. Their expanded hearts seemed to be bursting through their breasts, beating in their throats, tossing madly about, as if crying aloud in terror with blood-filled voices. But their eyes looked down at the shaking floor and their ears heard the wheels turn ever more slowly, slide, then turn again, and suddenly stop.

The train had halted.

Here the dream began. It was not very terrifying but rather unreal, unfamiliar, and somehow strange. The dreamer himself seemed to stand aside, and only his phantom moved about fleshlessly, walked noiselessly, spoke soundlessly and suffered without suffering. As in a dream they alighted from the carriage and grouped themselves in twos, inhaling the peculiar, fresh, wood-smelling spring air. As in a dream, Yanson resisted dully and feebly and was dragged out of the carriage in silence.

They went down steps.

"Are we going to walk?" asked someone almost cheerfully.

"It is not far," answered someone just as cheerfully.

Then, in a big black silent bunch, they walked through the forest on a rough, wet and soft spring road. A fresh, keen air blew from the snow in the forest. Their feet slipped and sometimes sank deep in the snow, and hands would involuntarily clutch a friend. Breathing heavily and loudly, the guards moved forward on both sides over the untouched snow. Someone's voice said angrily, "Why couldn't they clear the road? Fancy having to tumble about in the snow!"

Someone apologised guiltily, "They did clear it, your Honour. Only there's nothing to be done about the thaw."

Consciousness returned, but not fully, in strange scraps and fragments. Now the mind suddenly confirmed the fact in a business-like manner, "Of course they could not clear the road."

At times everything became a blank again and only the sense of smell remained: the unbearably fragrant smell of the air, of the forest and of melting snow. At times everything became abnormally clear: the forest, the night, the road, and the fact that this very minute they were going to be hanged. Snatches of restrained conversation flashed out in whispers.

"It is almost four."

"I said we left early."

"It is dawn at five."

"Yes, of course, at five. So that's why it had to be . . ."

They halted in darkness in a little meadow. At some distance, behind the sparse trees, transparent in their wintriness, two small lanterns moved silently. There stood the gallows.

"I have lost a galosh," said Sergey Golovin.

"What's that?" said Werner, not understanding.

"I have lost a galosh. It's cold."

"But where's Vassily?"

"I don't know. There he is!"

Vassily stood dark and motionless.

"And where is Mousia?"

"I am here. Is that you, Werner?"

They began to look round, avoiding the direction of the two little lanterns, which continued to move silently and with terrible significance. On the left the denuded forest was thinner and through it could be seen something large, pale and flat; a damp wind blew from thence.

"The sea," said Sergey Golovin, inhaling the air through his nose and mouth. "There's the sea."

Mousia responded in deep tones, "My love, which is as boundless as the sea."

"What are you saying, Mousia?"

"The shores of life cannot contain my love, which is as boundless as the sea."

"My love, which is as boundless as the sea," repeated Sergey thoughtfully, carried away by the sound of her voice and the words.

"My love, which is as boundless as the sea," repeated

Werner, and then cried in joyful astonishment: "Muska, what a girl you are still!"

Suddenly, at his very ear, Werner heard Tziganok's hot, suffocated whisper, "Sir, I say, sir! The forest! Oh, Lord, what's that? And there, where the little lanterns are, that's the peg for hanging us on, isn't it? What is it, I say?"

Werner looked up. Tziganok was in the throes of approaching death.

"We must say good-bye," said Tanya Kovalchuk.

"Wait, they have still to read out the sentence," replied Werner. "And where is Yanson?"

Yanson lay on the snow and people were busied about something around him. Suddenly came a pungent smell of ammonia.

"What is it, doctor? Will you be long?" asked someone impatiently.

"Nothing much, just an ordinary faint. Rub his ears with snow. He is already coming round. You may read the sentence."

The light from the dark lantern fell upon the paper and the white hands without gloves. Both trembled a little and so did the voice, "Gentlemen, perhaps there is no need to read the sentence. You know it? What do you think?"

"No need," answered Werner for all of them and the dark lantern was soon extinguished.

The services of the priest were also refused.

The dark broad silhouette moved back quickly into the darkness and disappeared. Apparently dawn was approaching; the snow grew whiter, the figures of people became darker and the forest looked sparser, sadder and less mysterious.

"Gentlemen, you must go in twos. Stand in pairs according to your choice, but please be quick."

Werner pointed to Yanson, who was now standing up, supported by two guards. "I'll go with him. And you, Seryosha, take Vassily. Go ahead."

"Good!"

"Shall we go together, Mousechka?" asked Kovalchuk. "Come, let us kiss each other good-bye."

They kissed each other quickly. Tziganok's kiss was firm

and one could feel his teeth; Yanson kissed softly and flabbily with his mouth half open, scarcely realising what he was doing. When Sergey Golovin and Kashirin had already gone a few steps, the latter stopped suddenly and said loudly and distinctly in a completely strange and unfamiliar voice, "Good-bye, comrades!"

"Good-bye, comrade!" they answered.

They went off. Everything grew quiet. The little lanterns behind the trees became motionless. They expected to hear a scream, voices, a noise of some sort; but it was as silent there as with them and the little yellow lanterns remained motionless.

"Oh, Lord!" someone cried out hoarsely and wildly. They looked round; it was Tziganok in the throes of approaching death. "They are hanging them," he cried.

They turned away from him and again all became quiet. Tziganok writhed, clutching the air with his hands.

"How is it possible? Gentlemen, I say! Am I to go alone? It is livelier to go in company, gentlemen! What do you say?"

He grasped Werner's arm with his fingers, tightening and then relaxing them as if in play, "Sir, dear, cannot you go with me? Eh? Be so kind, don't say no!"

It hurt Werner to refuse, but he answered, "I cannot, my friend, I am going with him."

"Oh Lord! That means I have to go alone. How am I to do it? Oh, Lord!"

Mousia stepped forward and said in a low voice, "Come with me."

Tziganok recoiled and rolled the whites of his eyes at her wildly, "With you?"

"Yes."

"Look at her! Such a little girl! And you are not afraid? I'd better go alone. Never mind."

"No, I am not afraid."

Tziganok grinned, "Look at her! But I am a murderer. Don't you despise me? Better not come with me. I won't be angry with you."

Mousia was silent. In the dim light of dawn her face looked pale and mysterious. She suddenly stepped quickly

up to Tziganok and, throwing her arms round his neck,
kissed him firmly on the lips. He took her by the shoulders
with his fingers, pushed her away, shook her, and then
kissed her on the lips, nose and eyes, smacking his lips
loudly.

"Come along, then!"

Suddenly the soldier standing nearest seemed to sway,
opened his hands and let his gun drop. He did not bend to
pick it up, however, but remained motionless for a while,
then turned sharply and walked like a blind man over the
untouched snow towards the forest.

"Where are you going?" whispered another soldier in a
frightened voice. "Stop!"

But the other went on silently, trudging painfully through
the deep snow. He stumbled over something, apparently,
for he waved his arms and fell face downwards. There he
remained lying.

"Pick up your gun, grey coat, or I'll do it for you!" said
Tziganok threateningly. "You don't know your duty!"

The little lanterns began to move busily again. The turn
of Werner and Yanson had come.

"Good-bye, sir!" said Tziganok loudly. "We shall meet
in the other world; when you see me, don't turn away! And
bring me some water to drink. I'll be having a hot time!"

"Good-bye!"

"I don't want to be hanged!" said Yanson weakly. But
Werner took him by the arm and the Estonian made a few
steps forward on his own. Then they saw him stop and fall
down on the snow. Someone bent over him, lifted him up
and carried him away; he struggled feebly in their arms.
Why didn't he shout? He had probably forgotten he had a
voice.

And the little yellow lanterns stood motionless again.

"And I, Mousechka, must I go alone?" said Tanya Kovalchuk sadly. "We have lived together, and now . . ."

"Tanechka, dear . . ."

But here Tziganok intervened excitedly. He held Mousia
by the hand, as if afraid she might be taken from him, and
spoke in a rapid, business-like tone, "Oh miss! You can go
alone, you are a pure soul and can go anywhere alone. Do

you understand? But I can't. As a murderer . . . you understand? It's impossible for me to go alone. 'Where are you going, you murderer?' they will ask. I have even stolen horses, by God! But with her I am as if . . . as if with an infant, do you see? Don't you understand?"

"I understand. Well, go together. Let me kiss you once more, Mousechka!"

"Go on, kiss each other," said Tziganok approvingly to the women. "You are made that way; it is right to bid each other a hearty farewell."

Mousia went forward with Tziganok. The woman walked carefully, slipping now and then, and, from habit, held her skirt off the ground. The man led her to death, holding her arm firmly, uttering cautions and feeling the ground with his foot.

The lights stopped moving. Around Tanya Kovalchuk was quietness and emptiness. The soldiers were silent, all grey in the colourless quiet light of the rising day.

"I am all alone," said Tanya suddenly and sighed. "Seryosha is dead, Werner is dead and Vasia. I am all alone, soldier boys; soldier boys, I say, I am all alone. Alone . . ."

The sun was rising over the sea.

The bodies were put into boxes. Then they were carried away. The necks were elongated, eyes bulged madly, and a swollen, blue tongue, like some unknown terrible flower, stuck out from the lips, flecked with bloody foam. The bodies were taken back by the same road along which they had travelled when alive. And the spring snow was just as soft and fragrant, and the spring air was just as fresh and keen. And the galosh which Sergey had lost lay wet and trampled, a black spot in the snow.

Thus did men greet the rising sun.

THE LAUREL DOSTOYEVSKY
Introductions by Ernest J. Simmons

CRIME AND PUNISHMENT

One of the most compelling novels in all literature by the man
André Gide called "the greatest of all novelists." 75c

THE HOUSE OF THE DEAD

Dostoyevsky's unforgettable account of a man condemned to
ten years of penal servitude for murdering his wife, based on
the author's own prison experiences. 60c

THE POSSESSED

An outstanding treatment of political conspiracy. Includes the
rarely published Tikhon chapter in a brilliant new translation.
95c

NOTES FROM UNDERGROUND, POOR PEOPLE
and THE FRIEND OF THE FAMILY

Three short novels which illustrate the remarkable diversity
and range of Dostoyevsky's genius. 95c

A RAW YOUTH

The story of a young rebel. Uprooted, disillusioned, and with a
tendency toward corruption, he presents a brilliant parallel to
the conflicts of today's youth. 95c

THE BROTHERS KARAMAZOV

The Constance Garnett translation in an authoritative modern
abridgment by Edmund Fuller. 60c

THE IDIOT

One of the best portraits in all fiction of a rare and difficult
subject: the good, truly moral man. 95c